REID KISSED HER BARE SHOULDER.

"I'm not laughing, Shanna," he told her in a whisper that made her very skin glow. He had shed his own clothes quickly. His body ripe with wanting her, Reid took her into his arms. "I'm smiling. Because I want you so much it hurts. And you're here with me now."

Placing both of his hands, palm up, against hers, he laced his fingers through hers, binding her to him. "Make love with me now, Shanna."

She tilted her head, awed at his words. "You're asking me?"

"I'm asking," he assured her, and she knew that even now, if she said no, he would back away. Shanna cupped his cheek with her hand, her fingers feathering along his bronzed skin.

"Yes."

CHOICES

Marie Ferrarella

HarperPaperbacks
A Division of HarperCollinsPublishers

This is a work of fiction. The characters, incidents, and dialogues are products of the author's imagination and are not to be construed as real. Any resemblance to actual events or persons, living or dead, is entirely coincidental.

HarperPaperbacks   *A Division of* HarperCollins*Publishers*
10 East 53rd Street, New York, N.Y. 10022

Cover photograph by Herman Estevez

First printing: October 1993

Printed in the United States of America

HarperPaperbacks, HarperMonogram, and colophon are trademarks of HarperCollins*Publishers*

❖ 10 9 8 7 6 5 4 3 2 1

To Jessica Lichtenstein,
with Deepest Gratitude for Sticking with Me

1

It didn't feel right. Her life, by every rational assessment known to society, was picture perfect. But it just didn't *feel* right, like a blouse that was supposedly made of silk, yet felt scratchy. There was a vague emptiness in the pit of her stomach, as if what she was living wasn't real. Or maybe she wasn't the real one and all the rest of this was.

Why wasn't she satisfied? Was there something lacking in her? Why wasn't she happy?

Because something was missing, some nebulous, unformed "something" was wrong. She could feel it, almost taste it. Almost touch it. But whatever it was, it was just out of reach.

And she hadn't a clue as to what "it" was.

A frustrated philosophy major, she thought with a sad smile, that's what she was. Maybe this was all just a proverbial tempest in a teapot.

But she had a feeling that it wasn't.

Shanna Brady Calhoun sat very still before the ornate antique vanity table. The table had been a gift from her father on her sixteenth birthday. Everything in the vast, exquisitely furnished bedroom where she had slept until two years ago was a gift, bestowed upon her thanks to the life fate had thrust her into by the whimsical happenstance of birth. She had done nothing more to earn any of this but be born Shanna Brady.

She knew that millions of women, millions of *people* would have given anything to be in her place. But this emptiness kept crowding her, ambushing her mind when she least expected it, drumming impatient fingers on her soul. And sitting in this chair, immobile, left Shanna nothing else to do but dwell on it.

The woman known to an adoring and vastly overcharged clientele as Alexandra was working on her face, making her into something she wasn't. Alexandra, a gnome of a woman, was a genius with makeup. She could take a plain face and make it beautiful. A pretty face and make it magnificent. She was the typical genius, petulant, opinionated, and exceedingly short-tempered. If Shanna were to so much as blink twice in succession, Alexandra would have interpreted it as being uncooperative and Shanna would be forced to listen to a diatribe on how lucky she was that Alexandra had deigned to make the trip out here personally rather than to leave her to the ministrations of an underling. Alexandra always said exactly what was on her mind. Others might be impressed that Shanna could trace her lineage back to the *Mayflower*, but it meant less than nothing to Alexandra.

Which was why Shanna liked her. The woman didn't see heritage or power by association when she looked at her. Alexandra only saw Shanna.

So Shanna sat there, motionless, thinking, silently wishing herself somewhere else. Wishing herself to be someone else. Someone with an identity that belonged exclusively to her and not to a surname or to a relative. Nothing but her eyes moved as Shanna passed the time watching dust motes do a lazy minuet within the confines of the sunbeam that shone through the huge bay window to her right.

If Alexandra wasn't working on her lips, Shanna would have smiled. She wondered if the dust motes knew they weren't allowed here. Her mother didn't tolerate such plebeian things as dust in her house. As if Brady Manor could ever be labeled with a title so benign as "house." Mausoleum was more like it, a cold, joyless mausoleum. Why her cousin Cydney wanted to be married here was beyond Shanna.

A lot of things seemed to be beyond her these days, she thought in mild irritation, like a student puzzling over a difficult algebra problem.

God, she felt so stifled, so directionless. So purposeless. She was going to be twenty-four next January. Twenty-four, going on ninety. At least she felt that way. A ninety-year-old formless lump.

Looking back, Shanna knew she had *always* felt that way. In the midst of luxury, in the eye of the public since the day her parents, Rheena Fitzhugh and Roger Brady, the only son of financier Alfred Brady, had announced her conception to a squadron of sensation-hungry reporters and eager photographers, Shanna felt that she had always been struggling to find a proper place for herself. It was a classic case of the poor little rich girl, on the inside looking out.

Or perhaps it was that Shanna was on the outside looking in. Looking in and searching for acceptance in a world that thoughtlessly would always compare her to her mother. And find her lacking.

She heard Alexandra hiss between her slightly

uneven teeth, her hands incredibly soft and gentle as she touched, smoothed, blended.

"Raise your chin, child," Alexandra commanded in a grating, nasal voice that held echoes of her native Poland, even though she had emigrated to the United States more than forty years ago. "I can't do my work if you're all hunched up like that."

Shanna obligingly lifted her head as she shifted in her chair. Pain danced through her, poking at her with pointy, scratchy fingers. Exercising extreme control, Shanna did her best not to wince. Her shoulder was still sore where she had hit it against the doorjamb yesterday. Her own fault, she thought. She had a habit of moving quickly without looking first.

"You're always rushing off without looking where you're going, Shanna. How did I ever get such a graceless child?"

The words replayed themselves in Shanna's head. She had been the object of her mother's criticism a thousand times during her childhood. And each time disappointment had dripped from every syllable. It was almost the first thing Shanna had ever been aware of: her mother's vast disappointment in her. Marriage hadn't altered that, although her mother finally seemed to see the merit in her choice.

How could she not? Shanna mused even as she searched for the surge of happiness that used to come whenever she thought of Jordan. It wasn't there, at least, not with the same intensity it used to be.

Something *was* wrong with her, she thought in annoyance. She had a good life, a beautiful house, a handsome husband who had singled her out in a crowd of gorgeous, wealthy women. What more was there supposed to be?

Something else, a small voice whispered within her.

Shanna bit her lower lip and heard Alexandra grumble

under her breath. Not wanting to agitate the woman, Shanna quickly relaxed her expression.

Yet with all this, her present life felt artificial somehow, like beautiful roses made out of plastic. There was this persistent feeling that what she was living wasn't real. That it was all mounted on very pretty paper, without depth, without substance.

Maybe she was still suffering from the aftermath of the flu, Shanna thought, almost desperate for a rational explanation to this hollowness that hounded her. The bout she had had at the beginning of the month had left her so weak and miserable she had wanted to die. Depression was known to hang on for a while even after a person recovered. Maybe that was what was wrong with her.

"Lean back a little, Shanna. You don't have to sit up so stiff."

Shanna obliged on command.

Like a programmed robot, Alexandra thought as she took out another tube from the creased black leather bag that she always carried with her. It was her one superstition. The bag always had to be within reach. Now crammed with her own special personally mixed makeup, forty years ago it had carried a single change of clothing as she had disembarked from a navy ship bringing European refugees to America. She had been smuggled by relatives from Poland to Germany after the war. Fate had brought her to the New World, where a natural ability and a quick mind had transformed Bella Perkowski into Alexandra, the darling of high society.

Alexandra looked at Shanna. She had known her, child and woman, for over twenty years, ever since she had been summoned to attend to Rheena's personal toilette for an inaugural ball. Widowed twice, Alexandra had no children of her own and had never wanted any.

Children were nasty little problems that grew up into nastier big problems. But there had been something about Shanna, something about her lost, waiflike quality that had won Alexandra over from the very start.

Shanna let out a long, cleansing breath and suddenly realized just how rigid she'd been. Every muscle in her body was tense, as if she was waiting for something to happen. Lately, she thought, she was always braced, waiting. Anticipating. But she didn't know for what.

She closed her eyes, scarcely feeling what the woman was doing to hide the tiny imperfections that her mother always found a way to magnify. She concentrated on Jordan. Sweet, handsome Jordan. If she tried, Shanna could still see him the way he had looked when he had first literally waltzed into her life. That, too, had been at a wedding.

Yolanda's. A distant aunt. Being related to the Bradys and the Fitzhughs meant having more cousins than any sane person could ever want. The Bradys, whose ancestors included Diamond Jim Brady, had a certain flash that appealed to the public at large and served them quite well in the realm of politics. Rheena Fitzhugh brought old money and respectability with backing. A perfect marriage. At least on paper.

Not like her own, Shanna thought with a genuine smile, ignoring Alexandra's murmur of disapproval because she had dared to change expression. A feeling of disloyalty for her previous petulance washed over Shanna. She should get down on her knees and thank God that she had been finally given something so rare as a stable marriage in this jaded world of politics and cotillions that she existed in. A stable, strong marriage. From the first moment Shanna had seen Jordan looking at her, he had completely taken over her world. She had stood very still, the way they had in the romantic old movies when two lovers find each other, watching as he walked in her direction. As he walked *to* her. Her heart had hammered so hard, she was certain everyone in the room heard it.

Silently, smiling into her eyes, he had taken her hand and then in a voice that rippled under her skin, he had asked her to dance. She had just numbly nodded. After that, he hadn't allowed anyone else to cut in the entire evening. It had all been like a glorious dream. He had been so attentive, so quick to try to please her. Six months later Shanna was having a wedding of her own.

Her mind drifted back to that day.

"Are you sure, Shanna? Are you really, really sure?" her mother had asked her sharply, even as the strains of the wedding march were swelling through the vast church that held hulking security guards at every possible entrance to keep out the paparazzi.

Yes, Shanna had thought then, she was sure. She was in love. Wildly, happily, blindly in love. For six months she and Jordan had been almost inseparable. And he had treated her as if she mattered, really mattered. As if she were a beautiful goddess.

No one had ever treated her that way, most especially not in her mother's presence. People tended to ignore her in favor of currying Rheena's favor. Rheena Fitzhugh Brady, the belle of every ball, the chairwoman of five major charities. The perfect partner for a politically motivated charmer whose eyes looked toward the country's most-sought-after position. Quick to smile, quick to laugh, her mother had been a raven-haired beauty in her youth and, at nearly fifty-one, was still considered stunning. Indeed, Shanna had heard her mother referred to as the embodiment of the eternal woman. Rheena had a lush figure and lustrous skin that never seemed to age thanks to creams and the clever scalpel of a skillful doctor who was content with his anonymity and his exorbitant fees.

Shanna had slowly smoothed down the skirt of her beaded wedding dress, the cost of which, she had thought guiltily, would have fed a small country for a month. Her mother had picked it out for her. Her mother had insisted on it.

A full head taller, Shanna had smiled confidently for perhaps the first time at her mother. Rheena had been a vision in lavender. The mother of the bride wore deep lavender in order not to be missed, Shanna had thought wryly. As if anyone ever could. But as she looked at her Shanna had been surprised by what appeared to be the flash of concern in her mother's famous cornflower-blue eyes.

"Of course I'm sure, Mother. Why wouldn't I be?"

Rheena shook her head, mindful not to muss her carefully arranged hair. "I don't know. Call it a feeling." She shrugged as an attendant carefully spread out Shanna's ten-foot train. She offered her only daughter a small, tight smile that hid a caldron of mixed emotions. "I just want you to be happy, that's all."

Do you, Mother? Do you really? Shanna wondered. Or was it just that her mother was jealous that she wasn't the star of this gathering?

No, that wasn't entirely fair or accurate. Her mother was unable to render the fabled "mother love" that Shanna had longed for when she was growing up, but Shanna knew that Rheena cared about her in the only fashion that she was capable of. And there was certainly no denying that her mother would always be the center of attention no matter where she was. Rheena Brady attracted attention the way nectar attracted honeybees. It was as natural as breathing to her. She thrived on it and expected it, never having known another way.

Shanna couldn't fault her mother for something she had no control over. She just found an expression of concern about her happiness at this late date difficult to believe, coming as it did from a woman who slipped in and out of her life like daylight savings time. Periodically, but with little effect beyond the very basic and the very obvious.

So she had married Jordan despite her mother's doubts and was, even now, trying very hard to "live happily ever after."

Shanna felt her neck cramping up and shifted ever so slightly as Alexandra continued working at her slow, steady pace. With her faded carrot-red hair, Alexandra looked like an extra from a thirties screwball comedy instead of the highly paid artiste she was. It was another thing Shanna found appealing about her. Alexandra didn't care what people thought.

Alexandra tapped the girl's shoulder to get her attention. "This is how you do it, child." She dabbed something soft and translucent along Shanna's cheekbone, then blended it upward. "Hides a lot of imperfections you don't want nobody to see."

Alexandra spoke as if the only English she had a nodding acquaintance with was the brand learned on the Lower East Side, but Shanna knew she was capable of speaking the king's English if she wanted to.

The woman saw the stubbornness rise in the young girl's eyes. She recognized resistance when she saw it. "You know, you should try harder. There's nothing wrong with using makeup to look pretty."

Shanna shrugged. The art of illusion had never been a goal for her. She was what she was. "I don't want to compete with her."

They both knew who she was referring to. "Why not?" Alexandra's tone was blasé. "Competition is what keeps us all alive."

Maybe you, Shanna thought, but not me. "Funny, my father said the same thing about winning."

Alexandra nodded sagely, dispelling her comical appearance. "Smart man, your father."

"Yes, he is."

Alexandra took that as capitulation. "So listen," she instructed as she launched into a short, precise narrative about makeup application.

Shanna tried to absorb what Alexandra was telling her. Jordan would undoubtedly appreciate the effort on her part. It meant so much to him to have her looking her best. He was very image conscious, perhaps a little too much so. Being at the right place at the right time with the right people seemed to have become his credo of late. He'd been the one to make her accept this invitation. He had made her accept all the invitations to these gala affairs when all she wanted to do was stay home with him. When it came to attending functions of any sort, Shanna much preferred her father's political gatherings. There, sharp ideas were exchanged, not meaningless talk about possessions or fashions. Her mind seemed to shut down and drift like a leaf in a summer breeze when she was exposed to that kind of conversation.

Alexandra frowned as she dabbed more makeup around Shanna's eyes. With a careful pass of her hand, she applied the final strokes. This, she knew, was as good as it got. The girl had good lines, but she wasn't a classic beauty.

"You don't have your mother's face," she said aloud without thinking, committing the same sin that everyone else did around Shanna.

Surprised, stung, Shanna pulled back a fraction. She hadn't expected this from Alexandra.

Alexandra shrugged, her expression never changing,

even though she saw the hurt in Shanna's eyes. She could have bitten her tongue off. She hadn't meant to hurt the girl's feelings. "But hey, who does?" she tossed off. "That's what makes her Rheena Brady and the rest of us peasants."

With a sigh, Alexandra returned her little army of tubes, brushes, and cotton balls to the interior of her black bag and snapped it shut. She stood back to survey her work. Not bad.

"Best I can do, Shanna." She wiped her hands on a tissue then wadded it up as she tossed it into the recesses of her bag.

Alexandra retreated to the door, her bag securely tucked under her arm. Her assistant was working on the bride and two of the bridesmaids, but Rheena was expecting her. And no one ever kept Rheena waiting. At least no one who wanted to continue to work for her. Though her list of clients was extensive, Alexandra knew better than to offend someone as powerful as Rheena. She turned toward Shanna as she was leaving.

"And I'd think about competition if I were you." She gave Shanna a knowing look as she turned to leave. Her path was blocked and she looked up, then recognized the man in the doorway. "Out of my way, handsome." Placing a bony hand against his chest, Alexandra neatly pushed him to one side. "I have desperate women waiting for me."

As, I am sure, do you, Alexandra added silently as she passed Jordan on the way out of Shanna's room.

2

Shanna turned, surprised. "Jordan, what are you doing here?"

She would have expected him to be downstairs. Her father had invited so many of his friends to this wedding that it threatened to turn into a semipolitical affair. Politics had turned into almost an obsession with Jordan in the last year. Shanna hadn't been aware of it before they were married. It was only after they had exchanged vows that his keen interest in the political scene had come to the surface. It pleased her because it gave them something of major importance in common.

Jordan, resplendent in a black tuxedo, placed his hands on his wife's bare shoulders and eased her around until she faced the mirror. Always alert beneath a deceptively languid exterior, he detected something different in the way she looked at him. The adoring eyes appeared uncertain, confused, perhaps even questioning. He wondered what had triggered it. A slight prick of tension had his stomach muscles tightening. Had his preoccupation shown? Did she suspect?

No, she wasn't clever enough for that. Not nearly as clever as he. It was probably only some trivial female thing. But just to be on the safe side, he'd pour on a little more charm, smile a little more broadly. Perhaps even make love to her tonight and behave as if her responses were exciting to him instead of incredibly mundane and boring.

He feathered one hand along the slope of her neck seductively. "Why, to escort my wife downstairs to the wedding, of course. Why else would I be here? They're almost ready to begin. If Douglas has any more champagne to fortify his nerves"—Jordan thought of the weak-chinned groom and smirked—"they're going to have to conduct the ceremony horizontally."

Shanna didn't want to go down to the wedding. She wanted to be alone with Jordan. She wanted assurances that she was just imagining that things, that *he* had changed in the last few months, slowly, subtly. She wanted to know that everything was just as it had been. Yet like a small child facing that closet door, wanting to open it to set fears aside and verify that it was empty, she was afraid. Afraid of the monsters that might be lurking behind it. So she said nothing and left the door closed.

"You don't have to escort me." Shanna saw the dark look enter his eyes and then disappear just as quickly. She wondered if she was just imagining it the way she was sure she had that time she'd turned and caught him staring at her as if she wasn't there at all, as if she was a chair or a lamp.

"I know that there're people down there you want to talk to, mingle with. You don't have to be here, dancing attendance to me. I can certainly find my way downstairs alone." Her hands fluttered to her honey-blond hair, held back with combs that were liberally studded with pearls. It had taken the hairdresser her mother had summoned a half an hour of fussing and muttering in Russian before he had declared the hairdo a success. "Besides, I'm not ready yet."

Jordan's expression tightened, as did his fingers on her shoulders. He hated to be kept waiting. "Nonsense, darling, you look perfectly ready to me. Besides, you know you're an asset to me. People want to see you, not me. You're the senator's daughter. I'm just his chief administrative aide."

Was it her imagination again, or was there something about the way he said "just"?

No, it wasn't her imagination, not this time. It was just his inherent impatience. Shanna realized by now that Jordan was anxious to get to where he was going, where he saw himself going. She understood the feeling. She'd seen it countless times before in her father's camp, in her father's circle of friends. So many people eager to be someone, to make their mark upon the world.

Because she loved him, she sought to soothe what she knew was a surge of gnawing insecurity. That, too, she was well acquainted with, on a very personal level.

"You're not 'just' anything, Jordan. My father relies very heavily on you. You know that. In the last two years you've found ways to become utterly invaluable to him and he appreciates that." Her father, even sharper now than the day he had stepped into the political arena, took nothing for granted. Though he had said nothing to her, Shanna was certain her father appreciated Jordan's dedication.

"I certainly hope so." Jordan smiled. The expression, just barely reaching his eyes, transformed him into someone who appeared almost celestial in bearing. Someone who wouldn't lie, or cheat, or betray anyone's trust.

It was, Jordan thought with pride, catching his reflection in the mirror, his chameleon mask. It represented all the things he wasn't. All the things he couldn't afford to be if he was to meet the destiny he had so carefully plotted out for himself. Later there'd be time to atone for whatever might need atoning for and to be a pillar of righteousness. Now there was the illusion to create. The flash and fire. Substance he would provide later. The public would never be any the wiser.

It was enough to assuage his conscience, such as it was.

Jordan Calhoun had materialized on the Washington scene literally out of nowhere. He had turned up a little more than two and a half years ago, fresh out of a Midwest law school he had put himself through, doing whatever it took to raise the money, to get the grades. Integrity was a word, he believed, for people with the funds to provide it. It wasn't anything he allowed to get in his way. If it raised its head, all he had to think about was where he had come from, of the poverty and smell of stale liquor, of the drunk old man who worked sporadically and of the angry, belittling woman whose hands always seemed to find him no matter where he hid to avoid the blows. Integrity couldn't have saved him from that. Only his wits could.

And his looks.

Jordan knew that and used them, just as he used his hands and his feet, automatically, without conscious thought. He relied on his looks and his charm to help him win confidence and gain access to places far more hardworking, plainer men could not reach. His looks helped absolve him of sins and made him privy to information not readily shared with others. The right incentive had him easily striking up friendships with people he loathed, they none the wiser about his feelings. It

was a gift of nature he used shamelessly from the time
he was fourteen and Miss Allison had passed him on to
the next grade after he had spent two hours delivering
groceries to her house and satisfying hungers that
couldn't be satiated with things purchased from a super-
market shelf. Shame was for losers. And Jordan had no
intention of being a loser. Ever.

He had come to Washington, D.C., with a suitcase
full of pride and a briefcase full of recommendations
signed by law-school professors who would have been
surprised to see their names affixed to documents of
such high praise for a man they had never met. It had
taken Jordan a painstakingly long time to compile those
letters. Faceless women he had slept with had supplied
the letterheads. He had used a great deal more patience
than he thought himself capable of forging his trail to
Shanna's door.

He had carefully chosen her as his best tool. She had
both lineage and money of her own. And a father who
was held in high regard in the right circles. Senator
Brady was in contention for the position of majority
whip. Jordan had wined her, dined her, and used every
wile at his disposal to make Shanna fall in love with him.

In the end, it had been almost ridiculously easy. Lost
in the shuffle all her life, outshined by a glamorous
mother and a charismatic father, Shanna was literally
starved for genuine affection. All Jordan had had to do
was supply it. Or pretend to. And he had. In spades.

Jordan's eyes narrowed as he looked down at her
again. The little bitch owed him. Big time.

Shanna saw the unguarded look in his eyes and shivered
involuntarily. "What's wrong? You looked so strange for a
moment."

Damn, he was going to have to be more careful. It
was just that sometimes—sometimes he got so agitated,

waiting for it all to really get under way, like a power hitter waiting for his turn at bat. He ran his hand over his carefully combed hair.

"Sorry, Shanna. Just edgy, I guess. I'm so damn bored." He looked at her pointedly. "It feels like the future is taking forever to get here."

"It'll be here before you know it," she said reassuringly.

"Yeah, sure," he murmured, threading his fingers through her hair. He watched the fine strands rain from his fingertips. Why couldn't she be beautiful, he wondered absently, like her mother? At least then he could be diverted for a while. Even her hair was different from her mother's. Rheena's was thick, luxurious, black like a tempest. Shanna's was blond, fine, straight, like a baby's. He was saddled with an infant.

But not forever, he promised himself. Not forever. Just until she served her purpose. And then no one would ever laugh at him again. He'd show all those fools back in Beauregard, Louisiana, where he had grown up. They'd still be grunts, working at their penny-ante jobs, while he'd become senator, planning his way up even higher.

He'd show them all.

Jordan looked at himself in the mirror. He was twenty-seven years old already. Looks didn't last forever. That garbage about men getting better as they grew older was just that, garbage. He wanted to make use of what he had *now*. He didn't want to wait until he "mellowed" or got "character" in his face. He wanted success in a hurry. He wanted to enjoy it all, not struggle toward it an inch at a time and wait until he was an old man to achieve what should be his now. There were plenty of young congressmen and senators. He intended to join their ranks. Soon. How else would he ever reach his ultimate goal? He intended to use his looks with the women and his charm with the men, just as his father-in-law had and did. Jordan's favorite saying was Seize the day. He planned to do just that.

Jordan took out a half-empty pack of cigarettes from his pocket. He saw Shanna wrinkle her nose in unconscious disapproval as he lit up. A certain perverseness danced through his soul like beads of water on a hot frying pan.

"Sorry, darling, just one." He tossed the pack onto her vanity table. "Being around your family always makes me a little nervous." In a way, it was true. Though he needed these people, though he intended to pick their bones for his own purposes, he was afraid of being found out. Afraid that they would discover that he was a sham, a cardboard front with nothing behind it, like a soundstage in a movie. There was always that, haunting him. He was constantly on stage, pretending, assessing every word he said, every action he took, and it was beginning to take its toll on him in small, telling ways.

Shanna reached up and took his hand in hers. A delicate hand, she thought. One that belonged to an aristocrat. "What would you have to be nervous about? They all envy you."

He gave a short laugh. "Because I have you." He kissed her cheek.

She should have felt warmth, she thought. But she didn't. Odd how cold his kiss felt. Shanna forced a smile to her lips. "No, because you're young and vital and are going places."

He allowed just enough honesty to show through. "Not nearly fast enough."

She released his hand. "Patience, Jordan. You have to have patience."

Easy for you to say, he almost said angrily, but bit the words back. Instead he took a long drag of his cigarette.

She had been born to luxury, he thought, careful to keep the resentment from his face. She didn't know what it was like to be mired in spirit-disintegrating poverty. To have others laugh because your clothes were castoffs, because your mother shopped at thrift shops stocked with other people's throwaways.

His eyes narrowed as he looked at her, pretending to squint over the cigarette smoke. *You didn't turn up wearing Billy Hathaway's jacket with the torn inside pocket and have kids at school throw mud at you, calling "pretty boy, teacher's toy" as they chased you.*

But he said nothing, though the words burned on his tongue. This wasn't a part of the past he had told her about. It wasn't part of the life he had fabricated before he had ever stepped onto D.C. soil.

Jordan crossed to the bathroom and pitched the cigarette into the commode, then flushed.

It was out there, he thought, waiting for him. Success. He could almost taste it. And Shanna was the key he needed to unlock the door. He just had to remember to be clever about it.

Walking back, his smile in place, he stood behind her again and looked at her reflection in the mirror. His deep blue eyes showed nothing but warmth.

A gift, he thought with pride as he glimpsed his own reflection. He clearly had a gift for this sort of thing. It would serve him well in the years ahead. The public was a collection of dolts who gravitated to the boob tube, nursing cans of beer and petty grievances they'd accumulated in their mundane throwaway lives. They would be easily won over. All he needed to do was be in the right place at the right time.

Running his hands along her bare shoulders, Jordan detected the tension she was trying so hard to hide. "You're tense, honey."

She had no explanation for it and didn't know what to tell him. He wouldn't understand. She didn't understand. "No, no, I'm not."

"Don't lie to me," he purred, sliding his fingers lightly along her skin. It was a purely sexual move that had her aching. He knew it would. "I know you inside and out."

I wish I did, she thought. "It's the wedding, I suppose. I hate being on display like this. The society hounds are out in full force down there. And Cydney loves them."

It was the wrong thing to say. Shanna realized it as she uttered the words. She saw a line tighten in his jaw. Damn, why didn't she think before she spoke? She knew how much he wanted to be in the public eye. She was supposed to be a help to him, she reminded herself.

"I—I mean . . ." she fumbled, her voice trailing off as she searched for the right words.

"You need to unwind. To have some fun." He knelt down beside her chair, holding her prisoner with his eyes. "I know, what we need after this is over is to get away. Just the two of us. Some quiet, romantic beach." He saw the hopeful glint enter her eyes and knew he had her.

She twisted around, looking at him. "Really, Jordan?"

"Really." He stroked her shoulder. "Right after Senator Whitney's little bash."

Shanna sighed inwardly. She knew how much being invited to that affair meant to him. Senator Whitney, one of the grand old men of the party, was having a private party at the end of the month, inviting only the most politically potent people. Her father and mother were on the A list. Jordan didn't even merit a footnote. Her heart ached for him.

She pressed her hand against his cheek. "Honey, we're not invited."

Jordan's blue eyes darkened for just a moment. He

turned the palm of her hand around and slowly stroked the sensitive center with his tongue, his eyes on her face. "Then get us invited, my pet."

Warm fingers of desire danced through her and she grasped at them the way a drowning man did to a life preserver. Or a dying man to a straw. "It isn't that easy—" She would have liked an invitation as much as he, but it wasn't in her nature to be pushy.

Long, tapering fingers dipped along her neckline, softly gliding along her breast. He heard the sharp intake of breath. It was too easy, he thought with satisfaction. Too bad Whitney wasn't a woman instead of a pompous ass of a senator. "It could be, for you. You're the senator's daughter. And I'm your husband."

"Couldn't we just have our own party?"

He laughed. "A little barbecue, perhaps? I wasn't meant for plebeian things, my pet. I was meant for finer things. That's why I married you."

There it was, she thought, finally solidifying. The "something" she had been afraid to face all this time. Had he married her because he loved her? Or because she was someone's daughter? Was she still doomed to play in other people's shadows, never being recognized for who and what she was?

Now what? Jordan stifled his annoyance. "Hey, you're frowning." With the tips of his fingers, he smoothed back her brow. "The future first lady can't have wrinkles." His lips followed the path his fingers had taken. "I won't allow it."

Shanna straightened. "Future first lady? Of what?" It was the first time he had ever mentioned plans so grandiose. Was he joking?

"The country."

No, he was serious. "The country?" she echoed incredulously.

"Your problem, Shanna," he said, still keeping his smile fixed in place, "is that you don't think nearly big enough. The country's had one young president, it's time they had another. And I *can* get there from here." He put out his hand, waiting for her to rise. His tone left no room for her to demur. "Ready?"

Apparently not nearly as ready as you, she thought, taking his hand. She smiled as she looked at him and told herself that ambition was a good thing.

So why did it leave her feeling so cold, so bereft, as if she had just stumbled onto a deep, dark secret?

3

For a woman who barely topped the sixty-inch mark, Rheena Fitzhugh Brady cast an enormously long shadow of influence and power. It engulfed everyone who came in contact with her. She was like a solar eclipse, blocking out the sun, taking its place. Except that her effect didn't pass in a matter of minutes. It remained in place until she permitted slivers of sun to shine through. Rheena could advance a career or ruin one with a well-placed word in the right ear. In her own way, Rheena wielded more power than the senator did. By blood and connections and money, she had avenues open to her that not even the powerful senator from Illinois had at his disposal.

Despite the fact that she had been raised to expect her every whim to be fulfilled, Rheena was first and foremost an astute businesswoman, capable of taking care of every aspect of life. Very little managed to get past her. She was definitely not a sheltered, pampered empty-headed socialite with no concept of the real world. On the contrary, she was very aware of it. She always had been. She refused to be uninformed and surrounded herself with the best sources of information, listened, then made her own decisions. She knew and understood people, their motives, their desires, and instinctively never fell victim to unscrupulous supercilious hangers-on, of which there were many in the twin worlds of society and politics. She was very much her own woman.

Her abilities to see past showy veneer allowed her to recognize her son-in-law for exactly what he was. A smiling, conniving opportunist who knew how to use people and situations to his advantage. Had he not been married to her daughter, Rheena might have even enjoyed sitting back and watching him at work. But he *was* married to Shanna and what he did directly reflected on her and all the Fitzhughs who had come before her. That colored the picture considerably.

Rheena looked at the redheaded woman hovering over her as she worked so carefully to polish the portraitlike face. Rheena's famous, pouty lips were drawn into a hard straight line.

"You're taking too long."

Alexandra hardly bothered to give Rheena any acknowledgment as she selected another lip brush. "I have more to work with these days."

"Watch your tongue, Alexandra."

Alexandra snorted. "You want to hear empty, flattering words? Talk to that pretty son-in-law of yours. If you can get past that outer ring of adoring women he's always attracting." Displeased, she replaced the lip brush and chose another. "Your daughter certainly has her hands full with that one." A wicked smile split her face.

The fabulous blue eyes shifted to look at the woman in the mirror. Alexandra looked like a grinning toad.

Rheena smirked. "You're old enough to be his grand-mother."

Alexandra lightly swirled a larger brush over a smat-tering of pink powder. "Age is a state of mind. It has nothing to do with one's birth certificate." She caught Rheena's eye in the mirror. "And we both know that."

Rheena's eyes sharpened. Did the old crone know? It had been just a temporary dalliance, lasting no more than a week. The cabana boy had only been twenty-one and had made her feel the way Roger never had, not even in the beginning. She couldn't remember his name anymore, but his lovemaking had the same effect as a vitamin B_{12} shot. It made her feel vital, energized. Her mouth curved into a smile as the memory warmed her.

But then Rheena's mouth hardened. What if Alexan-dra spread this tale? She lifted her chin as Alexandra applied the powder to her cheeks.

To attack rather than to wait and be forced to defend was the first lesson Rheena had taken to heart. "Why don't you do something with your hair, for heaven's sake?" She waved her hand at the untidy mess atop the other woman's head. The riotous hair was partially held in place with plastic, mismatched barrettes. "You're a beautician. Use some of your talents on yourself."

The criticism rolled off easily. If Alexandra hadn't developed a thick hide, she would have shriveled up years before she had ever crossed the ocean. "Picasso never looked like any of his work, either."

Touché, Rheena thought as she laughed. It was a lively, lusty sound that testified to her wholehearted involvement with life. "You know, you old bat, you're the only one who I'll allow to smartmouth me."

Alexandra pulled a tissue from the pocket of her oversized green smock. "That's because you're too old and too lazy to break in a new makeup artist."

It was a careless remark that struck a very real chord. And only Alexandra could have made it and survived with her skin intact. "Not old, Alexandra," Rheena whispered quietly.

Resting her hands on the arms of her chair, Rheena leaned forward and looked into the huge mirror that took up one half of the wall. Before her she saw the same stunning eyes that had belonged to the sixteen-year-old who had made her social debut on the arm of a Kennedy cousin. She had sworn to herself then that she would never look old. And she didn't. Very little had been necessary in the way of surgery, but she had gone that route gladly. The rest had been capriciously granted by nature. She turned heads wherever she went and she intended to continue to do so for a great many years to come. Looks were not something she would give up easily, not while there was an alternative.

"Never old," she repeated more lightly. Satisfied that Alexandra was doing her usual excellent work, Rheena relaxed and sat back again.

Pointy shoulders rose and fell beneath the smock. "Have it your way. Cary Grant looked pretty damn good, too, no matter what his age."

Rheena detected the worshipful note in Alexandra's voice. It was the first time she had heard it from the normally cynical woman. Alexandra had rubbed elbows with the rich, the titled, and the adored alike and never once had Rheena noticed that it affected Alexandra in any way. This reaction intrigued her. "That was different. He was a man."

Alexandra paused, allowing a genuine smile to crease her pinched lips. "Yeah, he sure was that."

Rheena studied the older woman. "You sound like a star-struck teenager."

Again, Alexandra shrugged, then carefully picked up

her brushes and selected one to use for Rheena's eyelids. "I was, with him."

Rheena thought back and smiled. A vision of a balmy
night and a very boring party in Buenos Aires came to
mind. Boring until he had taken her hand and led her
away. Or perhaps, they had led each other. "I met him
once, you know, when I was very young. It was at a party
for the American ambassador in Buenos Aires." Her
smile grew softer as the memory grew more vivid. "He
had a nice technique."

Alexandra's eyes narrowed, her work forgotten. "You
didn't."

Rheena shrugged carelessly, a world of meaning in
the simple gesture, in the full-mouthed smile she
offered. "If you say so."

Alexandra dropped the thin lip brush. "You did?"

Rheena merely nodded her regal head.

Alexandra moved closer. Rheena could smell the
mint she had been chewing. It mingled with the scent of
cigarettes. "How was it?" Alexandra whispered.

"Beyond description." Rheena let out a long, languid
breath as she remembered. "Something to drag out on a
lonely winter's night and remember forever."

Alexandra cocked her head and looked at Rheena
suspiciously. "Were you married to the senator at the
time?"

Rheena sighed. Grant had made her wish she hadn't
been. She had fantasized for months after that what it
would have been like, married to someone who knew
how to make a woman *feel* like a woman. But then, perhaps it was better to live with a dream than to marry it
and have it turn out to be a reality. Reality had ugly
edges to it and never lived up to expectations.

Rheena laughed in response to the question. "A lady
never tells." *That should keep her guessing*. Rheena

waved the other woman on to her work. "Now stop drooling and finish me. I'm told that the groom is busy changing the liquid composition of his body into ninety-eight proof. I want to get down there before they wind up pouring him into a glass."

Douglas would probably look better that way, she mused. Money only went so far in compensating for faults that nature had bestowed. "This is Cydney's third marriage and she's hoping it'll stick. I'd wager if she keeps the bars in her houses well stocked, she'll hang on to him." Rheena shook her head, wondering what it was that possessed these young women to chose such unsuitable men for themselves. One married with an eye out for lineage and the family name. The thrills came from different sources.

The knock on the door had her frowning in annoyance. Someone sent to hurry her along, no doubt. Rheena liked to set her own pace and didn't react well to being rushed. Time was gauged according to her, not the other way around. Cydney could wait, she decided. "Go away, whoever you are. I'm not ready."

Despite the dismissal, the door opened slowly. Shanna slipped in, leaving Jordan in the hall. Since the topic of Senator Whitney's soiree had come up, Shanna thought it best to lay the groundwork for getting an invitation. Her mother, though she loathed to ask her for anything, was her best bet. As far as she knew, her father hadn't arrived yet. The last-minute meeting about the president's veto was obviously still going on.

Shanna offered Rheena a slight smile, immediately feeling inferior the way she always did in her mother's presence. "Mind if I come in, Mother?"

"Come." The slightly beckoning gesture was befitting of a queen. Rheena kept her persona intact with everyone, even with her daughter. At times, especially with her daughter. She tilted her head and studied the girl's face. "You look a little peaked, darling."

It shouldn't hurt by now, Shanna thought. After so many years of offhand, belittling remarks, the words shouldn't hurt her anymore. But they always did.

"I did the best I could," Alexandra murmured, removing the long, navy-blue bib from about Rheena's neck.

"I wasn't talking about the makeup," Rheena snapped irritably. "She looks tired, drawn." She continued to regard her daughter's face. "You need a little fun in your life, Shanna." She gestured vaguely around, casting about for something tangible to work with.

She rose and moved toward the window. The three-thousand-dollar original whispered reverently like solemn monks praying in an abbey, echoing her movements. "Perhaps a party instead of a three-ring circus," she mused, glancing out. From her vantage point, she saw Alicia McNichol's husband leading a woman who definitely wasn't Alicia behind the gazebo. Rheena shook her head and hoped that they'd have the decency not to be discovered.

Her mother's suggestion caught Shanna by surprise. It was the opening she was looking for. "A party. That's what Jordan said."

Rheena pursed her lips, keeping the displeasure from her face. She avidly disliked her son-in-law, but on the surface, they made a nice family portrait and appearances were extremely important to Rheena. They always had been, to the exclusion of feelings and other people's wishes.

"Well, for once, Jordan and I seem to be in agreement. So," she said pleasantly, "why don't you find one to attend? Or better yet"—Rheena smiled, her eyes narrowing— "give a party yourself."

The suggestion was met with the expected response. She saw the uncomfortable expression Shanna sought vainly to hide. Nothing but a disappointment, no matter which way she viewed the girl. Rheena gave an impatient sigh. "You're never going to learn how to be a proper hostess, Shanna, if you don't host something." The disapproval dripped from her voice.

Didn't her mother understand that she didn't *care* about being thought of as a proper hostess? That standing around, making certain that everyone was suitably engaged in idle conversations that no one would remember tomorrow was totally unimportant to her? If she never gave a society party in her life, she would be vastly relieved. When it came to gatherings, her father's world held far more interest for her. She remembered the joy she had felt when she discovered that she and Jordan had this important factor in common.

Shanna took a seat on the white Italian leather sofa. It felt more like soft cream against her skin than a fabric. The leather whooshed seductively along the back of her legs, caressing them as she sat down. Aware of the annoyance in her mother's face, Shanna reluctantly pushed forward. This was for Jordan and she could put up with her mother's displeasure for his sake.

"I was thinking more in terms of Senator Whitney's party at the end of the month." Her mouth felt dry and she swallowed, hating the way her mother always made her feel. "Could you speak to Dad about getting us invited?"

Rheena turned slowly and looked down at her daughter. "Isn't that a little out of your league, dear?"

She was tired of everyone telling her where she belonged and didn't belong. Shanna lifted her head and dug in. "It's not out of Jordan's."

Rheena sighed. She might have known he was behind this. "That is your opinion."

Because the disparaging tone was aimed at Jordan and not at her, Shanna rose defensively. "Mother, he wants to become someone."

"Isn't being a gigolo enough for him?" Rheena saw Shanna cast an agonizing look toward Alexandra, flushing.

She'd forgotten about the other woman. Her faux pas had Rheena annoyed. She had no patience with mistakes, especially her own. She never let outsiders overhear such personal matters. "Oh, don't look at me with those hurt-filled eyes, you know what he is."

Alexandra coughed, clearing her smoke-clouded throat. Shanna drew back, collecting herself. She didn't like spilling her emotions like this, especially in front of someone else. Alexandra pretended to be occupied with gathering her things together, but Shanna knew better. Both women waited until Alexandra left the room.

"Until the next time," the woman murmured, closing the door.

Shanna laced her fingers together, forcing the words out. "I know what he could *be* if he only had the chance. If he was ushered into the right crowd, taken under the right wing, there's no limit—"

"To his ambition," Rheena murmured, patting her hair into place. She surveyed herself in the mirror and nodded her approval. The long, peach gown made her look five pounds thinner. She'd make certain all the wedding pictures were taken before she ate.

Shanna could see that her mother's mind was already elsewhere. She thought of her husband, standing beyond the door. Placing a hand on her mother's arm, Shanna tried to regain the woman's attention. "He needs to be seen, Mother."

Rheena thought of the report the weather-beaten, whiskey-voiced detective had dropped on her desk yesterday. It contained a rather lengthy list of the women

Jordan had bedded in just the last year. If sexual prowess was any yardstick, Jordan Calhoun had the makings of a marvelous politician.

"I would think that Jordan's been seen enough." Rheena disliked politicians. At times, even her husband was included in the group. But the prestige was alluring and the White House not out of reach, so she endured, the smiling wife. And played discreetly when she could.

Shanna looked at her mother, confused. "What?"

A baby-smooth hand cut through the air, waving away the statement. "Nothing, only talking to myself." The report was for her benefit, not Shanna's. Rheena meant to know everything that went on around her. Possibly she'd use the information someday to her advantage. For now it would remain her secret.

But someday Shanna was going to have to know. She felt sorry for her daughter. Rheena took Shanna's hands in hers. "Would that make you happy, attending the senator's party?"

It would make Jordan happy and that mattered a great deal to Shanna. "If Jordan has what he wants, then I'll have what I want and I'll be happy."

Rheena let her daughter's hand go, quickly bored. "I thought you just wanted to be married."

"Yes, that and happy."

Don't we all, Shanna. Don't we all?

Rheena straightened. "Ah, well, I can only help you attend the party. Happiness is a private affair. Very few of us have it." With a nod, she declared herself ready to join the vast crowd of people waiting below. "I'll speak to the senator about it."

The way her mother said it confused Shanna. "Dad?"

So bland and uninspired. How had she ever given birth to this lackluster child? "No, goose. Whitney himself. Why take the roundabout route when you can get farther being direct?"

It sounded like something Jordan might have said to her. Her mother and Jordan had more in common than either one would have liked to admit, Shanna speculated.

Well, at least that was over. She let out a sigh of relief. She had dreaded the idea of going begging to her father. It wasn't that he turned a deaf ear to her requests. He didn't. But he always treated her as if she were a simple-minded little pet to be humored.

As did her mother, she thought, glancing at the woman as she moved toward the door. But when her father did it, it hurt a great deal more. Her father's opinion still mattered.

Rheena smiled, a superior, self-satisfied expression spreading over her classic features. "So if I were you, I'd start shopping for my gown, Shanna. You're as good as invited."

She was still toying with her, Shanna thought. "And Jordan?"

Rheena shrugged casually, one hand on the doorknob. "You'll need an escort. He'll do as well as any. At least I won't have to be there to see him."

Shanna looked at her in surprise. "Aren't you going to attend?"

Rheena gave a short laugh as she shook her head. Her presence was no longer required at these hideous political receptions, thank the gods. Roger had stopped asking her to come along. She was not one to suffer in silence. "Not on your life. I find those things deadly dull and boring."

Shanna thought of the talks she had been privy to. As far back as she could remember, there had been politics in her background. She had grown up playing quietly in corners while florid-faced men with cigars made plans that cast the foundations of history as the country knew it. "I don't. I find them exciting."

A pitying look flittered over Rheena's features. "You always were a little odd, darling."

Rheena opened the door and found her son-in-law in the hall, a few feet away. He'd probably been listening to every word. She fixed a brittle, purposely insincere smile on her face. "Oh, Jordan, standing guard, I see."

"No, just waiting for the two most beautiful women in Washington to open the door." Smiling, he presented one elbow to Rheena, the other to Shanna.

Because he was devastatingly good-looking and she liked to draw envious looks, Rheena threaded her arm through his and turned toward the stairs.

For the moment, Shanna thought, taking his other arm, there was peace. She couldn't ask for more.

But she could always want more.

The wedding was as flamboyantly, as elaborately orchestrated as Shanna knew Cydney was capable of. The attending news media loved the display and saved it for posterity.

There were myriad camcorders and society reporters snaking their way through the celebration. Early on, she had gotten separated from Jordan. He had remained at her side for the ceremony, but as soon as the reception was under way, he had gotten involved in a five-way discussion about the recently proposed trade bill. She was getting used to this sort of thing happening, his inattentiveness to her at parties. He had pointed out to her that he was in the process of trying to further his career and, he had added, he was doing it for both of them. But she was beginning to have doubts about just how much she was included in his reasons. After all, they were more than financially comfortable enough to let things evolve slowly career-wise. If the situation had been reversed, her pace would have been a lot slower.

Except that to her, their relationship was of paramount importance. Everything else was secondary. She was beginning to suspect that in Jordan's mind, their relationship came second. And for all intents and purposes, it was a very distant second.

Nodding at several people she knew as she passed, Shanna sought a quiet spot where the society photographers weren't likely to bother her as they snapped photographs of the rich and famous who were attending the wedding of the week. She saw her grandmother sitting on a lawn chair off to the side of the gazebo where the couple had exchanged their vows. She cut through the throng to join her.

Eloïse Fitzhugh, her skin bearing testimony to an excessive love of the sun when she was a young girl, laced spidery fingers over the head of her gold cane as she watched the goings-on through sky-blue eyes that were still sharp. Eloïse had been Shanna's haven during her childhood, the one person, Shanna felt, who saw her as a complete entity, an individual, not an extension of anyone or anything. Though she was formal and undemonstrative, there was no mistaking the fact that Eloïse loved her only granddaughter. Shanna had always been secure in that, if in nothing else.

"Hello, Grandmother."

Eloïse raised her eyes as Shanna dropped into the white chair next to hers. "Surprised they didn't have trained seals and jugglers," she muttered with a shake of her head.

Shanna leaned over and kissed the parchmentlike skin. Eloïse was as careless of the rituals of skin care as Rheena was a slave to them. "You didn't like the doves," Shanna guessed. Cydney had ordered a flock of white doves to be released just as Douglas had said, "I do."

"Doves," Eloïse repeated disdainfully. "Pigeons in

whitewash, that's all they are. I hate pigeons. Messy, dirty creatures that relieve themselves on everything they pass over." A shadow of a smile creased her lips as she looked toward Cydney's new husband. One hand was around his bride's waist, the other was wrapped around a champagne goblet. "Perhaps it's fitting after all. That boy was born with a half-empty glass in his hand." Her eyes narrowed as she looked at Shanna again and verbalized the prophesy that was on almost everyone's mind. "It's not going to work, you know."

No, probably not, but it didn't hurt to hope. Shanna still liked to believe in hope, though for some reason, it was getting harder to do. "Grandmother, that's not very optimistic."

"I'm not a very optimistic person. Never have been. No cause to be."

No cause. Her grandmother's words struck closer to home than Shanna cared to admit. They echoed her present mood. Shanna fought vainly to shut it out and deny its existence. "How can you say that? You've had everything you've ever wanted."

The thin brows rose. "What do you know of it, child? What do you know about what I wanted?" Realizing her mood was getting too dark, even for her, Eloïse retreated, striving for a slightly lighter tone. "Besides, have you ever heard the old saying about being careful about what you wish for because you just might get it?" Shanna nodded. "I wished for your grandfather and I got him. Worst thing that ever happened to me."

Shanna didn't understand. She had always assumed that her grandmother had loved the big, blustering Thomas Fitzhugh. "But—"

She was too young, Eloïse thought, looking into the smooth, fresh face. Too young to know, but never too young to learn a valuable lesson. "Your grandfather was a very wealthy man who valued things, not people. I was his prize possession, and he took good care of all his possessions, kept them on a shelf to take out and admire at will. In return, I had every wish fulfilled. There was no reason to dream anymore, to make an effort," Eloïse said wistfully, murmuring the words to herself. She smiled sadly as she patted the girl's cheek. "And dreams are what keep us alive. Remember that."

Before she could comment, Shanna heard voices growing louder around them. She looked up and saw several people near them step aside as they hailed a greeting to someone. She smiled as she saw her father parting the sea of people, working his way over. He had missed the ceremony, but was making up for it now, playing the genial host. No one but her mother would be annoyed with him for being late.

"How did the caucusing go?" Shanna asked with genuine interest as soon as he was within hearing range.

Roger Brady reached for his mother-in-law's hand, enveloping it in his own two large ones. "The override is in our pocket," he said with a wink. It never failed to surprise him, after all his years with Rheena and his own sisters, whenever Shanna expressed an interest in the actual machinery of politics rather than the high gloss and sheen that went with it.

Turning cobalt-blue eyes on the only woman, in his estimation, worth a damn at the reception, he pressed a kiss to the soft, gnarled skin on her hand. Shanna smiled to herself as she saw her grandmother act as if she didn't care. She did, Shanna knew. Very much.

There was genuine affection in the senator's eyes as he looked at his mother-in-law. "How are you, Eloïse?"

She withdrew her hand from his and folded both

primly in her lap. The voice that answered his query was strong and clear. "Still breathing, still here."

Roger laughed as he took a glass of white wine from a passing steward. He allowed himself one sip before he told Eloïse, "And we're all very grateful for that."

Eloïse had always thought that Roger was too good for her daughter. Roger was a decent human being. Rheena hadn't really fallen into that category for a long time. Raising her chin, the older woman pinned him with a look. "Don't start practicing your campaign charm on me, Roger. You've always had my vote."

They understood one another, he and this old woman whose father had found ways that were not completely legal to make his fortune. But sins were forgiven if money was eventually used for good, and Calvin O'Hara, a robber baron in his youth, had died a beloved philanthropist. Roger bent and kissed the heavily lined cheek. "And you've always had mine."

Shanna glanced up to see the cool annoyance in her mother's face as Rheena directed her steps toward the trio. She was clearly annoyed that the senator had arrived so late and that he hadn't bothered to seek her out first. She looked from her mother to her husband, utterly ignoring her daughter.

"What a very touching scene." She presented her cheek for Roger to kiss as she grazed the air next to his cheek with her mouth. The frown was in her voice, if not on her lips. "You're unfashionably late, Roger, for your own niece's wedding."

Roger took another sip of wine, wishing for something stronger. "I'm sure Cydney will have another one for me in a couple of years and I'll make it up then."

Though she remained seated, Eloïse Fitzhugh had the ability to dwarf everyone else around her. It was a family trait that had yet to trickle down to her, Shanna thought, suppressing a smile as she watched her grand-mother come to her father's defense.

"This isn't a 'scene,' dear, this is real." Reaching up, she touched Roger's hand in a show of alliance. "Scenes are things that are played out before audiences, Rheena. But I suspect that you probably know all about that."

"The sound of pistols being cocked at close range has always been my cue to leave," Roger announced lightly. He downed the rest of his drink and set the glass on a nearby glass-top table. "You look beautiful, as always, Eloïse." He bowed to the older woman. "Rheena, I'll go mingle with our guests as I'm sure you'd want me to."

Roger turned before either woman could say anything more to him. Shanna was aware that once again, her father had absently ignored her presence. It was something that happened with frequency, but she never became used to it.

For a moment she thought there might be further fireworks between her mother and grandmother, but then she saw Rheena withdraw like a soldier retreating rather than risking defeat. Someone in the distance was trying to get her attention and Rheena was on again. She spared her mother one last fleeting glare. "Let me know when you want someone to take you home, Mother."

"I'll make sure you're the first to know." Eloïse said the words to her daughter's retreating back. The clear blue eyes glanced in Shanna's direction and she shook her head. "I wish I could say she was adopted, but the sad truth of the matter is, she's mine." Eloïse made a conscious effort to shed the topic. For her, Rheena was a lost cause. She took Shanna's face in her own hand. "So, when am I getting great-grandchildren?"

Shanna shrugged vaguely, remembering Jordan's annoyed look when she had tried to broach the subject. "Jordan doesn't want children just yet."

It was obvious that Eloïse found the excuse both flimsy and absurd. "So? A girl can forget to take one of those damn silly little pills once in a while." A man's wishes had never gotten in her way, and she had moved about in much stricter times. "Things happen."

Shanna cocked her head, enjoying the exchange. Her grandmother would have made a wonderful suffragette. "That would be deceitful."

Defeat was not a word Eloïse recognized. "Or cunning. Adjectives are provided, child, by the person telling the story. And the victor gets to write the story that's read." There was so much she wanted to tell Shanna, so much the girl needed to know. And there was so little time left. That bright young doctor who had attended to her last month had tried to sound optimistic when he had told her the news, but she knew better. The end could come at any time. If it weren't for Shanna, Eloïse would have been more than ready to go. But she worried about her, about how she could get along, a vulnerable innocent dolphin in a world of sharks.

Eloïse took Shanna's hand in hers and motioned her closer. "I want to tell you something, child. Something you need to know."

Shanna was used to her grandmother's stern expressions and solemn speech, but there was always a liveliness in her eyes before. The liveliness was gone now and it worried her. "What's the matter? Are you feeling ill?"

"At my age, why should I feel well? Everything's breaking down and there are no spare parts."

Shanna looked around for her father. "Maybe I should—"

Eloïse tugged at her hand for attention. "Maybe you should just sit here and listen when I talk."

Shanna sat down obediently, knowing that the best way around her grandmother was to appease her. "Yes, Grandmother."

"Do you know what life's about, Shanna?"

It was an odd question. Was she teasing? "In twenty-five words or less?"

There wasn't a hint of a smile on the old woman's face. "I'm serious. It's not about this." She waved a hand at the reception. "It's about choices, Shanna. It's always been about choices. Some we can make, some we should make, but don't, and some are made for us." She narrowed her gaze and everyone else disappeared except for the two of them. This was the most important part, the part Shanna needed to understand. "But you are never the prisoner of your destiny. Don't just lie down and hope life will get better. *Make* it better. You can either float or set a course." Eloïse leaned closer and placed her hand over Shanna's, as if trying to will her own experience, her own strength to her granddaughter. "Set a course, Shanna. Be sure to always set a course."

Dragging in a deep breath, Eloïse rose, leaning heavily on her cane. Shanna jumped to her feet and took hold of her grandmother's elbow, trying to support her as best she could. The old woman was unsteady and so very frail. Eloïse smiled up at her.

"And now a tired old lady is going to go home." She looked around the vast yard and sternly ordered, "But don't tell your mother. It would make her entirely too happy to be rid of me."

Someone jostled Shanna as they moved by and slurred an apology. Shanna hovered protectively over her grandmother. "You don't like Mother much, do you?"

Eloïse raised her head proudly. "She's my child. I love her. But no—"she let out a breath—"I don't like her. She was born jaded. All the Fitzhugh women were."

Shanna carefully guided her grandmother toward the double French doors at the rear of the house. "You weren't."

A raspy little laugh struggled out. "I'm an O'Hara, darling, not a Fitzhugh." Eloïse stopped for a moment and looked at Shanna. "But the curse skipped you, and for that I am eternally grateful." If asked if there was anyone she truly loved in this world, Eloïse would have quickly and singularly pointed to Shanna, the only drop of virtue she saw in a sullied, stagnant pond.

"I love you, Grandmother," Shanna whispered.

She expected nothing less, but it did gladden her heart to hear the words. "And well you should. Besides your father, I'm all you have in this cesspool."

Shanna was well aware of the fact that her grandmother deliberately had refrained from including Jordan in the small, tight circle. But that, she told herself quickly, was probably because for Eloïse it was too soon to tell. Her grandmother never passed judgment quickly. She waited, and watched.

"Why don't you wait here?" Shanna suggested. "I'll have your car brought around."

Eloïse dismissed the words with a wave of her unadorned hand. "Don't trouble yourself. Huxley will take care of me," she said, nodding toward the butler in the distance. She looked around the yard with its profusion of expensively dressed people eating, talking, drinking. It reminded her of a picture she had once seen depicting Rome before its fall. Yes, she would be well rid of this soon. "You go and try to have some fun, Shanna. You don't have nearly enough fun."

She knew that, small or large, there was never any arguing with her grandmother on any stand she took. Shanna stepped back, allowing Eloïse her dignity. "Yes, Grandmother."

Shanna watched Eloïse slowly make her way into the house, Queen Victoria taking her leave of the masses. As she watched she wondered what had prompted the sudden lecture her grandmother had delivered. Did the old woman see things within her that she had as yet failed to clearly express to herself? Did her grandmother sense the vague dissatisfaction that was taking seed within her? Eloïse always did have the ability to cut to the heart of the matter. Maybe she'd go and visit her grandmother in a few days and have a real long talk with her.

The thought buoyed her spirits. Shanna turned to look for her husband, humming under her breath.

Jordan was right where she thought he'd be, next to Senator Kyles, listening, absorbing. She saw the way Jordan's hand tightened on his glass just before he spoke, seizing an opportunity to state his opinion. The right opinion obviously, because Kyles slapped his back and laughed.

Jordan had incredible timing, she thought as she hung back on the perimeter of the circle, hesitant to intrude. She knew he was a novice, knew he had only these last three years emerged from law school, but he had a polish, a verve, that made him seem as if he had been practicing his whole life for gatherings just like this, for moments just like this.

"So here's the little girl who wants an invite," a loud voice boomed in her ear just as a large arm fell heavily on her shoulders.

Shanna didn't have to look up to know that Senator Hugh Whitney had joined her. "Hello, Senator," she said warmly. Out of the corner of her eye, she saw that Jordan, still animated, was now also watching her.

With his shaggy leonine white hair and the salt-and-pepper eyebrows that sprouted like tufts of cotton in an untended field, Senator Whitney always reminded Shanna of a portrait she had seen of Mark Twain in his later years. All the senator needed, she judged, was a white suit and panama hat to complete the picture.

Whitney, the slight smell of bourbon on his breath, inclined his head toward Shanna. His arm remained firmly around her shoulders. "Your mama tells me that you're eager to gladden an old man's heart by gracing his humble little party."

Shanna grinned. The senator from South Carolina had bounced her on his knee when she was still in diapers and had bought her a pony for her fifth birthday. He was generous, loud, and, she knew, oftentimes crude, though he had never used anything but pristine language around her. Conservative, old-fashioned to a fault, Whitney still believed that "ladies" belonged on pedestals and out of the way of men unless they were summoned. But he enjoyed playing the magnanimous grand old uncle when the whim moved him.

With effort, Shanna threaded her arm around the man's thick waist. "There's never been anything humble about you, Senator, and we both know it."

He laughed heartily and pulled her closer to him, giving her a squeeze. "Still my favorite lady, even though you broke my heart and married that pretty fella." He gestured vaguely in Jordan's direction with his empty glass.

She knew the game and played along. For all his rhetoric and sly winks, the senator was absolutely harmless and devoted to his wife of thirty-two years. "You're married, Senator."

"I know." He sighed mightily. "But I was hoping to hold you in reserve. Annabel's been threatening to leave me since before you were born. Someday she's going to make good on her promise." He winked. "I'll need comforting then."

He gave her one more squeeze then released her. "Until then, if you want to listen to a bunch of stuffy old men trade opinions, you're welcome to come. I just thought someone as young as you would be bored to tears. Annabel always is." His eyes lit up as he saw a waiter approach in their direction. Beckoning him over, the senator traded his empty glass for a full one. It made no difference to him that it was full of champagne instead of bourbon. Liquor was liquor and had the same end result. He had been raised on moonshine, he liked to brag, and it had given him a cast-iron stomach. "As is your mama."

Being compared with her mother bothered Shanna. Of late, she found herself actively rebelling against it. Her smile slipped a little as she looked at the senator. "I'm not my mother."

Spirit, that's what it was, Whitney thought as he saw something flash in Shanna's eyes. He had always admired spirit, in horseflesh and in women. "No, that's for dang sure. You're a whole other act, Shanna." He grinned broadly. "I'll be sure to have them set a place for you at the table come Friday."

She saw that Jordan had stopped talking and was watching, though a young blonde was trying to snare his attention. "Two places?" Shanna pressed Whitney.

He toasted her and fleetingly envied Jordan the match he had struck. "Two places," Whitney confirmed before taking a long pull of his drink.

With a small inward sigh of relief, Shanna turned and gave Jordan a high sign as soon as the senator had walked away from her. She supposed she was in debt to her mother.

The smile that lifted Jordan's lips was positively beatific. It erased any bad feelings she had about the means she had used to gain the end.

5

Streams of moonlight floated in through the windows on either side of the bed where they had made love only twenty minutes ago. Lighting only parts of the room, the silver threads gave it an ethereal glow. The shaft from the window on the left lightly danced along Jordan's naked body as he lay sleeping, the tangled sheet gathered about one leg.

So now he even glowed in the dark. A sad smile grazed Shanna's lips.

She pulled her legs in under her on the chaise longue as she sat, staring at Jordan, letting herself see him for perhaps the first time the way he was, not the way that she wished he would be. She hugged herself for warmth, for comfort, in a fruitless effort to drive away the aching, empty feeling that was growing within her.

Jordan had made love to her tonight. Wildly, frantically. Quickly. And then within a few moments he had fallen asleep, completely spent. The very same action that had drained him and then lulled him to a sound sleep was keeping her awake.

They had made love, or was it that they just had had sex? She wasn't certain anymore that she knew the difference, although she thought she had once.

Shanna balled her hands into fists as she kept them crossed, pressed against the sides of her breasts. She just couldn't shake the feeling that in those few, private moments that should have been so special, it hadn't really mattered to Jordan that it had been her in his arms and not someone else. There had been no expression of love from him, no words of endearment to differentiate her from any one of a number of faceless women who drifted in and out of Washington society looking for a few hours of companionship and anonymous gratification. It hadn't felt personal somehow. He had treated her as if she was just a willing body and nothing more.

Shanna pushed her hair back from her face with fingers that were still shaking. She had to stop this. *Of course there was more, idiot. He's your husband. He loves you, remember?*

Lord knows Jordan had said it often enough. I love you. I love you. I love you. So why didn't she feel it, inside, where it counted? Why didn't she feel happy, protected, loved? Perhaps it was because the words had been too smooth, had sounded too rehearsed.

Even on her wedding night, she had felt there was something lacking. There were no soft, languid moments building up to the crescendo she thought she was to anticipate. She had come to Jordan a virgin on her wedding night, something that had completely astonished him. A twenty-one-year-old virgin was a rarity, but she had been determined to save this one individual thing, this one true shred of her own identity, and give it as a precious gift to the man she married.

She closed her eyes and remembered the overwhelming stab of hurt she had felt when she had seen the amused look in his eyes. He had almost laughed when she had told him, then quickly said that nerves were responsible for his insensitive reaction. His words. "Insensitive reaction." It had appeased her. Especially when he seemed so sincere as he swore that he was as nervous about pleasing her as she was about pleasing him.

The first time. A lifetime of anticipation and it had been over with so fast. Was this all there was? Was this what she had been daydreaming about, looking forward to? Frenzied movements? The tearing of her dress and groping hands? The thrusting invasion that was followed so closely by pain? And then nothing? That was it? That was the reward for the yearning, the pounding pulses, the expectations and desire?

Her disappointment was overwhelming.

She had absolutely no frame of reference to work with. There had been no one to compare feelings with, no close girlfriends to share that kind of an experience with. Awkward and trapped in her isolated world, Shanna felt more at ease with old politicians than with young women her own age. Consequently, she had nothing but a belief that somehow there should have been something more than this used feeling.

Shanna let out a shaky breath as she drew herself up into a tighter ball. In the background she heard his steady, rhythmic breathing and wished that she could sleep as easily as Jordan did. She wished she could take her pleasure as easily as he did. She shrugged. Maybe she had read too many books, seen too many movies, dreamed too many dreams.

Dreams are all we have, Shanna.

Her grandmother's words echoed in her brain over and over again, like an old melody that refused to die once it had found a place. She believed in them.

Dreams were an integral part of life as was the struggle to realize them.

Jordan murmured in his sleep and she narrowed her eyes, focusing on his face. He looked innocent, sweet. She was making too much of this.

Jordan had dreams, she thought defensively. His, it appeared, were just on the threshold of becoming reality.

So why couldn't hers? They were far narrower in scope. Or were they?

"I had them in the palm of my hand, Shanna!" he had cried out enthusiastically this evening as they had walked into the expensive Georgetown house that had been a wedding gift from her father. Exhausted, enormously pleased with himself and the evening in general, Jordan crossed straight toward the bedroom. As he went he threw off his jacket and dropped it on the floor behind him.

Following, Shanna picked it up and brushed it off. Entering the bedroom, she carefully hung the jacket on his clotheshorse.

"Yes, you did," she agreed with no small pride.

She had seen the way the other men at the party had sat back and watched Jordan tonight. Once he had begun talking, a spark had traveled through the room. There had been envy in their faces. Envy because he was young, and with their backing, the political arena would just be opening up for him. Opening with possibilities that they no longer had because they were old and the quest for leadership was ever in search of the young and the strong.

Jordan kicked off his shoes, one in one direction, the second in another, and then crossed his arms and watched. Shanna retrieved the expensive Italian-made shoes and placed both in the closet on his side. He frowned slightly at her mundane and predictable behavior.

But the evening had been too much of a success for him to dwell on what a colorless drudge his wife was. He yanked at his bow tie and the sides drooped down like tired black streamers. He replayed the highlight of the evening in his mind. All had grown quiet to listen to the debate he went on to win.

"Put that old codger in his place, didn't I?"

She waited until he pulled the bow tie from his collar and then took it from him and put it away. Of late, she had a crying need for things to be more orderly than they were. This small part she could control.

She hadn't liked seeing Jordan like that this evening. For one moment, as he cut Rawlings down, Jordan's tongue had been rapier sharp. She had glimpsed a ruthlessness that would have frightened her if she hadn't loved Jordan as much as she did. If she hadn't known him. Still, it had been a cruel thing to do. "That 'old codger' has twenty years of experience in government behind him."

She would defend a wimp like that. The old fool was right up there in her league. "Stale experience," he pointed out. "History, Shanna. The past." Jordan swiped at the air with his hand as if to catch something that she didn't see. Something that was visible only to him and meant a great deal. He opened his hand, fingers slowly unfurling, palm up. He offered it to Shanna like a tangible gift. "I want the future."

He was high, she thought. But not on alcohol. Jordan was very careful to abstain from all but the barest of sips. He touched his lips to the glass for form's sake only. He wanted nothing to cloud his mind, nothing to get in the way of opportunities that might cross his path. No, this high was more than that. She recognized it for what it was and tried not to let it upset her. Jordan was high on the promise of power.

It was a revelation she didn't like.

Removing the pins that had fastened her hair, she made a conscious effort to sound cheerful. She knew she should be happy for Jordan, for the success that appeared destined to be his. And yet, as his goals were beginning to appear within reach, he seemed to be metamorphosing into someone she didn't know.

She tossed the pins on the vanity table. "Dad sounded pretty positive just before we left. It looks as if they're really going to consider running you for the seat that Gallegher is vacating." Adam Gallegher had held the congressional seat for four terms and was calling it quits at the end of this one. Poor health had caused him to grow tired of the constant fight.

Jordan came up behind her and slipped his hands around her waist. Her father had been instrumental in raising his name during the discussion tonight. It was time to keep his daughter happy.

"Why shouldn't they?" He thought of the roomful of movers and shakers, men who "found" proper backing and money for the candidates of their choice. Candidates who could win the public vote while furthering the party platform. As well, he thought with a smile, as serving private ends. He saw nothing wrong with that tactic. It suited his needs just fine.

Jordan nuzzled the crook of Shanna's neck, feathering a few kisses along the slope. "I'm young, dynamic. Ready." With the tip of his finger, Jordan began sliding the zipper of her dress down her bare back. He smirked to himself as she moved against his touch like a kitten gathering warmth at the hearth. "Who better than me?"

Shanna thought of the dedicated man who had come to work in Gallegher's office during the last term. "Jack Peters, for one." She felt Jordan's fingers release the zipper and momentarily tighten into a fist along her back before he relaxed them again.

Jack Peters. The suggestion was laughable. He was a pasty-faced do-gooder who was nothing more than fodder for men like him. "That droopy-eyed jerk?" Jordan muttered a curse he knew Shanna particularly hated and felt her stiffen slightly. "The guy's got as much color as a black-and-white monitor."

Looks weren't everything, she thought defensively, seeing her own reflection in the mirror through her mother's critical eyes. "He's sincere," she pointed out stubbornly. It wasn't right that someone like that should be dismissed because he didn't have the proper "image," the proper "look."

"He's a loser," Jordan insisted, annoyed that she was defending the man.

Shanna opened her mouth to point out Jack's record as an assistant DA, then closed it again. What was she doing, arguing with Jordan? This was the beginning of his big moment and she *was* happy for him. It just bothered her that she couldn't wholeheartedly approve of the method that left bodies in the wake of his first triumph.

She turned and smiled at him over her shoulder. "And you're not."

That was better. His mood shifted. "Damn straight I'm not a loser. Never have been, never will be," Jordan pronounced vehemently, yanking the zipper down the rest of the way. It broke. The gown fell about her feet as he turned Shanna around to face him.

Standing nude before him, except for a pair of panty hose, she felt a blush rising and looked down at the floor. Even now, after two years of marriage, she couldn't get over the feeling of embarrassment whenever she was undressed. The zipper and the metal dangling from it stared up at her. She picked the gown up and held it up to him. "You broke it."

He pulled the dress from her hands and tossed it aside. "What do you care?" He heard the hard edge in his voice and masked it with a smile as he placed his hands possessively on her shoulders. "You've got lots more. I just want to get my hands on you, gorgeous."

Her head jerked up. She couldn't stand for mockery, not from him. "Don't call me that."

Damn it, now what was the matter with the little bitch. "Why?"

"Because we both know I'm not."

So, she wasn't as stupid as he thought. But still not as smart as he was. The boyish grin that had worked for him with a league of women spread over his face.

"Sure you are. Besides," he said softly, "we're in the world of politics, Shanna. Everything is an illusion." He stripped off his shirt, letting it fall on top of her torn gown. When Shanna made a move to pick it up, he caught her by the arm and gave her a slight shake.

"Leave it."

Shanna bit her lip. She had never learned to emulate her mother's careless disregard for money and possessions. "I just wanted to—"

"I said leave it," he ordered, his voice stern.

It pleased Jordan to be able to cast off expensive clothes without a second thought, assured that there would be more when he wanted it. That there would always be more when he wanted it. He had paid his dues for that privilege. Over and over again.

After all but ripping off her panty hose, Jordan shed his trousers and deliberately kicked them over toward the rest of the clothing. That one small pile represented more money than a factory worker in Beauregard made in a year, he thought with pure satisfaction. He threaded his fingers through Shanna's hair. His breath stroked her face, making her vibrate.

"The maid'll take care of it," he whispered as lust began to demand its release. In the dark, one woman was as good as another, and as far as bodies went, Shanna's was ripe and firm, even if she was uninspiring in every other way. "Right now I have something more pressing than folding clothes to take care of."

To emphasize his words, he pulled Shanna even closer to him, moving his throbbing body against hers. He studied her eyes, waiting to see the desire bloom. It never ceased to feed his ego, watching women respond, watching women want him.

The grin he flashed her was slightly lopsided and sent Shanna's pulse racing. Perhaps this time she'd reach the pinnacle, too. Perhaps—

Jordan kissed her hard, bruising her mouth as he bit her lip. With a groan, he pushed her onto the bed. He was over her as the breath whooshed from her lungs, never giving her a chance to catch it. His hands were everywhere, raking over her like familiar, used territory. Seeking something she didn't know how to give him.

She felt his teeth as he suckled at her breast and tried to push him back. She wanted nothing more than to make him slow his pace just a little. Just until she could catch up. A sob began to rise and grow within her.

She needed time, she thought desperately. Time. She wanted to build up to the fever pitch that always seemed to seize Jordan instantly. She wanted to share in this, not be on the outside, not be just a vessel for him.

"Jordan, wait," she pleaded against his mouth, but her words were swallowed up as he continued to savage her lips.

He raised himself on his elbows. He had heard her, felt the words vibrate on his tongue. His eyes were dark, prophetic, and for a moment he was a stranger.

"I'm never waiting for anything again, Shanna." And

then he thrust himself into her so hard she cried out loud from both the pain and the surprise.

Jordan rode the crest he had created until its end, then fell, exhausted, over her. When he made love with other women, it always lasted longer for him. But there was nothing about Shanna to inspire him, to drive him to new heights, so he did it quickly, enjoyed himself, and moved on.

"Did I hurt you?" he muttered into the pillow. Vaguely he was aware of her crying out, but there hadn't been the sound of ecstasy ringing in it. The bitch was nothing more than a damn robot.

Shanna blinked back tears that had suddenly sprung to her eyes. She didn't want him to see her crying. He wouldn't understand. "No," she whispered.

"That's good." He gave her a quick kiss for good measure. Women wanted tenderness after the fact, or some garbage like that, he remembered. "If I did, I didn't mean to. It's just that I wanted you so much." The last words faded from his lips as he fell into a deep, almost druglike sleep.

It should have made her happy to know that he wanted her so fiercely. But it didn't. He had rolled off her and was instantly asleep.

Upset, feeling as if she was adrift, Shanna stared at the ceiling, wishing she knew what was wrong with her, with them, and how to fix it. She shivered. The shiver grew and she couldn't control it. Afraid that she would wake Jordan up if she stayed there beside him, she rose and put on a nightgown.

She couldn't stop the shiver that danced insistently through her even when she pulled the heavy blue flannel robe from out of the closet and then wrapped herself up in it.

Shanna sat down on the chaise longue. Taking a slow,

deep breath, she tried to steady herself as she rubbed her hands up and down her arms, waiting for the warmth to return. Waiting for her body to stop shaking.

Shanna sat there for a long time, waiting.

6

As Jordan began to take full advantage of the machinery that had been made available to him to help ensure the success of his first campaign, Shanna saw her heretofore rather pacific life pitched into the outer rim of a hurricane. It wasn't as if she was totally unprepared for it. Her father had first run for office when she was six years old and he hadn't been out of politics once in the ensuing eighteen years. Election fever, in one form or another, was a condition that had always been a part of her life.

But she had never been the wife of a candidate before, never been completely aware of or appreciated the hundred and one things that were required of her in order to be supportive of Jordan's efforts. As a candidate's daughter Shanna had been relegated to the sidelines, brought in for photographs and the occasional human-interest story.

Her mother had never entirely gone the route that now stood before Shanna, because that would have pushed her into the background. She would have appeared to be standing in her husband's shadow and that was something Rheena would have never allowed to happen. She pulled her own strings for Roger from a position she was supremely comfortable in. The center of the court.

Shanna had no connections of her own, no affiliations to draw on in order to help Jordan. Despite that, she made up her mind to be an asset to him, to make every effort count. She would help him, she thought as she stood beside him when he had announced his candidacy to the press, through sheer dedication and hard work. Beginning uncertainly, she decided to throw herself wholeheartedly into assisting him in formulating his campaign strategies. Or tried to.

To her surprise and subsequent disappointment, Shanna realized quickly that behind the scenes, Jordan regarded her as far more of a hindrance than an asset. He didn't listen when she tried to make suggestions. Rather than having her share as a partner in his plans, Jordan obviously wanted her in the role of the supportive little wife who dressed well, said empty words, and smiled.

She was to attend social events and fund-raisers and, when asked to speak, was to parrot cheerful words that had been prepared for her by someone else. Under no circumstances, Jordan had warned her, was she to elaborate on topics on her own, even if she felt that they shared a common opinion.

She was to be, she saw, a puppet. It was her name, her lineage that counted. Not herself. Hurt, Shanna made the decision to ride it out and hope that eventually she could change things around and have her opinion count for a change.

Jordan had no time for Shanna's trivial input and her soft, bleeding-heart approach to issues she thought should be given priority. There were congressmen to cajole, mayors to rally to his side, money to find. And people to cull and, he added silently, to gull.

"Why don't you do something really useful," Jordan said to her after returning home from a grueling meeting that involved his father-in-law and several other senior members of the party. His patience had worn thin after hours of being affable and agreeing with his mentors. "We've got an apartment in Virginia, but I think we'd do better getting a house. It gives us an air of stability. Yes"—he thought it over—"I need a house if I'm to represent the fair state of Virginia's people adequately."

He allowed his lips to twist in a cynical grin that vanished quickly, replaced by the innocent expression he showed to his future constituents. "Find us a house."

At least that much she could do for him, she thought, resigned. "Any place in particular?"

"Virginia." Couldn't she get anything straight?

The seventh district was large. "I know that, I meant where in Virginia."

"Use your head, Shanna. I want some place private, but I don't want to appear too inaccessible." He remembered to give her a quick kiss on the cheek before retiring to his den. There was still a speech to rework. He needed better writers than he had, he thought. They were all plodding idiots who had no idea how to appeal to the masses. He was better off writing his own speeches. "Don't want the voters to know that we're out of their league now, do we?"

"No," she murmured, wondering if it had been a slip on his part, or if he really thought of himself as above the people he was seeking to represent. He was becoming a snob, she thought sadly. He *was* changing.

The next morning, she telephoned her mother's

social secretary Denise to ask if the woman knew the names of any real estate agents that she could get in contact with in Virginia.

"Moving, Shanna?" the woman asked warmly. "We'll miss you around here." Denise, a single mother of three, had tenaciously stayed on with Rheena, enduring fire and brimstone and a salty tongue, for ten years.

"Jordan's going to run for a seat representing the seventh district in Virginia." Congressman Calhoun. It did have a nice ring to it. "We have an apartment there now, but we'd both rather have a house."

Denise understood. "I'll see what I can do," she promised.

Shanna expected a call back that afternoon, or possibly the next morning. The last thing she expected was a visit from her mother the following day. She was already running half an hour behind schedule. She was to take a commuter flight to Virginia and meet Jordan at a rally in a large business center in the heart of the seventh district.

"Mother, what are you doing here?" Shanna whirled around as she saw her mother's reflection in the mirror. Her mother had a key to the house and used it whenever the whim hit her. Shanna never felt as if the house was completely hers.

Rheena stood in the doorway of her daughter's bedroom and critically looked over the pale blue suit Shanna had on. She shook her head.

"You don't like it," Shanna said needlessly.

"Makes you look too old, too conservative. The reason they picked that husband of yours is because he's so damn engaging and youthful looking." She frowned. "Stop dressing like his mother."

Just once she would have liked to hear something positive, Shanna thought. But that was probably asking for the impossible. She looked around for her purse. "I'm going to be shaking people's hands on a busy street corner, Mother. I'm not going to a cocktail party."

Elegant shoulders rose and fell beneath the designer jacket. "Have it your own way. What do I know about being the wife of a successful politician?"

Nerves already brittle, Shanna felt her temper fraying at the ends. "Did you come to look me over or was there another reason for this visit?" Finding her purse on the bureau, she opened it and put her wallet and keys inside. As an afterthought, she threw in a roll of mints.

Rheena eyed her daughter with a superior smirk. "You've gotten testy now that you've got someone to warm your sheets. And here I am, on a mission of mercy. I came to give you this." Rheena produced a photograph of a two-story colonial house from her clutch purse and handed it to Shanna.

Dumbfounded, Shanna stared at it. It was happening again. Her mother was making decisions for her. When was it ever going to stop?

"Denise told me you were looking for a suitable house in Virginia. I called Hawley and Holmes, my realtors and they faxed me the particulars on several houses." A scarlet nail tapped the top of the photograph in Shanna's hand. "I had someone take this photograph for you after I made my decision. This place will be perfect for you and Jordan. I've put in a bid for you."

Shanna felt her throat constricting. *Stop it, Mother. Stop taking over my life.* Shanna kept her voice steady. "I haven't seen it yet, Mother."

Rheena frowned at the quiet, firm tone her daughter used. She wasn't used to opposition, least of all from Shanna. "So?"

This couldn't continue to go on this way indefinitely. Somewhere along the line, she was going to have to take a stand. It might as well start today. Shanna took a breath. "So I might not like it."

It hadn't really occurred to Rheena to consult Shanna or that she might have an opinion. It wasn't as if the girl had ever displayed good taste, or even good sense for that matter. "I like it."

Then you live in it. Shanna slowly threaded her purse strap over her shoulder, struggling to keep the irritation that throbbed within her breast from breaking through like a creature trapped beneath thin ice. "Fine, and I probably will, too."

She turned to face her mother, searching Rheena's face for a shred of understanding. Didn't her mother see that she had to be her own person? That she was perfectly capable of making decisions? That she wanted to lead a life that wasn't tied to the Bradys or the Fitzhughs or any other pseudo-dynasty?

No, her mother didn't see anything of the kind, Shanna realized. She found only annoyance in her mother's eyes. "But I just want to see it first, Mother. With Jordan."

It was obvious that the girl only wanted to argue for argument's sake. Stupid. "You haven't got that much time," Rheena pointed out.

Shanna refused to give in. "I've got enough time to see the house I'll be living in."

Exasperation raised Rheena's brows even as her eyes narrowed. Her daughter was a stubborn idiot, just like her father. "The realtor wants an answer before the weekend. There's another couple who's interested. You have two fund-raisers and a banquet to attend between then and now. Just how do you propose to manage seeing the house? With Jordan," Rheena tagged on sweetly as an afterthought.

So she knew her itinerary. Shanna had no idea that her mother was suddenly keeping such close tabs on her life. She thought of all the lonely years she had spent as a child, longing for her mother's attention. Was that what it would have taken to get it? The potential of spending life in the limelight? She felt the bitter taste of bile in her mouth. "We'll squeeze in the time. I want to know what the kitchen looks like, Mother, and where the bedrooms are."

Rheena turned to leave. She'd had enough of Shanna's obstinacy. Did the silly little twit think she had nothing better to do with her time than find a suitable place for Senator Brady's daughter to reside in? She placed her hand on the doorknob and looked at her daughter.

"You want a house. What difference does it make what the kitchen looks like?" Rheena's full mouth curved into a malicious smile. "And I'm sure Jordan will break in the bedrooms one by one soon enough."

Shanna stiffened at the implication. There was no use trying to make her mother understand anything. "I just want to see it all for myself."

Rheena shrugged carelessly as she opened the front door. "Have it your way. If you lose the house, you lose the house. I was just trying to help." Making an exit, she slammed the door in her wake.

The house shook as the sound echoed throughout. "Yes," Shanna murmured to herself as she stared at the door, "I suppose you were." But she didn't want the kind of help her mother had to offer. She didn't want to be herded like some mindless entity, she wanted to be consulted. As an intelligent equal.

Of course first, she knew, she had to prove that she *was* Rheena's equal.

It was going to be a tough, uphill fight.

°   °   °

His forearm hurt from the hands he had had to firmly grip and his face felt as if it had permanently tightened into a smile. And now she was whining about some house her mother was arranging for them to live in.

Jordan couldn't afford to scowl in public at his wife, but with very little urging, he would have gladly throttled her someplace where no one could see them. He ignored the photograph she had tried show him during a lull in the campaigning and fervently wished he could ignore her as well.

"Look," he told her softly, taking care not to be overheard, "any place is fine as long as it gives off the right kind of message."

Shanna slowly flexed her fingers. She had only been with him for half the time he had spent here at Hampton Plaza and every joint ached. She knew the kind of message he was talking about. Old money. Respectable. Everything she was supposed to represent. Was that why he had married her? she wondered. Because she sent out the "right" sort of message to voters?

The streets began to fill again as another throng of people approached them. It seemed as if the people moved about this area in spurts. Shanna braced herself for another round of politicking. All around them, the busy plaza was filled with Jordan's campaign volunteers. They wore bright blue armbands that echoed the color of his eyes. His name was written in white across the azure field, branding the volunteers as they cheerfully passed out flatteringly worded literature about Jordan. Behind them was a background of white placards with startling royal-blue letters that proclaimed: JORDAN FOR CONGRESS.

Jordan, his smile widening as he grasped a distin-

guished elderly man's hand and introduced himself, said
under his breath, "Your mother has probably picked out
just the right place."

How could she assert herself when everyone seemed
to be bent on not letting her? Was she being so unrea-
sonable about wanting to see the house before they
moved in? She didn't know anymore. "But—"

What was the matter with this woman? "Rheena has
taste, Shanna, and breeding," Jordan pointed out, his
stern, whispered tone at war with the boyish smile on
his face. "We'll go with the house she's picked out and
that's the end of it." He had allied himself with this family to reap the benefits that such an association would
harvest. Why was Shanna constantly trying to sabotage
that?

Jordan stepped forward to seize another hand and
pump hard. With the flat of his other hand against the
small of her back, he gave Shanna a slight push toward
the tall stranger.

"Hello, I'm Jordan Calhoun and this is my wife,
Shanna." For just one beat, he looked at Shanna, smile
never drooping, then shifted his eyes to the man whose
hand he still held. "I'd like to be your representative in
Congress because I think I can best understand your
needs."

Shanna shook hands with the thirtyish man and
smiled as warmly as she could. She had always disliked
crowds. There was something overwhelming about a sea
of bodies, surging, vying for position. But this was for
Jordan, she kept telling herself over and over again, so
she tried her best.

And as she stood beside him, exchanging pleasantries
with men and women she would never see again, all
commemorated on video cameras from the local news
stations for the evening report, she surrendered another

tiny bit of herself. After this was over, she would return home and call her mother to tell her that Jordan wanted the house.

As always, her mother, not she, prevailed. She felt herself slipping farther into the shadows.

No.

The word formed rebelliously in her mind. No, she'd give her mother Jordan's message *after* she went to see the house for herself. The house they occupied in Georgetown had been given to them by her father. She didn't want this house to be purchased completely on Rheena's say-so. She had a right to her own choices, her own opinions. She had to make a mark before she was completely swallowed up by the world around her.

"I'll tell her," she said to Jordan as another hand clutched hers fleetingly.

To get herself through the ordeal, Shanna made a conscious effort to step back mentally and become a spectator at the goings-on taking place before her. The sea of faces eventually merged into one huge blur as she shook hands, smiled empty smiles, and shyly murmured, "Hello."

By gradual degrees, she became aware of the man. At first, he was just a grayish blur in the distance. As she focused on him he appeared almost stark against the vivid background of well-dressed business people and tall, angular, chrome-and-glass office buildings. He was out of place here, sitting beside the rectangular marble fountain. In tattered, baggy worn clothes and a ripped coat, he would have been out of place anywhere. His complexion was yellowed and partially hidden by white grizzly stubble.

Shanna tried to guess his age and couldn't pinpoint a year, or even a decade. He was anywhere between thirty and fifty. It was hard to tell just where, hidden as he was beneath the despair and the defeat that stained him far more cruelly than the grime that was on his clothes and face.

Jordan signaled to one of his men, and within moments, the black limousine his father-in-law had provided for his use was being brought around. They had another busy plaza to stand in, another crowd to win over. But as the chauffeur opened the door for Jordan, Shanna turned away. Jordan caught her arm as she began to cross the street toward the homeless man.

"Where are you going?" Jordan demanded in a low voice as he returned a wave to a woman in the distance. "Hi, how're you doing?" He tightened his grip on Shanna's arm, waiting for an answer.

"I want to give him some money." She nodded toward the man across the street.

"Why? He can't vote." He couldn't look annoyed in public, he told himself. "Your job is to stay here with me, remember?"

Her heart ached when she looked at the man's hopeless face. "But he's hungry, Jordan."

Jordan scarcely glanced in the man's direction. "He's a deadbeat." Jordan knew his tone was harsh and he tried to temper it. He wasn't through using Shanna by a long shot and she was more easily managed with kindness than with harshness.

"Look, I know you're softhearted, but what are you going to do? Give everyone of these shiftless drifters five dollars?" He couldn't help the condescending laugh that came. "Even your father doesn't have that much money. Besides, there're jobs out there." He motioned her toward the limousine. Shanna climbed into the backseat reluctantly. Jordan used the persuasive tone he had used with voters. "They just don't want them. They don't want to work, they want to drop out of society and be taken care of."

From the interior of the car, Shanna shifted forward in her seat and watched the scrawny man in torn khaki trousers shuffling slowly down the block. People moved to the left or right of him as if he didn't exist.

A nonentity. Shanna felt a wave of empathy. She understood what it was like to be treated as if you didn't exist. "Maybe," she said quietly. "But whether or not he tries to get a job tomorrow doesn't change the fact that he's hungry now."

Jordan straightened his tie and glanced critically at his clothes. He knew he had to look fresh for the next stop. "So someone else'll feed him. He's not your problem, Shanna. This election is the only thing you should be thinking about. Right?" He waited until she nodded her head. It was like trying to train a stupid pet. He placed his hand over hers on the seat. "When I get elected, I can look into what we can do for these homeless people."

A campaign promise, she thought. Her husband was making her a campaign promise in order to appease her. She wondered if he thought of her as one of his constituents. In either case, it served no purpose to argue with him.

Liz Conway, Jordan's campaign secretary, leaned in on Shanna's side. The woman was incredibly well built and consciously dressed to accent her main assets. Her turquoise sweater was so tight, Shanna wondered how the woman managed to breathe at all.

Liz handed Shanna a clipboard and nodded for her to pass it to Jordan. Beyond that, she ignored her. "Here's your schedule for the rest of the afternoon, Mr. Calhoun." She indicated the plaza with her eyes. "It looks like we made a pretty good impression here."

"Couldn't have done it without you."

Liz beamed in response to Jordan's words.

Impulsively Shanna pulled a bill out of her purse. She was vaguely aware that she had twenties and fifties in her wallet, but didn't bother to verify the denomination as she handed it to Liz. "Here. Give this to that vagrant across the street."

Jordan muttered something about her wasting money on fools as he signaled the chauffeur to leave.

Liz stood, staring at the fifty in her hand as the limousine turned a corner. "What vagrant?" she asked aloud as she looked around. All she saw were the men and women Jordan had come to charm. In the distance she thought she saw a hunched old man scuttle off.

With a shrug, she slipped the bill into her own pocket. She wasn't about to go running off on some fool errand. Jordan might need her.

At least she could hope so.

A *gust of wind* accompanied Shanna as she pushed open the large ornately carved mahogany door and hurried inside the French restaurant. It took a moment for sensation to return to her cheeks. The tops of her ears stung painfully as they registered the sudden change in temperature.

I'm defrosting, she thought with a grin as she slowly peeled off her black leather gloves. The ambience soothed her. Chez Charles felt like an old, kindly friend as the familiar surroundings enveloped her.

"Ah." The Mediterranean-looking maître d' clapped his hands together softly and crossed the short distance from his desk to the entrance. His smile was warm and genuine. "You have arrived a little early, Mrs. Calhoun." He took her hand and bowed at the waist.

Even in that position, he was able to look her straight in the eye. He was tall, she thought, and so thin. It always amazed her that someone surrounded by food could stay slender.

With practiced grace, he helped her off with her heavy winter coat.

Shanna slipped her gloves into her purse. Her fingertips were beginning to thaw. Washington, fresh out of one snowstorm, was just on the threshold of another. For once, the weatherman had been right in his forecast. This time Shanna would have gladly welcomed another mistake. She hated snow in the city.

"No one keeps my grandmother waiting," she answered pleasantly. She looked around. There was an inviting fire burning in the hearth. The winged armchairs that faced the fireplace were, as yet, empty. Only a few people were in the restaurant.

"I take it she hasn't arrived?" The maître d' shook his head as he placed Shanna's coat into her hands. Shanna frowned. She shouldn't have agreed to meeting her here. What if something had happened? The chauffeur's reflexes weren't what they used to be. "The weather's so awful, I hope everything's all right."

Behind her, the heavy door creaked slightly as the wind picked up, whistling mournfully. When Eloïse had called this morning, asking to meet her for lunch at the French restaurant they had frequented ever since Shanna had been a small child, Shanna had suggested coming to her grandmother's house instead. The weather promised to be much too nasty for her grandmother to venture out. But Eloïse had been adamant and, as always, got her way. Shanna wished now that she had insisted.

Taking a menu from his desk, the maître d' was quick to reassure her. "It is undoubtedly only a matter of traffic impeding the fine lady." His eyes lit as the front door burst open, propelled by the force of the wind and guided by a human hand. "Ah, I am right again." He gestured with a flourish behind her.

Shanna turned as the door yawned closed. Her

grandmother, seated in the mobilized wheelchair that had become part of her daily life shortly after Thanksgiving, approached her. Mildred, the matronly black woman who was her companion—Eloïse refused to refer to the woman as a nurse—followed directly behind her.

Seeing Shanna, Mildred smiled, shaking off the remnants of snowflakes that were melting into her hair. "Your grandmother is a stubborn old woman, Mrs. Calhoun." Mildred opened the top two buttons of her coat and loosened her scarf. "I couldn't get her to listen to reason."

Eloïse shifted the control on her wheelchair, turning the vehicle just enough to look up at Mildred. With the determination that was the hallmark of her life, Eloïse had spent hours practicing in the wheelchair until her turns were butter smooth and the chair's movements steady and flawless. Despite the hard-won expertise, she hated the damn vehicle, hated what it represented. That she was growing weaker. She knew eventually she had to surrender to the inevitable and it made her angry.

"No one's been able to do it for seventy-nine years, Mildred, why should you?" Turning on what seemed almost a dime's worth of space, she faced the maître d'. "So, André, is our favorite table ready?"

"Always." André smiled. Eloïse Fitzhugh had been coming to his restaurant ever since he had first opened it with the money she had discreetly loaned him. A place of honor remained set aside for her even on the busiest nights. It was her table and no one else's. "Right this way, Mrs. Fitzhugh."

He led them to a table that looked out on the Potomac. Today, the river was dark and restless, its choppy water fruitlessly slapping at the oncoming snow.

André pulled out her chair for her and Shanna

exchanged light pleasantries with the man until he left. As always, he had personally taken their order for hors d'oeuvres and drinks.

"I still don't see why I couldn't just come over to your house, Grandmother," Shanna said after Mildred took Eloïse's fur wrap, quietly leaving the two women alone. Mildred had murmured something about getting a little shopping done while they had their lunch. Shanna knew it was just an excuse and was grateful. She didn't feel like sharing Eloïse with anyone today. Visits were so few and far between that their time together was precious.

Shanna glanced at the menu out of habit, though she knew everything on it by heart. It rarely changed. The restaurant's attraction was in its excellence, not its variety. "Alice could have made us a little lunch and—"

Eloïse waved away the suggestion impatiently. "I'm tired of Alice's cooking." She nodded at the young waiter as he brought their hors d'oeuvres, a basket of bread, and their beverages. When he was gone, she continued, "Tired of sitting at home. Tired," she murmured with a sigh. She saw the concerned expression on Shanna's face. She hadn't asked her here to look for pity. "I was born and raised in Minnesota, child," Eloïse reminded her. "I don't break apart in cold weather." Softening, she winked. "Humor me."

Shanna grinned as she broke off a piece of the loaf. She had an incredible weakness for warm French bread. "I'd be afraid not to."

Eloïse lowered her fork as she looked at her granddaughter sharply. "Don't be."

Shanna swallowed her first bite quickly. She saw no reason for the sudden change in her grandmother's mood. "What?"

She was overreacting, Eloïse thought But this was not the time for benign, halted actions. There might not be another time after today. She could feel it. "Don't be afraid, Shanna. Never, never be afraid. Fear is for the weak."

The look in her grandmother's eyes worried her. Shanna searched for a way to lighten the conversation. "You were never afraid?"

Eloïse snapped out the answer. "No."

And then she smiled, momentarily transcending the wrinkled and sagging skin to look like a young girl with a naughty secret. "At least not so anyone would ever notice. Otherwise," Eloïse added more seriously, for this was the crux of everything she believed in, the crux of what she wanted Shanna to realize, "I would have been trampled on."

She covered her granddaughter's hand with her own. Now there was no strength left to give the girl, only warmth, Eloïse thought sadly. A last few precious moments of warmth. "The way I'm afraid that you will be." She watched the surprised look bloom in Shanna's eyes. "See, I am afraid of something, but I'll only admit it to you."

The waiter arrived with Shanna's hot chocolate. It was a treat she liked to indulge herself in around her grandmother, for to sip hot chocolate and sit by Eloïse was to be surrounded with wonderful memories she shared in this place. Jordan had laughed at her habit, saying that hot chocolate was *not* the sort of thing she was expected to drink at parties. Image, always image. So she never drank hot chocolate around him.

She reacted now to the concern she saw in her grandmother's face. She didn't want the woman worrying about her. She had enough to deal with with her failing health. "Grandmother, I'm all right."

Her grandmother's thin lips pressed into a hard line. "No, you have the *potential* to be all right. The

power. But you have to take control of your own life."
She signaled Shanna to be silent as the waiter
returned.

"Is everything all right?" he asked solicitously. When
he received an affirmative answer, he took their order
and retreated. He returned shortly thereafter with their
main course.

Food no longer interested Shanna. She tried to dis-
cern what Eloïse was driving at. Was her grandmother
referring to the way she was living now, with Jordan's
campaign throwing everything on its ear? There were
complete blocks of days when she didn't see him at all.

"Are you talking about Jordan's campaign?" She
knew she had, for all intents and purposes, stepped into
the shadows as a human being, but that was only temporary. That always happened with a candidate's wife,
except perhaps for Eleanor Roosevelt and Jacqueline
Kennedy. And her mother. But they were the rare
exceptions. Other candidates' wives licked envelopes,
made speeches, and stood in the background, cheering
their husbands on.

If it was only a matter of that, perhaps it wouldn't be
so bad. But Eloïse knew it went a lot deeper than that.
"I'm talking about your whole life, Shanna. God gave
you a fine father who was too busy to realize what a
treasure he had produced and a mother who was too
vain to take the time to love you the way you should
have been loved. Even I've failed you—"

"Grandmother—" Was that what this meeting was
about? Guilt? Her grandmother was responsible for all
the happy memories she had of her childhood. Shanna
reached for the woman's hand, but Eloïse pulled it
back. She was far from finished.

"And as for your husband—"

Eloïse's look was as dark as the storm outside threatened to be. So, she had made up her mind about Jordan, Shanna thought sadly. She picked at her food. "You don't like him, do you?"

Eloïse looked at the prettily arranged plate of coq au vin and found she had no appetite either. "I don't feel that anyone is good enough for you, but I would have been willing to compromise if I felt that Jordan really loved you. If I saw love in his eyes."

Her protests, she knew, would have only fallen on deaf ears and Shanna had always respected her grandmother's natural instincts. "Why, Grandmother, what is it that you do see?"

"Someone wrapped up in himself."

Shanna thought of the small, tender moments during their whirlwind courtship, the way he had made her feel when he told her he loved her. No, it couldn't be true. He couldn't have treated her that way and not cared. "You're wrong, Grandmother."

The girl had a stubborn streak. There was hope, Eloïse thought. As long as the stubbornness wasn't coupled with blindness. "I sincerely hope so."

The slight feeling of nausea that had been ebbing and flowing within Shanna all morning suddenly reared up violently. The world around her shrank to a tiny black pinprick. Shanna went numb.

Eloïse looked up as Shanna's fork clattered to her plate. The girl had turned white as a sheet. Eloïse grew alarmed. "Shanna, what's the matter?"

Shanna fought her way back up to the surface, pushing aside the darkness that had momentarily enshrouded her. After a beat, the restaurant came back into focus. She realized that her grandmother was talking to her.

"Hmm?" Shanna dragged air into her lungs, trying to steady the frantic beating of her heart. She ran her

hands over her face. "Oh, I'm sorry. It's nothing, really."
She didn't want to make a big thing out of this. "I just
felt dizzy again."

"Again?" Eloïse's concern changed gears, from worry
to interest. She peered more closely at Shanna's face,
looking for a sign.

"It comes and goes." Shanna shrugged, relieved that
she hadn't made a fool of herself and passed out. "I even
fainted once last week." She stared down at her plate
and decided that she really couldn't eat what she had
ordered after all. She turned her attention to the cup of
hot chocolate the waiter had refilled. "There's a lot of
flu going around this time of year."

Eloïse leaned forward and grasped Shanna's wrist.
There was more strength in the small, frail hand than
Shanna would have thought. Maybe her grandmother's
health was improving after all. At least she could hope
so. "Have you been feeling sick in the morning?"

In the last fourteen days, misery had hopscotched
through her life, attacking every other day. "Yes, that
is—" She saw the light that came into her grandmother's
eyes. She knew exactly what the woman was hoping for.
Shanna hated to disappoint her, but there never had
been any lies or half-truths between them. "Oh, Grandmother." She shook her head. "I'm not pregnant."

Eloïse guessed at the reason. "You're still taking your
pills."

"Yes, I am."

Eloïse refused to be convinced. She knew what she
saw. "They're not foolproof, you know, and considering
the fool you've been sleeping with—" Shanna opened
her mouth to refute her reference to Jordan. Eloïse
released her wrist, waving her hand. "Yes, yes, I know,
he loves you," she agreed impatiently, then softened for
Shanna's sake when she saw the uncertainty in the girl's

eyes. "Perhaps he does, but I would like to see proof with my own eyes."

She leaned back and sampled the wine sauce her chicken was swimming in. She was certain that it was excellent, but her taste buds had all but faded. Another curse of old age, she thought, disgruntled. One of her passions had always been eating fine foods, though she had managed to remain whisper thin over the years. Well, she'd be food herself soon enough. Food for worms.

She leveled an intent look at Shanna. "Is he considerate of your feelings?"

"Yes," Shanna answered quickly, then reiterated more slowly. "Yes, he is."

Her taste buds might have been fading, but not her hearing. "I hear a 'but' in your voice. What is it, child?"

Shanna shrugged. "It's nothing."

"I've always preferred to judge things for myself."

Shanna hadn't voiced this aloud and maybe she needed to. "I don't know. I feel like there's something missing." She gestured helplessly, palms up. Maybe she was just crazy, demanding too much. "I can't even put it into words."

Eloïse understood what she meant perfectly. "When something is right, you know. Without words."

It went against her grain, but she found that she couldn't leave her granddaughter without a shred of hope. Shanna did love that narcissistic idiot of a husband of hers. "Maybe it'll take time," Eloïse said, though her tone said that she doubted it. "In the meanwhile, I want you to take care of yourself." She looked pointedly at Shanna's small waist. "And my great-grandchild."

Shanna laughed, casually passing her hand along her flat stomach. It did no harm to humor her grandmother, though she knew that she just had a touch of the flu.

Besides, what harm would it do to pretend? She couldn't think of anything she wanted more than to have Jordan's child. To have a baby that smiled up at her with Jordan's wonderful smile. "I promise if it's a girl, I'll name her after you."

Eloïse looked at Shanna as if she'd lost her mind. "You'll do nothing of the kind."

"Why not?"

"I may be vain, child, but I'm not vengeful. Picture how unhappy that girl will be, saddled with a name like Eloïse." She shuddered just from the thought of it. "I always hated that name, though it was far better suited to my generation than to yours."

"I never knew that." When her grandmother looked at her quizzically, Shanna quickly explained. "That you hated your name."

Eloïse chuckled softly. Too late. It was too late to share so many things she would have wanted to share. Hindsight wasn't wonderful. It was a curse. "There's a lot of things about me you don't know."

Shanna leaned forward, her head propped on her closed fist, her dinner plate carelessly pushed to one side. "Tell me."

There was too much to tell and too little time. Besides, it was all running together in her mind, like a chalk portrait left on the sidewalk in the rain. "I'm a boring old woman, Shanna."

A feeling of urgency suddenly danced through Shanna. She didn't believe in premonitions, but just this once, she decided to act on it. "Not to me."

Yes, Eloïse realized, and that was one of the reasons Shanna had always meant so much to her. Shanna loved her just for herself.

"All right." Eloïse sat back, getting comfortable in the padded armchair. "You asked for this."

Eloïse's voice drifted through the quiet restaurant as all around them, patrons began arriving for lunch. Outside, the snow continued to fall on a city that never rested.

Shanna listened in rapt attention, pleased with the image she conjured up, envisioning her grandmother as a young girl. Eloïse talked on for almost an hour before Mildred finally returned. When it was time to go, Shanna was sorry that the afternoon was over. It had been one of the most peaceful afternoons she could remember spending in a long, long time.

"I love you, Grandmother." She kissed the worn, rouged cheek just before she stepped back to hold the door open for Mildred.

Eloïse nodded. It was her due. Yet she felt in her heart that no one else loved her. "Yes, I know."

"I'll see you soon," Shanna called after her. The chauffeur had come to the restaurant entrance to help Mildred usher Eloïse quickly into the waiting limousine.

"Perhaps," Eloïse murmured to Shanna, knowing her granddaughter could no longer hear her. "Perhaps."

Her words were eaten up by the wind.

8

The shrill, persistent noise wouldn't go away. It peeled off the layers of haze around Shanna one by one until she finally opened her eyes. Stiff, disoriented, she shifted her shoulders and realized that she was still sitting on the living room love seat. Exhausted from a full day, she had sat down here at ten to wait for Jordan to return home.

The book that had only marginally held her attention was lying facedown, next to her feet. In the background the television set she had turned on for company in the overly quiet huge house had on a yellowed-looking black-and-white movie. The crackle of the film almost drowned out the actors.

Focusing, she looked at her watch: 2:00 A.M. The noise that had woken her was still demanding attention.

The telephone. The telephone was ringing. She caught her breath as the sound finally registered.

She checked her watch again. *Oh God, something's happened to Jordan.*

She accidentally kicked her book aside as she hurried

to the telephone. She had no idea how long it had been ringing. What if the person hung up before she answered? Shanna snatched the receiver from the cradle and held it in both hands as she pressed it to her ear. "Hello?"

"Mrs. Calhoun?"

Shanna vaguely recognized the voice, but couldn't connect it with a face. Her heart was pounding in anticipation. There was something about the dark that always intensified unformed fears. "Yes?"

"It's Mildred Harlow, Mrs. Calhoun." The voice was authoritative and professional. But there was an underlying pain within it that the speaker didn't bother to mask. "Your grandmother's nurse." Mildred added when there was no response.

Shanna was instantly wide-awake. She clutched the receiver even more tightly in her hands, as if it were a lifeline connecting her not to Mildred, but to Eloïse. Fears began to take a definite shape.

"Why are you calling? Has she taken a turn for the worse?"

There was a pause, as if the tiny increment of time could somehow make saying the words easier. But it couldn't. "She's passed away, ma'am."

No!

Shanna wanted to scream the word, to make Mildred admit that she was playing some horrible prank. Her grandmother couldn't be dead. She was too real to die.

"But I just saw her. Monday. Two days ago," Shanna insisted, waiting for Mildred to confess that she was lying.

Mildred's voice was soft, comforting. She'd been in this very same position so many times before. It never became easier. "Yes, I know. She knew she was dying and she wanted to see you one more time."

"But how . . . ?" Words evaporated from Shanna's

brain like small beads of moisture in the desert. Dead. Her grandmother was dead. Shakily Shanna sat down on the floor, the large living room shrinking down to just herself and the telephone she held in her hand.

Now that Eloïse was gone, there was no reason for secrecy any longer. "It was her heart, ma'am. It just gave out on her. The doctor told her that she didn't have long. There was no possibility of a transplant. Her body wouldn't have supported one."

Cold traveled up from her toes until it encompassed all of her. Shanna felt frozen. When? How? There'd never been any mention that she was going to die soon. That she was dying. "I had no idea."

"She didn't want you to know. She didn't want anyone to know. She said she couldn't have abided being the target of pity."

Shanna nodded numbly, though the other woman couldn't see her. There was nothing her grandmother tolerated less than pity, unless it was weakness and deceit.

Now there was nothing to tolerate.

Dead. *Grandmother's dead.* Shanna pressed her hand to her mouth to keep a sob from escaping. Eloise wouldn't have approved of her carrying on. She tried to focus on what Mildred was saying to her.

"—Mr. Stewart's the executor of her will," Mildred continued, referring to Eloïse's lawyer. "He's to handle all the funeral arrangements." For a moment there was silence as Mildred looked for words. "I'm sorry to have to be the one to tell you this, Mrs. Calhoun, but Mrs. Fitzhugh wanted you to be the first one to know if anything happened."

Because she loved me, Shanna thought and felt sobs rising again. She struggled for control. "I'll be there in the morning, Mildred." From somewhere far within, years of training took over. "And thank you for calling."

"I wish I could say it was my pleasure," Mildred answered, and there was genuine sorrow in her voice. "She was a fine lady. Good-bye."

Shanna murmured good-bye, or thought she did. Reaching up, she dropped the receiver into the cradle. She sat on the floor a long time, too numb to move, too lost to think coherently. Somehow, despite the woman's frail state, despite the necessity of the wheelchair, Shanna had always believed that her grandmother would go on forever. Her spirit had always been so strong, so indomitable. So unconquerable.

And now something had conquered her. Death.

Shanna felt abandoned.

"You should have told me," she whispered as the tears, hot and desolate, began to fall, trickling down her cheeks. The tiny drops were absorbed by the folds of her flannel robe. "You should have let me know."

The sound of the key in the lock registered vaguely in the back of her mind. Shanna, still sitting on the floor, looked up just as Jordan entered the living room. With his overcoat draped over his arm, he crossed the threshold, making a conscious effort to be as quiet as possible.

He stopped when he saw Shanna on the floor.

Damn! He had thought that she'd be fast asleep by now. Jordan drew closer, looking at her face. Terrific, she was crying.

Impotent anger rose within him. Had some "well-meaning person" seen him going to Liz's apartment earlier tonight and called Shanna because she "had a right to know," or whatever it was that gossips used to justify their actions? Shit, he had thought he'd been so careful. It didn't matter that they had recently moved to this exclusive two-acre estate and that the phones had been changed. Gossips always found you. Jordan braced himself for damage control.

Jordan threw his coat on the sofa as he crossed to his wife. He braced himself for the accusations he knew would come. Standing over her, he put out his hand to her. "Look, Shanna, I know I'm late, but the strategy meeting ran over and then we—"

Shanna wrapped her fingers around his, but stayed where she was for a moment, gathering strength. Her legs felt as if they couldn't fully support her if she rose. "She's gone, Jordan."

She? Who the hell was Shanna talking about? He hadn't the vaguest idea.

When Shanna suddenly rose, flinging herself into his arms and sobbing, he instinctively stroked her hair. One arm around her shoulders, he rocked her against him. At all costs, Shanna had to be appeased, though tonight and the other nights that had come before were really her fault. If she was just better in bed, maybe he wouldn't be so attracted to other women.

And then again, he mused, knowing himself too well, maybe he would be anyway.

"Who are you talking about, honey?" he coaxed gently. "Who's gone?"

Shanna wanted to lose herself in the folds of his gray jacket, like a little girl hiding in the closet until everything was all better. But she wasn't a little girl. She hadn't been for a long time, and life had to be faced. "Grandmother."

Jordan could have shouted with relief. Shanna didn't know anything about his affair. God, that was a load off his mind.

And then Shanna's words penetrated. So the old woman finally bought the farm. He suppressed a smile. The old bitch had been crazy about Shanna. That meant

she probably had left her a hefty chunk of money in the
will. He felt nothing but elation at the news. Eloïse
Fitzhugh had never liked him and now she was dead.
Good. Things were really going his way.

"Oh, honey, I'm so sorry," he murmured into her hair
as he stroked it. "I really liked her."

Shanna raised her head to look at him. Her eyes were
bright with tears. To know that he really cared about her
grandmother was extremely important to her. "Did you?
I always got the impression that you didn't."

He read the look in her eyes easily. "It was she who
didn't like me," he pointed out innocently. "You
couldn't very well blame me for being a little on the
defensive side."

"No." She sighed. Stepping back, she dragged her
hand through her hair. Her voice was still shaky. "I
guess not." She dropped onto the sofa.

Jordan glanced toward the bedroom. All he really
wanted to do was collapse in bed and get some sleep.
Liz had been a wildcat tonight. He had had to grab her
hands twice to stop her from leaving telltale marks on
him. He was completely drained and had used his last
ounce of energy just getting back here.

But there were motions to go through, so he sat down
beside Shanna. Draping one arm around her shoulders,
he pulled Shanna against him.

Shanna leaned her head on his chest. There was safety here, she thought, and warmth. She silently thanked
God for Jordan. "I'm going up tomorrow to help with
the funeral arrangements. Will you come with me?"

"I can't." He looked at her apologetically as he lightly
stroked her arm. "But let me know when the funeral is
and I'll have Liz clear my schedule."

Shanna slipped her hand into his. "I can't believe that
she's gone."

Jordan kept his smile to himself as he held her. "Neither can I, honey. Neither can I."

The funeral was large and ostentatious and everything Eloïse had come to hate. It took place two days later. Shanna moved through both the wake and the services in a haze of alternating disbelief and bereavement. It had taken every ounce of strength she had to look down into the casket and see her grandmother lying there. When she finally went up to view the body, she had gone alone. Jordan had managed to melt into the crowd and she couldn't find him.

Looking down at the face she loved so much, Shanna suddenly felt dizzy. Frantically she clutched at the side of the casket to keep from falling.

From out of nowhere, she felt a hand come up behind her to support her elbow.

"Don't make a fool of yourself by fainting," Rheena hissed between lips that hardly moved.

Steeling herself, Rheena looked down into the casket as well. As soon as she had heard of her mother's death, she had had Alexandra flown in, insisting that the funeral-parlor director use her to do her mother's makeup instead of the regular girl.

Alexandra hadn't been happy about the task, but knew better than to decline.

Rheena studied her mother for a moment before ushering Shanna away. "I think she looks better now than she did when she was alive."

Taking offense for Eloïse, Shanna pulled away. "I didn't care what she looked like. I just wanted her to be here."

Fighting the continuing waves of nausea that kept assaulting her, Shanna searched for Jordan. How could

Rheena have said something so flippantly callous? Shanna thought angrily. Her mother had just died. Didn't she have any feelings at all?

Shanna knew the answer to that. Her mother and grandmother had never been on good terms. There was no reason to believe that the funeral had changed her mother's attitude toward Eloise.

What would she feel when it came to be her mother's time? Shanna wondered as she picked her way through the crowded parlor. Would there be this blasé performance before an audience, with no feelings behind it? Would she be this indifferent? God, she hoped not.

During the services, her father was a great comfort to her. He was sincerely saddened by Eloïse's death. But it was to Jordan that Shanna turned when they stood in the church. He provided the support she needed. Except for short periods of time, he remained at her side throughout most of the morning. Liz had reworked his heavy schedule, he told Shanna, so that he would have this time free to pay Eloïse the respect she deserved.

He saw Shanna's grateful smile when he told her and was satisfied that he had made a good move. Besides, there were people here it wouldn't hurt him to meet. Being the bereaved grandson-in-law gave him an instant excuse to initiate conversations with several financiers and wealthy industrialists he might not otherwise have gotten a chance to speak to. Ever charming and gracious, Jordan worked the room with his future foremost in his mind.

After the service at the grave site, everyone returned to the senator's house in Georgetown for a lavish reception. Rheena would have it no other way. Shanna felt more out of place than usual and found the milling

crowds too stifling. She responded gratefully to the condolences that came her way. But she slipped away the
first opportunity she had. She needed some time alone
with her grief.

Her old room seemed to be the best place for her to
go. There were people everywhere as she made her way
up the stairs. She couldn't help wondering if they had all
known her grandmother, or were here merely to see
and be seen. Another circus sideshow.

As Shanna opened the door to her room she heard a
soft sound. Sobbing. She cocked her head, trying to
determine where it was coming from. She could have
sworn it was coming from her mother's room. Crossing
to it, she listened at the door and heard it more clearly.

Hesitating, she eased the door opened slowly. Her
mother was going to be furious when she heard that
someone had gotten into her room. Maybe she could
get whoever it was out before her mother found out.
Shanna was completely unprepared for what she saw.

"Mother?"

Rheena looked up from where she was sitting on the
bed, a startled expression on her face. She made a
furtive move to wipe away her tears, then stopped.
What purpose did that serve? She had been caught.
"She got in the last blow, you know."

Her mother's voice was raspy, as if she'd been crying
for a while. Shanna sat down beside her and took her
mother's hand in hers. She couldn't remember ever
holding her mother's hand before. There had always
been a nurse or a nanny to take her hand, never her
mother. Rheena's fingers felt icy now.

"You mean Grandmother?"

Rheena nodded. She stared straight ahead, as if
unable to acknowledge Shanna's touch. Rheena wadded
her handkerchief in her other hand.

"I didn't think it would hurt when she died. I thought that I'd be relieved that I was rid of her. She was always so damn critical of me and I could never do anything right to please her." Rheena let go of a ragged breath. "And now that she's gone, I thought I'd be free of that feeling, free of needing to somehow try to garner approval." Another tear slid down.

Shanna stared at it in fascination. Feelings. Her mother had feelings.

"But all I feel is this overwhelming sorrow that I never got the chance to hear her say she was proud of me." Rheena shrugged helplessly. "And now she never will. So she won."

Shanna wanted to hug her mother, to hold her, but she knew that Rheena would never allow that. "Nobody wins at something like that." Shanna rose, her own heart aching. "Can I get you anything, Mother?"

Rheena shook her head, still not looking at her. "No, it's too late for that."

Shanna slipped out and closed the door behind her. "It's never too late to find out that you care for somebody, Mother," she whispered. "Don't you know that?"

9

Shanna sighed and slowly looked around the room where she had spent so many hours spinning soothing fantasies for herself as a child. Outside, the weather had turned cold. More snow on the way, probably. She felt a little of the cold seep in through the corners of the multipaned window. Or maybe she just felt cold because of the funeral.

She leaned against the wall framing the window-seat alcove, staring out of the window into the blackness beyond. She had sat here so many times before, always feeling protected. Then the dark world outside had been held at bay by the window. The image of her room had been mirrored on the windowpanes, diminishing the unknown. It had made her feel protected as a child. But no more.

Now she felt that the real world was beyond the glass, not contained before it. The dark, unknown, cold real world, where a single instant of time could bring dramatic changes into one's life.

Rubbing her hands up and down her arms, Shanna

rose from the window seat. She felt restless here. It would be impossible to sleep tonight.

Her father's suggestion to spend the night had seemed logical. They had both felt, albeit silently, that the familiar surroundings might help her cope with the tragedy of her loss. Though words were his stock and trade in public, at home her father had always demonstrated difficulty with expressing any kind of emotion. He had nothing to offer his daughter now that might help, other than his physical presence. So he had invited her to stay rather than drive home tonight and Shanna had accepted.

She had assumed that Jordan would remain with her here, but he had begged off. Clearing the first part of the day had left him with a myriad of details to catch up on. The primary might still be six months away, he'd pointed out, but they both knew that it would be here in less than a heartbeat. Neither of them wanted anything less than a landslide victory.

Jordan had kissed Shanna tenderly at the door before he left. There had even been, she thought, a trace of subdued passion evident in his parting.

Growing more restless as she thought, Shanna wandered around the room now, trying vainly to ward off a chill that refused to leave her.

Maybe it was selfish of her, but she hadn't wanted him to go. She *needed* him right now, needed to feel his arms around her, needed to feel his support. Why hadn't he sensed that? Having him here wouldn't have changed the fact that her grandmother was gone, that she'd never again spend a snowy afternoon talking to the old woman over lunch at their favorite restaurant, but somehow it would have helped her get through the night.

Flopping down on the bed, Shanna stretched her feet

out in front of her, rubbing one bare stockinged foot
against the instep of the other. There was no use brood-
ing about the fact that he hadn't been sensitive to her
needs. She should have said something. More than that,
she should have just gone home with Jordan. She had
stayed here because this was where most of her childhood had taken place and her childhood had been the
time when her grandmother was very alive, very vital.

She realized now that her reasoning had been faulty.
Shanna knew she didn't belong here anymore, not the
way she had before. She wasn't Shanna Brady any
longer. It was more than just a name change. Part of her
would always be a Brady, of course, and a Fitzhugh. But
she was no longer a child, no longer just the daughter of
the senator and the socialite. She was a wife now. Possibly a congressman's wife, if everything went well in the
next few months. And eventually she would just be
Shanna, someone of her own making. She just had to
find out who that someone was.

The thought pleased her. Even though that eventual-
ity was still far in the future, the fact remained that she
had taken a step up, a step forward. She had grown away
from all this. She belonged with Jordan now in the
house they had bought together. This room wasn't her
haven any longer.

Making the decision to go home, she couldn't wait to
leave. Hastily she pulled out the few belongings she had
brought with her for her stay out of the closet and threw
them on the bed. Satin padded hangers fell unnoticed
as they flew out, raining on the carpet. She took out her
suitcase and packed without bothering to fold.

She was going home.

With her coat unbuttoned, Shanna made her way
downstairs, suitcase in hand. She looked around for her
father. She didn't want to leave without telling him she

was going. He was exactly where she thought he would be. In the den.

For a moment Shanna leaned her shoulder against the doorjamb and just looked in. It always smelled the same. Leather and lemon oil. Books lined two of the walls from floor to ceiling. As a child, she had been incredibly impressed by all the knowledge that was crammed into this room. She had been certain that her father had to be the smartest person in the whole world, thinking that he had read every one of the books on the shelves.

While Congress was in session, they lived here. The house in Illinois was a place they retreated to in the summer. Her memories were here. She had seen him like this countless times before, in that exact same position, sitting at his desk bent over a speech he was to give or a report that he needed to read in order to make a decision on a pending vote.

She was proud of him, she realized, feeling a small, surprising surge at the thought. She only wished she knew him a little better. But she doubted that the opportunity would ever materialize now. Jordan needed her, and once he was elected, she knew the rush of Washington life would take her with it. There'd be precious little time to spend with her father and certainly not alone.

Brady felt that odd, vaguely uncomfortable feeling that came over a person when someone was watching them. When he looked up and saw Shanna standing in the doorway, he pushed back his chair, surprised to see her. She had looked so exhausted before, he was certain she had gone to bed.

And then he saw the suitcase. "Are you going somewhere?"

Shanna took a step into the room. The den was warm, cosy. She realized that it made her feel the way Chez Charles did. "I'm going home, Dad."

"I understand, Shanna, I really do." Brady crossed to his only child and took her hands in his. He felt a little hypocritical, playing the father-daughter scene. But he *was* her father and he did love her, even though he'd never really had the time to show her. "But the weather bureau's predicting snow again. Why don't you wait until morning?"

It was a very sensible request. But there was a sense of urgency nagging at her, as if she *had* to get home. Not tomorrow, the way she had planned, but tonight. It was as if something outside of herself was making her go.

Shanna shook her head. "I'll be all right." She saw the furrow form between his eyes. "It's not that I don't appreciate your concern, Dad, it's just that—"

The senator stopped her. There was no need for her to explain. He could read her thoughts. "I know. You're a big girl now and belong with your husband."

He continued to hold her hands in his for a moment longer and just looked at her. Really looked at her. She had grown up without his ever having noticed the process. He had been at a rally in Texas for her fifth birthday, at a party convention for her sixteenth. Telegrams had taken his place. And he had missed her twenty-first birthday party by three days. He'd only remembered the fact a day after it was over. She'd taken his belated call of congratulations without reproach, intensifying his guilt. But there was always something else to see to, some situation that demanded his attention immediately instead of a quiet little girl who always waited.

All those years, gone in an instant. Shanna had done all her growing up without him and he now regretted it, but there was no getting back the past. There was only now. "Call me if you need me, Shanna."

Shanna gave him a little squeeze before she withdrew her hands. "Thanks, Dad. I will." She left, humming.

° ° °

The storm that was just on the horizon lingered there and the air tingled, feeling crisp and clean as she hurried home. She drove ten miles over the speed limit all the way, one eye in the rearview mirror, watching for dancing red-and-blue lights. To her relief, none appeared. She didn't want to waste time while a policeman wrote her a ticket.

The sense of urgency, of a need to go home, was increasing. It came, she thought, from a need to count her blessings. Her grandmother's death had made her acutely aware of how precious life was. How much all the good points should be savored. Shanna pressed down harder on the gas, slowing only when she came to patches of ice.

It was almost one in the morning when she finally pulled up in her driveway. For the first time the imposing two-story custom-built Tudor house with its lofty rooms and manicured landscaping actually felt like home to her. Up until now, it had been the house her mother had selected for them. It had suited Jordan instantly. But it wasn't until this very moment that Shanna felt she belonged here as well.

An ironic smile lifted the corners of Shanna's mouth. Her mother had been right after all.

Getting out, she left the overnight case in the car. She'd get it in the morning. Right now all she wanted to do was slip into bed beside Jordan. She decoded the security system next to the front door and let herself in. As she closed the door quietly behind her she automatically reactivated the system. It started to snow again.

Given the hour, Jordan was probably asleep. Though Shanna wanted to wake him, to talk to him and have him hold her, she knew that would be selfish of her. It would be comfort enough for now just to lie next to him.

A wave of sadness washed over her, sneaking up from out of nowhere. She pushed it aside. Her grandmother was gone, but life went on. That was what Eloïse had always said to her. No matter what, life went on and you had to go with it or get swept aside by the undertow.

She slipped off her shoes and quietly crossed to the bedroom. The sound of voices made her stop. She strained, trying to make out the words. It had to be the television set. He was up, watching a movie. Maybe he missed her and couldn't sleep. She grinned. At least she could hope.

Still wearing her coat and holding her purse, she hurried the rest of the way to the bedroom. But she stopped just before opening the door. The voices weren't coming from the television set. That was Jordan's voice. And a woman's.

In her bedroom?

Shanna's heart began to hammer as her breathing quickened. No. It was the television, it had to be. She bit her lower lip hard as she slowly pushed the door open, hoping. Afraid.

The bedroom was dark except for the light coming from a lamp on the nightstand. Shanna saw nothing else but the two tangled, naked bodies on the bed.

Jordan, his body sleek with sweat, balanced himself on his elbows as he looked down at the woman who was currently satisfying his almost inexhaustible carnal appetite. Liz Conway, his campaign secretary, was the latest in a long string of women that went back some thirteen years. Except for a redhead named Nona in Gary, Indiana, Liz had proven by far to be the most superior lover he had ever had. She could do things with her mouth that made him groan just to think about. Too bad she wasn't as well connected as she was well built.

The ache in his loins was growing again, demanding

release. His hips moved in mounting agitation as he laughed at Liz's weakly stated suggestion that perhaps she should leave.

"There's nothing to worry about, I tell you." With a hard thrust, he watched her eyes widen, watched the hunger take over. His ego and his lust fed on the look of urgent desire on her face. "The silly little bitch is spending the night in Georgetown at her parents' house, so prostrated with grief she can't even put on her shoes, much less drive over here. We've got the rest of the night to ourselves. Don't waste it thinking about her."

Shanna opened her mouth to cry out in protest, as if the very act would erase the scene she was watching, but at first no words would come out.

Everything crystallized. It was true, all of it. The rumors, her mother's snide remarks, her grandmother's instinctive dislike. True. All true. Jordan was using her. He didn't love her. How could he have done this to her? Betrayed her when she loved him so much?

She wanted to crumple in a heap on her knees and sob her heart out. She wanted to hurl something at the two grotesque bodies on the bed who mocked everything she had believed in, mocked the world she had created for herself. She wanted to hurt him physically for slashing her heart out so carelessly, without remorse, without thought.

She wanted to throw up.

Tears lodged in her throat, strangling her. She gasped and the bodies on the bed jerked apart, startled as they looked in her direction.

"Goddamn you to hell, Jordan!" Shanna screamed, spinning around on her stockinged heel.

"Shanna!"

In one instant Jordan's world shook on the foundations he had so carefully built up over the long years. Panic, rage, frustration all sliced at his awareness. He had to fix this. He had to. He shoved Liz aside as if she were an inanimate object in his way.

"Oh God, Shanna."

Jordan leaped from the bed as if he had been hurled by the force of a detonating bomb, a bomb that could destroy everything that was just now coming within reach. He stumbled, tangling in the sheet that clung to his leg. Cursing vehemently, he kicked it aside and ran after his wife, not even bothering to pull on his pants.

Behind him, Liz scrambled into the bathroom. Articles of clothing dripped from her arms as she turned to slam the door behind her.

Jordan forgot she was even there. "Shanna," he cried as he chased after her. "Wait. I can explain."

He had a golden tongue. He had talked himself into her life, into her heart. She wasn't going to give him the opportunity to talk again.

"You don't have to," she spat over her shoulder. "One picture is worth a thousand words, 'Congressman.'"

"Shanna, please, I'm sorry. She doesn't mean anything. I was lonely, upset by the funeral. She started coming on to me and I weakened."

The lie made her physically sick and she almost retched as she fled. He managed to catch her by the arm just as she reached the hallway. Shanna turned, swinging. Catching him off guard, she hit him squarely in the face and he fell backward, releasing her. She didn't want to talk to him. She didn't want to look at him.

She didn't want to live.

Her entire world was completely shattered. There was no place to turn, nowhere to go. No one to care.

Shanna tore open the front door and the security

alarm went off, a shrill sound piercing the air. She ran outside.

Jordan had cut the corner of his brow when he fell. The blood trickled down his face unnoticed. Naked, genuinely frightened for his future, he stood in the doorway, shouting after her to come back.

Still barefoot, Shanna ran through the fresh crisp snow to her car. In her hurry to see Jordan, she had left it unlocked. She threw herself behind the wheel, frantically trying to thrust the key into the ignition. Her hand was shaking so badly, she missed the first time. She jabbed at it again, afraid that Jordan would come after her and pull her out before she had a chance to get away.

Above all else, she had to get away.

Shanna needed time to think, to find something, *anything* to hang on to. Somehow she was going to pull the pieces of her life into some semblance of sense. She couldn't do that if Jordan got a chance to talk to her first, to mesmerize her with his words, with his eyes.

"Jerk. Stupid, stupid jerk." She blinked back tears, not knowing if she meant the term to apply to him or herself. Or to both.

Spinning the car around on what felt like two wheels, she heard the tires squeal in protest as she peeled out of the driveway and drove into the blackness beyond her house. The blackness that now represented her life.

Behind her, the siren still screeched, drowning out the sound of Jordan's hoarse, impotent cries as he called for her to come back.

10

Shanna drove, unseeing, down the long, winding road that led away from the house. She had absolutely no idea where she was going, she just knew that it had to be as far away from Jordan as was physically possible. She was shaking so badly she turned on the heater in the car all the way up. Fumbling with the switch, she took her eyes off the road.

A car traveling in the opposite direction just narrowly missed ramming into her. The driver leaned on his horn, cursing her stupidity.

"Your lights, shithead! Put on your damned lights!"

Muttering an oath, trying to clear her mind, Shanna turned the wrong switch and the wipers came to life, scraping at the windshield. She stopped them and found the lights. Twin golden beams formed and merged, illuminating the path directly in front of her.

Damn him! She swiped the back of her hand across her cheek to wipe away the flow of tears. She couldn't control them. She couldn't control anything. She just continued crying.

And damn her for believing that someone who looked like Jordan could fall so easily in love with her. Damn her for needing so much to *be* loved.

She shook her head, blinking, trying to clear away the tears that clung to her lashes, blinding her as she drove. She swerved and gasped. Regaining control of the car, she looked down at the speedometer. Seventy-five. In her agitation, she had the gas pedal almost down to the floor. Shanna eased her foot off.

How could he? Damn it, how *could* he? How could Jordan *do* something so heinous to her, and on the day of her grandmother's funeral. Didn't he have any sense of decency at all?

She knew the answer to that. Anger churned within her as she pressed down hard on the gas pedal again without realizing it.

A large navy-blue sedan appeared at the cross street at the bottom of the hill, running the stop sign. Shanna slammed on her brakes. Her car swerved, fishtailing along the icy road. It was another narrow escape. She didn't care.

Shanna kept driving, trying to outrun her feelings. If she went fast enough, maybe she wouldn't ache so.

It was impossible.

A fool, a stupid little fool, she thought bitterly as she went through a red light, that's all she had been. She had closed her eyes to the signs that had been all around her. She'd loved him unconditionally and thought that he loved her. Her mother's blatant references, other people's sly innuendos, the way women had fawned on him, she had whitewashed it all. Excused it time and again with flimsy lies to herself. Because she'd wanted to believe that what he told her was the truth.

That he loved her. That he wanted to spend the rest of his life with her.

Finding him in bed with that woman was the final straw. She had to open her eyes.

They had all been just campaign promises, the words he had said to her. Campaign promises made in order to get elected to the lofty position of Senator Brady's son-in-law. It was all suddenly looking glass clear to her. It had been a clever plan, laid out with the strategy of a Napoleon. A Napoleon taking advantage of an attention-starved Josephine.

She hated herself for that, for being so weak. And she hated him for being so cruel and using that for his own benefit without any thought to what it might do to her.

Why should he? He didn't care. Tears choked her.

A beam of light bounced off her rearview mirror and exploded within the car, blinding her. Squinting, she looked into her rearview mirror. She could just barely make out a truck suddenly coming up behind her. The driver had his brights on to illuminate the almost pitch black path.

Unable to see, Shanna lowered her head to get away from the glare.

She didn't see the icy patch ahead.

Her car went into a skid. Frantically Shanna twisted the wheel to the left before she remembered that she was supposed to drive into a spin, not out of it. Panic clawed away the hurt and despair that had been her companions a second ago as she felt the car going completely out of control. In less than a moment she was tossed into a cacophony of sounds. Tires squealed as glass shattered and metal groaned. She thought she felt the jolt of something huge moving into her.

The scream she was only vaguely aware of as she tumbled into complete, overwhelming blackness belonged to her.

White.

Nothing but white. It surrounded her, then ripped apart, cut through by flaming scissors of pain that slashed ruthlessly into her consciousness.

Shanna desperately attempted to rouse herself, to pull free. To pull free of the pain that oppressively weighed her down.

A multicolored mosaic of incidents, feelings, sounds swirled through her brain and she tried to make sense of the shards. There was no whole, no picture, only fragments. Jordan, his sensuous mouth laughing at her, growing larger and larger as hideous sounds echoed around her. Her grandmother, wan and pale, fading farther and farther away as Shanna tried to reach out and touch her. Lost, she was lost, running, searching to find her way. A light appeared in front of her and she ran toward it, until suddenly it blinded her. It was a car and it was heading directly toward her. She was going to die. She tried to scream, but no sounds came out.

And then nothing.

Was she dead?

No, she hurt too much to be dead. Being dead wasn't supposed to hurt. Was it?

Shanna struggled against overwhelming weight to open her eyes. She felt as if there was something incredibly heavy pressing down on her lids, drugging her senses. If she just gave in, it would be all right. She wouldn't have to struggle, to fight.

But she wanted to open her eyes.

"Choices, Shanna, make choices," her grandmother's voice whispered in her ear.

I made a terrible choice, Grandmother. I married Jordan.

Had she uttered the words? Her lips weren't moving. Was she just dreaming? Nothing moved except the pain as it steamrolled over her body in passes that took Shanna's breath away and threatened to press her further into the chaotic world she found herself in.

Definitely alive, she thought. What a pity.

Pity.

Her grandmother's voice filled her head again. *Nothing I can't abide more than pity, Shanna. And the worst kind is self-pity. It'll unravel you as surely as if you were a skein of wool.*

No, no more pity, Grandmother, I promise, she vowed, bowing before the dancing lights that shielded her grandmother from her view. *No more pity. No more weakness. No more Shanna Brady, or Shanna Calhoun. No more Shanna anything, Just Shanna.*

Shanna felt a smile and couldn't tell if she was forming it on her lips or if there was something smiling down at her. It didn't matter. It was going to be all right. Her grandmother was here to help her get over this.

"Grandmother?" she whispered hoarsely. Dry, her lips felt dry, cracked, as if someone had taken a knife and cut little notches along them.

Something, no some*one* moved just next to her. She could sense it. A voice drifted to her from very far away, growing louder with each word.

"No, it's Mother, Shanna. Can you hear me?"

This time her eyelids did lift when she tried to move them. The stark whiteness she had sensed started to take shape. It was the curtain near her bed. But everything else was a blur. There was someone there with her. Shanna labored hard to focus.

A lady in a white coat. A white fur coat. Raven-black hair spilling down on the collar. Perfume that smelled of exotic flowers.

Mother.

"Can you hear me, Shanna?" Rheena repeated urgently, squeezing the cold, pale hand she held in hers.

What was that pain? Shanna lifted a hand that seemed incredibly heavy and touched the side of her head. She couldn't reach her temple. Something thick and rough was in the way. A bandage?

"I can hear you, Mother." Shanna attempted to turn her head so that she could look around. A thousand arrows sliced her scalp. She bit her lip to keep from gasping and felt the sickly taste of blood again. "Where am I?"

"Georgetown University Hospital. I had you transferred here as soon as the police called me." Rheena, thoroughly shaken, had just lived through what had seemed to her to be the most horrible twelve hours of her life. Anger rose in response to the fright she had felt and the fear she had been warring with for half a day. "What the hell were you doing, driving in that weather? You could have been killed. Are you out of your mind?"

For once, her mother's anger didn't disturb her, didn't make her want to shrink away. She was past all that now. "Jordan—" she began weakly, then stopped. How did she go about summarizing the devastating pain, the shattered dreams in one sentence?

"Right here, honey."

No, not here. I left you behind me, at the house. Naked. That other woman's sweat dampening your body.

Jordan, his eyes filled with concern, a day-old stubble on his handsome face, stood on her other side. He took her hand in his and she winced as she pulled it away.

So, she was still angry. But he wasn't going to let her be difficult about this. Time, it would just take a little time, he thought, swearing inwardly. He'd behave like the contrite, atoning husband, promising her anything if she would just forgive him. She'd be eating out of his hand again within the week.

Next time, he promised himself, he'd have to be more careful.

He touched her face tenderly. "You had me so worried. I thought—"

No, no lies, Jordan. Not anymore.

From somewhere, she summoned her anger and held it up like a shield to ward off his ploys. She wished she could pull herself up into a sitting position, but knew she hadn't the strength. She saved it for her words.

"Get out."

Jordan shrugged helplessly at Rheena, his expression never faltering. Taking Shanna's hand again, he looked lovingly into her eyes, mentally cursing her soul to hell. "Shanna, honey, you're delirious, you don't know what you're saying—"

With a surge of strength that immediately left her gasping, Shanna pulled away her hand. It hit the IV stand, causing it to totter. Jordan caught it before it could fall over.

"Shanna, be careful," Rheena cried.

Ignoring her mother, Shanna struggled for breath, for control. She wasn't going to be hysterical and she wasn't going to surrender her consciousness to the terrible pain she was experiencing and pass out, not before she made him leave her room. She never wanted to see his face again as long as she lived.

"I know exactly what I'm saying, Jordan, and I want you to get out. Out of my room, out of my life. Now."

Jordan's facial muscles tightened. He glanced nervously at his mother-in-law as he tried to calm his wife.

"Shanna, please—"

"Don't plead, Jordan," Shanna said, her voice cracking. There wasn't a part of her that didn't scream for relief. "It doesn't become you. Now go away." She turned her face into the pillow, away from him. "I'm tired, I want to be alone."

Jordan nodded, grasping at the excuse. He crossed to the door. "I understand. This has all been a terrible ordeal for all of us, but everything will be better soon. I promise," he added vehemently. He looked at the pale face. Why hadn't she just died? It was just like her to live and give him grief. "I'll be back to see you soon," he told her just as the door closed behind him.

When hell freezes over. She turned her head slowly, realizing that her mother was still in the room. "I'd like you to go, too, Mother."

"Not just yet." The little scene that had just transpired had Rheena speculating. She arched her brow as she moved forward to her daughter. "I admit that I'm not much of a mother, Shanna, but I almost lost you last night and I want to know why."

It was on the tip of her tongue to tell her mother to get out again, but there was a note of sincerity in the other woman's voice that had Shanna weakening and tears rising to her eyes.

No, no more tears. No more pity.

"I came home," Shanna began slowly, each word burning in her throat. Betrayed. Jordan had betrayed her love, her trust. Who was she going to trust now? No one. There was no one. There was a huge void within her that was so overwhelming she felt as if she was going to plunge into a bottomless chasm. "I came home," she repeated again, measuring each syllable, fighting the natural urge to hide her shame. Her mother, studying her face, remained silent and waited. "And found him in bed with some woman."

It had to happen sooner or later, Rheena thought. The report she had locked in her safe from that detective had labeled Jordan a modern-day satyr. Rheena began to say something about it and decided not to. What purpose would it serve to hurt Shanna, especially now, while she was lying broken and bleeding in a hospital bed?

"I see." Rheena sat down on the side of the bed and leaned forward, taking Shanna's hand in hers. It was a warm, bonding gesture. "And you ran."

It sounded so cowardly, Shanna thought. She was through being a coward, through keeping to the shadows. "I just wanted to get away. There is a difference."

Rheena thought of the way she had felt when the call came in from the police. Of the way fear had spasmodically clutched at her heart. "Getting yourself killed would have made quite a difference," she said cynically.

Shanna was in no mood for a lecture, especially not from her mother. "I'm still alive." She tugged on her hand, but her mother's grip only tightened.

"And what do you intend to do about it?"

Shanna tried to focus on the question. The noise in her head was amplifying as the pain increased. "About being alive?"

"Yes, and about Mr. Hot Pants." Personally, Rheena would have liked nothing better than to see him tied to the rear end of a car and dragged, naked, over broken glass. The feeling of revenge warred with her inherent desire to avoid the hint of scandal.

"Divorce him."

Her daughter's answer surprised Rheena. She realized that she was waiting for her daughter to say something ineffectual about forgiving Jordan because he was under so much stress or something equally lame. She looked at her daughter with new respect. "No second chances?"

The corners of Shanna's mouth lifted in an ironic smile that hurt for more reasons than one. "I think Jordan's been living on second chances for a long time now, Mother."

Well, well, well, the worm has turned. It's about time. Rheena's smile was warm, almost maternal. "You're a lot smarter than I gave you credit for, Shanna." She rose, still holding her daughter's hand in hers. It was her turn to offer comfort. "It'll be his loss."

"I know." Her headache was now unbearable. Shanna pressed her lips together as a sudden excruciating pain claimed the top of her skull.

Shanna gripped her mother's hand more firmly than Rheena had thought she was capable of, given the circumstances. "Pain?" she asked, concerned.

"Yes," Shanna whispered.

Rheena let go of Shanna's hand as she turned toward the door. "I'll call for the nurse. She can give you something for it."

Tears slid down Shanna's cheek. She was too weak to hold them back any longer. "They haven't got anything for this kind of pain, Mother."

"Of course they do, Shanna," Rheena said firmly, trying to infuse her daughter with the will that had always seen her through her own travails. "They call it time. I'll let you rest now. Your father's on his way to Illinois. I left a message at all three offices and the house. When he arrives, I'm sure he'll turn around and get the next flight home again. Together we'll cut your about-to-be ex-husband into little bloody ribbons." She smiled, relishing the thought. "He'll wish he was never born."

"No, Mother."

"Second thoughts?" Shanna's spirit had had a short life, Rheena thought in disappointment.

"No, no second thoughts. He's just not worth the

effort, that's all. Besides, I don't believe in revenge."

"A pity," Rheena murmured, her hand on the door. "I always have."

"I know," Shanna mumbled as she slipped into a merciful sleep. "But I'm not you, Mother."

As she fell into a deep sleep Shanna could have sworn she heard the word *bravo*. It sounded like her grandmother's voice, but it could have been her mother's. She wasn't sure and much too tired to wonder about it any longer.

11

Shanna slept intermittently for the next thirty-six hours. Her sleep was dreamless and her body mended. To ascertain the extent of her internal injuries, the doctor ordered a series of tests performed on her.

Her mother returned, this time with Shanna's father. The senator's face was deeply lined with concern. Shanna couldn't remember ever seeing him look so old or so worn. It touched her that he cared so much. It made the emptiness within her not quite so vast.

Her mother had told the senator that Shanna wanted a divorce. The reasons why she left for Shanna to explain.

The senator wasn't happy about the idea of a divorce in his family. Despite the times, he had a very old-fashioned view of the institution of marriage. He was mystified that Shanna actually wanted to leave Jordan. She had appeared to be so much in love with the man.

"Perhaps there could be a reconciliation," the senator suggested gently.

She had made up her mind. It was the only thing she had to hang on to. Shanna slowly shook her head, promising herself that this time she wouldn't cry. "No, no reconciliations."

She looked so pale, Brady thought, lying there. So frail. Perhaps it was just her confusion speaking. "You're sure?"

Shanna pressed her lips together and nodded. "I'm sure."

Brady took his daughter's hand, patting it. He felt horribly awkward. It was a new role for him. Part of him still thought of Shanna as a child. Perhaps it was because he had never gotten to know her during that period. And now she was a woman. How did one parent a woman? What did one say? "Perhaps after you've recovered—"

"I have recovered," Shanna answered with a sad smile. "From Jordan." Her father's kind blue eyes urged her to go on, but she didn't want to recount the sordid details. What was the point? "I don't want to be married to him anymore, Dad. Please don't ask me why."

Brady glanced at his wife, but Rheena, for once, refrained from speaking what she knew. Gossip was fine about others, but not about her own. Rheena shrugged. "She's apparently made up her mind."

Funny, just a little while ago, he would have commented that Shanna had no real mind of her own. She merely conformed. Now he knew otherwise.

"If that's what you want." He sighed, thinking of the primary. "It makes it rather awkward, backing him for the election when my own daughter's rejected him."

Nothing would ever be publicly awkward for her father, Shanna thought. That was what made him Senator Brady. "Love and politics have nothing to do with each other, Dad. You've always said that. Back him if you believe what he says. Withdraw if you don't."

Brady studied his daughter silently and made a mental note to have Haggerty look into the situation. If Shanna didn't want to tell him what was going on, someone else would. There was always someone willing to fill in the details in Washington. For now it was enough that Shanna was alive and apparently recovering. He had seen a photograph of the car she'd been driving that night. It was mangled beyond recognition. He refused to entertain the possibility of what might have been.

Test after test was run. It seemed to Shanna that they left no stone unturned in an effort to pinpoint just what sort of damage had been done by the accident. Her vision was still blurry and the doctor had ordered a CAT scan of the head to determine the extent of the optic-nerve damage, if any.

"I feel," she muttered to her nurse as she was being wheeled out of one of the X-ray labs that catacombed the ground floor of the hospital, "as if I'm having a complete overhaul."

"Think of it as a fine-tuning. Besides, nothing's too good for the senator's daughter," the nurse added cheerfully as she pushed her wheelchair into the elevator.

The words left a bitter taste in Shanna's mouth, quite the opposite of the nurse's intent. Shanna knew that her parents had donated a large sum of money to the hospital. It seemed that everywhere she turned, her lineage was there to haunt her, even though it wasn't meant to.

Just something else to come to terms with, she told herself.

Bringing her to her room, the nurse left to see about getting Shanna a late lunch, since testing had run past lunchtime. Shanna struggled back into her bed. Behind her, she heard the door to her suite being opened again.

Another test, she wondered wearily, another set of hands to poke and prod and find nothing? It was amazing how many working parts there were to the human body, she mused as she pulled the cover around herself.

"I'm not going for any more tests," she said half seriously before looking in the direction of her visitor. "I've just been shaken up, not apart."

Her smile froze.

Jordan stood in the doorway. He held a cut-glass vase with three dozen long-stem yellow roses arranged in it. His smile was warm, loving, and left her completely cold.

"Hi, how do you feel?"

She stiffened and pain lanced through her at the minor movement. She didn't want Jordan here, why did he persist in returning? She scowled at the flowers. Yellow roses. They were her favorite. He was using, she thought, every weapon at his disposal. Was he that afraid? "Like I was hit by a car. Inside and out."

Jordan placed the vase on the table next to Shanna and took her hand. She balled it into a fist. He held it for a moment longer, then released it. This was going to take time, he counseled himself. "Shanna, there's a lot to explain," he began.

She looked at him. His shoulders were sagging, like a man who'd been beaten, a man who had come to beg forgiveness. He always knew just how to play an audience, she realized suddenly, just as he had always known how to play her. She had been disgustingly easy for him.

"I don't think there are enough words in the English language for you to explain with, Jordan. I asked you once to get out and I meant it."

He wasn't going to give up so quickly. It had been an uphill battle to get where he was, a fierce fight against poverty, against abuse. He wasn't about to be licked by a bitchy spoiled brat. There was a way out of this.

"You were distraught when you said that, Shanna. You weren't thinking clearly—"

She avoided his eyes. Mesmerizing, beautiful, they had always been her downfall. She was probably part of a large club, she thought bitterly. She knew now that he could charm the skin off a mink without making an incision. And she had to be very, very careful not to fall back into the trap. She didn't pretend to deceive herself. She was still susceptible to him, still vulnerable. Everything she had felt when she fell in love with Jordan was still there within her. All the insecurities, all the needs. She just had to find a way to rechannel them.

"No, Jordan," she said firmly, "I am thinking very clearly, probably more clearly than I have in the last two and a half years." Digging her knuckles into the mattress on either side of her battered body, she pushed herself up against her pillows. It gave her leverage and seemed to help somehow. "I mean it. I want you out of my life."

Jordan wished again that she had died. It had been his first thought when the police had called to notify him of the accident. If she had, he could be playing the bereaved widower right now before the press. It would have undoubtedly garnered him the sympathy vote in the primary, perhaps even the election. Instead he was standing here, trading words with a vengeful little mouse who unknowingly held his future in her hands.

He touched her cheek, the way he knew she always loved. This time she pulled back. A growing panic began to fray his temper.

"Shanna, darling, you can't throw everything we've had together away because of one stupid mistake, one mindless indiscretion. She'd been after me for the last few months, hounding me." He lowered his head while raising his eyes to her face. It was a look calculated to be appealing. "A man can only resist for so long. But it's over, I swear. I fired her."

When Shanna appeared unmoved, he felt a bead of sweat winding its way down his spine. Who could he get to back him if Shanna told her father about this? Though he was ingratiating himself to several other financial backers, he was counting on Brady's support to win him this primary.

It amazed her how sincere Jordan could appear while he lied. A mirthless smile rose to her lips. The effort hurt her face. Rumors crowded her head, rumors she had always refused to acknowledge. "One? One indiscretion? Just how stupid do you think I am, Jordan?"

He wanted to strangle her. Was she doing this on purpose, getting her revenge, making him dangle this way? Didn't she realize that this was his life she was threatening to cut short? All because of her goddamn injured pride.

A muscle in his cheek twitched as he sat down on the bed next to her and took her hand again. It felt cold, lifeless. The way she had in bed, he thought. The way his political career would be if he didn't find a way to make her take him back. He cursed the lust that sent him questing from one warm, willing body to another. Most of all he cursed her.

"I never thought you were stupid, Shanna."

He sounded so well rehearsed. All his words did. Why hadn't she seen it before? Why had she been so blind? "When do you stop lying, Jordan? Or have you lied so much that you don't know what's true and what's not, what's real and what's illusion?"

His patience shredded and he dropped her limp hand.

"Spare me your Psychology 101 crap, okay?" Jordan snapped and then realized what he had said. Blowing out a huge breath, he dragged a hand through his hair. "I was out there in that frigging hallway half the night, just waiting to find out if you were going to live or die. Do you know what that's like, do you have *any* idea? Wondering if you were a widower? Knowing you were responsible. And then to come in and hear that you don't ever want to see me again? Goddamn it, Shanna, you've pitched me straight into hell without so much as a backward glance."

For one moment she believed him. He sounded so hurt, so sincere. But then, he always had. She forced herself to recall what he had said to that woman when she stood in the doorway of her bedroom, unnoticed. He had called her a bitch. For no reason at all except that she existed and she loved him. A bitch.

She clutched the term and it helped her rally.

"Drama." She nodded her head slowly as if appraising his performance. "You do drama very well." Jordan got to his feet and began to pace, watching her as she spoke. He reminded her of a caged panther at the zoo, looking through the bars, looking at freedom and knowing it wasn't to be his.

Oh, Jordan, if you'd only been honest and loved me the way you said you did.

"That's why you've gotten as far as you have. That's why I fell in love with you. You were so dynamic, so forceful, so much bigger than life." She folded her hands in her lap and then raised her eyes to his face. "But you're a lot smaller than that, aren't you, Jordan?" Shanna asked quietly.

He was losing and he knew it. He couldn't twist her around the way he always had before. He'd pushed her too far. Desperate, he tried another approach. "What's gotten into you?" His voice cracked with feeling. He congratulated himself on the touch. "It's that blow on the head, isn't it?" He looked at the bandage on her left temple. "It's making you talk nonsense."

She laughed and the sound rankled in him.

"Maybe I had to be literally hit over the head to finally see what other people have been hinting at all along."

"Who?" he demanded heatedly. "Who's been telling you things? Give me names, goddamn it. Tell me who's been spreading lies about me!"

Agitation was causing tiny fissures to snake through his facade. It was crumbling right before her eyes. She felt absolutely no satisfaction. She was just tired.

"It doesn't matter who, Jordan. What matters is that it was the truth. You can't keep secrets in Washington, Jordan. You should know that. There's always someone to see you, someone to know."

Jordan ran his hand over his mouth. He had to have time to think, to regroup. Things would work themselves out once he got her home. He'd give her the attention she wanted, take a couple of days off from the campaign, maybe take her on a second honeymoon. And made sure that Liz was kept the hell far away. Yes, that would be the way to go.

He leaned over the bed, one hand on either side of her, defining her space. His eyes on her face, he slowly slid his hand along the length of her body, petting, fondling. But the look of longing, of desire, didn't come. She looked at him with pity and contempt. He fought the urge to hit her for it.

Straightening, he gave her a warning look. "Look, get some rest and we'll talk about this in the morning, or when you come home—"

She was grateful he had stopped. She wasn't certain how much longer she could have resisted him. Despite everything, he still affected her. "Don't you understand,

Jordan? There is no home for us. There'll be your home and my home. Two separate places."

"I'm sorry, Shanna. I'm sorry," he cried. There was nothing there in her face. Nothing. God, what did it take to make her come around? "You can't do this!"

No, she wasn't going to cry, she promised herself. Not until he left. He didn't deserve to see her tears. "Why? Because I'm meek and mild? Because I'm plain and you're beautiful? Because I should be grateful that someone like you ever looked my way?"

He had never seen her like this before and had no idea how to handle her. She had stripped him of every weapon he had. "No, but—"

"I *know* why you looked my way, I just never wanted to admit it to myself." She wadded the bedclothes under her hand, digging deep for courage. Her grandmother's courage. "It's because of my parents, of who they are, not who I am. But I won't be used anymore, Jordan. I do have some pride left."

He stared at her, completely appalled at her words. He tried again, trying to tap into her compassion. "Shanna, if you leave me, I don't know what I'll do—"

She didn't believe it for a moment. "You'll go on. You're a survivor, Jordan. You'll go on." Her mouth twisted into a cynical smile. "You won't get any Boy Scout merit badges for the way you do it, but you'll survive very nicely."

She saw the dark look that came over his face and knew exactly what he was thinking. Now that she knew the truth, it was easy. "I won't go to the press with this, if that's what you're worried about. I want a scandal even less than you do. Perhaps not less than my mother, but less than you. I'm not particularly partial to letting the world know that my husband's been having affairs. I won't damage your chances at the polls."

Yeah, right. Jordan had never believed in the kindness of others, not when it came down to the bottom line. Then it was everyone for himself. It was one of the first lessons his father had taught him before giving him the back of his hand. He'd been about three or four at the time. "The divorce'll do that."

"Why should it? We have 'irreconcilable differences.' It happens all the time." She couldn't resist adding, "You'll get more women voters—both at the polls and in your bed."

"Your father—" He thought of the backing he would lose, of the money, and gripped her hand.

"I didn't tell him why I'm divorcing you. You strike your own deal with him—without me in the middle."

Her father would never stay, once he knew. And Jordan didn't believe for one moment that she was telling the truth. He knew people. She would like nothing better than to go crying to her father about his "betrayal." "I can't let you do this."

No, we're passed the point where you have the right to tell me what you want me to do. "You can't stop me from doing this." Shanna stared him straight in the eye and lied, wishing fervently that the words were true. Maybe someday they would be. "You don't mean anything to me anymore."

His look was angry, foreboding. She hadn't loved him any more than he had loved her. "Just like that?"

Shanna raised her chin. If she could, she would have walked out. Her mother would have appreciated this as an exit line. "Just like that." Pain seared through every fiber of her being. It far outweighed the physical pain she felt. She still loved him, even though she couldn't stand the sight of him anymore.

Jordan searched her eyes, looking for evidence of a lie. They were flat, unfathomable. He'd been right. "You always were a cold bitch."

The pronouncement ripped through her like a knife, but she managed not to show how much it hurt. She still had her integrity. Perhaps it was the only thing she had, but it would have to do.

"If you believe that, you never got to know me at all." She felt her lower lip begin to tremble and bit the inside of it to keep it still. "Your loss, Jordan, not mine."

Swearing at her, he hit the vase with the side of his hand and left the hospital suite. It smashed into a multitude of pieces. Roses fanned out haphazardly on the floor like broken dreams.

The sound of the vase crashing brought her nurse running into the room. The young woman looked at the shattered vase in surprise. It was a good distance from the bed. "What happened here?"

Shanna sighed. She felt so hollow, so devoid of everything. Would she ever be able to pull herself together again? "A minor earthquake."

The nurse looked at her quizzically before she shrugged away the strange explanation. "I'll get an orderly to clean this up right away." The woman glanced at her wristwatch. "Time to take your blood pressure anyway." She uncoiled the blood-pressure reading apparatus from its storage place on the wall. "Lunch is on its way. So, how are you feeling?"

Shanna looked at the door that Jordan had stormed through. "Like I died." Listlessly she raised her arm. The nurse wrapped the gray cuff around it tightly, then pumped the bulb in her hand, inflating it.

Mechanically she listened for the beat. When it began, she smiled, watching the gauge. It was normal. "No, you're far from dead, my dear." She removed the stethoscope from her ears, letting it rest around her neck. "Luckily neither one of you is."

Shanna stared at the woman as she let her arm drop

against the bed. Neither one? What was she talking about? "Excuse me?"

"You're both going to be fine," the nurse assured her cheerfully.

"What 'both'? I was the only one in the car." Was the woman referring to someone else? "Do you mean the man who hit me?"

The nurse returned the blood-pressure cuff to its wire cage on the wall. "No, he got away without a scratch. I'm talking about the baby."

Shanna's throat went dry. "What baby?"

The nurse turned as she picked up the clipboard at the foot of Shanna's bed. She pulled her pen out of her skirt pocket. "Why yours, of course." She jotted down the latest reading, then stopped and looked at Shanna. "Do you mean to tell me that you don't know?"

They'd done so many tests, had one of them been a routine pregnancy test? Oh God, had it turned out positive? "Know what?"

Please, it can't be true, not now.

The nurse beamed at her. She'd gotten a look at Shanna's husband yesterday. Stubble and all, the man was gorgeous. They made a nice couple. "Why, that you're pregnant, of course."

Her grandmother's voice echoed in her head. *They're not foolproof, you know. And considering the fool you've been sleeping with—*

Talk about timing, she thought helplessly, her hand unconsciously splaying over her stomach.

12

Reid Kincannon sighed as he stretched his legs out before him on the white beach chair. Behind him was the Hotel Lorraine, an exclusive resort where only the very wealthy could afford to stay. His own hotel, far less expensive but suiting his needs adequately, was farther down along the beach. He was partial to the view here.

He burrowed the tips of his toes into the white sand and sighed. Heady stuff, he mused languidly, for a farm boy from Iowa.

The balmy air caressed the length of his body with warm, seductive fingers. Back in D.C., the temperature was a crisp forty-one degrees with rain forecast for the rest of the day. He'd checked the newspaper first thing this morning. Knowing he was here instead of there increased the almost innocent pleasure he felt, even though he would be back in D.C. all too soon.

It was like being in another world here in the Bahamas. And he didn't take it for granted, not even for one moment. Each minute, filled with nothing but relaxation, was far too precious not to savor. Doing nothing, he was actively purging the stress that had brought him to this point in time.

This was the first vacation Reid had ever allowed himself. There had never been enough time or money before. Even now, there were just four short days in the sun before plunging back into the hectic world of studies and part-time jobs meant to hold body and soul together until he got his degree.

Reid smiled to himself. He was older than most of the students who sat beside him at the university, older by probably a good ten years. It hadn't been easy, getting started in life all over again at his age. But things didn't always fall into place on a timetable when you were poor and without resources. The only way he could have gotten the education he craved as much as food and water was to give the army a piece of his life first. So he had. He had done his part, now the army was doing its share.

It hadn't been so bad, being in the army, he mused, and it had given him shelter for a while and hidden him from Tyler Poole's family.

A waiter walked by and eyed him, apparently wondering if he was one of the guests of the hotel. Reid only smiled at him and nodded. *Guest* was always such an odd term to use when you had to pay, he thought. And he had paid, paid dearly for everything he had. For everything he intended to have.

The GI bill was helping him get through school. The GI bill and a host of odd jobs that threatened to leave a permanently bloodshot tinge to his eyes as they whittled away at his natural stamina. He had been keeping this pace up for three and a half years now, working two shifts in the summer to save up money for the fall. But a man could only keep going for so long. Eventually he had been faced with a choice of either stopping for a few days, or dropping dead in his tracks. So he had taken a trip to the islands. It was a necessary shot in the arm that had dangerously depleted his emergency fund.

Today was his last day in the islands.

A new semester was beginning at the end of the week. Besides, four days was all he could afford to take off without pay. Part-time help was only paid when they showed up.

He heard sea gulls crying in the distance. Reid glanced at his watch. Eleven o'clock. It was time.

He turned to the right, anticipating her arrival.

Like clockwork, the tall, honey-blond-haired woman with the sad eyes appeared. She was dressed in a modest light pink maillot. She moved effortlessly and unselfconsciously, as if she had no idea that she had a very beautiful shape. She had stirred his fantasies, such as he allowed himself, from the very first. She was alone as always and completely oblivious to her surroundings.

As she had for the last three days, she spread out her turquoise beach blanket on the white sands, propped up her striped, small chair on top of it, then sat down to watch the ocean, her long limbs stretched out before her. There was no radio, no book, no magazine to distract her. She simply stared straight ahead. For hours.

She was staying at the Hotel Lorraine. He had seen how the waiters all danced to her attention and wondered if she was anyone special, or just another pretty woman on a vacation. He wished he was staying at the same hotel as she was. It would have provided him with an excuse to start a conversation. Or perhaps wait to bump into her in the lobby. But the Hotel Lorraine was completely out of his price range, even for a day.

Still, the beach was free and even a cat could look at a queen, he mused, watching her.

Who was she? he wondered again. And why, looking the way she did, with everything apparently at her disposal, was she so unhappy?

He knew he'd never see her again, but he couldn't help wondering about her. People had always intrigued him, the way they thought, the way they acted, and what made one person happy while the same set of circumstances made another miserable. Nursing the tall lemonade in his hand, he watched her and let his mind drift.

Shanna squinted as she looked at the sea gulls that cried out as they flew overhead. She wished she could be that free. She wished she could just glide on the wind and not feel anything but the cool air around her, enveloping her body.

She sighed and looked back at the ocean. She hadn't told anyone. When she had left the hospital last week, she still hadn't found the words, or perhaps the courage, to tell her parents that she was pregnant.

She laughed quietly under her breath, though there was nothing funny about it. She had just now found the courage to admit it to herself. The doctor, of course, had given her conclusive proof. He had brought her the test report when he saw the doubt in her eyes. Her mind had still refused to accept it. A baby. Something she had always wanted, and now it dragged her down like a heavy iron chain.

Her physician had gone on to confirm her suspicions about her vision. It had been permanently affected by the blow to the head she had received, but glasses or contact lenses would easily correct the problem.

Nothing else, he had assured her cheerfully, was wrong.

A lot he knew, she thought.

Pregnant. She was pregnant.

Oh God, what did she know about being a mother? She was just now learning how to be a human being, how to deal with things on her own. How could she possibly be responsible for another tiny life? She'd never even had a pet before. At least, she recalled with a small smile, not after the goldfish kept dying.

This wasn't going to be like having a goldfish.

Two lovers, holding hands, strolled along the beach in the distance. The sound of their intimate laughter carried on the wind. As Shanna turned to look they stopped to embrace, then kiss. Shanna didn't even bother pretending to herself that it didn't bother her. It did. Horribly.

But she would get over it. She clenched her fingers together so hard, she felt her nails digging into her palms. She would get over it, she swore.

Her mother had suggested that she get away to the islands, had even offered to come with her, but Shanna had turned Rheena down, saying she wanted to be alone. To her surprise, Rheena took no offense. She seemed to understand. Her mother wasn't as remote, as feelingless as she had thought. Learn something new every day.

She had come the the islands to think, to try to sort things out, but so far her mind was one huge blank. Just as formless as the ocean was before her. It seemed to roll out to forever, coming in contact with nothing. There was a solution out there for her, but she couldn't see it any more than she could see the land that existed on the other side of the ocean.

But she still knew it was there. That much hope she hadn't lost.

A long shadow spread over her. She turned her head, squinting, and found she had to look up a long way to see the face of its creator. Her eyes traveled along the length of a hard, muscular male body wearing nothing but bathing trunks. The bathing suit was just that, trunks, not the skimpy little briefs that Jordan had favored.

The man standing next to her had a body that had taken time to perfect. Rough, sturdy, it matched his face, which was all planes and chiseled angles. It bespoke character. She wondered if the same thing could be said of the long, thin scar that ran along his side. A racing-car accident? Perhaps something involving a motorcycle or hang gliding. It would have suited him. There was something dangerous and reckless about him. He had black hair and he wore it longer than was fashionable, a dark, unruly mane like a lion. That's what he reminded her of, she thought, a lion, staking out the boundaries of his domain.

God, she wasn't interested.

She looked at him, then very deliberately looked away. Just a few weeks ago she wouldn't have been able to do that. A few weeks ago, she thought, she'd been a timid soul afraid to voice an opinion too loudly, afraid to offend. But the timid had plagues visited upon them that ravaged them dry. Plagues like Jordan.

She was a cool one, Reid thought. But her eyes belied her facade. Besides, it was his last day. What did he have to lose but a little time? He gestured casually around him, his voice friendly. "It's a beautiful beach."

"Yes, and a large one."

Shanna's meaning was very clear. She'd never had enough courage to be rude before, never had the desire to be rude before. But now she just wanted the world to leave her alone, to let her think in peace. To let her forget how to feel. She was absolutely in no mood for intruders, especially not good-looking males who thought that reason enough to barrel in. She lowered her sunglasses, as if creating a barrier between them.

"I like this section." Reid folded his long legs beneath him, tailor fashion, as he sat down on the sand beside her. "I notice that you do, too." She had a delicate profile, he thought. Like a Dresden doll. He found himself wondering if her emotions were close to the skin and what it would take to awaken them.

The last thing she wanted was for a man to try to pick her up. She glanced down at her hand. She still had on her rings. Somehow her hand had felt too naked without them. Besides, wearing them had afforded her some safety. Until now.

"So does my husband." She held up her hand. She waited for the man to retreat. When he didn't, she let her hand drop back into her lap.

Reid looked at the diamond engagement ring that had cost Jordan half of his savings.

"Very impressive." He could take a hint, he thought, amused. Reid rose, brushing the sand from his legs. It fell like tiny droplets of white rain to his feet. "He doesn't come out much, does he?" He saw the puzzled look on her face. "Your husband. I haven't seen him with you when you come here."

"He's in the hotel room," she said quickly, then raised her sunglasses and stared at Reid. "You've been watching me?" Perhaps he wasn't just a harmless man trying to find a meaningless good time for the night. Maybe he was something else. Kidnapping was a threat she had lived with all of her life. Rather than cringe, she decided to brazen it out. She knew she had to. There was no one here to turn to. No one, she amended, in her life to turn to. Not anymore.

"Why?" she demanded.

That was an easy one, Reid thought. "Because you're lovely. And sad." He was tempted to touch her face lightly to see just how delicate her skin really was. He didn't. "And I wondered why."

No, he didn't strike her as a kidnapper. Maybe one of those horrid magazine reporters, the ones who filled the tabloids at the checkout aisles with distorted half-truths that titillated the public. She grew angry at the invasion of her privacy he represented. "That isn't any of your business."

"No," he agreed easily. "It isn't. But I still wondered why."

Since he made no further move to leave, Shanna decided that it was time for her to go. Otherwise she knew she'd have no peace. With a huff, she reached over for her beach bag.

Automatically Reid placed his hand over hers, stopping her. The glare she flashed had him immediately releasing her and withdrawing. He raised his hands, palms up as he took a step back.

"No, stay." He saw the way she eyed him suspiciously. "I'm going in. I have to pack anyway. Today's my last day here."

She lowered her sunglasses back into place and turned her face toward the ocean. She wondered if he was lying. More than that, she wondered if she could ever believe anyone again, even about the simplest of matters. "Have a nice trip back."

"I'll do that."

Reid grinned to himself as he began to walk away. A very nice piece of work, he thought. He'd bet her husband had his hands full with her. She seemed like a spitfire beneath those long, cool looks.

But she was right, it was none of his business. There

was no place in his life for entanglements at the moment, however brief and pleasing they might be. Not until he got his life into the order he wanted it. First things, he promised himself, first. There were grades to raise and a degree to earn. After that, he could turn his attention to more earthy needs.

Shanna watched him leave out of the corner of her eye, pretending that she was still looking out at the ocean. He was undoubtedly part of the idle rich, she surmised, with nothing but time to work on his body and to satisfy his appetites. Was that what there was in store for her? Idleness? A life of combing beaches and hot spots, seeing and being seen? And having nothing to show for it at the end?

Even in the beginning, she hadn't wanted to live that way. But she hadn't done anything about it. She had gone to college and, to her regret, just floated along until Jordan had come to fill her world.

No, he hadn't quite filled it, she reminded herself, not even when she was head over heels in love with him. She recalled the restless feeling she had had that came to a head at Cydney's wedding. She had felt something wasn't right, as if all the pieces to her life weren't in their proper place or hadn't been found yet. That had been less than a year ago. Cydney was already getting a divorce. Irreconcilable differences.

Well, they had that much in common, Shanna thought philosophically, she and Cydney. They were both getting a divorce, both citing the same trite, tired phrase to explain their responsibility for hopes gone awry. Her mother told her that Cydney was flying to the Riviera to recuperate.

She was going to fly back home, Shanna decided. There was no point in sitting here on the beach, watching wave chase after endless wave. It was time to be an active participant in life, not just a passive one, meekly hoping things would work themselves out without any intervention on her part.

It's time I took your advice, Grandmother.

After all, she was living for two now, not just herself. It was time she started to set an example. It was time, she thought, rising, to live.

Reid turned to look at the Dresden doll one last time before he went in. But when he looked around for her, she was already gone.

Probably to her husband. Lucky guy, Reid thought, turning around again.

13

The decision was made on her return flight. During her stay in the Bahamas, all those days on the beach, she had carefully sifted through her life, through all the things that meant anything to her. Despite efforts to the contrary, her thoughts continued to return to Jordan's campaign. At first, she tried to block it out. She didn't want to think about anything that reminded her of Jordan at all. Yet memories of that short period of time kept poking through. Because she was naturally shy, she hadn't liked the crowds at first. But after a few days a change had set in. She discovered that she enjoyed being out and meeting people, talking to them. She had felt more alive, had felt a greater sense of purpose then than she had at any other time in her life.

She hadn't really ever thought of herself as being outgoing. Yet she found herself getting caught up in the personalities of the people she met. Some had spilled out problems to her in hopes that once elected, Jordan

could help. Shanna had wanted to help them. She
wanted to help make a difference. Politically.

Rather than having the taxi take her from the airport
to her house in Georgetown, Shanna checked into the
Hay-Adams Hotel. She couldn't bear the thought of
staying at the house, staying alone with the memories.
She had no idea where Jordan was and she didn't want
to know. All she did know was that she didn't want to
run into him.

The desk clerk at the hotel gave her a third-floor
room with a clear view of the White House. Stopping
only to remove her coat and kick off her shoes as she
walked into the suite, Shanna headed straight for the
telephone. She placed a call to the realty company that
had handled the purchase of her house in Virginia.

Another loose end for the lawyer to take care of, she
thought as she pressed the series of numbers that would
connect her to the real-estate office. Asking to be put
through to Hawley, she was connected and politely
endured the perfunctory small talk before describing
what she was looking for in an apartment. The man
promised to get back to her quickly.

Having set the wheels in motion, she then called her
family lawyer. A little more than half an hour later, after
consuming only half of the ham-and-cheese sandwich
she had had sent up to her room, Shanna was ready to
launch phase three of her plan.

Senator Roger Brady had subconsciously acknowledged the knock the first time he heard it, but didn't
answer. He had no time for interruptions. When the
unwelcome sound was repeated, a little more insistently

this time, he knew he was going to have to talk to whoever was on the other side of the office door.

Where the hell was Ellen? He had told her that under no circumstances was he to be disturbed. He had only forty-five minutes to get through this report before he met with Whitney and planned their strategy for the preliminary vote being taken by the Education, Arts, and Humanities subcommittee today. There were three people sitting on the fence on this one, three people to see and convince before the session began. He had no time for any unscheduled crisis.

Stress had always been part of the political game, and normally he rather thrived on it. But lately, he had to admit, it was getting to him. Running for reelection while juggling the issues that were important to him was getting to be a little too much at times.

Maybe, he mused, he was getting old. He had never thought it would happen to him.

The knock came again. "Yes, what is it?" He caught himself just before he snapped the question. He had never lost his temper, not in public and not in private, since he had passed the age of fifteen. That was probably why he was nursing an ulcer, he speculated. But after exercising outer control for a lifetime, he knew he wasn't about to change now.

When the door cracked open, Brady was surprised to see his secretary, Ellen Hale, looking in. His watchdog had turned out to be the offender.

Ellen, a small, squarish woman who favored long gray skirts and unflattering blouses, smiled hesitantly at him. "Senator, I know you're busy—"

He looked down at his desk. So much work, so little time. "*Very* busy, Ellen. I thought I asked not to be disturbed."

After working with the senator for over twelve years,

Ellen instinctively knew when to bend the rules. One of those times was now. "Your daughter's here to see you, Senator."

Brady took off his glasses and rubbed the bridge of his nose. Why couldn't anyone invent glasses that didn't feel like glasses? he wondered absently as Ellen's information registered. "My daughter? She's in the Bahamas." What was Ellen talking about?

"No." Shanna came in and stood behind Ellen. She smiled at her father. "She's right here." Crossing to his desk, she leaned over and kissed him lightly on the cheek. "Hi, Dad."

Surprised, concerned, Brady nodded at Ellen. The woman left, softly closing the door behind her. Brady frowned slightly as he looked at his daughter. Something was wrong. "You came back early. I wasn't expecting you until next week."

She wasn't early, she thought, looking around the office. By her own calculations, she was late. Twenty-five years late, but all that was going to change. "I have my life to get on with."

He nodded, not completely certain he understood where she was going with this. It was one of those vague, philosophical things people said when they had no answer. He thought he remembered that she had taken philosophy in college. Majored in it, wasn't it?

"Why didn't you call me or your mother? I would have sent someone with the car to meet you at the airport."

Nice and safe and well taken care of. It was a tender trap. But it was time to struggle out of the nest. High time. Shanna sat down in the black leather chair opposite her father's desk and slowly took off her gloves. The D.C. air was still sparring with a cold snap. "I got a cab. That's part of getting on with my life, Dad. I'm twenty-five years old. It's about time I started doing things on my own."

He didn't want her to feel as if she was alone. He hadn't been there for her before, but he wanted to be there for her now. She was a grown woman and he knew how to speak to adults. The child she had been before had rather frightened him. He knew that now. "You'll stay with us, of course."

She shook her head. "I'm at the Hay-Adams for the time being. I've got Mother's realtor looking into getting me an apartment." She saw her father's frown deepen and hurried to pacify him. Maybe she *was* trying to find her own identity, but it was still nice knowing that her family cared. In a way, it was rather a revelation. She had always thought she hadn't mattered, except as an appendage, an extension of the dynasty. "Perhaps I'll live at the Watergate for a while until I figure a few things out."

The senator leaned against his desk. "What about the house in Georgetown?" He thought he already knew the answer to that, but he let her say it.

"It'll be part of the settlement." She'd have to go there to pack the few belongings that still remained, but it couldn't be helped. As for the house in Virginia, she'd face that when her resolve grew a little stronger. "It'll be sold."

"I see." He studied her face. He had always been rather good at reading people. It was time, he realized, to use his ability on his own daughter. "Still want to go through with it? The divorce?" He certainly couldn't blame her, not after what he'd found out about Jordan since the accident. Still, people had a way of working things out when you least expected it.

"More than ever."

It was time to ask. She felt a slight tension enter the pit of her stomach and told herself she was being silly. This was her father and she wasn't a little girl anymore, seeking a favor of the great senator. She'd aged a hundred years in the last two weeks.

Taking a breath to calm herself, she began. "On the night of Grandmother's funeral, you told me to come to you if I ever needed anything."

"Of course." Now they were getting to it. She'd never come to his office before. He thought it odd for her to start now, out of the blue. "What is it you need? Another place to get away?"

She shook her head, a smile forming. He'd never guess. Why should he? He didn't know her very well, even if she was his flesh and blood. For that matter, she was just getting to really know herself. It was a shaky journey, but one she was beginning to find satisfying. "A job."

His eyes narrowed. "A what?"

She leaned forward, her momentum growing in the face of her uncertainty, as if to speed things along before he turned her down. What if he did refuse, for some reason? What if he thought it wouldn't look right or something equally immaterial but annoying? People had strange reasons for doing things, or not doing them. "A job. Here, with you."

He'd never pictured her working. Rheena would have a fit. Not that that would stop him. It might even make things interesting. But was Shanna serious? "Shanna, I think—"

She could hear the refusal coming a mile away. Shanna held up her hands, stopping him.

"Just hear me out, Dad. I wasn't cut out to be a bored heiress. I want to do something with my life. My education doesn't qualify me for much except standing on a street corner and spinning theories about life."

"If you just transfer that to a party atmosphere, then you're all set." He smiled, then saw just how serious

Shanna was. He crossed his arms before him, ready to listen to reason. "Go on."

Maybe it *was* going to work. "I never felt more alive than when I was working on Jordan's campaign committee. Even the little details, they were all important. They all went into making up a whole. And it felt good being a part of that."

He saw the light that came into her eyes. It intrigued him. So, she had a taste for politics. He had suspected it, on occasion, because of the questions she asked and because she seemed to like to linger and listen when he and his colleagues discussed politics. But he hadn't expected her interest to go this far. "Well, a candidate's wife—"

She shook her head. "It wasn't just being his wife, Dad. Of course I went into it to help him, but it got to be more than that. It meant more than that to me. For the little while that I was working, I felt really good about myself." She rose, placing her hand on her father's shoulder. It was the first time she could remember approaching him on a one-to-one level, as an adult. "I want that feeling back, Dad. I want to make a difference." She smiled. "And I really do believe in you."

He was touched more than he thought was possible. Lightly he covered her hand with his own and patted it. He'd been the recipient of a lot of praise over the years, some genuine, a good deal not. The senator couldn't remember ever being this moved. "Nice to hear after all these years, Shanna."

Talk was very cheap in politics, they both knew that. People traded it for favors all the time, buttering up, kissing up. She wanted him to know that she was being sincere.

"I really mean it. And it's not because you're my father and it's not because you're charming." He inclined his head slightly at the compliment and she smiled for the first time since she had walked in. "It's because you stand for something, for integrity." She thought of Jordan. "That's not an easy thing to do in Washington. Souls get sold all the time for a vote."

Though it was good for the voters to think of him in this light, Brady didn't want his daughter getting blinded. He was only mortal. "Don't put me on a pedestal, Shanna. I'm not lily-white."

She liked him, she thought. She genuinely liked him. It was a nice thing to find out about your own father. "No, you're a man and human. But you'll never be accused of being corrupt, either. And I know your record," she pointed out. "I know you've made a difference more than once. I want to help you keep making a difference."

"Very heady stuff to hear this far into my career." He sat down and turned his chair to face her squarely. For a moment he forgot about the work, the vote waiting for his support and his influence. What was happening here right now might not change the course of national events or history, but it was important to him.

He made his decision, knowing he couldn't have said anything else. "All right, you're hired. As it happens, I need a new aide. See Haggerty about placing you in the office."

Brady saw Shanna's relieved smile and realized that she had been afraid he'd turn her down. His own daughter? Did they really know so little about one another? He supposed so. It never ceased to amaze him. He probably knew more about Haggerty than he did about Shanna. But now that she was here, it was something he would have the opportunity to remedy, God willing.

He rocked back in his chair, a forefinger against his

cheek as he studied her. "What is it that you can do?"
Something else he didn't know.

She shrugged. "Anything that needs doing." She
thought of Jordan's headquarters. Someone else had
taken the title, but she had done the work. "I'm a hell of
an organizer. And I'm not too proud." As she remembered Jordan and the way he had been the last time she
saw him, her mouth hardened slightly. Pride had kept
her from forgiving him. That, and good sense. "At least
not when it comes to working."

He laughed, then nodded. "That's good to hear. On
both counts." Brady glanced at the report on his desk.
There were responsibilities waiting and he could put
them off only for a fraction of the time that he would
have liked. "Now, if you'll excuse me." He raised the top
two files. "I have to—"

She had to tell him everything. Now that she was
working for him, he'd know soon enough anyway. She
gripped the arms of the chair, as if that would help the
words come out. "There's one more thing you should
know."

There was something in Shanna's tone that had him
raising his brow, not quite knowing what to anticipate.
"And that is?"

She said the words in her head before she said them
aloud. Dress rehearsal. "You're going to be a grandfather."

It was the last thing in the world he had expected,
even less than her application for a position in his office.
He looked at her incredulously. "What? How . . . ?" For
a moment speech failed him.

Shanna shrugged, striving for humor. "The standard
way. Birds and bees." But her father wasn't smiling.

"Jordan's?" Brady saw the surprise mingled with hurt
that came into her eyes and quickly waved his hand. It'd
been the wrong thing to say. He never said the wrong

thing in public. But this was personal. "Yes, yes, of course it's Jordan's. I'm sorry." His apology was in his eyes. "It's just that I'm completely off guard here."

He wasn't the only one. "Tell me about it." Shanna laughed sadly.

He wondered if Rheena knew about this. "Are you keeping it?"

She smiled and pressed a hand to protect the tiny being that lived within her. She had come to terms with that, too, on the flight back. In a way, she knew she had from the very first. There could have been no other decision. "Yes. Possession is nine tenths of the law and I have squatter's rights."

This put everything in a different light. Except his love for her. "Does Jordan know?"

She raised her chin. He was beginning to recognize the familiar move. It reminded him of Eloïse.

"No."

"Are you going to tell him?" he asked more gently.

"Eventually I'll have to." There was no way around that. Jordan had a right to know of his one legitimate child. She wondered how many others there were born "on the wrong side of the blanket." "But it doesn't change anything." She searched her father's face. "Does it?"

This was where the support came in, he thought. He wasn't about to let her down. "Not a thing. Like I said, report to Haggerty. At your convenience."

She saluted as she rose. "Will do, Senator. Now is fine." Smiling, she let herself out.

It took a lot of concentration for the senator to get back to his reports, even though he knew that the sub-committee would be waiting.

14

It was Shanna's intent to fill all the empty spaces, all the tiny openings in her life with work. She threw herself into it from the first moment she entered her father's D.C. office. The first week was a whirlwind of orientation that left her breathless, exhausted, and hopeful. The pace limited the amount of time she had to dwell on the almost stark bleakness of her personal life. The only time she spared for it was to make sure her divorce was under way.

Stealing an hour from the office, Shanna emphatically informed her attorney that she hadn't changed her mind about the divorce. She wanted it to be quick and neat. Furthermore, there was to be no quibbling over possessions. Whatever Jordan wanted, within reason, would be his. The houses, the furniture, she didn't care what it took. She just wanted him out of her life. Permanently.

Though appalled at the idea that she apparently was giving in on all counts, John Stewart agreed to take care of the matter as discreetly as possible. He did, however, draw the line at Shanna's money.

"You can't just give that social-climbing scoundrel what he wants," Stewart insisted from behind his two-hundred-year-old intricately carved desk.

It sounded as if he had been on the phone with her mother, and recently, Shanna mused. What was left of her breakfast was making itself uncomfortably known and she wanted to cut the meeting short. Besides, she had to be getting back to work.

"No," Shanna agreed. "The money belongs to me. And the family. Whatever Jordan earned and saved during our marriage is his to keep." When last she looked, Jordan's bank-account balance had been abysmally low.

Shanna rose, hiking up her purse strap on her shoulder.

Stewart looked down his long, thin nose at her. He had been retained by the family for more years than he cared to count. He felt as if he had a vested interest in their affairs. By association, what transpired with the Bradys reflected on him. He rather liked Shanna and wouldn't want people thinking of her as a meek little fool. "There, at least, you're showing some sense."

Shanna smiled. "Thank you, Mr. Stewart. It's taken me a while, but I'm learning."

As she walked out of his office she left behind the impression of a young woman who was on her way to becoming someone to reckon with. Stewart hoped he'd live long enough to see it happen. These things often took a great deal of time and he was far from a young man.

Something to look forward to, he thought, lighting up the one imported cigar he allowed himself each day. He buzzed his secretary. "No calls, Miss Jacobs," he instructed, then leaned back and enjoyed his only vice.

Shanna returned from the lawyer's office and plunged into work. She wanted to forget about the divorce, forget about everything that had come before. Her life began now, today.

Except, of course, she amended, for the little detail of her pregnancy. That tied her to the past. She fervently hoped that she wouldn't look down at her baby's face each day and see Jordan looking back.

Gathering together the bound copy of the latest data she and another aide had complied on the present housing shortage in her father's home state, Shanna brought them to his office. She knew his itinerary better than her own. There wasn't any conference scheduled.

She walked in on a friendly conversation between her father and Senator Whitney. The latter, sitting back comfortably on the leather coffee-and-cream-colored sofa, looked a bit more jowly than he had when she and Jordan had attended his soiree. He grinned broadly when he saw Shanna enter, then shook his head in disbelief.

"Well, now, how about that? Your daddy said you were working here, but I didn't believe him." Whitney eyed Shanna compassionately. Brady had told him about the divorce. "How are you holding up, honey?"

She placed the five-inch-thick report on her father's desk. "Here's the statistics you wanted on the housing shortage, hot off the presses." She turned toward Whitney. Though she appreciated his concern, she didn't want to be the object of pity. "Just fine, Senator. I'm working at becoming indispensable." She glanced at her father. "Right, Dad?"

Brady had turned to a page of the report at random and was very satisfied with what he saw. He looked up in response to her question.

"Absolutely." He saw the indulgent smile on Whitney's face. "I'm serious. She has this knack I never knew about." He ran a thumb over the report's binding. "People talk to her. She can get to the bottom of things and get things done."

In a paternal move that was becoming increasingly more familiar to him, Brady slipped his arm around Shanna's shoulders. He was a head taller, but they had the same slender, wiry build, the same color hair. He was beginning to see a lot more of himself in her than he ever had before. But then, he realized, he'd never really looked before. "She's a godsend to the office. Pretty damn good at canvassing on the streets, too, and talking to the voters."

Whitney listened, impressed. No matter what, Brady had never been one for empty praise. "Come by my office." The elder statesman winked broadly at Shanna. "I could use a pretty little face around there."

Shanna patted the man's baby-smooth cheek affectionately. There were few people she felt as at ease with as she did with Whitney. "Just look in the mirror, Senator."

Whitney roared appreciatively. As a young man, he had been "downright ugly," he liked to say. His wife, he maintained, had married him strictly out of pity and the depth of her good heart. Now, as age advanced and gave his face character, he was not nearly as self-conscious of his appearance. When Shanna had once likened him to Mark Twain, he had all but glowed.

"She's gotten sassy, Brady." He nodded twice at his assessment. "Nothing wrong with that. Just don't let her get fat." He pretended to leer, raising his shaggy white eyebrows comically up and down. "I like my women on the thin side. Meat I can get from a turkey."

Shanna glanced down. Her waist was still small because of her almost daily communion with the toilet bowl. But morning sickness would stop eventually. When it did, she had a feeling that her body would explode, expanding two dress sizes up.

"Better look now, Senator," she advised. "I won't be thin for long, I'm afraid."

Whitney looked from Brady to Shanna, then cocked his head to one side. "How's that?"

Her father hadn't told him. She felt grateful for his respect of her privacy. "You're going to be a great-godfather," she told Whitney, keeping a smile fixed on her lips. She watched anger bloom in the florid face. Whitney was a dangerous man when aroused. She was glad she had never been on the receiving end of his disapproval.

"That son of a bitch!" he huffed, embarrassed at his slip, but his anger remained. "Pardon my French, Shanna." It was the first time in all the years he'd known her that he had ever cursed in front of Shanna. "He left you pregnant? Where I come from, they've got ways of dealing with scum like Calhoun."

He made her sound as if she was a castoff, and while she knew he hadn't meant anything by it, she was determined to correct the image she had unwittingly had a hand in creating.

"Please get something straight, Senator," she told him quietly. "Jordan didn't leave me, I left him." She raised her chin. "It was my first act of independence and I'm proud of it."

The outrage against Calhoun still vibrated within his chest and Whitney wasn't certain what to say to Shanna. In some ways she was like his own daughter. "But—" he looked at her stomach.

She knew he meant well. "No 'buts.' There're lots of single mothers in this country, Senator. No big deal. I've just become another statistic."

It wasn't nearly as simple as that. There were things to consider. "And your ex's name has just become mud. He's not going anywhere in this town." He glanced at Brady, annoyed that this had been kept from him. Goddamn it, he was practically family. "'Least not on our coattails, your daddy's and mine."

Shanna placed a restraining had on Whitney's arm, her expression serious. "I don't want anyone 'fighting' for my honor, Senator. I can take care of myself. This is between Jordan and me." Her expression softened to an affectionate smile. "I don't want anyone taking him behind the woodshed and giving him 'what-for.' Or ruining his reputation. He'll do that on his own, just give him enough time."

Whitney looked at Brady, who shrugged, indicating that it was out of his hands. "Sassy *and* stubborn. Quite a gal you've got here, Brady."

Brady smiled the wide, beguiling grin that his constituents had all come to know and trust. "I'm just getting to find that out."

The time slipped by so quickly, Shanna had difficulty remembering which month she was in. There was the business of maintaining the office on a day-to-day basis, plus her father's reelection campaign had wound up to almost a fever pitch. There were rallies, speeches, reports, not to mention sessions of subcommittees to help him prepare for. There wasn't a moment's peace, an island of time to seize and savor.

It suited her needs perfectly.

Initially she had been assigned to doing very little at the office. Aaron Haggerty, the man who had run the senator's office ever since Brady had arrived in

Washington, had known Shanna almost as long as Whitney had. Brady tended to attract people who remained loyal to him. Consequently, they all operated like a well-oiled machine. Shanna's capabilities were an unknown when she joined, much like the law students who came to apprentice in the summer months. Haggerty had no idea if she was just temporarily on the scene, satisfying some desire to dabble in the world of the working class, or if she intended to stay on. He observed her progress carefully. As her proficiency became evident her work load increased. At her insistence, her responsibilities became even greater. Fast, efficient, and eager, she doggedly undertook and managed to do the work of two.

Haggerty's natural skepticism turned into concern that she would wear herself out. Everyone who worked for him was his responsibility. Shanna, though the boss's daughter, was no exception.

"Damn it, Shanna," he muttered, his bushy red mustache quivering as he took a huge pile of books she was struggling with out of her arms and followed her to her desk. "Damn it, Shanna," he repeated, "you're pregnant." He set the books down with a thud that echoed his annoyance.

Easing herself into her seat slowly, Shanna kicked off her shoes as she stared down at the mound before her. She had grown bigger than she had expected in the last few months, but had refrained from getting clumsy and awkward. She had made a conscious effort not to and that seemed to help.

Choices, just like her grandmother had said. It was always a matter of conscious choices. She just never realized that she had them.

She laughed now at Haggerty's disgruntled concern. "Tell me something I don't know."

He gave himself a moment and straddled the seat next to her. "I mean, shouldn't you be taking it easy now, maybe slacking off?"

"Sitting around with my feet up, knitting booties?" she suggested with a twinkle. "Uh-uh. Not my style, Aaron." She took a deep breath and reached for the first of the books. There was another report to get out by the end of the week. "Now that I've gotten into the work mode, I don't want to stop." Without thinking, she propped the book up on her stomach. It made for a handy shelf. "When I think of all the time I wasted, it makes me shudder."

"They wouldn't have let you come to work at ten," he pointed out with a paternal smile. "Child-labor laws." He was married with four daughters of his own, all older than Shanna. Only Angela had turned out to be a work-aholic, just like he was. After he'd made this admission, recognizing the signs in others had become easy.

Shanna looked up at Haggerty as he rose again. "You're not supposed to make fun of the boss's daughter, you know."

Haggerty folded his arms before him. One of his sleeves came undone. He pushed it back up on his fore-arm, tiny red hairs marking the path. "I thought that wasn't supposed to matter at the office." The corners of his mouth rose.

"Only when I want it to." Her stomach rumbled insistently. Shanna looked at the pile of books and was torn for a moment. But it had been over a week since she had had anything but an uninspiring sandwich sent in for lunch. Using her toes, she felt under her desk for her shoes, then slipped them on. "C'mon, a lowly aide will buy you lunch, Mr. Haggerty."

He pulled back her chair as she got to her feet. "There's never been anything lowly about you, Shanna."

No, she thought, only my own self-esteem. But it's getting better all the time.

Haggerty glanced down at her feet as they walked out of the office. She was wearing three-inch high heels. Even if she wasn't pregnant, he couldn't think of anything more torturous to do to her feet. "How can you walk in those things?"

"Easy." She walked through the door ahead of him. "Besides, it's by choice. I look like a duck in flats."

Shanna made a deliberate effort to avoid running into Jordan. In square miles, Washington, D.C., was a small town, crowded to overflowing with politicians. Paths tended to cross on a regular basis. She made sure that theirs didn't.

She wasn't running, she told herself. She was just making certain that she wasn't taking any unnecessary risks, that's all. Shanna wanted to be absolutely sure that she was completely over Jordan before she met him again. Though the face that looked back at her in her mirror each morning appeared radiant, with a healthier bloom than she ever recalled seeing before, she knew in her heart that she would feel like a clumsy ugly little duckling if she was in the same room with Jordan. It would be a case of beauty and the beast, with her playing the part of the latter. It was something he had done to her without saying a word, a way he made her feel. Huge with child, she didn't need that now. Or ever.

She had heard that though her father and Senator Whitney had completely withdrawn their backing from Jordan's campaign, Jordan had found other people to be his mentors, other people to finance his campaign. Other people who knew people who owed them favors.

He always knew how to take advantage. In a very short time, Jordan had become an accomplished student of networking and had found his place in the system. No matter what, he always knew what to say and what to do.

And he always came up smelling like a rose, she thought as she entered the suite her father had reserved for his people to watch the telecasts of the primary results.

But it took fertilizer to grow roses and fertilizer was just a polite term for the manure Jordan was standing hip-deep in. Someday she knew that Jordan would get what was coming to him. At least she fervently hoped so.

But someday apparently wasn't tonight.

A wall of almost deafening noise surrounded her as Shanna entered the crowded suite. All the people she worked with seemed to be here, along with their families or friends. It made moving around very difficult, especially in her present shape. Scanning the large room, she saw her father on the far end. He was talking to Haggerty and Whitney. He waved to her. Her mother, she knew, would put in an appearance later on in the evening, just before they all went out to eat. This sort of political assembly always irritated her. Rheena preferred less noisy, less frenzied gatherings.

Shanna liked the noise, the enthusiasm she felt crackling here like raw, unchanneled electricity. She stood for a moment, just absorbing it. It was dress rehearsal. The real showdown, for them, came in November. Her father was the unchallenged incumbent and wasn't involved in a primary. But a lot of the people he was backing were.

Tonight Jordan's fate would be decided, too.

It was an election year and there almost seemed to be more candidates than voters. Different faces were periodically flashed on the various television monitors her father had arranged to have brought into the suite. Everywhere she turned, there was another commentator making predictions that would affect so many people's lives based on one percent of the tally.

She turned, trying to find a way to reach her father, when the monitor on her right caught her attention. Jordan's face, innocent, beguiling, was on the screen. Sitting before it, a blond, sophisticated woman commentator read from her teleprompter and told the audience that Jordan Calhoun appeared to be a shoo-in in his first primary. She was smiling broadly as she said it.

Another woman who fell under his spell, Shanna thought, feeling a twinge of pity for all the women that he would carelessly use during his political career. She felt a sense of relief that she had gotten out in time.

Shanna felt strong hands bracket her shoulders. "He's leading," her father said needlessly, standing behind her. There was a note of apology in his voice.

Shanna continued looking at the screen as Jordan's image stared back at her. She hadn't looked at a single photograph of him in the last six months. All the albums from Georgetown and the Virginia residence were locked up in storage. All traces of Jordan, save the one growing within her, had been erased. As she looked at his face now she waited for the pain to come, and found, to her relief, that it was less than a whisper now.

"I never expected anything else," she told her father. She had to raise her voice in order to be heard above the din.

Brady leaned forward and said just next to her ear, "He won't get far, Shanna."

Shanna turned around. "Why not? He has the perfect

qualities to be a successful politician. It's you who's always been the dark horse. It's harder to win being fair and honest."

Brady laughed and kissed the top of her head. "That's what I love, unbiased support." He looked at her in concern. All around them, people were jostling one another for space. This was no place for her. "You should get some rest. Want me to have someone take you home?"

She shook her head. "No, but I will leave." She had only meant to stop by for a moment, because she had promised and he would have worried if she hadn't. "I've still got a few loose ends to tie up at the office tonight."

Her answer didn't please him. The sea of people parted as he ushered her to the door. "They'll keep until morning. I don't want you taking any unnecessary chances with your health. I don't want you taking any chances at all."

She shook her head as they gained the doorway. "Never happen. Besides," she reminded him, "I'm still a month away from my due date."

He never had much faith in those kinds of projections. The senator had lived with the unexpected for too long. "You never know."

"I feel like I've been pregnant forever now." She patted her belly, then winced as the baby kicked. "It can't happen soon enough for me."

Shanna became quiet as she remembered that Jordan had once used the exact same words when talking about getting into office. Shaking off her mood, she brushed a quick kiss on her father's cheek.

"I'll see you later, Dad, have a nice dinner. Look." She pointed at the screen closest to them as a new image appeared. "Walters is the projected winner in his district." The man was one of her father's protégés and had once worked as an aide in his office. "Congratulations."

Brady rubbed his hands together as someone else in the room, seeing the projection, began to lead a cheer. "One down, twelve more primaries to go. Still," he almost shouted to her, "you never know." He never counted his victories until after they happened.

"No," she agreed as she left, thinking of all the turns her life had taken recently, "you don't."

15

Oh no, it couldn't be!

Clutching both arms of her chair, Shanna haltingly attempted to stand. A sharp pain shot through her. The intensity surprised her and she fell back in her chair. Braced for the worst, lungs filled with air, all muscles tensed, she tried again. This time there was no pain. She pushed herself away and turned around to look at the seat.

Please, please, let it just be my imagination.

It wasn't.

The muted beige-and-brown cushion on the chair had a large, fresh round stain in the middle. Feeling behind her, she located the wet spot on the back of her navy-blue dress. Shanna closed her eyes. She sank down in the chair again, disregarding the dampness. Her legs felt as if they could no longer support her weight.

She wasn't just having discomfort. She wasn't having premature contractions. Her water had just broken and she was sitting in the middle of her father's deserted office at 7:30 at night in labor.

"Calm, I've got to stay calm," she said out loud, trying to talk herself out of the acute anxiety that was hovering over her. "Billions of women have all gone through this before."

Yes, she thought as the panic refused to disappear, but none of them had ever been her.

This was too soon, it wasn't right. "You're not supposed to be here for another month," she told the child in her womb accusingly.

The pain returned, causing beads of perspiration to pop out along her forehead.

Thoughts raced through her head, colliding with one another. She should be timing this. God, she wished someone else was in the office with her. Why had she been so stubborn and insisted on working? Everyone else was back at the hotel suite, partying.

Shanna waited until the contraction subsided, then looked up at the large office clock on the wall opposite her desk. She watched the minute hand spasmodically move from number to number. She held her breath in dreaded anticipation. She knew the day, the time to have her baby would come eventually, but not now. Not tonight. She wasn't ready.

It felt as if it took an eternity before the next contraction came. But when it did, it swallowed her up and held her prisoner in its iron jaws, sapping away her breath. She kept her eyes trained on the clock, curling her fingers into her palms.

Ten minutes. Ten minutes in between contractions. She brushed back the hair from her face. Perspiration had plastered down her bangs, curling the tips upward.

This was serious, wasn't it? Why now? Why tonight? Tonight was the night of Jordan's first political victory.

Maybe she was being childish, but she didn't want her baby being born now.

She splayed her hand over the huge mound that somehow, inconceivably, contained a small human being. "I guess you're not in any mood to listen, huh?"

Sweat formed between her breasts and trickled down, coming to rest in a tiny pool on her expanded abdomen. Shanna hurried to call her doctor's number before another contraction began rolling in. Instead of her doctor, she got his answering service. The irritatingly calm woman on the other end of the line took down all the pertinent details from her, then told Shanna that she would try her best to reach the doctor. When she did, he would return her call.

Here comes another one, Shanna thought in alarm, grasping the edge of her desk. "No offense, but I don't think your best is going to be fast enough. Tell Dr. Miller I'll meet him at the hospital. Soon."

She dropped the phone into the cradle. She breathed slowly and deeply. Initial panic was subsiding. Reality had set in. She knew she had to act quickly and calmly.

Staying very still, she waited for the contraction to hit and run its course. When it did, it was relatively mild. It gave her a measure of hope. Maybe she was overreacting. There was time. There had to be.

Grabbing her purse, Shanna was halfway to the door before she remembered her shoes. "Maybe I'll just glue them to my feet from now on," she muttered, jamming the pumps on. More than anything, she wanted someone to be with her. She didn't deny that she was afraid. But everyone she knew was probably on their way to dinner now. She had no time to go and check.

All she wanted, she thought, jabbing the elevator button impatiently, was a healthy baby. And a taxi.

°   °   °

It had been a long shift. It felt twice as long tonight, what with the primary night traffic on the street and his anticipating what was waiting for him right after he got off. Well, it would all be over by tomorrow, Reid Kincannon thought. He leaned over in the front seat and was about to flip on his off-duty sign when he saw the pregnant woman standing in front of the Senate building. She was waving frantically at him.

"Oh, no."

His better instincts warred with the fact that he had a class to get to and a final to take. If he stopped to pick up this fare, there was no doubt in his mind that he would be late for his exam. Unless, of course, she was heading for the university.

Seeing her condition, he rather doubted that.

To stop or not to stop, that is the question. And he knew his answer.

"Damn it, Ma," he muttered under his breath, "why'd you raise me to have a conscience?" If he didn't stop, the woman would haunt him all night. With a sigh, he left his sign on and pulled up to the curb next to the woman.

Shanna could have cried with relief. She yanked open the door and awkwardly tumbled into the backseat. She had begun to feel wobbly and it felt wonderful to be off her feet again. "Thank God."

He turned to look at her. Well, he had made the right choice for one of them, he thought sarcastically. "Always glad to ride to the rescue. Where to?"

Shanna gripped her purse so hard, her knuckles felt as if they were going to break through her skin. Another contraction had just slammed into her. "The hospital."

He glanced at her abdomen. The lady was ripe. "Which one?"

"Any one." Shanna was panting. This was absolutely awful. She felt as if a pair of huge unseen hands were trying to rip her apart. She realized that the taxi wasn't moving and that the driver was still looking at her, waiting for a real destination. "No, I mean Georgetown University Hospital."

It was all he wanted to hear. "You got it."

Reid turned the car sharply to the right. Tires screeched in protest as he took the corner. Before him, the traffic light had gone yellow. He stepped on the gas, but the signal turned red a full two seconds before he managed to get to the corner. As he waited impatiently for it to turn green again, he turned around to get a better look at his fare. There was something vaguely familiar about her and it nagged at him. It was rare that he forgot a face. "Do I know you?"

She squeezed her eyes shut as the end of the contraction finally came. She couldn't go on like this. "I don't think so." She slowly took in a lungful of air. "I don't know any taxi drivers."

"A snob, eh?" It was a teasing remark meant to lighten the tension that was beginning to fill the interior of the cab.

"A hermit," she bit off. At least that's what she should have been nine, no eight months ago.

There was something about her voice, the slight bit of distance in her tone, that kept gnawing at his memory. He turned again to look. The lighting wasn't very good at this corner and the interior was dim. "Are you sure we don't know each other?"

"Positive."

What was he trying to do, pick up a pregnant woman? What kind of a degenerate had she hailed?

"It's green. The light, it's green." She jerked a hand toward the signal, then sucked in her breath. Another contraction was coming. How could that be? How could ten minutes go by so fast? "Drive," she ordered in a voice she scarcely recognized as her own.

Reid turned around and stepped on the gas. She was definitely scared. "First baby?"

And last. "Yes."

The field of red taillights up ahead looked brighter than they should. That could only mean cars were braking. Another jam? He hoped not. "They say first babies are usually late."

She clutched her stomach with both hands, wishing she could just squeeze the baby out and be done with it. "They lie." Shanna clamped down on her lower lip to keep from yelling out. That much control she still had.

Her moan at the next red light had him turning around again. The woman's head was thrown back against the cushion. Light from the street lamp was streaking in and Reid was able to get his first clear look at her face. And then it came to him.

"The Bahamas."

Shanna opened her eyes. Weren't they ever going to get there? "What?"

"The Bahamas," he repeated. "I met you in the Bahamas five months ago."

It was ebbing away. Thank God the pain was ebbing away again. She let out a huge sigh, feeling only marginally human. She dragged a hand through her hair, moving it away from her face. "I don't remember."

But he did. Hers wasn't a face to forget easily. He wondered what she was doing out here by herself at this time of night in her condition. Where was her husband? "Your husband still in the hotel room?"

Her head jerked up. Leaning forward, she touched the plastic surrounding the identifying photograph on the back of the front seat. She stared for a second at the smiling face there before looking up at Reid, her eyes opened wide in recognition.

"You."

"Me. Small world, isn't it?" His mother had always been a firm advocate of destiny. Until this moment he had never believed in it himself.

Shanna leaned back in the seat as she braced herself again. "Could we please save the reunion for later and get to the hospital? This baby doesn't want to WAIT!" She shrieked out the last word as the contraction crashed into her like a doubled-up fist. She could have sworn she felt the baby trying to kick its way out through her side. The front of her abdomen began quivering uncontrollably and wouldn't stop.

Shanna struggled to hold back her sob.

They had slowed to a crawl. Before them was what looked like the mother of all traffic jams. Reid let out a breath through his teeth, thinking. They weren't going anywhere for a while, that was obviously clear. He wondered if the woman could hold out. The strangled cry from the backseat answered his silent question and had him debating driving on the sidewalk. He was game, but there wasn't enough room to do it. The alley up ahead on his right led to a dead end. There was no alternate route. This was it. They were stuck.

He draped his arm over the back of the seat as he turned toward her. She looked bad, he thought. What the hell was he supposed to do with her? "Primary night isn't a good time to be out on the road."

It sounded like an accusation. Maybe he thought this was fun for her.

"It wasn't exactly up to me," she snapped. Another wave, larger, more powerful than the last, began to build on the heels of the one that had just passed. She clutched at the folds of her dress, wadding them, desperate to hold on to something.

Panic was growing with each wave. "I think the baby's coming."

It was about three miles to the hospital from here. They were never going to make it in time. Reid looked around anxiously for a policeman, but there wasn't a single one in sight. Nothing but cars and blaring horns. She certainly wasn't in any condition to walk, and gallant though the thought might be, he couldn't carry her there. She'd probably give birth right in the street.

Or in the car.

He glanced toward the alley and made up his mind. Leaning on his horn until the driver in front of him turned around, Reid pointed to himself and then jerked his thumb in the direction of the alley. The car in front pulled up as far as it could, moving to the left.

There was hardly enough room to maneuver, but with two tires bumping along on the sidewalk, Reid managed to pull the taxi into the alley. He went as far as he could, then cut the engine.

It was a narrow alleyway between two relatively old apartment buildings. Uncovered garbage cans pockmarked the area. It didn't smell very good, either, but then, he doubted that the woman in the backseat would really care about that right now. He was trying to give her as much privacy as he could.

When he got out of the car, Shanna's distress was ripe, ready to explode. He wasn't just going to walk away and leave her here, was he? "Where are you going?" she cried.

He knew panic when he heard it. "Nowhere. I'm right here," he said softly. He opened the rear door and got into the backseat next to her. "First baby, you said."

She stared at him with wide eyes, shrinking into the

corner of the car as far as she could. She had no idea what to think. "Yes."

He smiled encouragingly at her as he took her hand in his. "That makes two of us."

Was he saying that he was going to . . . ?

When he reached for the hem of her dress, she pressed her palm down over it. "No!"

He was all for modesty in the right place, but this wasn't it. Circumstances had plunged them both beyond polite niceties. "Lady, I don't want to do this any more than you do, but right now I'm all you've got."

He was right. She was going to give birth inside a filthy cab in a filthy alley. This was more awful than anything she could have imagined.

"Have you ever done this before?" she asked suddenly. Maybe he had training in assisting at childbirth. Policemen did, didn't they? Maybe taxi drivers did, too. Her thoughts began winking in and out, making no sense as they chained together.

"I've never delivered a human baby, no. I helped my dog have puppies, once. I was twelve at the time." He saw horror mingle with pain in her eyes. He reached over and took back the clenched hand into his, holding on tightly. For now, the best thing he could do for her was give her comfort. "Don't worry, these things have a way of never leaving you." His eyes were warm, as was the feel of his hand. "Like riding a bicycle."

She had no idea who he was, or even his name. She had glossed over that because his face had startled her when she had looked at his photograph. For all she knew, he could be some closet homicidal maniac or a rapist.

But there was something about his eyes that made her trust him. Besides, she had no choice.

Shanna hated the fact that it had been taken out of her hands. Again.

As another contraction slashed through every fiber of her being, making her want to scream, making her want to beg for mercy, she damned Jordan with the last breath within her exhausted soul.

Shanna tightened her hold on the taxicab driver's hand and held on for all she was worth.

16

Reid knew he would be sweating it out before the evening was over, but he had thought it would be because he was wrestling with difficult questions on his final exam, not sitting in the backseat of the taxicab he drove, trying to assist a pregnant woman deliver her first child.

Who would ever believe this? He could just envision the look on his professor's face as he told him he missed his exam because he was helping a lady give birth in an alley. Talk about truth being stranger than fiction.

He looked at her face and saw the fear. "Lady," he said softly. Her eyes darted toward his face, bewilderment and apprehension reflected in them. He sought for a way to reassure her. His fingers were still tangled up with hers and going numb fast. The intensity of her grip was constricting the flow of blood. "It's going to be all right. I promise."

"Easy for you to SAY."

The words were torn from her by the jolt of intense

pain, which, once there, refused to weaken. She was certain that she was going to die in its grasp. Death was actually becoming a preferable alternative to what she was going through. There didn't seem to be an end to this agony, just wave after wave of excruciating pain. She couldn't cling to respites, gathering her strength for the next onslaught. There weren't any respites. The pain no longer came and went. Now it decreased only slightly and then intensified with a vengeance. She wasn't going to make it.

She had an incredibly strong hold for someone who looked as thin-boned and delicate as she did, Reid thought. He began to wonder if he'd ever be able to flex his hand again. "What's your name?"

Her lids felt heavy as she struggled to keep them up. "Why?"

"Because we're going to be getting very close here in a few minutes and I can't keep calling you 'lady.'"

Reid eyed the hem of her dress, hesitant to raise it even though he knew he had to. This wasn't exactly how he had pictured getting to know her when he had sat in his beach chair five months ago, watching her stare off into the ocean. Obviously staring wasn't the only thing the woman had done.

"Shanna," she bit off, tears rising of themselves to her eyes. Tears created by pain. She started to give him her last name, then stopped. Which one? Brady? Calhoun? The divorce wasn't final yet. "Just Shanna."

She didn't trust him, he thought. He couldn't think of a single reason why she should, except that she really didn't have much of a choice. If the situation had been reversed, he wouldn't have been happy about it either. It was a hell of a position to find yourself in. It was probably frightening enough just to give birth for the first time without having to do it in an alley, with no hospital or doctor, just a total stranger for help. She had to be terrified.

"All right, 'just Shanna,' my name's Reid." He tried to smile at her encouragingly. His own insides felt a little like Jell-O over what was ahead, but he wasn't about to let her know it. "Who would have ever thought that when we met on the beach in the Bahamas, we would wind up in the back of a cab, waiting for your baby to be born."

He was making jokes while she was dying right in front of him. Didn't he have any feelings? "I take it driving a cab is only temporary work until you get a job as a stand-up comic." Startled by the magnitude of this contraction, she yanked hard on his arm. "OH GOD!"

"He's not making house calls tonight, Shanna." If she kept this up, he wouldn't be able to do anything to help her. She would have pulled out his arm. But he let her go on holding his hand. "Now think. What did they teach you at your childbirthing classes?"

She hadn't gone. There hadn't been anyone to go with her and she had been too embarrassed to ask her mother. "To say no next time."

He looked around outside the car. The apartments on either side were still dark. No windows had been thrown open. No one was hanging out, prompted by curiosity as to what a taxi was doing, parked nose-first in the alley. At least that part was good. "Maybe you should be the one to get the job as a comic," he suggested gently.

Reid saw her eyes dilate as her hands flew out, grasping at the air as if there was something there that could pull her out of the spiraling pain. Then as he watched, her eyes rolled back in her head. He shook her. She couldn't pass out on him. "Hey, hang on, Shanna. Don't pass out on me now. You'll miss all the fun."

His words penetrated, drifting slowly to her mind.

She fought to stay conscious. She had no intention of passing out. No intention, she kept saying over and over in her head. "A man would say that," she panted.

"A scared man, yeah."

She looked at him. "You're scared?"

He couldn't afford to have her lose confidence in him. Reid managed a grin. "Let's call it opening-night jitters, okay?"

As politely as he could, he pushed her dress up to her thighs, then slipped off her underwear. He purposely kept his eyes on her face, trying to spare her as much as he could.

"It's going to be all right, Shanna." His voice was now low, soothing. Just the way it had been when he had talked to Judy as he held her. Except that with Judy, it hadn't been all right. She had died before the doctor could arrive. Reid had been too late, had bandaged her slashed wrists too late. She had lost too much blood to be saved. The woman he had adored, the woman who had jilted him, had died in his arms.

Reid shook his head, as if to shake off the memory. He couldn't think about Judy now. This woman needed him. He looked around helplessly, wishing that there was a blanket or something within the cab that he could use to make her comfortable. But there wasn't. Not even the bare necessities. She didn't even have enough room to lie down properly.

He smiled encouragingly at her. "Times like this, I wish I was driving a stretch limo."

A stretch limo. Luxury. "With champagne to toast all this." She was getting delirious, she thought, perspiration pooling all along her body. She clamped her teeth together to imprison the scream that was escaping and it was transformed into a guttural moan.

Reid reached up and switched on the overhead light

in the car. It helped a little. Positioning himself where he was needed, he thought he saw the crown of the baby's head, but he wasn't sure. He wasn't sure of anything. Wasn't this too soon to be happening?

He looked up at Shanna as she tried to suppress another scream. "Do you have an urge to push?"

She nodded, swallowing, then gasped for air.

This much he knew. "All right, I want you to lean forward as best you can, hold on to your knees, and push the next time you get the urge." He prayed that nothing would go wrong.

"Is that what you told your dog to do?" She was babbling nervously now, but couldn't stop.

"It was a well-trained dog." He became serious. "I keep the TV on in the background when I study. Public-television broadcasts mostly. You pick up things occasionally that help."

She had only heard one word. The rest had faded, swimming off somewhere into the background. "Study, study for what?"

"My degree. I'm a political-science major." He suddenly remembered the exam. He glanced at his watch. "That's where I'm supposed to be right now, taking my final. Up to twenty minutes ago I thought that was going to be one of the most difficult things I'd ever have to face. Now it seems like a piece of cake." He saw the anxiety tighten her features. "We're going to get through this."

"What 'we'? Only one of us is pregnant."

"Shanna, if sympathy pains mean anything," he assured her, "we both are."

"Reid?" She clawed at his arm again.

"Right here, Shanna," he said in a voice someone used to reassure a small child that there were no monsters living in the shadows of her room. "Right here."

"Oh-oh-OH!" Arching against the racking pain, she

felt as if her pelvis was being cracked apart like the shell of a lobster.

Show time, he thought. Unconsciously he sucked in his own breath as he spread his hands wide beneath her. "Okay, push, Shanna. Push!" He heard her grunting, but nothing was happening.

She fell back, her head hitting the side window. She was exhausted beyond words. "I can't, I can't. It won't come out."

There was no time for niceties, no time for trying to spare her embarrassment or his. With quick, probing hands, Reid felt the shape of her stomach. "I'm no expert in this, but it feels as if there's nothing out of shape. I don't think it's breech."

In a haze, she was still surprised at his assessment. "Breech? How would you know?"

"I grew up on a farm," he told her, then flashed a quick smile at her before repositioning himself again, "if that makes you feel any better."

"Only if I was a chicken." Another urge came, more demanding than the last. She didn't think she had enough strength to follow through, but the pain was insistent.

Unable to stop herself, she let loose with a scream that sliced through the heavy, humid air like a sharp hunting knife.

Reid blinked back his own sweat as it fell into his face. He never lifted his eyes. It had to be any second now. That *was* the crown he saw. "If that doesn't bring the police, nothing will." Even if they were arriving, sirens and all, he wouldn't have heard them. All Reid's concentration was trained on the opening that was beginning to stretch.

And then it was happening.

"Okay, okay, you're doing it, you're doing it." Reid's own excitement was almost overpowering. "He's coming, Shanna. He's coming. The head, Shanna, the head's out," he declared, feeling triumphant for both of them. "All right, now push again."

She couldn't. There wasn't an ounce of strength left within her. "I can't." Even saying the words was difficult for her. She was so drained, so very drained.

He looked up at Shanna. There was no way he could take the child from her. He had nothing to hold on to but the tiny head. She had to push the shoulders out before he could help. She couldn't stop now.

"Push, goddamn it. You don't want him knowing his mother's a quitter, do you?"

It was the right thing to say. She squeezed her eyes shut tight as she mentally cursed the man in the taxi with her, heaping every name she could think of on his head. Not a single one made it to her lips. She didn't have any breath in her to say them out loud. Every ounce of energy was focused on ridding her body of the invader that was subjecting her to this torture.

She squeezed every muscle in her body, pushing, then collapsed against the window again.

The baby's shoulders were free. Reid slid the tiny form out completely, hardly believing what was happening. He was holding an actual tiny newborn in his hands. There was blood everywhere, on him, on the baby, in the cab. He didn't notice. All he knew was that he had to keep this little person safe.

"And we have a winner," Reid cried.

It was over. Thank God, it was over. "Is he, is he all right?" she gasped out the words, barely conscious.

Reid cradled the tiny life against him. It was slippery and dirty and he had never seen anything so beautiful before. He felt incredibly moved. There was a lump in his throat that he had to work past before he could answer her. "Yes, except for one thing."

There was something wrong with the baby. Oh God, there was something wrong with her baby. Hysteria bubbled, making her dizzy. "What?"

"We're going to have to stop referring to the baby as he. It's a girl, Shanna." He smiled as he looked at her now, over the baby's head. "You had a daughter."

"A girl?" she repeated numbly. Slowly the information penetrated. A daughter. She had a daughter. "Thank you, God," she whispered so softly, she wasn't certain she had said the words at all.

He had never seen eyes so alert before. And such a bright shade of blue. "Yeah, you know, one of those cute little people of the female persuasion who is destined to break men's hearts."

Because there was absolutely nothing to wrap her in, he took off his shirt and tucked it around the baby as best he could. It wasn't much, he thought, but it would have to do for now. "I guess you'd like to hold her." He was almost loath to give the baby up. In those few moments when he had been the first to hold her, he felt as if he had bonded with the brand-new human being.

Shanna couldn't answer, she could only nod. For the moment emotions swirled within her, making it completely impossible to talk.

Reid gently placed the small, wriggling bundle into Shanna's arms.

"I can't do anything about the cord," he apologized. "Let's see if we can get you to the hospital and have someone with a little more knowledge than mine take care of that part."

She nodded again, tears brimming in her eyes. It was over and she was holding her daughter in her arms. Her *daughter*. It didn't seem real. "Reid?"

"Yeah?"

"I don't know how to thank you."

He smiled as he lightly touched the baby's cheek. It was a miracle, he thought. One hell of a miracle. "You just did."

Shifting, Reid got out of the taxi. He took in a deep breath of fresh air, not even minding the fact that there was a stench of garbage in the air. Every muscle in his body was tense, like the string of a bow that had been pulled back as far as it would go. The humidity in the air only added to the coat of sweat he already wore. He didn't notice. It was great to be alive.

He let out a long breath, trying to relax. It was over and they were both alive. A damn good accomplishment, he told himself. Reid looked into the backseat of the cab and saw Shanna cradling the baby against her. Damn good.

The light from the interior of the car bounced off his wristwatch. He held it up, wiggling it until he could see what time it was. Eight-fifteen. The exam would be almost over by now. Maybe he could get a makeup. Reid smiled to himself. He had a hell of a good excuse for missing it, but the professor was probably never going to believe it.

Right now it didn't matter. She was alive.

Stretching, he arched his back before getting back into the taxi, this time into the front seat. He turned for one last look before starting up the car. "Everything okay back there?"

She had been so exhausted just a moment ago. Where had all this new energy come from? Shanna looked up at Reid and smiled. "Perfect."

It was all he wanted to hear. Turning on the ignition, Reid backed the taxi out of the alley slowly, then edged onto the street.

To his relief, the traffic jam had mercifully broken up. Cars were moving at a slow, steady pace. Traffic was still heavy, but not impossible. But the emergency was over, so he wasn't in a hurry.

Wasn't that always the way, he thought. Behind him, the baby made a whimpering, sucking noise.

He had delivered a baby tonight. Damn, it felt good.

"What are you going to call her?"

"Jessica." The name came to her out of her past. An imaginary childhood friend she had invented to keep her company. Now she had a daughter to do the same. "Jessica Eloïse," Shanna said, smiling down into the tiny, wrinkled face of her daughter. She knew her grandmother would have approved.

17

"You'll be okay?" Reid asked as he brought the cab to a stop at the curb before the hospital emergency entrance.

"I'll be fine." Though there was no real reason for it, his concern made her feel warm, safe.

He nodded. "Good, I'll be right back."

Moving quickly, Reid hurried to the emergency-room entrance. He dashed through the electronic doors just as they began to pull apart. Scanning the large room, he found the registration desk. There were three chairs, partitioned off from one another at a long desk. Only one opening was unattended. He saw a man, a day-old stubble on his face, his shirttails hanging out, shuffling from the large waiting room and heading toward the desk. The man wore a pinched expression and he was holding his stomach as if it would fall off at any moment and explode.

"Sorry." Hurrying, Reid got to the desk ahead of him. "This is a real emergency."

"Hey, my gut's on fire, man," the man complained, then grew silent as he looked Reid up and down. He took a step back. Reid was still shirtless and there was blood on his jeans.

Reid leaned over the desk, noting that he and not the man behind him had the registration clerk's full, rapt attention. "I've got a woman in the backseat of my cab who's just given birth." He jerked a thumb toward the parking lot. "She says her doctor's on staff here."

Reid had no idea whether or not Shanna did have a particular physician at this hospital, but he knew that saying so would get him the desired results. Less than a minute later, summoned by the clerk, an orderly and a nurse were rushing out to the parking lot with a wheelchair for Shanna.

"Hey, be careful with her," Reid called after them, remembering. "I didn't cut the umbilical cord."

Before Reid could get out to the parking lot to join them, Shanna and Jessica were being brought into the hospital. He moved aside, giving the orderly room. As he watched, mother and daughter were taken away to the bank of elevators in the rear of the building. Reid was left standing alone in the emergency room.

"Bye," he murmured to them under his breath.

He turned and saw that the few people who were in the waiting room were staring at him. He looked down and remembered that his shirt was still in Shanna's possession, wrapped around Jessica.

"Great."

He couldn't return the taxi to the dispatcher looking like this. He'd have to go home and get something to put on. Well, so much for his getting to the college in time to catch his professor, he thought. He'd have to see about calling the department in the morning and hopefully arranging for a makeup exam. His degree depended on it.

Hell of a night, he thought, running his hand through his unruly hair. He saw another woman staring at his bare chest as he approached the exit. She seemed totally oblivious to the fact that her mouth was hanging open.

Reid grinned. "Careful," he warned her as he went past, "they take the shirt right off your back around here if you give them half a chance."

Whistling, he walked to his cab.

Hell of a night.

Another wave of exhaustion took hold and Shanna fell asleep as soon as she was helped into bed. She slept as if she were dead until the following morning. Waking at six, she felt like a different person from the woman who had flagged down the taxi last night. Her fatigue had all but vanished. She was achy and incredibly sore when she tried to sit up, but all that would pass soon, she thought. There was no point in dwelling on it. It was time to think and to make plans.

Plans for the two of them. She could hardly believe that she was actually a mother now. All those months, walking around with that bulging growth in front of her, it had still seemed like a fantasy. But the fantasy had become reality. She had a baby.

A baby. Hers. Incredible.

Shanna looked up as the door to her room opened slowly. "Someone's hungry," the nurse said, entering the room. "Are you up to a feeding?"

In lieu of a reply, Shanna stretched her arms out toward her daughter. The nurse placed the baby into them carefully. "Ring when you want me to take her back," she said cheerfully as she left.

"Never," Shanna murmured under her breath as she looked at her daughter.

It was the first time she had seen Jessica in daylight. She lightly probed one small hand and felt love flooding through her as the tiny fingers closed over hers.

"Hi, I'm your mom. But I guess you already know that." The baby watched her quietly with wide eyes. She appeared to be really listening. "So, how do you like the world so far? Big, huh? It shrinks down to size after a while, I promise."

Shanna raised Jessica slightly, bringing her closer to her face, and took a little whiff. "You smell good." She laughed. "I can't believe you're really here." Shanna closed her eyes as she pressed her cheek against the baby's. Jessica protested with a whimper. Shanna lowered her again. "You're going to have to get used to this. I've never been a mother before. But then, you've never been a baby before, so I guess that makes us even."

Sitting here, with her daughter in her arms, she felt as if she had fallen into a fairyland. Her room was painted in soft pastels. It was soothing and beautiful. It was easy to think that all of life would be like this. But Shanna knew better.

Diametrically opposed emotions struggled within her. She was full of awe at what had just transpired. She had given birth to a beautiful baby girl. A perfect baby girl. She already loved Jessica so much that it hurt. But her love was entwined with a twinge of depression, with concern for her child. Would this tiny baby grow up to make the same mistakes as she had? And what kind of a mother would she make? Rheena had felt that Eloïse had failed her. And Shanna had spent her childhood longing for her mother's love and attention. Was the pattern destined somehow to continue?

No, she swore to herself. She was going to be different. If nothing else, she could give her daughter the life she had always yearned for. A life filled with love.

"I promise to do the best I can." Memories of a lonely childhood echoed in her mind. "To listen to you and to love you no matter what." Her mouth curved in a smile as she thought of the "differences of opinion" she had had with her mother. "I also promise that you don't have to give a single society party if you don't want to, or make your debut or do anything else that a Brady-slash-Fitzhugh is supposed to do. You can be your own person."

She took a good look at her daughter, memorizing each tiny feature. Jessica had delicate, almost translucent pink skin, a rosebud mouth, and an entire mop of fine, very light blond hair.

Jordan's hair.

A surge of sadness shuddered through Shanna. She had never told Jordan that she was pregnant, never wanted him to share in this moment with her. She had felt better sharing Jessica's birth with a total stranger than she would have with Jordan. Perhaps it wasn't fair not to tell him, but she didn't feel like being fair. Besides, she instinctively knew that he wouldn't have cared anyway.

Jessica whimpered again. "Sorry. Breakfast coming up," Shanna promised, slipping the hospital gown off one shoulder. There were more important things to do than feel sorry for herself, she thought. Her daughter needed her.

Roger Brady had a meeting scheduled with a Senate Judiciary Committee member at two. He had his secretary arrange his itinerary to provide enough time to take a slight detour before his appointment and visit with his daughter and new granddaughter.

She had done nicely for herself, he thought, looking

around Shanna's new apartment. When Shanna and Jessica had left the hospital, he had offered to have them stay at the house. But Shanna had refused, determined to maintain her independence. She had hired a nurse to help her with the baby and gotten herself settled in a larger apartment nearer the office. In the two months since she had given birth to Jessica, his daughter had gotten her life in order and was going full speed ahead.

Who would have thought it?

He looked up and smiled at her as she placed his cup in front of him on the black marble coffee table. When she was growing up, during the infrequent times he had spent with her, it had never occurred to him to be proud of her. He felt pride now.

He made himself comfortable on the boldly blue-and-mauve-flowered love seat. The coffee was hot, rich, and dark, just the way he liked it. She knew a good many more things about him than he did about her, he mused. He had spent the last twenty minutes playing with Jessica, until the nurse had taken her away for her nap. Now it was just the two of them, Shanna and he.

"So, how is everything?"

Shanna settled down next to her father. "Wonderful. I have an excellent nurse for Jessica and things are beginning to finally fall into place." Taking a sip of her own coffee, she watched her father. "Jane will be coming with me to the office at first. If you don't mind."

Brady raised a quizzical brow. "Jane?"

"The nurse." She nodded in the direction of the bedroom. "I'm going to continue feeding Jessica until she's about six months old." Her father cleared his throat, embarrassed by the delicate subject. Shanna couldn't help smiling. "It'll be hairy for a while, but nothing we can't all handle if we try."

He set the cup down thoughtfully. "Does that mean you intend to come back to work for me?" Nothing would have pleased him more than having her there, but he hadn't wanted to pressure her. In the few short months she had been at the office, he had come to look forward to seeing her. And she was an asset to him.

Savoring her coffee a moment, Shanna grinned. "Try and keep me away, Senator."

"I wouldn't dream of it." He took her hand in both of his, enveloping it. "I've missed you, Shanna." He thought of the work she had spearheaded on the homeless problem in Illinois just before she had gone on maternity leave. "The projects are beginning to fall behind."

She was eager to get back. Eager to work again. "You could bring some of the data and reports here. My computer is compatible with the one in your office."

He held up a hand to stop what he knew was coming. "I didn't mean for you to think you had to work at home. I just want you to know that you're needed and missed. But there's such a thing as burning the candle at both ends, you know."

She knew that, but she also knew that she needed to work. She needed the cleansing feeling that being involved in things she felt were important brought her. She still needed to justify her existence, if only to herself. The project her father had put her to work on was the means to that end.

"I've got a lot of 'wax' stored up, Dad. Twenty-five years' worth."

"That doesn't mean you have to go up like a Roman candle." He realized that he was making fatherly noises and it felt good. "If you had listened to me and not gone back to work primary night, you would have given birth to Jessica at the hospital instead of the back of some filthy cab."

Shanna nodded vaguely. Her father's reference brought Reid's image back to mind, the way he had looked as he placed Jessica into her arms, his shirt wrapped around the infant. She found herself thinking about Reid a lot these last two months, her thoughts sometimes turning to him when she least expected it. She had waited for him to come to see her in the hospital and had been disappointed when he didn't show up. She still wondered who he was and if she would ever see him again. She remembered that he had said he was a political-science major. If he found work in D.C., maybe she would run into him again someday. She wanted a chance to thank him properly for helping her bring Jessica into the world. On a whim, she had asked to keep his shirt as a souvenir, rescuing it just as the nurse was about to dispose of it.

Shanna became aware that her father was looking at her and had stopped talking. "Well, the result is still the same," she told him lightly. "One way or the other, you would have still wound up with the most gorgeous granddaughter on the face of the earth."

Brady smiled, finishing the last of his coffee. "That's what your mother says."

"Mother?" Shanna couldn't picture her mother acting the part of the proud grandmother if her life depended on it. Though the woman had come by several times to visit and to bring gifts, she had remained the regal Rheena Brady, socialite, throughout.

Brady knew exactly what his daughter meant. "She doesn't exactly refer to Jessica as her granddaughter. That part of the relationship is glossed over rather rapidly. Your mother's still not sure what she wants Jessica to call her."

"Well, Mother's got at least nine months to come up with an alternative." Shanna studied her father's face.

"How about you? Want Jessica to call you something other than Grandfather when she finally learns how to talk?"

"Not a chance." He laughed. He looked down at the gold-framed photograph on the table. It was a close-up of the round little face and clear blue eyes. He hoped the eyes wouldn't change color. It was something he and Jessica shared. He'd only recently realized how important it was to share things. "I'm looking forward to it." Glancing at the photograph again, he grew serious. "Have you told Jordan?"

"Yes." She toyed with the empty cup, wishing she had more coffee. "The first week Jessica was born. I wrote him a letter."

"And?"

She shrugged. She had lived in fear for a month before she had relaxed. "And nothing."

Brady couldn't believe what his daughter was telling him. "Jordan hasn't even bothered to try to get in contact with you?"

She set the cup down on the saucer and folded her hands in her lap. Ambivalent feelings traveled through her. She wanted Jessica to have a father, wanted Jordan to realize that he owed his daughter something besides genes. But she still didn't want him in her life, didn't want him laying a claim to the infant.

"Not a word. Now that he's won the primary, he's undoubtedly too busy with his election campaign." She thought of Liz Conway. Talk had it that the woman had been replaced, both as Jordan's campaign secretary and his lover. Shanna found no solace, no feeling of revenge in the information. "Or his women."

Brady placed his hand on top of his daughter's, trying to offer her as much comfort as he could. "He wasn't worthy of you, Shanna."

Shanna raised her chin. "Not for a moment," she agreed, an easy smile on her lips. It was nice having her father in her corner.

She was going to be all right, he thought, relieved. Remembering his appointment, Brady looked down at his watch to check the time. It was getting late. "Well, I'd better be going."

She walked him to the door. "Thanks for stopping by, Dad." He turned and looked at her, a puzzled expression on his face. "I really mean it."

His visits shouldn't come as such a surprise. There were years to make up for, he thought. "I'm sorry it took so long."

She didn't understand his meaning. "For what?"

"For me to become a father."

She threw her arms around his neck and hugged him, deeply touched. Then she jumped back, afraid she'd wrinkled his suit. He had a dapper reputation to maintain. With a fond smile, she straightened his collar. "Better late than never, Dad."

He touched her cheek, grateful for this second chance. "My thoughts exactly."

"And send me a few of the reports on my pet project, will you, Dad? I'm getting restless. I need something to do."

"With a newborn around?" he asked skeptically. Rheena, of course, had never gotten immersed in motherhood for one moment, but that was Rheena. Shanna was an entirely different matter.

Shanna glanced back toward her daughter's room. "She sleeps a lot. Besides, I don't ever want to become part of the idle rich again."

"Whatever you want. I'll send them over with Haggerty. He's looking for an excuse to come by and visit you, anyway. This'll give him one."

Shanna smiled to herself as she closed the door. She tried to picture the hulking manager of her father's office acting like a common messenger boy and failed.

18

It had been a long haul, Reid thought, to get to this point in time. It was almost 9:00 A.M. and he was on his way to a brand-new job. Anticipation and excitement rippled through him. He quickly walked up the stairs leading to the Senate building, smiling to himself. A long haul, but he was finally here, after one false start, on the threshold.

His professor had turned out to be a great deal more understanding than Reid would have thought he'd be that night he missed his final. After leaving the hospital, Reid had raced home to change out of his bloodied clothes, dropped off the taxi, and taken the metro to school. He had made a last-minute decision to try to catch his teacher.

Professor Howard was just locking the classroom door when Reid came hurrying down the hall. There had been nothing beyond an icy silence while Howard had listened to Reid relate his story. And then, for the first time, Reid actually saw the wizened old man smile.

Howard unlocked the door and motioned him inside. While the professor sat at his desk, reading the evening edition of *The Washington Post*, he allowed Reid to take the test he had given the rest of the class earlier. Reid graduated with his class that summer.

It seemed hard to believe that a year had passed since that night. A year since he had helped Shanna give birth to her daughter. He thought of her occasionally, wondering where she was and if she ever thought of him at all. He had wanted to visit her at the hospital, but what would have been the point? He found her very attractive. He had the first time he saw her on the beach. But she was married. The feeling pulsing through him when he looked at her was far too sexual, at least for him, to believe that only friendship would be at the end of the line. Besides, he had never learned her last name and he couldn't have very well gone from room to room on the maternity floor, looking for her.

He knew he would have, if she had been single. But the fact remained that she wasn't single. Some things, he knew as he walked to the first bank of elevators, were better left alone.

The elevator arrived and he moved just inside it, to the right of the door. Six other people quickly filed in behind him, jockeying for position in the small cubicle. He recognized a congressman from a newscast the other day. It felt good to be here.

Still, Reid mused as the doors closed, he did think about her, especially when the winter nights had stretched out endlessly until morning's first light. He thought about the way she had looked when he first saw her on the beach, the way she had raised her eyes to his when he had placed her baby in her arms. No, there was nothing platonic at work here. What he felt when he thought of Shanna came strictly under the heading of desire.

The elevator opened on the third floor. This was it. He got out. A sign on the wall pointed him down the right corridor. Before applying for this position, he had spent a total of ten months working for Congressman Calhoun. Young, dynamic, and an obvious winner, at first glance Jordan Calhoun seemed to be the type of up-and-coming politician Reid wanted to be associated with. Since Calhoun's office was almost as new to the scene as Reid was, he'd thought it was a good place for him to start and get himself oriented to the ins and outs of the political world in Washington, D.C.

But Reid found that he didn't really care for Jordan. It wasn't actually something he could put his finger on. The words were sincere, the grip was warm, the smile bright. But there was something lacking about the man, something in the eyes that told Reid he was in the presence of a great showman and nothing more. It was like looking into a window of a store and seeing a host of wonderful goods, only to discover that it was nothing more than a cardboard mock-up. Calhoun gave him that impression.

Principles were something that could be easily bought and sold, but Reid wanted to hold on to his for a while. Naive though he knew it might sound, he didn't want to work for someone he didn't really believe in. He couldn't write speeches for a man like that and know it was only so much rhetoric, said only because the people wanted to hear it, not because the speaker believed in the words.

So when a friend of a friend told him that there was an opening in Senator Brady's office, he had jumped at the chance. The position wasn't what he wanted, but there was no doubt in Reid's mind that, given time, he would work himself up to being one of Senator Brady's speech writers. And Reid wasn't afraid to work.

It would actually help him in the long run, he thought, to learn the daily routine of the Senator's office. Eventually it would all dovetail with his goal of being a political speech writer. Admiring Brady the way he did, Reid now felt he should have set his sights on getting a job at the man's office to begin with.

Part of Reid felt as if things were happening too slowly for him. He was almost thirty, and at thirty, a lot of men already had a family and had spent five years at their chosen career. Still, some never got the opportunity to follow their dreams at all and he was getting his chance. That was something. He realized that he was, in a roundabout fashion, building his success due to a tragedy. He hadn't wanted it that way, but he had always tried to make the best of everything.

Except once.

Then he had almost succeeded, he thought wryly, in getting himself killed. He had had no intention of getting killed at the time. It was Tyler Poole he had wanted dead. Even now, eleven years later, when he thought of the spoiled, only son of Hemitsville's first family, he felt his fingers curl the way they had that night around Tyler's throat. He supposed in a macabre sort of way, he had Tyler to thank for getting him to this point. If Tyler hadn't showered Judy with gifts and attention, if he hadn't turned her head and won her away from him, maybe things would have turned out differently for everyone concerned.

The memory still left a bitter taste in his mouth, like spoiled almonds. He had loved Judy, really loved her. And they would have been married if it weren't for Tyler. There had always been an inherent rivalry between them and Tyler had enjoyed stealing Judy's affections away from him. It was done with no more thought, no more sense of responsibility than he would have used if he was choosing a shirt to wear for the day.

Judy, captivated, overwhelmed, had fallen completely

under Tyler's spell. Within a month she was pregnant. Tyler had denied the baby was his, saying she was just after his family's money. His parents had been quick to echo the sentiment. Tyler had even gone so far as to spread lies that Judy had gone to bed with half a dozen other men during the time he had been seeing her. Judy had been totally shattered. She felt that she had no other way out except to take her own life. Reid had been the one to find her, lying on the floor of her room, blood flowing from the wrists she had slashed in a frenzy of despair. He had frantically tried to bind up her wounds. It had been no use.

Grief-stricken, he drove around looking for Tyler. He found him in one of his father's clubs. Tyler was there, surrounded by his hangers-on, boasting about his sexual prowess. Confronting him, Reid had almost lost control when Tyler pulled out a knife and slashed him, leaving a long, bloodied line along the right half of his torso. Enraged, knocking the knife from Tyler's hand, Reid would have killed him if the others hadn't pulled him off Tyler's battered body.

Tyler swore revenge. There was no doubt that the Poole family had enough power to have Reid put away for a long time, if not killed while he was behind bars. Reid's mother had begged her only son to leave town. He joined the army the next day and never came back.

Yes, he supposed he had Tyler Poole to thank for all this, but the words wouldn't be coming soon. Reid had no use for the spoiled, indulged offspring of rich parents.

Shanna peered over her assistant's shoulder as the older woman sat at her computer. On the screen was a colorful spreadsheet depicting, in bargraph form, statistics it had taken Shanna and her committee three

months of intensified research to compile. It was all to
go into a booklet Brady wanted to have distributed in
order to gain support for a new bill he was proposing
to curb taxation. It was a lofty proposition at best, popular with the people, unpopular with legislators and
government departments that survived on continually
increasing budgets.

"Looks good, Shirley." It would be a good addition to
the report. "Now I need those graphs finished and on
my desk by noon. Otherwise I won't have time to go
over them today."

Shirley turned from her computer and looked at
Shanna, clearly bewildered. Shanna was amused by the
woman's expression. She knew exactly what Shirley was
thinking. Shanna had steadily built up a reputation for
being a workaholic. She *always* had time to look into
another source, to revise another report, interview
another person. It was sleep she never had time to catch
up on. Everything else she managed to juggle, including
always finding a way to fit her daughter into the scheme
of things, no matter how hectic things became.

Shirley turned the swivel chair to face her supervisor
completely. "You mean you're not going to burn the
midnight oil for a change?"

Mentally Shanna was already halfway to the printer's
with the pages that were available. "Nope."

Shirley splayed a hand over her ample bosom. "Shanna,
I'm shocked. What's the matter, you have to go in for
your hundred-thousand-mile tune-up?"

Shanna took no offense at the teasing words. When
she had returned from maternity leave, it was Shirley
who had turned down a promotion to offer her services
to Shanna. Shirley who mothered her on the very few
occasions that she needed someone to listen. The older
woman could have easily resented her for coming in and

taking over, but she didn't. Shirley was a loyal friend and Shanna was grateful to her.

Shanna crossed her arms before her and leaned her hip against the edge of the desk. "Don't you remember about the party?"

"Another political fund-raiser?" Shirley guessed, failing to recall what Shanna was referring to.

"Birthday party," Shanna corrected. "My daughter's one year old today."

God, it had gone so fast. A whole year. A year of first smiles, first words, and first teeth. And she had been there for almost all of it. Jessica was the only reason Shanna ever slowed down. She made sure that Jessica would never once, even now at this tender age, question whether her driven mother loved her. Shanna swore to herself daily that though the pace she had chosen for herself kept her racing madly through life, Jessica would never feel neglected. Her determination to keep her promise was the main reason Shanna stopped every afternoon at four to go home and have dinner with her baby before coming back to work. Right now Jessica might be too young to appreciate the fact, but Shanna knew. And that was what counted.

Shanna looked down at Shirley's soft brown eyes. "So, are you coming?"

Shirley Sinclaire was fifteen years older than Shanna. She had worked at the office for nine years, content with her position. There were a lot of people who worked for the senator with ambitions to rise eventually to a high position within the political hierarchy. Shirley's ambition was to do her job well and collect her paycheck. Her husband was a bus driver and she had no desire to attain a loftier position than he held. She was, as Senator Whitney liked to term it, "good people." It was one of the reasons Shanna enjoyed her company so much.

Though she had visited Shanna's apartment on several occasions, Shirley had never socialized with the Brady family beyond the gatherings on election night. She frowned skeptically at Shanna. "Me? I don't think I have anything suitable to wear—"

It was a strange comment, coming from Shirley. As far as Shanna was aware, Shirley didn't really care about making any sort of a fashion statement. "What's wrong with what you have on?"

Shirley looked down. She was wearing a simple black skirt with a raspberry-colored silk blouse she'd gotten on sale. "This isn't exactly what you'd wear to hobnob with socialites."

Shanna shrugged. "It is when you're coming to my place."

Shirley looked surprised. "The party's at your apartment?" She had naturally assumed that since Jessica was the senator's granddaughter, the celebration would be at the Brady house.

"Sure."

Shanna had politely but firmly scotched her mother's original plans to hold Jessica's birthday party at the house. There were to be clowns, balloons, and a pony. And a host of people who belonged to Rheena's far-reaching circle of acquaintances. Shanna vividly remembered parties like that from her own childhood. She had gotten lost amid a forest of people, all ignoring her except to give her an occasional, fleeting smile before returning to their conversations. She didn't want more of the same for her daughter. Things were going to be different for Jessica, right from the beginning. Rheena had fussed and fumed and, eventually, agreed reluctantly.

"Well, if it's at your place," Shirley answered, "count me in."

Shanna nodded, pleased. "Terrific. It's at six." She rose. "Bring Robert."

It was going to be a terrific party, she thought happily. She had to remember to stop at the bakery on her way home to pick up Jessica's cake. Jane had volunteered, but Shanna had turned the nurse down. She enjoyed doing these little things herself. It made her feel as if her life was real. Sometimes she needed that, needed to find reasons for her existence. Her work at the office was part of it, as was Jessica. If there were times in the middle of the night when she woke up, yearning to have someone there next to her, someone who would love her just because she was there, just because she was Shanna, well, no one ever had everything they wanted. And she came pretty close.

As she turned to hurry on her way she collided with a muscular wall. As she sprang back, mumbling, "I'm sorry," her eyes grew wide.

Reid.

Haggerty saw the strange, dazed expression on Shanna's face and wondered if she wasn't feeling well. He was taking the new man and introducing him around the office. Though he could easily have delegated the job to an underling, Haggerty enjoyed doing things like this personally. It kept him visible and aware of what was going on. "Shanna, I'd like you to meet—"

"Reid—" she said, her voice low and breathy with surprise.

"—Kincannon," Haggerty finished. He looked from the new man to Shanna. "You two know each other?" Reid hadn't indicated that he knew the senator's daughter when they had spoken during the interview last week. The fact that he had refrained from name-dropping reinforced Haggerty's feelings that he had made the right choice in hiring him. He liked his staff unassuming.

Reid smiled warmly at Shanna. So, they'd met again. *Yeah, Ma, destiny does exist.*

"In a way," he told Haggerty, his eyes on Shanna. She had grown thinner since the last time he saw her, he thought. It wasn't just her body, it was her face. She was almost gaunt. It gave her one hell of a sexy air.

Instinctively he looked down at her hand, She wasn't wearing a wedding ring anymore. And the rock she had flashed at him on the beach to ward him off was gone as well. All he saw was a small, delicate hand with neatly pared fingernails and no jewelry whatsoever.

Destiny, he thought, was looking very good indeed.

"We've just hired Reid on to take Edwards's place. He came with some pretty strong letters of recommendations," Haggerty told Shanna. He was getting the feeling that he was inadvertently intruding on something very personal, judging by the look that passed between the two people. "He's starting out as an aide until he gets himself oriented with the senator's platform. Reid's eventually going to write a few earth-moving speeches for your father."

Reid's smile faded slightly, giving way to confusion. He looked questioningly at Haggerty. What was he talking about? "Her father? I thought that I'd be working for Senator Brady."

Haggerty looked at Reid. Was it possible that he didn't know? "You will be. Senator Brady's Shanna's father."

"Oh." Reid's smile vanished completely as if it had never existed and his eyes darkened as he continued looking at Shanna. He nodded formally. "Pleased to meet you, Ms. Brady."

The greeting had frost all over it. Why? She stared after Reid as Haggerty took him away and introduced him to another group of people in the next section.

You would have had to be a dead person to miss the antagonism that had suddenly sprung up. "What's the matter with him?" Shirley asked.

"I haven't got the slightest idea," Shanna said slowly, then looked at Shirley. "But I sure as hell am going to find out."

If he was judging her for something, and it was more than obvious that he was, she had a right to know what. She stood in no one's shadow anymore, not even her father's.

Shanna forced her attention to her work. There was time enough to find out the reason for Reid's scowl. "After I get back from the printer. Hurry up with those graphs, will you, Shirley?"

She hurried out the door.

19

"*I see you did get* to take your final." It wasn't much of an opening line, Shanna thought as she came up behind Reid. But it was the best she could come up with in the half hour it had taken her to get to the printer and return.

After the pertinent introductions had been made, Aaron Haggerty had left Reid's further orientation to a junior aide who had been on staff a little more than a year, Bryan Jennings. Bryan had just begun to give Reid a more intensified view of office procedure when Shanna walked up. A slight young man with an even slighter chin, Bryan smiled brightly at Shanna. The smile was in sharp contrast to the somber expression Reid wore.

Another spoiled brat, making it on her parents' good graces and far-reaching influence. Reid couldn't help the look of disdain that came over his face as he turned toward Shanna.

The eyes that looked at her were not the ones she had drawn strength from that night a year ago when they had been together in an intimate, bonding situation. One that she would have thought had left a mark on both of them. It had on her. Those weren't the eyes of a friend who had shared something precious with her. Those were the eyes of a stranger, judging her as if she were hateful and only partially human. Shanna felt both confusion and ire rising within her in response.

"Yes, I did," Reid answered coldly.

The words just hung there, awkwardly strung out in the air like forgotten party streamers that had gotten wet in the rain.

Temper took a larger bite out of her. Well, if that's the way he wanted it, fine. The last thing in the world she wanted was to deal with a boorish male who was devoid of manners. She turned to leave.

But something kept Shanna standing where she was, stuck to the floor as if flypaper had trapped her shoes. All right, she'd give it one more try. Maybe he was just experiencing a first-class case of nerves. Or he was intimidated because she was Brady's daughter. She had encountered that situation before. Once upon a time, Shanna remembered, she had been intimidated by that fact herself.

"I'm having a birthday party for Jessica tonight." She smiled, though the expression felt a little forced at the edges. "You're welcome to come, seeing as how you were the first person to ever see her."

She saw Bryan listening to all this and felt awkward at having the scene played out in front of a third party. But the very fact that she was talking in front of someone else should've shown Reid that there wasn't a basis for his feelings toward her, whatever the cause might have been. She had done nothing and had absolutely nothing to hide, certainly nothing worth condemning her for.

For a moment Reid was tempted to accept. It would

be interesting to see the tiny child he had held in his hands that night again, to see how she had grown. And perhaps recapture some of the awe he had felt at life's simplest, yet greatest miracle.

And there was no denying the physical attraction he felt for the child's mother. But there were other things he felt, things that materialized from his past to haunt him. Feelings that had been burned into his soul the night he had held Judy as she had taken her last breath. A rich man's son had robbed him of her twice, once when she had jilted him and once when she had taken her life. He had little use for the offspring of the rich. "If you don't mind, I'll pass."

Shanna felt the iciness in Reid's reply as if it had taken actual form in shards of cold steel hurled in her direction. Bryan looked down at his desk, embarrassed at being a witness to what was transpiring. He liked Shanna far too well to see her humiliated this way.

She squared her shoulders, her tone formal. The look she gave Reid cut him dead from the knees on up. "Sure. It was just an idea." She turned and started to walk toward her office.

No, damn it, she wasn't going to retreat like a whipped dog with her tail between her legs because someone had scowled at her. That was the old Shanna, the Shanna whom Jordan had used with her unwitting permission. She wasn't going to let anyone hurt her again in any manner, shape, or form. That included this big oaf.

She turned and retraced her steps to Reid's desk and tapped him on the shoulder, her finger poking hard against the ridge of muscle. Bryan chose that moment to investigate something in one of the hanging files located in the back of the office. It was still close enough to hear, but far enough to remove him from immediate view.

Reid looked up at Shanna. He half expected her to snap out something to the effect of did he realize who he was dealing with and that she could have him fired immediately. If she could, if the senator was swayed so easily by the demands of a spoiled brat, Reid knew he didn't want the job. "Yeah?"

Insides trembling, Shanna nonetheless planted both feet on the floor, her hands on her hips. "What's your problem?" she demanded, her voice low. There was no way to keep her temper at the same level. It was there, in her eyes, flashing.

She looked magnificent, he thought, finding himself stirred despite his feelings about her. He had to focus himself on exactly how he felt about people like her. "Excuse me?"

"Your problem," she repeated, biting off the word. "What is it? You're obviously judging me and I want to know why."

Next, she'd undoubtedly be throwing a tantrum. The best way to answer her was to be blunt and be done with it. If there were consequences, well, he couldn't help that. He had no time to put up with people who hadn't gotten to where they were by virtue of the sweat of their own brows. "Maybe I just don't like spoiled rich kids."

His words were like a heartless slap in the face. She drew herself up and glared at Reid. How dare he? She'd spent a year and a half trying to establish herself as her own person. A year and a half and he had dismissed it all with a careless phrase. He hadn't the right. He hadn't the slightest idea who or what she was.

"And maybe you're just a big jerk. If you'll excuse me, I thought you were somebody I knew. Obviously I was mistaken." With every scrap of haughty dignity she could gather, Shanna turned and walked away.

Bryan took his cue and returned, the hanging file

drawer left partially open behind him as he took his seat next to Reid. He frowned in disapproval, his chin disappearing completely.

"Pretty stupid of you, mouthing off at the boss's daughter."

The boss's daughter. He wondered if she enjoyed throwing her weight around. Did the others work with an eye out to pleasing her for fear of losing their jobs? He thought of Tyler Poole and bile rose in his mouth. It had a bitter taste. Tyler had been that kind of a bully, flaunting his money, his position, and what he could do to people who didn't see things "his way."

Reid shrugged, unaffected by Bryan's meaning. If he lost this job, there'd be another. The political arena was large and he'd find his place in it eventually. He greatly admired Brady, but things didn't always work out the way one planned. He'd learned that early in life.

"Yeah, well, I've done stupid things before. This won't be the last time."

He started to read through the pamphlet Bryan had given him, but the words remained just words, unconnected with any sort of meaning. She was on his mind even though he didn't want her to be. He glanced at Bryan, who was still looking at him dubiously. "What does she do around here, anyway?"

"Shanna?" Bryan grinned at Reid like a lovesick puppy. The aide's greatest fantasies all included Shanna in various stages of undress and willingness. "Work her tail off, mostly."

Bryan looked serious, but Reid didn't know the man well enough to be sure. "That a joke?"

"No." Bryan pushed his wire-rim glasses up the bridge of his short nose. "An observation. She started working here right after her marriage to Calhoun fell apart."

Reid's eyes narrowed. "That wouldn't be Jordan Calhoun, would it?"

The phrasing struck Bryan as odd. "Why wouldn't it?"

Calhoun? What kind of a woman would have married Jordan Calhoun? The man was all flash and promises, but very little substance. It was a proven fact, as seen in the last election, that he could draw voters like bees to honey, but there was an emptiness behind the smile. There was a self-serving, calculating ego there, if Reid wasn't mistaken. Only a woman of the same ilk would consent to be his wife. It told Reid that he hadn't been wrong about his judgment of her just now. There was a great deal of truth in the "birds of a feather" adage.

"No reason. Go on, you were saying," Reid urged Bryan on.

Bryan shrugged, apparently not knowing what Reid was fishing for. If it was something disparaging about Shanna, he wasn't going to get it from him. Bryan thought she was nothing short of terrific.

"She started out doing what you're doing, more or less. Junior office aide." Bryan waved a vague hand at the material spread out on the desk. "The senator's got her working on the homeless project, as well as half a dozen other things now. She worked her way up to that. Earned it. Dunno how she manages. I sure as hell couldn't work in the fast-forward mode all the time. It's almost, you know, like she's got something to prove, doing all this." Bryan warmed to his subject, exploring the theory. "Like she's got to prove that she's good enough to be working here or something." The young man grinned. "She doesn't have to prove a thing to me."

"Is she seeing anyone special?" The question had absolutely nothing to do with anything that concerned him, Reid thought stubbornly. Yet it was there, just the same, begging for an answer.

Bryan shook his head. "Not unless she's got something going with a pilot. She's always flying back to Illinois for the senator, to get more statistics, do more research, canvass the area for him. Like I said, I don't know where she gets the time, or the energy, but I sure wish I could get her to spend some of it on me."

"I heard her say she was taking off early today." Reid pointed out the contradiction to the man's assessment. Workaholics didn't take off early.

"That's 'cause it's her daughter's birthday. You know, the party she invited you to." Bryan looked at him pointedly. "The kid gets top priority over everything. Cute kid. Shanna's brought her in a couple of times, just to show her off. Now there's a real mother for you." Bryan's expression sombered slightly. "Mine was always serving us frozen dinners and rushing off to meetings."

The description didn't match the portrait of Shanna Reid had just been trying to paint for himself. It did, however, match what he had felt, looking at the woman who had ridden in the back of his taxicab that night a year ago.

Reid stared off thoughtfully in the direction Shanna had taken.

She wasn't going to let it bother her, Shanna swore under her breath, again. What some throwback Neanderthal type thought of her wasn't going to bother her. Not in the slightest. She was past that, past caring what men thought of her. What people thought of her. She had spent so much time and energy carefully building herself up in her own eyes. As well as building a wall around herself so that remarks like this wouldn't hurt. So that she'd never again be prey for or vulnerable to men like Jordan again.

Dear God, she had wanted to kill herself then.

Shanna carefully picked her way through the noonday traffic, heading to her apartment, the wide birthday cake safely strapped into the backseat with a seat belt. The idea still astounded her when she thought of it. She had actually considered killing herself that night because of Jordan. What an incredible waste that would have been. She would have snuffed out two lives without even knowing it. Hers and Jessica's. All because she had been heartsick over the fact that her husband didn't think enough of her to be faithful.

Driving off blindly into the night during a storm had been a stupid, stupid choice on her part. It wouldn't have played that way if the same set of circumstances had happened today. She might not be able to control what other people thought of her, but she could certainly control her own reactions.

So why did it hurt now? she thought irritably as she parked beneath her building. Why had that cold look in Reid Kincannon's green eyes cut her in half that way? She didn't even *know* the man, for God's sake. She'd only been in his company an hour, an hour and fifteen minutes tops, if she counted both occasions. What was an hour measured against a lifetime? Nothing. Boring speeches went on for longer than that.

She slammed the car door and it echoed throughout the parking structure. The birthday cake was large, requiring two hands to hold. And her attention, she reminded herself. She had a party to get under way and a daughter to dote on. She had absolutely no place in her life or in her head for the likes of one Reid Kincannon and his groundless, obviously prejudiced, stupid remarks.

°   °   °

Shanna leaned in the doorway of her kitchen, absolutely exhausted and completely pleased with herself. She took a deep breath before taking another step into the room. It was incredible how so many people had managed to fit into her apartment tonight. A warm, satisfied glow emanated from her. It had been a terrific party, just the way she had planned it.

Jessica wouldn't remember, but it was all recorded on videotape for her to look at when she grew older, thanks to the combined efforts of Haggerty and that sweet-faced office aide, Bryan. For four solid hours, Shanna's apartment had been a hub of activity with countless people passing through if not actually staying for the duration. It had been a comfortable mixture of her old world and her new one: people she had known while growing up, such as Senator Whitney and his wife, and people from the office, like Shirley and her husband.

Her mother had initially cast a disapproving eye at the mixed "pedigree" of the people who were at the party. But she had stayed throughout, for once not even arriving fashionably late. It had touched Shanna deeply to see her parents arriving together for a change. Rheena Brady, consummate socialite, had wound up in a corner, talking to Shirley and finding common ground, of all things.

Yes, Shanna thought as she moved about the kitchen, wondering where to start first, tonight was an unqualified success.

If there was just the tiniest bit of a hollow feeling within her, well, that would pass.

She bit her lower lip. It was late, but she didn't think she could sleep, exhausted though she was. Her mind was too keyed up. Maybe if she addressed the mountain of dishes tonight instead of hiring a cleaning service to take care of the mess in the morning, she could work through this slight bit of agitation she was feeling. She was glad that Jane had long since retired to her room. She wanted to be alone with her thoughts.

Alone.

As she was a great deal of the time, she mused, then pushed the feeling aside. Hot dishwater was undoubtedly the cure for this kind of self-pitying, maudlin mood. Reid had brought it on, she thought, roundly cursing his soul for having shown up in her life again this way.

She had just begun stacking dishes in the sink when she heard the doorbell. Frowning, she wiped her hands on a towel and crossed to the threshold. It was almost eleven. She had no idea who would be stopping by this late. She had specified that the party was at six.

Shanna glanced around the living room as she passed it to get to the front door. It was pretty much in a state of turmoil. Maybe someone had left something behind.

"Who is it?" she asked cheerfully. Her smile froze when she heard the answer.

"It's Reid Kincannon."

20

Shanna opened the door a crack and kept her hand firmly on the doorknob. She resisted the urge to slam the door in Reid's face. If she did, she'd never know what prompted the man to show up on her doorstep at this hour of the night, and she wanted to know, if for no other reason than to satisfy her own curiosity.

She frowned at Reid, making no effort to conceal her displeasure at seeing him standing there. "What are you doing here?"

"Haggerty told me where you live." He wasn't good at apologies, and this one burned on his tongue. Reid looked past Shanna's head, inside the apartment. "Mind if I come in?"

"Yes, I do mind." She was annoyed with him and with herself for caring. Yet if she didn't hear him out, she'd be no better than he. She relented, stepped back, and opened the door further. "And just why would Haggerty do that?"

"Because I asked him." Reid looked around as he walked in. It wasn't what he had expected. This was no palatial residence, ostentatiously crammed with obvious signs of wealth. It was an apartment. A rather messy apartment from what he could see, but an unpretentious one. "I guess he thought I was coming to your party."

She felt herself tensing, as if for battle. Her heartbeat quickened. She could feel each beat in her throat. She suddenly questioned her judgment. This man was basically a stranger and she was letting him into her apartment. A wave of anxiety washed over her, but faded as she remembered the look on his face when he had handed her daughter to her.

Another look, the one he had worn this morning, came to her. "But you really just wanted to come and continue our scintillating conversation from this morning, is that it?" she asked sarcastically.

He deserved that, he reasoned. That and more. He turned to look at her. She looked a little frazzled. And incredibly sexy. The dress, though simple, flattered every curve and the color brought out her eyes. He thought of how good she had looked on the beach that day almost eighteen months ago now. He found himself wondering what she looked like without that dress on. A slight smile creased his face. Thank God humans weren't telepathic or he'd be in a lot more trouble than he was already.

The way he was appraising her didn't go unnoticed. It made her feel nervous, yet in a way she liked it. Now he was smiling. No, it looked as if he was trying to stifle a grin.

"Do you find something amusing?"

"No, not amusing." He looked down at his offerings, suddenly remembering the reason for his visit. "I came to give you these."

"These" were two boxes. One was wrapped very attractively with a huge multicolored bow and a tiny teddy bear attached to it. The other was far less fancy. His handiwork, no doubt, she thought. The slightly wrinkled shiny green paper was taped around what appeared to be, judging from the shape, a shoe box. He held them both out, waiting for Shanna to take them. She could have sworn he felt awkward about it.

Shoe on the other foot, she thought. Good.

Shanna raised her eyes to his face, perplexed. She didn't want gifts. She wanted an apology.

"The pretty one's for Jessica," he explained. "The other one's for you. I wrapped that one," he added needlessly.

She stared down at the packages. Did he think he could buy off rude behavior with gifts? Yet not to accept them would be just as rude. "I guess that means I should open it."

"Actually I wish you would. It's rather important for a couple of reasons."

Doubly confused, Shanna sat down on the sofa and gestured Reid toward a chair opposite the coffee table. "Sit down if you like."

Instead of the chair, he sat down beside her on the sofa, his eyes watching her face as she neatly, slowly removed the wrapping from the box.

"You must have been a lot of fun at Christmas," he murmured, impatient for her to be done.

She raised her eyes, but not her head. He felt a dryness in his mouth. "I like to savor things."

"Nice to know," he said softly, almost to himself. Shanna lowered her eyes again, vaguely unsettled by his comment.

Laying the neatly removed paper aside, she stared down at the gift. It *was* a shoe box. A man's shoe box.

Was this a joke? She lifted the lid. There was a single black loafer inside. It was worn, but freshly polished.

Setting the box aside on the coffee table, Shanna held the shoe aloft and looked expectantly at Reid. He didn't look weird, but looks were deceiving. Jordan had looked like an angel and he was clever as the devil and twice as heartless. "What's this?"

"This is the shoe that fell off my foot when I had it surgically removed from my mouth this afternoon."

She laughed and shook her head as she handed the shoe back to him. She nodded at it. "Is that your way of apologizing?"

He looked chagrined. "That's my way of saying I'd like to start over."

She forgave him. Temporarily. It was in return for the compassion he had once shown her. "I wouldn't."

"Oh." He supposed he deserved that, too.

She smiled. It appeared that for just one moment she held the upper hand, yet she felt shy. Nothing more than a paper tiger, she mused. Perhaps she hadn't changed as much as she had thought. Dismayed, she took a deep breath. No more shy, shrinking violet, not for her. Not ever.

"We already have a history, Reid, and I don't particularly want to erase that." She saw the relieved look in his eyes and it made her smile widen. "What I do want is an explanation."

He owed that to her. It didn't make the telling any easier. "For this morning."

She nodded. "Good guess. What made you change direction, midstream? You looked like you hated me."

"Not you, exactly." It was hard looking into her eyes and remembering the feelings he had had this morning. "What you stood for."

"Which is?" she asked quietly. Even though she suspected that she might not like what she was about to hear, it had to be said in order to be cleared away.

Reid avoided her eyes and looked down at the shoe he was holding in his hand. All at once he felt extremely foolish. He wanted to get up and leave. No, he needed to make amends with this woman. He had hurt her and she hadn't deserved it.

He looked around at the living room, noting the different scraps of wrapping paper and boxes that hadn't been cleared away. As he did so he listed Tyler's offenses out loud. "Privileged class, having everything handed to you. Never having to work for anything. Taking unfair advantage of situations." He thought of Judy. "Of people."

Nothing new. She'd heard all that before, loudly, unjustly whispered behind her back. "I've been fighting against that sort of stereotyping all my life. That and shadows." Shanna paused, replacing the lid on the empty box. "Who did you know like that?" He spoke with too much feeling for this to be just a random opinion he harbored. He'd been hurt, somehow, made to bleed.

Though he thought he was able to do it, Reid found that he didn't want to talk about it. He shrugged. "Someone in my past." He looked away. "It was a long time ago."

"A woman?"

"A man." *Who took away my woman.*

She suspected he wasn't about to tell her anything further and perhaps she didn't want to know. She was too tired for long stories, too tired to look into someone else's bedeviled life. She was carrying too much emotional luggage from her own.

She changed the subject. "I've got some birthday cake left over in the kitchen. Would you like some?"

Nervously she rose and started for the kitchen before Reid gave his answer.

Reid got to his feet. He was grateful for the respite. If she had pushed, he wasn't certain what he would have said. The wound was still too private to share, still too raw to expose. He hadn't realized that until this moment. "That'd be nice, but I'd like to ask a favor, first."

She stopped, waiting. She couldn't help the suspicion that sprang up within her. Jordan had done that to her, she thought. He had taken away her innocence, her trust. And inadvertently made her find her backbone. But he had stripped her of an important part of her soul. She could forgive him more for his infidelity than for that.

"I'd like to see Jessica."

Then why didn't you come to the party? Shanna found she couldn't make the accusation. Instead she motioned for Reid to follow her. "You'll have to be quiet. She's asleep."

He crept softly behind her, watching the way her body moved seductively without her even knowing it. "It's eleven-thirty at night, what else would she be?"

Shanna looked over her shoulder. "You don't know much about children, do you?"

"Just how to deliver them."

She turned at the bedroom door right next to hers. "You said you only knew how to deliver puppies." She recalled what he had told her just before Jessica had fought her way into the world.

He grinned. "You expanded my repertoire."

Shanna cracked the door open slightly, then tiptoed in. A small night-light in the shape of a smiling fairy cast a cozy, warm glow within the room. Jessica was lying tummy down, in her crib, fast asleep and madly working her pacifier.

Reid pointed it out to Shanna. Energy temporarily on hold. He bet Jessica was more than a handful awake. "She's like you."

"No," Shanna whispered, love shining in her eyes as she looked down at her daughter. "Not like me. She's beautiful."

Reid wondered if Shanna ever took a real look in the mirror.

Shanna led the way into the kitchen. She cut a large piece of cake for Reid, placing it on one of the few remaining clean plates she had, then went back to stacking the dishes.

Reid took a forkful of the fudge marble cake as he watched her work. He wondered if she was doing it on purpose, to make him feel even worse for his remark. Did she really work this hard? He remembered what Bryan had told him. "Don't you have help?"

She pushed a fistful of forks together on the counter. "I have a nurse for the baby."

He shook his head, indicating the dishes and surrounding bedlam in the blue-and-white room. "I mean a housekeeper or something."

His words echoed her mother's lament. "I like doing for myself." She looked for room on the counter to make another stack. Forks, glasses, and plates littered the area like toy soldiers in the aftermath of an imaginary battle. There was no space to be had. She turned her attention to the dishwasher rack and placed the plates there. "Too many people tend to get in the way."

She certainly didn't think like any of the wealthy people he had ever known. He pushed the subject a little further to see how she would respond. "There doesn't seem to be much point in having all that money and not enjoying it properly." Finished, he placed his plate on the nearest stack.

She wondered if he had a hang-up about wealth or if this was all just a ruse to throw her off her guard. It would have been a lot simpler being born to some average, middle-class couple who enjoyed summer barbecues and went to baseball games instead of "gala events of the season" and political rallies.

"It's my parents' money, not mine. I want to earn my own way."

He looked around pointedly. "Seems like a very nice apartment for someone on an aide's salary," he said innocently.

"Chief aide," she corrected. "And the co-op was bought with my inheritance from my grandmother." She threw her towel on top of the counter and looked at him. "Do you have a problem with that?"

He had gone too far again in testing her. He'd really have to watch that if he didn't want to set her off. "No, I have a problem with someone named Tyler Poole. And myself," he admitted.

The way he said it had her softening. Maybe she wasn't too tired for a long story. "Want to tell me about it?"

Yes, but he couldn't. "Someday, when we know each other better."

"We know each other now."

And she had no intention of knowing him, or anyone else for that matter, more intimately than she did right now at this moment. She had her work and her daughter and enough responsibilities to fill a thirty-hour day. She didn't want any more complications than she had. And certainly not the complications she suddenly saw in Reid's eyes.

Unable to resist any longer, Reid reached and touched her hair. "There're a lot of blanks to be filled in."

She moved aside. "I'll have an office bio printed up for you."

Now it was her turn to back off and grow cold, he thought. But he wasn't easily put off, though he did know the wisdom of an occasional retreat. He nodded at the large white box on the table. "Good cake."

She smiled, relaxing. "Want more?"

He shook his head. What he wanted wasn't on the menu. And at the moment, he had a feeling, wasn't allowed. "Need help with that?" He nodded at the dishes.

"No, I'll leave it all for the morning. I'm suddenly very tired. Besides, the noise might wake up Jane. Jessica's nurse," she clarified when Reid raised a quizzical brow.

It was late. They both needed their sleep. "I'd better be going, then."

Shanna followed him to the living room. "Thanks for Jessica's present. She'll love opening it in the morning. Unlike me, she rips into things."

Reid wondered if she was that cautious about life as well. She gave every indication that she was, except that she had been married to Calhoun.

Maybe that was the reason for her caution.

Shanna picked up Reid's loafer from the coffee table. "Oh, don't forget your shoe." She looked it over again. "Or should I have it bronzed?"

"I'd rather you didn't." He opened the box and Shanna placed the shoe inside. "It would make it kind of hard to walk in." He glanced down at the loafers on his feet. "I've only got the two pairs."

Obviously not a clotheshorse, she thought, remembering Jordan's obsession with buying expensive clothing and then treating it like thrift-shop specials.

Reid turned at the door. "Friends?"

"Why not?" Shanna placed her hand into his. When

he enveloped it, a strange feeling she couldn't describe briefly swept over her. She only knew it frightened her. She tried to keep the tension at bay. "No one's ever given me a single shoe before."

"At your age, I find that hard to believe."

The laughter that punctuated the absurdity of the remark died away abruptly as he looked at her. Old habits were hard to break, as were old prejudices, but he should have given her a chance before casting her in the mold. The fault was all his.

"I'm sorry, Shanna, really sorry for the way I acted. It's just that you stirred up a lot of old memories, none of which had anything to do with you."

"I understand."

He tucked the shoe box under his arm, not really wanting to leave. He wanted to stay and talk. To get to really know her. But she was already stepping behind the door. He wondered if he had ruined his chances, being hotheaded. "Good night, Shanna."

"Good night."

She closed the door, locking him away from view, and then leaned against it. There was absolutely no reason in the world, she told herself sternly, for her heart to be doing double time.

But it was.

21

Reid strapped himself into the seat next to hers, still somewhat surprised to find himself here. They were on their way to Illinois to do some legislative research. He'd only been in the senator's office a little more than a week. A week in which he had tried to absorb everything that was going on around him. A week in which he was always aware of Shanna's presence the moment she stepped into the room.

Uncustomarily unsure of himself, he had been attempting to work up enough courage to find an excuse to be alone with her. And then fate had taken over.

Bryan, who normally went as her assistant, had come down with a stomach ailment at the last minute, leaving an opening. Reid had happily volunteered to fill it. Shanna, at first, had hesitated, as if something was warning her not to accept. There was something different about Reid that set him apart from the other men she worked with, the other men who populated her life in various capacities. She had been aware of it from the beginning. But work came first and she had no right to let her personal insecurities get in the way. She had agreed to his taking Bryan's place.

The plane's engines began to rumble and so did Shanna's stomach. From anticipation, not hunger. A haze dropped its shroud about her, encasing her. It was the same one that always overtook her at takeoff. And landings. And sometimes entire flights. Shanna gripped both armrests as the small aircraft began taxiing down one of Washington National Airport's runways. She knew that statistically, she was supposedly safer in an airplane, even a small one like this, than on the ground, in a car. It did nothing to hearten her. She absolutely hated flying, but taking a train to Chicago would require entirely too much time. And time was the only thing she couldn't afford.

It's going to be fine, just fine. You've done this almost a hundred times now. Nothing's happened yet, right?

But it only takes once.

"How much do these research trips you go on cost the taxpaying public?" Reid asked absently.

She forced herself to turn her head slightly and look at Reid. Anything to take her mind off the takeoff. Bryan had always tried to distract her with card tricks that were miserably poor. She usually laughed so hard at his ineptness that she forgot to worry about the flight.

She wished Bryan was here now.

Shanna tried to focus on Reid's question. Was he trying to bait her, or was she reading more into the question than was there? In the last week she had purposely avoided being around him. There was a strong physical pull that she was trying to ignore. It made her keep her distance from him. One didn't tempt the gods.

"You sound more like an investigative reporter than a senatorial aide."

He supposed it was rather a crass question, but he was curious about Brady. Was the senator as altruistic as he sometimes seemed, or just a very good politician? Who better to shed light on the subject than his daughter? "Just wondering."

Reid's tone was inoffensive, so she took no offense. "Put your mind at rest. 'Citizen' Brady pays for the flight, not the public via a whim on 'Senator' Brady's part. This is his private plane, his private pilot." They were leveling off a little. She wished her stomach was. It was insisting on scrambling the light breakfast she'd consumed hours ago. "There are some advantages to being a millionaire in office."

He knew of a lot of wealthy men who were tightwads and relished saving even a small sum of money. Many of them, Reid was slowly becoming aware, held office. "Why does he do it?"

She would have thought it was self-evident. "To keep fingers from being pointed at him snidely, the way you were just doing." Reid shifted a little uncomfortably in his seat at her remark, but strictly for her benefit. "He doesn't want anything to get in the way of the good that's coming out of these projects he's backing. No dark shadows to obscure the light."

The plane dipped slightly before regaining altitude. Shanna's eyes widened as she swallowed a gasp. She didn't want Reid to hear her cry out. If she was going to die, there was nothing to be gained by having him think of her as a frightened fool.

Damn, why was she being such a baby about this?

She'd turned two shades paler. He glanced down at her hands. They held on to the armrests like claws belonging to a desperate animal about to lose its hold on a piece of driftwood and slip into the sea forever. "Do you know that your knuckles are turning white?"

The seat-belt sign had gone out and she sighed. Bill had gotten them airborne again. Here was hoping that he kept the trick up. She eased her hands off the arm-rests and into her lap. "They tend to do that on flights."

She was acting like someone on her first flight. "I thought you flew frequently." It wasn't a question. He knew she did. Bryan had told him.

Shanna was aware that he was keeping tabs on her. Shirley had gleefully informed her of the fact when the woman had overheard Reid talking to Bryan. Shirley obviously saw a match here. It was one of the reasons Shanna had been uncomfortable when Reid offered to take Bryan's place on this trip. That, and the fact that when he looked at her, something unraveled within her, a little more each time.

Shanna kept her face forward. The Dramamine was taking its time kicking in. "I do."

He studied her profile. Her jawline was rigid. "But you're still afraid."

She shrugged. There was no point in denying it. "Yes."

"Then why do it?" He still didn't fully comprehend the reason she worked so hard when she didn't have to work at all. "There're other people on the staff who could be doing this in your place. Why put yourself through all this agony each time?"

Agony. He'd certainly picked the right word. She turned to look at him. She knew she didn't have to answer, but she wanted to. It seemed important for him to understand. "I like to think I can do it better than the other people. Maybe it's vain, but I am striving to be the best that I can be, and sitting in this box, thousands of feet above the ground unfortunately is part of that program."

"The best that you can be," Reid repeated, shaking his head with a bemused smile. "You sound like a poster for army recruiters."

She laughed. Maybe she did at that. It still didn't diminish the fact that she was striving to achieve a level of perfection. "And you sound like a cynic."

He was trying to blunt those edges these days, but it wasn't always easy. "You get that way, after the age of ten."

There was a note in his voice she wanted to explore, a core of pain she hadn't heard before. Suddenly, after keeping her distance so carefully, she found herself wanting to know things about this man. She tried to ignore the fact that knowing was always the first step to real intimacy.

"What happened at the age of ten?" she asked softly.

"My father died." It was twenty years in the past. Saying the words still hurt.

"I'm sorry." She reached out and placed her hand on top of his, purely in a gesture of comfort. The contact rippled through both of them. There was nothing comfortable about it. Shanna pulled her hand away, momentarily disoriented and confused.

He'd felt it, too, and it had him slightly unsteady. And curious as all hell. Reid cleared his throat. "Yeah, so am I. He was a great old man." He reflected on his unconscious choice of words and laughed. "Actually he wasn't all that old. Thirty-nine. It just seemed old to me at the time." Reid thought back, remembering, and wished for just a moment of that time back, when he was young and his father was still there. "I just don't think it was fair."

She felt a touch of envy at the faraway look on his face. His expression was sad, yet oddly happy, too. "Good memories?"

The smile spread until it took over his whole face. "Yeah."

She'd guessed right. In a way, it made him wealthier

than she was. She had numbers in a bank account. What he had was priceless. "You're one up on me."

"You and your father don't get along?" It was a natural assumption to make because of the tone she had used. Up to now, Reid was under the impression that she and her father were friends. There seemed to be a genuine bond between them the few times he had seen them together. Was it just for show?

"No, it's not that. I really love my father." Her warmest memory of her childhood was the birthday party her father *did* make on time. "I just didn't get much of an opportunity to know the busy senator until the last eighteen months."

"Is that why you joined the office? To get to know your father?" What sort of person was Shanna Brady? he wondered not for the first time. What made her tick?

"No, it was because I discovered that I enjoyed the work. Getting to know my dad was a bonus. I enjoy politics." She saw that her remark amused him. "It doesn't have to be a dirty game, you know." She remembered what she had heard Whitney say a long time ago. "Representatives are supposed to be, and can be, the servants of the people. It's a pretty damn good system, when it works right." She smiled as another faraway memory floated to her. "When I was a child, I'd sometimes sit at the top of the stairs, listening to my father and his friends talk about different issues, bills that were up for a vote. What could be done if they could just find a way to bring a stubborn 'so-and-so' around."

Shanna glanced out the airplane window. The sky was a crystal blue, except for one pure white cloud. It was so close, she felt she could just open the window and touch it. There was a serenity to flying, if you didn't think about the fact that your life depended on a piece of machinery. And a thousand gears and whatnots. She shuddered slightly and looked away.

"I liked those times a lot better than having to endure my mother's parties." She sighed, remembering the endless boredom, the artificial airs. "All that vacant talk, who owned what, who was going where. Even at that level, it was always a game of one-upmanship. It doesn't interest me in the slightest, not then, not now."

Reid remembered the way Judy had talked about marrying into the Poole family the night she had jilted him. Being invited to dinner parties where women drifted in and out of conversations wearing expensive designer originals had been something Judy had aspired to desperately. How different they were, he thought. Judy had been shallow, easily led astray. There was a strength about Shanna he found very attractive. And very sexy.

"You know, you're one unique lady, Shanna Brady."

He could have sworn her complexion turned a deeper shade of pink at the simple compliment.

There was no reason to feel flustered. She wasn't a child anymore and he was just making conversation. People did that all the time, she told herself.

"Tell that to my mother sometime. She thinks her only daughter is some sort of a social mutant. I think she was hoping for a crown princess to help her reign over charities and gala social events." Abruptly Shanna remembered the concern on her mother's face at the hospital after the accident. "Maybe that's a little too harsh," she amended. "I think she is coming around a little. She did come to Jessica's birthday party even after I refused to have it at the house."

"The house?" he echoed.

"The mausoleum in Georgetown where I spent most of my childhood. It never looked as if people were actually living in it, just passing through. The maids kept it much too clean."

He thought of her life in comparison to his. He had had to work hard for everything he had, but there had always been love, if not enough to eat. He realized now that it made up for a lot of deficiencies. "Not like your place."

She grinned. "It doesn't always look as if a tornado hit it, you know. You've only seen it at its worst."

Reid spread his hands wide, palms up. "I'm an open sort of guy. I'm willing to reevaluate my opinion, given the opportunity."

She couldn't help being amused at his playful tone. "Are you asking for an invitation?"

"In the clumsiest way I know."

But it worked. She had to admit she liked the soft, unhurried approach, coupled as it was with a very persuasive pair of green eyes. She hesitated only for a second, the memory of another evening holding her back. But this wasn't some gay madness sweeping her off her feet. This was just friends, sharing a meal. She wasn't going to let Jordan's memory ruin the rest of her life, the way it had two years. Besides, there wasn't anything romantic about what she proposed. People saw each other socially all the time without it meaning anything. "Dinner, Friday?"

"You cook, too?"

She wasn't exactly qualified to undertake a cooking show on public television. "I put things in the oven. After that, they're on their own."

"You certainly know how to tempt a guy." The smile on his lips softened as he looked at her, her head framed with the bright sunlight shining in through the small window on her right. Yes, he thought, she certainly knew how to tempt a guy, probably without realizing it. "I'll be there," he promised.

Shanna stifled a shiver that nudged at her spine. Maybe she shouldn't have done that after all.

She was backing away. He changed subjects. "So, what's on the agenda for today after we land?"

Work. A nice, safe topic. An area in which she was secure. "We check in with my father's office in Chicago, see what's going on. Then we go to the homeless center. There are a lot of programs in the works that still have to be implemented."

He had wondered about the center Brady had helped build. A lot of politicians gave a great deal of lip service to how they felt about the poor. Like the weather, they talked about the subject, but *did* nothing. Brady seemed to be actively involved in the issue. Reid wanted to know more. "About this homeless center your father's back—"

She could see Reid's questions forming. He probably wanted to know if this was a sham, strictly just for show. She supposed it was a legitimate question.

"It's tax-funded, nonprofit." She thought of the almost constant scrambling for money. There were five on staff that handled only that and they were woefully overworked. "God, is it nonprofit. Dad does what he can to get government funding for it, though that keeps eroding. Mother's fund-raisers help out as well. Private contributions have been plugging the hole so far." She realized that this was the first and possibly only project that the Bradys had undertaken freely as a family. Maybe there was hope for them as a unit after all.

"It's going pretty well, actually. It's gone from being a run-down storefront shelter that was barely twelve by twenty, to a two-story building with facilities to house a hundred people, and more important, to educate them." She was warming to her subject. Of all her father's projects, this is what interested her the most, helping the homeless stand up for themselves. "Do you know how many homeless people are illiterate? The hope is that if we can teach them the basics, they can go on to help themselves. Education still is a powerful tool. Do you know how many of them don't know they can vote?"

Reid looked at her in surprise. He'd been under the same impression. "I thought you couldn't vote if you didn't have a permanent address."

She thought of Jordan's snide remark when she had wanted to give the vagrant money. "Why bother? He can't vote." *Joke's on you, Jordan. He can.*

She looked at Reid. "A lot of people make the same mistake. But homeless people can vote. They just need to be registered. They need to know they have a say in their own lives." She could well identify with that. It had taken her twenty-six years to realize. "It's a beginning."

"Why don't you quit politics and get into charity work completely? The National Alliance to End Homelessness is based in D.C. Why not join them? Or do you want to run for office?"

Though she was light-years away from the shy young woman she had been when she had first begun to work with Jordan on his campaign, the idea of standing before crowds of people, trying to convince them to vote for her did not appeal to Shanna.

"Not me. But I do think that government, eventually, can be moved to do something about this homeless issue. You have to make a noise on every level you can to be noticed, really noticed. But in the long run, you've made no progress unless things are changed legally. It's how our country works."

He crossed his arms before him as he smiled, bemused. He believed that he was actually in the presence of an idealist. "You really buy into that, don't you?"

"The entire apple pie," she answered seriously. "Don't you?"

He thought about it. He had left Jordan because of his own principles, hadn't he? And the chances of advancing quickly had been great, if he played it Jordan's way. "Yeah, I guess I do at that."

"How about you?" she wanted to know. "Any political aspirations?"

He shook his head. Running for office was the furthest thing from his mind. "No. I have absolutely no desire to constantly try and get myself reelected. I'd much rather be working behind the scenes. There's a lot of satisfaction in that."

There were many men who chose to stay out of the limelight for one reason or another and exercise control indirectly. Power for them was the main thing. Power was a mistress, an aphrodisiac that few could resist. "Like Richelieu with the king?"

Writing had always been his main passion. Writing with a purpose. "No, more like Will Rogers on salary. People need to hear language they can understand, statements that say something. Usually it's one or the other, not both. Not everyone has William Buckley's vocabulary. That doesn't mean they should be handed a bunch of platitudes that promise roses and say absolutely nothing about how those roses will be earned." The inflammatory speeches were like that, words that build on other words, images that fed into images. Beneath them all, upon close examination, was nothing more than air.

"And you're the man to write the speeches, make it all clear and good?"

He grinned. She was teasing him, but he played along. "I'm the man to do it."

Shanna grew serious. "Why did you choose to come to work for my father?"

Because I like the guys in the white hats. "Because he uses his own plane."

Her smile was warm and unsuspectingly seductive because of its genuineness. "I see."

22

"*I'm sorry, Ms. Brady,* but there's no way we can take off in this storm. I'm afraid we're grounded for the night."

Shanna looked away from the large bay window of the Ambassador Hotel. Shanna had made reservations for the three of them here, near the airport, when the storm gave no signs of relenting. Outside, the sky was a dark, oppressive gray. It appeared to be dusk, yet sunset wasn't due for another two hours. Rain was beating a fast, furious tattoo against the glass, like an angry hand trying to make her retreat from the window.

She nodded at the pilot's words, disheartened. There wasn't anything he could do about the weather. The rain had been threatening to come since they'd landed early this morning in Chicago. She had hoped it would hold off just long enough for them to leave. At two o'clock, her hopes had been squelched.

It was coming down in endless sheets, rattling the window and howling mournfully. Shanna shivered and wondered how many homeless people hadn't gotten shelter tonight.

"Thanks, Bill." She turned away from the window. She really hated not being with her daughter, but standing here, wishing it would stop, wasn't going to change anything. "It's not your fault." She sighed, running a hand through the blond hair that had curled quickly. Humidity always tangled it, giving her an almost frail, waiflike appearance. "It was bound to happen sooner or later."

Reid wondered what she meant as the pilot left them alone in the lobby. It was rather an odd thing to say. Maybe she was planning to burn the midnight oil again once she got back and felt thwarted.

He leaned against one of the chairs in the lobby, studying her. It had quickly become one of his favorite pastimes. He had memorized every curve of her body, every expression she had. They hadn't been alone together since the night of Jessica's birthday party, yet he felt at ease with Shanna. The silence between them was a comfortable silence. He didn't feel the need to weigh his words with her. There was no performing, no games. Everything was natural. He wondered if she felt the same way.

"Looks like you're finally being forced to kick back a little."

She smiled vaguely, her thoughts centering on Jessica, not on the conversation at hand. *I'm sorry, honey. The storm kept Mommy from you.* "I have my PC."

They'd been given this evening by a whim of fate and the weather, he thought, and he intended to make the most of it. He wanted to talk with her, not watch her fingers fly over a keyboard while she unconsciously worked her lower lip. "What if I steal your plug?"

She looked at him blankly, then realized what he was talking about. "My PC runs on batteries."

She was incorrigible, he thought, but they couldn't kill a guy for trying. "So do you, apparently."

She turned toward the window again, fervently wishing for a clear sky. She shivered as she ran her hands up and down her arms. The plum-colored sleeves crinkled slightly beneath her fingers. "It's not the work I'm concerned about."

Having watched Shanna in action and been told about her dedication, he naturally assumed that her main concern was the project she was putting together for her father. He drew a little closer to her. "What, then?"

She sighed. She was being foolish. Still, she couldn't help the way she felt. "I don't like being separated from Jessica at night. She needs me there to tuck her into bed."

He wanted to smooth away the furrow in her brow with his fingertips, to touch her soft, inviting skin. "You must have missed some nights."

"Not a one," she answered proudly. It hadn't been easy, but she had managed. And it had been worth every effort.

Reid looked at her, awe mingled with disbelief. "Since Jessica was born, you've never been away overnight?" It seemed almost impossible to believe, given her breakneck schedule.

Shanna shook her head. "Never." She shoved her fisted hands into her tailored skirt. "It's important for children to feel secure, to know they can depend on someone." She clenched and unclenched her hands, frustrated. But there was absolutely nothing she could do. "To be able to see the same face above them at night, when everything is dark and scary."

Her voice had grown wistful as she spoke. He suddenly wanted to take her into his arms and comfort her, but it wouldn't be right here. "You speak from experience?"

A sad smile played on her lips. "I speak from lack of experience. I had a parade of nannies wandering through my life. Some nice, some not so nice."

She thought of one in particular. A sharp-featured woman who had laughed at her fear of the dark and made her sleep without the light on. She'd spent six months facing each night in terror before the woman had been fired. Shanna had grown pale and wan and Eloïse had quickly determined the cause, then immediately brought it to the senator's attention. Thank God Jane wasn't like that. Shanna knew her daughter was in safe hands. That didn't make her feel any better about not being there, though.

"And all of them were paid to be with me."

Reid heard the echo of loneliness in her voice and felt sorry for the little girl she had been.

She shook off her melancholy and smiled at Reid. "If I don't give Jessica anything else, I want to give her that feeling of being loved. I want to give her a foundation that'll make her feel confident to walk out into the world and try things because she'll know that there'll be someone to catch her if she needs it and applaud her if she doesn't."

"Wasn't there anyone to catch you?" Reid saw by the look in her eyes that she wanted to call a halt to the conversation. Perhaps they had gone a little further than she had intended when she had begun to talk.

"My grandmother, when she was around." Shanna moved away from the window. "Well, if it's going to rain all night, I might as well go to my room and—"

He stopped her with just the slightest touch on her arm. "How about dinner?"

Maybe a sandwich from room service. Later. "I was

planning to start inputting the last statistics we've
received into my PC—"

He wasn't going to let her talk her way out of it. She
worked far too much. "You have to stop and eat sometime. You're already too thin."

She looked down, surprised at the observation. "I'm
too thin?"

Too harsh a word, he thought. There was still something within her that obviously became skittish at criticism. He smiled at her easily, still holding her arm. "All
right, slender, on the way to thin." His voice lowered
without his being aware of it, his eyes whispering along
her skin until they reached her face. "A man likes to
have something to hold on to."

With a deliberate move, she disengaged herself. "All
right, dinner. Let's get something at the hotel. That way
I can get right to work afterward."

He was already leading her toward the more expensive restaurant in the rear of the building, the one facing
the avenue. "Funny, I had the same thought."

She looked up at his face and saw things she didn't
want to see in his eyes. There was something dangerous
to her peace of mind there, and yet thrilling because of
it. "No, you didn't."

The smile on his face had her blood warming. "Ah,
you've found me out."

Shanna took her room card out of her purse and
inserted it in the slot above the doorknob. She preferred
a key, but there was no arguing with progress. Dinner
had lasted over two hours, far longer than she planned.
She turned as she opened the door, her body blocking
entrance to her room. "I had a very nice evening, Reid."

He didn't want it to be over. Reid glanced at his

watch. "It's only seven-thirty. That doesn't qualify it for an evening."

She could see why he thought he was able to write political speeches. He had a way of turning the simplest things into debates. "Oh?" she asked, amused. "And what are the guidelines?"

"You have to stay out until at least eleven o'clock. *Then* it's an evening." He was so close to her now, she was certain that he could hear her heartbeat. "Think you can put up with my company for another three and a half hours?"

She took a step back. He was definitely in her space, and having him there was crowding her more than she wanted. Yet she couldn't bring herself to withdraw completely. "If you'd like to come in for something to drink—"

He wasn't about to allow her to turn him down. Greed had him wanting her company for a little while longer. "I would."

After Jordan, she was suspicious of anything but a direct approach, not that she'd allow herself to fall into any emotional traps as a consequence. Once was more than enough, thank you very much. "Just say so."

He smiled easily. "I'd like to come in for something to drink."

No matter how hard she tried to resist, his smile worked its way beneath her barriers, as did his disarming manner. Whether he knew it or not, the man was pure smoldering sex appeal, and she had a feeling he knew it. She shook her head and laughed as she opened the door wide enough for both of them.

"Come on in." She crossed to the small bar in the sitting room. "I have no idea what they have readily available here."

It wasn't the drink he was after. It was her company.

He sat down on the sofa facing the bar and shrugged expansively. "Let's play it by ear. Surprise me."

The cabinet contained several magnums of different types of alcohol. Shanna took out a bottle of sloe gin, poured what she assumed was a shot and mixed in some seltzer until it looked more or less the right color. She had no idea about the proper proportions. She rarely drank, and when she did, someone else prepared it. Having watched once, she only had a vague idea what went into a sloe gin fizz.

"Bottoms up." She presented him with a tall glass of light pink liquid.

Reid eyed it dubiously before sampling. He coughed, made a face, and set the glass down on the coffee table with a finality that echoed through room.

Shanna couldn't help grinning at his pained expression. "You said to surprise you."

"I said surprise, not poison." He coughed again, then eyed the glass as if it would take off on its own at any moment. "What is this stuff?"

"A sloe gin fizz. I like them."

He pushed the glass a complete arm's length away on the table. "No offense, but you wouldn't have liked this one. Forget the surprises, just give me scotch on the rocks. Ice," he clarified.

"I know what rocks are." To prove it, she took out the ice bucket.

He eyed the drink she had just mixed. "I'm not taking any chances."

She served him his glass, then poured a little Kahlúa and milk for herself.

"Playing it safe?" He nodded at her drink.

She took a sip from the chunky glass before she sat down. "I like having my head clear at all times. That way I can always stay in control of myself."

Reid look a long, slow drink and savored the way the liquor wound through his body, friendly and warm. He studied her as he felt the alcohol's subtle effects. She sat perched on the edge of the seat, her legs tucked under her as if she was going to jump to her feet at any second. She held her glass in both hands. Control seemed to be a large issue with her, he decided.

He set his glass down on the coffee table. He had no need of alcohol, he realized, to bring on a warm feeling. Just looking at her took care of that. "Do you ever relax, Shanna?"

His scrutiny made her even more uncomfortable. "Of course I do. I'm relaxed right now."

He ran a hand lightly along her spine. She almost snapped in two. "You're sitting like a soldier at attention."

She looked down into her glass. She should have never let him come in. What was she thinking of? "Good posture's important," she mumbled.

"So is having fun." He sat back, crossing one leg over his thigh. His hand still rested on her spine. "Do you have fun, Shanna?"

She wasn't going to be backed into a corner, she promised herself. Jordan had always done that to her emotionally. There weren't going to be any more Jordans in her life.

"I thought that was what we were having this evening." Her eyes narrowed. "Or don't you call it that unless we end up in bed together?" He was just like Jordan, only after his own gratification. She'd been stupid to think otherwise, even for a moment.

It was evident that her ex-husband must have done a job on her. She bristled with scars. "Where we end up, tonight or some other night," he told her softly, "is not the point."

His voice was getting under her skin. *He* was getting

under her skin. She couldn't allow that to happen. Yet she sensed that he understood so much that wasn't spoken. If this was an act, he was one hell of a performer. She wanted to believe him, but hard-learned lessons were difficult to ignore.

"What is the point?" she asked, not nearly as forcefully as she would have liked.

He wound a strand of her hair around his forefinger. She tugged it away, wincing slightly as a hair caught on his finger. "That I think you're afraid to relax, to have fun. That you're afraid of what you're feeling."

She grew more rigid as she moved aside on the sofa. "How would you know *what* I'm feeling?"

"Because"—he slid a finger along her neck and watched her eyes grow dark with a desire she denied— "unless I miss my guess, it's what I'm feeling as well."

She rose. "Nice line." When cornered, attack. It was one of the first rules of survival she had learned in the political arena.

He took his time rising. When he did, his presence ate away at her space. She had nowhere to go. "I don't deal with lines. Not in the speeches I want to write, not in my life. Lines are for people who play games."

She looked down at the drink in her hands, avoiding his eyes. It wasn't a cowardly act. It involved self-preservation. "If you don't play games, how do *you* have fun?"

His body was a scant inch from hers. She could feel the heat from it. "By being honest. By selecting who I spend my time with."

She looked pointedly toward the door. "I think it's time you left."

Reid took the drink she was still holding from her hands and placed it on the coffee table next to his. "I don't."

Shanna searched for bravado, wishing her knees

didn't feel like whipped butter. "I really don't care what you think, or feel."

Reid didn't believe her. "Funny, I do."

"About yourself?" Why not? All men centered their feelings several inches below their belt line. Jordan had taught her that.

"No." Reid buried his fingers in her hair. "About what you think." His eyes drifted to her lips, his very look caressing her seductively. Shanna's breath grew shallow as her pulse began to drum madly at every available point. "And feel."

"What are you doing?" The question came out in a whisper.

The smile was tender, loving. It completely undid her. "If you have to ask, it's been one hell of a long time for you."

She curled her fingers about his forearms. She meant to push him away. She was holding on to him instead. "I don't want—"

He wouldn't let her finish. "I'm going to kiss you." The words slipped along her lips, causing a tremor within her.

She forced the words to her lips, though everything inside of her trembled. "I don't want you to." More than anything on this earth, she wanted him to kiss her. And nothing frightened her more.

Reid stopped and looked deeply into her eyes. "Honestly?"

He had pinned her with a look, pinned her so securely Shanna wanted to cry. She moistened her lips. "That is, I—"

"If you really want me to leave, I will. I only want to stay with you if you want it, too. This has to be mutual, Shanna, or not at all." Reid's voice belied the emotions that were churning within him, tearing him up for want of her. He had wanted her from that very first moment on the beach. "Just say the words. Tell me to stop and I promise I'll go away and leave you alone."

She wanted to. With all her might, she wanted to tell him to go.

With a sob, she pulled his face down to hers and pressed her lips against his.

She wanted this.

Oh God, how she wanted this precious, intimate contact with a man. She wanted more than anything in the world to feel like a woman, a whole woman. She wanted that heady rush that had been promised her light-years ago when her body had first yearned to be loved. The heady rush she had never found with Jordan.

It was absolutely illogical, bordering on insanity, what she was about to do. She was about to leap from a plane and free-fall. And she was going to do it of her own volition.

Without a parachute.

The only thing that was waiting for her was the ground below, and it was coming up at her at an incredibly fast speed.

23

It took everything Reid had to restrain himself, to draw away from the overwhelming pull of her kiss. Never had he expected so much passion, so much hunger. On both their parts. The magnitude of it devastated him.

Catching his breath, he lifted Shanna into his arms and carried her to the bedroom.

Her mind and body were reduced to the consistency of taffy left out in hundred-degree weather. He desired her, really desired her. She could feel it and it roused a flame within her.

But once Reid set her down on the floor, the old fears returned coupled with new ones. She didn't want to become intimately involved with anyone. Her relationship with Jordan had been too painful for her to risk trying another. There were no rewards at the end, only emptiness and feelings of inadequacy.

And yet . . .

And yet Reid made her yearn for it to be possible.

"Reid, I think . . ." She couldn't talk, though the need to protest was deep within her. Shanna's words faded from her lips like dewdrops sliding down a petal to the thirsty ground as soon as he touched her, as soon as he looked at her.

Longing fought with fear. Longing was stronger.

"Shh." With gentle hands, he smoothed her hair away from her face. Since he had first seen her on the beach, he had imagined her just like this, alone in a room with him, desire vibrating between them.

She found herself aching for his touch, wanting to feel it on every part of her body. It had been so long, so very long.

"I think—" she tried again, but without feeling.

He kissed each eye as it fluttered closed beneath his lips. "You think too much, Shanna."

Her lids felt heavy, her limbs drugged even as excitement pulsed through her soul. His mouth seemed to awaken every nerve ending in her face and neck. What was he doing to her? The merest touch and she felt herself falling apart. There were diametrically opposed reactions taking place all through her. Ready, yet hesitant. Weak, yet strong. She was solid, yet everything within her felt liquid. A complete caldron of feelings was all tumbling together.

"You don't play fair," she moaned. Only part of her was resisting the madness, the rush that was pulling at her. The rest was racing toward it, even though she knew only disappointment waited for her.

But what if perhaps, just this once . . . ?

"I don't play at all." Reid stopped and looked into her eyes, his own deadly serious. "I told you, no games, Shanna." Slowly he slid his hands along the length of her arms. "I've wanted you ever since I saw you sitting there alone on the beach."

It seemed like a million years ago and yet only yesterday. "But you didn't do anything about it." It had surprised her, she remembered, the ease with which he had retreated. "You just walked away."

"You were married then," he reminded her. Tilting his head, he lightly pressed his lips to her throat. The pulse there jumped and throbbed. Her reaction heightened his own arousal.

Her head swimming, she had trouble concentrating on what he was saying. "And that made a difference?"

"It did to me," he whispered against her skin, creating tidal waves of unquenchable desire within her.

Her body heated quickly, every part tingling. It had been over two years since she had experienced anything remotely like this, over two years since anyone had even so much as touched her. She hadn't allowed it. Now she was hungry, so incredibly hungry.

Yet something within her pulled back, remembering the way it had been. Remembering the yearning that went unfulfilled, the needs that had gone unsatisfied. She didn't want to rush toward a peak, waiting, wanting, only to find herself there alone. She couldn't bear that sort of disappointment again.

Make me trust you, Reid.

She splayed her hands against his chest, thinking that she was pushing him back while her fingers only managed to tangle themselves in his shirt. "Reid."

Panicky protest surrounded his name. She was afraid, he thought. He could see it in her eyes, hear it in her voice. Why? Had Jordan somehow distorted all this for her? Had he ruined what could be the most beautiful, giving act between a man and a woman?

Reid cupped her face in his hands, his voice low and gentle. "I'll go slow, Shanna, I promise. We'll take every step together."

He didn't lie.

He took her on the journey slowly, easily. But the fire came oh so fast. He wasn't just tearing off her clothes, eager to get into her body, eager to take his pleasure and be done with it. It wasn't just a singular thing for him. Reid was trying to give her pleasure. The thought burst upon her like a comet streaking across the darken sky.

Shanna wanted to cry.

It was a fantasy come to life. A dream. She slid her hands along his hard, muscular back, pressing him to her. No, it wasn't a dream. He was here, beside her, making love to every inch of her body just by skimming his hand along the length of it. He was doing it by kissing her face, her eyes, her throat. Each kiss he brushed along her lips bloomed, deepening, taking her to dark, exotic places where she had never been. This was more exciting, more wondrous than anything she had ever experienced. And they were still standing up. Weren't they?

Shanna forced open her eyes, hardly realizing, until she did so, that they had drifted shut. She wanted to look at him. "We're still dressed?" she asked incredulously.

She was so adorably sweet, he wanted to laugh, but he didn't. Somehow instinct told him that would be the worse thing to do.

"A situation that can be remedied. But not," he warned, "too quickly." Reid grinned wickedly as he toyed with the top button of her blouse, slowly working it free of the hole. "Remember how you unwrapped my gift? You said you liked savoring the surprise. I've given that a great deal of thought and decided that your approach definitely has its merits."

He watched her eyes as he undid each one of the buttons on her blouse. They grew huge with anticipation and darkened with untried passion. He felt her tremble beneath his hands. "I won't hurt you, Shanna. I

swear I won't hurt you." He touched her face for a
moment, wishing he could read her thoughts. "Do you
believe me?"

She nodded slowly as if hypnotized. Her eyes never
left his.

Her blouse was hanging open. He slipped it from her
shoulders in a gentle, massaging motion, until it was
completely off. It drifted from her arms to the floor
unnoticed. Her bra was a deep lavender, done up with
black lacings in the front. He kissed her temple lightly
and felt her sigh as he untied the lacing and slowly
tugged it out. He heard her slight gasp as the bra fell
open, exposing her breasts to his touch.

"Shh," he murmured, struggling to curb the heated
demands of his own flesh.

As much as part of him wanted her now, this instant,
he couldn't frighten her, couldn't give vent to what he
wanted selfishly. What was more important to him, what
he wanted more than simple sexual gratification, was to
bring her with him to the ecstasy that waited for them
both. He found no satisfaction with racing there alone.
The pleasure, the satisfaction came with seeing her
reach it just a heartbeat ahead of him. Of watching her
expression as she came with him.

He stroked her breasts, his long, patient fingers
arousing her almost beyond endurance. Anticipation
gripped her in an iron vise, banishing Shanna's fear to
some faraway, seldom-visited corner of her soul. The
only fear she had now was that he would stop kissing
her, that this fiery, lyrical dance between them would
end, casting her into cold, lonely despair.

She had never been sexually satisfied. Jordan had
been her first, her only lover, and he had always been
sated long before she could be properly aroused. He
had never taken the time to bring her with him.

She ached to feel Reid within her, to be one with him, yet she didn't want this wonderful sensation bursting along her body ever to end. This, this was the best part.

She couldn't remember when her skirt had pooled to the floor, or how she came to be standing before him completely nude. It was all happening within a hot haze of disorientation. Her only frame of reference in this strange, new world of fire and unspeakably wondrous sensations was Reid and the way he was making her feel.

When he had first kissed her, desire had been the instigator. He had given in to it, meaning to pleasure them both. He had wanted to give her something of himself for what he would take. But he was getting far more than he felt he gave. Far more than he had bargained for. He was just as awestruck, just as dazed as she by what was happening between them. There was an innocence in the kisses she ardently returned that almost humbled him. A hunger in her touch, in the way her mouth took his each time he kissed her lips.

"Slow, slow," he cautioned, knowing he wouldn't be able to hold out if she continued to press. So sweet, so incredibly sweet.

She felt his smile against her lips and drew back, stung. Memories returned to haunt her. "You're laughing at me."

The accusation stunned him. "Why would I do that?" He saw the hurt shining in her eyes. "Did he laugh at you?" he asked softly.

She remembered her wedding night. She'd been so clumsy, so eager, so frightened. And when Jordan had discovered that she was a virgin, he had laughed, saying something about it being just his luck to find the only twenty-one-year-old virgin in Washington, D.C. He'd quickly covered his remark, but it had rung in her ears, mocking her, mocking her attempts at lovemaking.

Shanna nodded, suddenly swallowing tears.

Reid wished he could have had Jordan alone in the room for just five minutes. Five minutes to make the man pay for turning Shanna into a mass of emotional scars and pain. But there was nothing to be gained by beating the man into a pulp. He had somehow to undo the damage the other man had heartlessly caused.

Reid kissed her bare shoulder. "I'm not laughing, Shanna," he told her in a whisper that made her very skin glow. He had shed his own clothes quickly. His body ripe with wanting her, Reid took her into his arms. "I'm smiling. Because I want you so much it hurts. And you're here with me now."

Placing both of his hands, palm up, against hers, he laced his fingers through hers, binding her to him. "Make love with me now, Shanna."

She tilted her head, awed at his words. "You're asking me?"

"I'm asking," he assured her, and she knew that even now, if she said no, he would back away. Shanna cupped his cheek with her hand, her fingers feathering along his bronzed skin.

"Yes."

He turned her palm up, kissing it. He saw her stiffen. "What?"

It had come back to her in a cold wave. Déjà vu. "Jordan used to do that."

Reid frowned. It wasn't going to work for them if there were going to be ghosts in the room. Didn't she see that?

"I don't want him here, Shanna." Reid tapped her temple. "I want you to banish him from your mind. He has no place here between us. Not now, not ever. Do you understand?"

She pressed her lips together and swallowed. The

hesitant look in her eyes remained. She was completely different from the competent woman he had seen in the office. It was as if a hurt child still lived within the woman she had molded herself to become.

"Let me show you how it should be done, Shanna," he urged more gently. "Let me love you the way you deserve to be loved."

Tenderly he laid her across the bed, then joined her, his nude body next to hers, primed, ready. Yet he waited for her to give a sign.

She felt the heat, the all-consuming heat along her body as his clever fingers found all her secret places, secret places she never even knew she had. She vibrated against his touch, arching, moaning, twisting so that she could feel him against her. He was causing things to happen. Strange things. Tiny explosions were erupting within her. Was this what making love was really like?

And still he held back, though it was taking almost superhuman strength to do so when all he wanted was to lose himself in her.

He made her ready for him. With his lips drugging her, his hand dipped down between her legs, slowly working her into a frenzy. He brought her up, each time higher. She gasped, her nails digging into his back, as the explosions increased in magnitude. She fell back, dazed. Her lungs felt as if they were bursting as she struggled to pull in air. And then he'd do it again. Agony and ecstasy, tangled together.

When he finally slipped into her, she felt herself spiraling upward to a place she had never been, had never imagined. Their hips joined in an ancient dance that was as new as the next sunrise, as old as the dawn of time. When she cried out, it was from joy, not from a plea for him to wait, the way she had with Jordan.

Nothing was the way it had been with Jordan.

* * *

"Where are you?" he asked, amused, as she opened her eyes. He had watched her lightly doze off and on for an hour.

"Wonderland. Paradise. Xanadu." She breathed out each location with a contented sigh.

He laughed softly, lifting her hand to his lips as he pressed another kiss there. "I take it it was good for you." He assumed a very comical French accent. "Eet was good for me, too."

"The best," she answered. And it was. The very best, exceeding anything she had ever imagined.

He shifted her so that she was suddenly on top of him. "Oh, no, the best, my dear Ms. Brady, is yet to be."

Her eyes opened wide as she felt him suddenly hard beneath her. "Again?"

"Again."

"Oh, boy."

He laughed, his arm tightening around her. "Spoken like a woman after my own heart."

She grew serious. She wanted him to know. To understand that she understood the rules. "I won't be," she promised.

"Won't be what?"

"After your heart. No strings attached. I know that. You don't have to worry that I think this means more than what it is."

He wondered if she was saying that for his benefit or for her own. In either case, they'd resolve that when they came to it. But not now. "Just shut up and kiss me."

"With pleasure." Shanna had never meant anything so wholeheartedly in her life.

24

"*Shanna, could you come* to my office, please?"

Shanna looked up from her computer monitor. She had been going from screen to screen, searching for a data file she had saved some time ago. The information there would help substantiate the conclusions of her report. The senator needed this report to support a legislation proposal he was putting forth. The report had to be as clear, as definitive as possible. Damn, where was that file?

Her father was standing in the doorway of the office she had occupied for the last six months. She had initially protested that she didn't need so much space. Now there was no available space left. It was all taken up with boxes crammed with files and various reports and pieces of information that hadn't yet been inputted into the computer.

"Sure. What's up?"

Normally he didn't stop by her office, unless it was to take her out to an occasional lunch. He was so busy that there wasn't time for a conversation during the day. If he wanted her, he just buzzed her on the telephone. Something was in the wind.

"There's something I want to discuss with you."

There was a pregnant note in his voice that made her curious. She wondered if it had anything to do with next year's national elections. So many people they both knew were stepping down or retiring, afraid to lose in the next public vote, or just tired of the stress that went hand in hand with the job if it was to be done well.

As she followed him to his office Shirley raised a quizzical brow in her direction. Shanna lifted her shoulders in response as she walked through the entrance of the corner office. She was just as much in the dark as her assistant.

Shanna crossed to the chair before his desk and sat down. It was the same chair she had sat in when she had asked him for a job. It seemed a lifetime ago. And it had been. Except for an occasional lapse, she no longer resembled the girl who had asked. Funny, she had anticipated a struggle with lapses. Yet it hadn't been that difficult for her. There had been a rough transition period. She had felt a little awkward at first, but that had been a normal reaction to a new situation, new people. It had passed quickly.

She had learned something about herself in the interim. She had met the real Shanna and was basically pleased with the woman she had found.

The senator closed the door behind him and walked slowly to his desk. Sitting down, he steepled his fingers before him and studied the only child he had ever created. He had provided good schools and good teachers, but she had more or less raised herself. And turned out pretty damn well. Far better than he knew he had had a right to hope for. By the time he had realized his error, she was a woman, more in need of a mentor than a father. She had made him proud.

But he had no way of knowing how she was going to react to his proposal. Never one to rush right in, he had given it a great deal of thought before arriving at this conclusion.

It had been a long time since she had seen her father this serious. "You certainly are making a mystery out of this." Was it his health? "Is something wrong?"

"Brideen's retiring."

So that was it. "You're kidding." Congressman Jack Brideen was her father's best friend. It was because of Brideen that her father had gotten into politics in the first place. They had been junior congressmen from Illinois together, bolstering each other's confidence in the early days as they learned the ropes. When her father had gone on to run for the Senate, Brideen had been his staunchest supporter. It was Brideen who had brought Whitney into their corner. It just wouldn't be the same for her father without him.

Shanna watched her father as he shifted in his chair. He looked old to her. His face was drawn and she could see where the years had touched him.

"No, I wish I was. Jack's tired of the good fight, he says." The senator leaned forward, studying her face. She was a good-looking woman. Where had that little girl gone? He had to stop this. He was beginning to behave like an old man. "He wants to pass the mantle to someone younger, someone with the same interests we share. Someone who would continue to fight for and push for the same things we believe in." Her father dropped his hands, palms down, on his desk. He made Shanna think of a preacher at his pulpit, about to come to the crux of his sermon. "Jack asked me to do some scouting around and see if I could find that kind of a person."

Did he want her to get involved in someone else's campaign? She already had her hands full. Campaigning along with what she was already working on would require an eight-day week.

She saw a smile begin to nudge away his serious look. "I'd say that by your expression, your scouting trip was successful."

"If you mean do I think I've found the right person, yes, I do."

Why was he looking at her like that? Unconsciously she placed her hands on the armrests for support as she leaned forward. "Who do you have in mind?"

Diamond Jim Brady's smile lived on in her father's face. It almost lit the room. Someone had once said that when he smiled, Roger Brady could have gotten a tree stump to vote for him. "You."

"Me?" He couldn't possibly mean that. She must have missed something vitally important in the conversation. "To do what?"

The senator rose, excited by the idea now that it was out in the open. He leaned on the edge of the desk, his arms crossed in front of him. Bradys in both houses of the government. It would be wonderful. "To take Brideen's place."

"Brideen's from Illinois. I don't live in Illinois." It was crazy, absolutely crazy. His best friend's departure had caused her father to temporarily lose his common sense. She couldn't possibly run for office.

Brady saw the stunned look in his daughter's eyes. She had absolutely no ambitions, he realized. All that dedication, all that energy, and no thirst for power. It made her perfect for the job. The party needed people like her.

"Technically you still live in Illinois. You're registered there, even though you live here. And you certainly put in enough time there. Besides"—he grinned—"you still get some mail at the house, don't you?" He was referring to the family residence. It was a rhetorical question, but she answered it anyway.

"A few pieces occasionally, yes, but—"

Run? For a political office? Her? It seemed absolutely incredible.

"That qualifies it as a place of residence," Brady concluded. His voice was soft, lulling. It was the same voice that inspired confidence and trust within his constituents. "The election is over a year away and we have primaries to face first. You have time to get a place of your own in Illinois to make it official."

He saw the doubt lingering in her face. She still wasn't convinced. Persuading her was going to take some time, but he was certain he had made the right choice. "Shanna, you care about the same things I do. I've seen you out on the street, talking to people during my reelection campaign. You weren't just not mouthing platitudes, you believe in what we stand for."

Believing wasn't enough. "I don't know, Dad." There were a hundred obstacles. Including her own insecurities. "I don't think that I'm that qualified to run."

"Because you're not a lawyer?" he guessed, knowing the way her mind worked. "Hell, Shanna, the government's filled up to here with lawyers." He passed his hand over his head, frowning. "A few honest, caring citizens are what's really needed, not lawyers. The original signers of the Declaration of Independence weren't all lawyers, they were people. People who cared enough to get involved." He could see by her eyes that he had her thinking and that was all he could ask, for now. "I know it's too soon for a decision, but at least tell me you'll think about it."

She rose and smiled. "I'll think about how crazy it all seems."

"No." Brady placed his hands on his daughter's shoulders just as she was about to walk out. "Think about the good you can do, Shanna. If the wrong person is elected, it can undermine all the good we've managed to do." He shrugged. "People have different priorities. They can see the allocation of funds as being needed in different areas. The educational and social programs we've worked so hard to implement can be cut in a year if I don't get the backing in the House that I need. Brideen's leaving means I'll have one less man on my side. One less person," the senator amended with a smile. "I need your enthusiasm working for me in the House."

"All right." She nodded reluctantly. It still sounded farfetched, but it was beginning to grow on her ever so slightly. And he was her father. This was the first time he had ever asked her to do something. Why did it have to be something so completely alien to her? "I'll think about it. But the idea of running scares the hell out of me."

He wasn't taking that as an excuse. They'd all been there. And he was convinced she was going to make one damn good congresswoman. "Good. Overconfidence is something I never trusted in a candidate."

She stopped in the doorway, one hand on the door. She had to know. "Then why did you back Jordan in the beginning?"

"Because he was your husband and I thought you wanted it," he said honestly. Though Jordan had the charisma to charm both the voters and his fellow politicians, Brady had had the feeling that Jordan would support anything, align himself with anyone, to achieve his goals. The end justifies the means was his credo. Watching the man's voting record in the last two years had proven him correct.

Her father's answer couldn't have surprised her more. "What about your principles?"

"Sometimes, when you love someone"—affectionately he stroked her cheek, thinking of all the time he had stupidly let slip by, time he could never recapture—"they get a little bent."

"I'll think about the proposition," she promised, touched.

Reid waited until after dinner when they were in her living room. She had been in a pensive mood all evening. It had begun in the office. He had hoped she'd volunteer the information on her own. When she didn't, it bothered him that he had to ask. She still didn't trust him enough to share her feelings, though she was sharing his bed and he hers on a regular basis. There were still barriers between them, barriers because of who and what she was and who and what she had been.

He waited until she sat down on the sofa beside him. "Something's been on your mind all day, what is it?" As if to emphasize his point, he traced a swirl of hair at her temple.

Shanna frowned, working her lower lip. She should have known he'd realize that something was wrong. He always seemed to know. It was a comforting thought, as long as she didn't allow herself to get carried away and fall into the tender trap. "Brideen's retiring."

He waited. It wasn't enough to put her in this mood. "I heard the rumor."

She laced her fingers together and took a deep breath. "My father thinks that I stand a good chance of taking his place." Her words had all come out in a rush, as if it was too fantastic to say slowly. She looked at

Reid, expecting to see the same shock she had felt at the suggestion. It wasn't there. "He seems so keen on it, I don't know how to let him down."

"Simple," Reid told her. "Don't."

Shanna stared at him. Had he lost his mind, too? "What?"

He didn't see her problem. Since the day she had told him how she felt about politics, he had seen this coming. He was amazed that she hadn't, that she actually needed convincing. "I think you should try for it."

"Not you, too," she groaned.

"Yes, me, too." He swept her hair away from her neck and lightly glided his tongue along the sensitive area. She shivered. "Maybe then you'll stop running," he murmured against her skin.

She pulled away. "Running?"

"Yes, running." He wasn't about to match her annoyed tone, even though the way she acted at times did annoy him. She worked too hard, tried too hard. It was, as someone had once commented about her, as if she was trying to validate her existence on this planet. "From demons and shadows. If you win, and you will"— he laid a finger to her lips to stop her protest—"you'll have your own shadow to cast. You already do, but maybe this'll prove it to you." He shrugged, leaning back on the sofa. "The choice is yours."

Choice. It had a familiar ring. She smiled fondly. "My grandmother told me that the last time I saw her."

Her eyes softened when she spoke about the other woman. This was someone, he thought, who had meant a great deal to Shanna. "She wanted you to run for office?"

"No." Shanna laughed. "She talked to me about making choices, the right choices." She studied his face intently. "You really think I have a chance?"

He saw fear mixed with excitement. She wanted this. All she needed was a push. Well, he could certainly give her that. "Sure. You actually believe in the system, you're dedicated, and you have me in your corner. What more do you need?"

He made it sound so incredibly simple. But he had never been through a campaign before. She had. "A miracle."

"We make our own miracles, Shanna." He took her into his arms. "Each and every day, choosing the right path, we make our own miracles."

Leaning over, he nibbled on her ear and watched with pleasure as her eyes fluttered shut. They'd been lovers now for three months, ever since that night in the hotel, and he still hadn't gotten enough of her. He doubted that he ever would.

Reid slid her onto his lap. "Now, if I could interest you in making a little magic, all my prayers would be answered. At least for the night."

She could already feel her pulse beginning to escalate. "Wait," she said with effort. "I want to talk." And she knew she couldn't if he turned her mind into mush.

"I can talk and nuzzle at the same time." Watching her eyes, he licked the tip of his finger, then slowly slid it along the outline of her ear. "I'm very talented that way."

Her limbs were starting to rebel against the calm she was trying to maintain. "No one's arguing with your talent, Reid, but I'm serious."

"So am I, a serious nuzzler." As he moved to kiss her again he saw the plea in her eyes. "Okay, first talk, then nuzzle." He let her slide off his lap. "So, what's bothering you?"

The whole idea. It was so frightening. "Will you really be in my corner?"

The question hurt. When would she ever trust him? "You have to ask?"

She shrugged. She hadn't meant for it to cause a rift. "It's just that it would mean leaving my father's office." She was thinking of his career, not hers.

"Not really. I can still continue working for your father and be there for you when you're giving your own speeches." Now that he was finally on his way up within the senator's staff, he didn't want to let that opportunity slip through his fingers. But he intended to be there for Shanna when she needed him. That was important in a very private way. "It won't be easy, but it can be done. The senator would probably encourage me with his blessings," he pointed out. "This was his idea, remember? I can lend you a hand with your speeches when you need it." He grinned at the thought. It was, after all, his goal. "I think I'd like that."

She chewed on a corner of her lip. She knew she wanted him with her on this, that she would feel better knowing he was there. But there were risks for both of them. "Are you sure? What would it do to your career to be associated with a loser—if we lose?"

She needed a severe dose of confidence. "Who says you're going to lose?"

Shanna studied his face, expecting to see a teasing grin. Instead his expression was one of encouragement. "You really mean that, don't you?"

"I told you once that I didn't play games, Shanna. I believe in you, in that big heart of yours that seems to have room for everyone." Except, at times he thought, for him.

Lowering his head, he pressed a kiss to her breasts. Even through the clothing, she could still feel the burning effects.

"You'll make a terrific congresswoman. And all those

homeless people that we registered, who do you think they'll vote for?"

She hadn't worked so hard to organize the committee to register the homeless for her own personal gain. That was for self-centered people like Jordan. And she didn't want to run on a platform that made them believe she could do things she couldn't. "I can't make their life better single-handedly."

"No, but you can try. And you can give them hope." He began to undress her as he talked. "Nobody can ask for more than that of anyone. You'll do it?"

She gave him the same answer she gave her father, though the words hadn't come out as breathlessly the first time. "I'll think about it."

"Good. Now here's something to do while you're thinking." He slipped his hand beneath her skirt as he teased her lips with his mouth.

Shanna struggled to hang on to her senses. He could wipe them out faster than she would have believed possible. "Reid, Jane might come out."

"I paid her off. She's in her room until the turn of the next century." He rose, then lifted her up in his arms. "Destination, bedroom. Any more arguments?"

She laughed as she laced her arms around his neck. "Not a one."

But it wasn't Reid who made up Shanna's mind for her, or even her father. It was Erikka.

She was a small, dirty child of about five or six, hanging on to her mother's torn coat as the woman stood on a busy street corner. In the woman's dirty hands she held a sign that read WE'RE HUNGRY. WILL WORK FOR FOOD. The woman had that faded, permanently brown, dirty look that people who lived on the street acquired.

There was still a pinkness to her daughter's cheeks, but color had long since fled from the woman's.

Shanna was driving by in her sedan when she saw them. They were standing on the opposite side of the street. Glancing to see that there weren't any cars in the way, Shanna made a U-turn and doubled back.

When Shanna pulled her car up at the curb, the woman shuffled over to her. She was twenty or perhaps thirty, and her red hair was matted against her scalp. A small tongue licked along lips that were cracked. "Do you have a job for me?"

The woman's voice was raspy, as if she was suffering from a deep chest cold. Shanna opened the passenger side. "I have a place for you to go."

The woman looked at Shanna suspiciously, obviously distrustful. She pushed her daughter behind her protectively. "I don't want no charity. Me and Erikka don't need handouts." The woman pulled her shoulders back beneath the baggy overcoat that hung about her like a cast-off gray tent. It had never been her size. Charity took away choices. You took what you were given, Shanna thought. "I'm strong. I can work."

"We'll find you something, I promise," Shanna said softly, looking at the little girl. "Come with me."

The woman still hung back, but Erikka, with bright, dark eyes that still hadn't lost their hope, climbed into the car and smiled shyly at Shanna. The woman had no choice but to follow.

If she was a congresswoman, perhaps she *could* help a lot of Erikkas keep their pride and get the simple things they were entitled to.

She would tell her father, she decided, that she was going to run in the primary. Right after she took Erikka and her mother to a homeless shelter she knew of.

25

She couldn't imagine that a body could feel this exhausted and live if she hadn't gone through labor. When Reid had unlocked the hotel door for her, it was all Shanna could do to put one foot in front of the other until she reached the nearest chair. She collapsed into it, barely having enough energy to kick off her shoes. Her right forearm felt as if it was cramping up and her fingers were painfully stiff from shaking what must have been an ocean of hands. The muscles in her cheeks felt as if they'd frozen in place permanently.

At least she would die smiling, she thought.

Reid had flown in last night to be at her side and he had endured today with her. He popped the top of her favorite diet drink she kept stocked in the hotel room and handed it to her. "Here, I think you might like this."

It was hard to get her fingers around the can. "Thank you." She closed her eyes and drank, as if the effort to keep them open was too much for her. She let out a long sigh and then drank again.

Reid sat on the arm of her chair. "You look wiped out."

She handed the can back to him. Her eyelids slipped closed again. "You are an extremely intuitive person."

He grinned. "It's a gift."

Whenever he could get away, he'd been at her side these last few months, editing her speeches and holding her hand when she needed it. The primaries were less than five weeks away, and though she appeared to be her party's front-runner, she took nothing for granted. She continued giving speeches to organizations, visiting shelters for the homeless, the abused, and the forgotten. Both ends of the spectrum. The message was always the same. Raising social consciousness and promoting education were the only keys to end morally embarrassing situations. People had to pitch in to help people. The government should be there to give them a start, but not to fix everything, for a government that controlled everything could someday take everything away.

It was an odd feeling, he thought as he looked down at her, being in love with a crusader. Well, he admitted to himself, there it was. He was in love with her. He hadn't planned on this happening, wasn't completely certain that she could even return his love. But it didn't alter the way he felt about her. For better or for worse, he was in love with her.

Right now he was in love with a woman under a great deal of stress, a woman who desperately needed to relax before the next round got under way. There wasn't much time. "Want me to draw you a hot bath?" Reid offered.

"No." She tried to wave her hand at the suggestion and only managed to move her wrist slightly. "I'll probably slide under the water, not have enough strength in my arms to pull myself out and drown."

He placed the can of soda down on the coffee table. "I never noticed, were you always this cheerful?"

She laughed weakly. How had she gotten herself talked into this madness? "Cheerful is for people who don't have to visit every single nook and cranny in the sixth district."

She rotated her neck, trying to work the kink out. It felt stiff and painful. When she felt his fingers on her back, she almost cried out. And then he began to massage, slowly, gently, working on her shoulders, her neck. She would have purred if she had enough strength. Heaven had come to claim her. Her head dropped back as the tension slowly ebbed away. "Oh, please, don't stop."

Reid laughed, slowly kneading the muscles along her spine. "Funny, that's what all the beautiful congress-women say."

"They'd better not. I'll scratch their eyes out."

"Why, Ms. Brady, I never knew you to be territorial."

She sighed as his fingers worked magic. "You haven't been paying attention, then."

Bending, he was about to kiss her when there was a knock on the door. Shanna groaned. "If that's anyone from the press, tell them I died. Story and photos at eleven."

"Not after all the work we've put in on your campaign, you don't." He kissed the top of her head like a child who needed encouragement before crossing to the door. "Die after the election."

All she could manage at the moment was to turn her head in his direction. Where was she going to get the energy to go to the next event? "That's just what I'm afraid of," she murmured as Reid opened the door.

"Afraid?" Doreen Priestly asked, her well-shaped eyebrows raised as she walked in.

Tall, stately, with short-cropped silver-gray hair, Doreen had been Brideen's campaign manager for his last three successful bids for Congress. She had reluctantly agreed to offer her services to Shanna when she had come out and announced her candidacy. It had begun strictly as a favor to Brideen and Brady. She was going to see what she could do to tailor Shanna's image for the public, then hand over the reins to someone else.

But after observing Shanna address several groups, after listening to her speak, Doreen had become a convert. Shanna, she felt, had something new and fresh to offer. Enthusiasm. Genuine enthusiasm. And she definitely wasn't of the "government owes me a living" persuasion. Doreen respected that. She gladly began to shape the rest of Shanna's campaign.

Doreen breezed into the room, stopping to take a sip of the soda on the coffee table. Her ever-present time-management gray binder was clutched against her perfectly flat bosom. She favored gray, all shades of gray, but there was nothing gray or subdued about her approach to things.

She looked down a long, angular nose that gave her face a sharp, birdlike look and had eluded the surgeon's scalpel despite her late mother's pleas.

"Successful candidates for office aren't afraid, Shanna," she chided. "They're supposed to fearlessly stand up against the odds." They had done well with the crowds today and Doreen was exceptionally pleased with the latest polls. They gave Shanna a six-percent edge over her closest opponent. Doreen planned to see that it stayed that way.

Shanna looked down at her bare toes. "Right now I'm not sure if standing up is in my repertoire."

Doreen flipped open her eight-by-eleven binder to the page marked Friday and tapped a line in the middle

of it. "You have an hour before your speech at the Wainwright Women's Club. Get it into your repertoire."

Shanna sat up, struggling to be alert. "Women's
club? Weren't we supposed to stop at the homeless
shelter next?"

Doreen shook her head, wide gold hoop earrings
swinging back and forth in rhythm. She checked the
schedule again before shutting the gray padded book.
"We were, but this fell into our lap. I thought I told
Claire to call you about it." She shrugged, annoyed at
her assistant, but not really worried. "You're good on
your feet. Use the speech you used for the Elks Club
and change it where it needs it."

"What about the shelter?" Shanna persisted. She had
made all the arrangements for the official visit herself.

"Only time for one, sugar. Even you can't be in two
places at once. You've got a press conference right after
that."

It would be a lot easier standing before a roomful of
smiling women than facing the heartbreak, the hope-
lessness that always resided within homeless shelters.
But she hadn't started on this road to take the easy way
out. She made her decision. It wasn't even close. "Okay,
reschedule the women's club."

Reid would have placed money that she was going to
say that. The woman had a one-track mind. Too bad, he
thought, that he couldn't divert the track in his direction
a little more often. But that, he had come to accept, was
what made her Shanna. And what made him love her. It
was the way she cared, her steadfast loyalty and principles, even if they weren't popular. He admired the fact
that she was so independent, yet worried that perhaps
that would be the very thing that would come between
them eventually. Only time would tell.

"No can do." There was a note of finality in Doreen's

voice. She knew what worked for candidates and where the important votes were to be found. The president of the Wainwright Women's Club was an influential woman in the area. A large fish in a small pond, Doreen thought with a smile. If she backed Shanna, it would have a rippling effect, like a stone cast in the water, creating rings that reach farther and farther out. People like that couldn't be ignored.

Reid glanced at Shanna, waiting. He knew what was coming next. "All right," Shanna agreed, "move the press conference."

This wasn't what Doreen wanted to hear. Her tone was steely. "To when?"

Shanna shook her head. "Not when, where. Let's take them to the shelter."

"That's damn depressing." But the woman wasn't really protesting the idea. Possibilities were beginning to formulate in her mind. Yes, this could work out very well. Even better than she had initially arranged. Shanna Brady, the candidate with a heart. Good press was always welcome.

"So is being homeless." Shanna got her second wind. She knew it was important to impress the right people to get elected, but she couldn't do it at the sacrifice of her beliefs. It would mean blunting the point of her platform. "Do it. Maybe if some footage gets on the local news, somebody'll be moved to donate time, money, a job, something. Anything. Every scrap helps. The public keeps thinking this is someone else's problem. It's not. It's everyone's problem. Because it can happen to anyone. Those people didn't start out being homeless. They started out with hopes and dreams."

Reid applauded. "Very good for a woman who's too exhausted to even stand up."

Doreen was furiously scribbling memos in her book. "I like that line." She made a note of the key people she had to call to rearrange things. "The one about it being everyone's problem." The book made a muffled thump as she closed it. "Be sure to use it at the press conference today."

Shanna looked at her sharply. She had no intention of coming off like a cheap politician, playing angles and saying things she knew people wanted to hear. She didn't want to play Jordan's game. She rose. "It's not a line, Doreen. I mean it."

Doreen patted Shanna's cheek on her way out. "That's why I'm here, sugar. That's why I'm here. I only work for the real McCoy." There was a smile on her face. The serious look was in her eyes. She turned to Reid. "Take care of her. I'll go see what I can do with our friends from the fourth estate." She closed the door behind her. Reid flipped the lock.

When Reid turned around, he saw Shanna had crossed to the window. He walked up behind her and slipped his arms around her waist. Shanna leaned into him. She projected determination. To those who didn't know better, she was a pillar of strength. But beneath it all, he knew she was still vulnerable, still in need of being protected. Maybe now more than ever because she had never put herself on the line before. All he could do for her was give her the support, real and emotional, that she needed. "Get you anything?"

It felt good to be held. It would be so nice if things were simple. If there wasn't this overwhelming drive within her to prove something, to *do* something. If she could just relax and let herself be loved. And just be. But she had things to accomplish and she'd seen what happened when she let herself fall in love. Her life became a shambles. Still, it *was* comforting to have him here. She placed her hands on top of his. "A little peace and quiet would be nice."

"That's not on the agenda for the next few years, I'm afraid."

She heard the regret in his voice. She had had an idea what she was in for, but she had never been at the center of the whirlwind before. The pace was incredibly grueling. It was a lot harder, she realized, when the product you were selling was yourself.

She sighed and turned to face him. He kept his arms around her. "Do you have any idea what I did with that speech I used at the Elks Club?"

He wanted some time alone with her, some time to be just a man and a woman, still at the threshold of discovering one another. He almost regretted having urged her to try for the nomination. But then, he knew she had to prove something to herself. They wouldn't be happy with one another until she did this.

He nodded. "It's on the desk." Most of the final input had been his, but the ideas were hers. "Just soften it a bit and it'll work."

Shanna frowned as she recalled the speech. "No."

"No what? You don't like the speech? I thought you did a pretty good job delivering it." He had to be getting back to Washington on the midnight flight. It was a little late for him to do a rewrite now, but it could still be managed.

"No, the speech was fine. But I won't soften it. My platform is my platform. I plan to stick by it no matter who it displeases."

He studied her for a moment, reflecting on his feelings as he ran his hands slowly along her arms. "Who would have ever thought I was going to fall for Joan of Arc? Okay, do it your way, but if they start getting a bonfire going, I'm coming in to get you."

She laughed. "My hero."

He took her face in his hands. "And don't you forget it." Just as he lowered his head to kiss her, there was another knock on the door. He sighed, dropping his hands. "Is there a camera in this room or something? Why is it people keep knocking every time I'm within an inch of your lips?"

"Maybe it's Jane and she forgot her key." Shanna had insisted on having Jessica and the nurse come with her. She couldn't put up with long separations from her daughter, not even to win the election.

Reid ran his thumb along her bottom lip. "To be continued."

Shanna sank back into the chair as Reid opened the door. They were both surprised to see Rheena standing in the hall.

Reid stepped back as he opened the door all the way. "Mrs. Brady." He glanced down the hallway in both directions. "Is the senator with you?"

The entrance her mother made seemed just a tad less dramatic than usual to Shanna. Maybe she was getting too used to them, she mused.

Rheena tossed her silver mink coat on the sofa carelessly. "I don't need anyone to walk me to see my own daughter. Escorts are for the theater." She turned to look Reid over appreciatively. This one was a lot better than the last. Loathing filled her when she thought of Jordan. "Reid, isn't it?"

"Yes," he responded, amused. She was quite a piece of work, Shanna's mother. He could see why Shanna would have had trouble finding her own identity with this to contend with.

"I never forget a good-looking face." Dismissing Reid, she looked at her daughter. "You, however, look awful."

Shanna didn't even bother to stand up. "Did you come all the way from Georgetown to build up my confidence, Mother?" She was surprised and rather pleased that there was no deadening within her at her mother's criticism. Nothing shrank away. She'd either come of age, she decided, or was so tired, nothing mattered.

"No, I just came to see you." Rheena saw the surprised expression on Shanna's face. *Didn't think I really cared, did you?* "And Jessica." She looked around the room for signs of her granddaughter's presence. "I think it's a sin to drag her around this way."

Shanna had no intention of being influenced by her mother any longer. If anything, she was pulling in the complete opposite direction. "I wouldn't get to see her otherwise." She looked at her mother pointedly, recalling the long vacations Rheena had taken away from her. "Or she, me."

Rheena looked away. The unfamiliar prick of guilt stung her. "Yes, well, maybe you're right."

There was something in her mother's tone that had Shanna relenting slightly. "I'm playing it the best I know how."

Reid looked at the two women. They were so different, yet far more alike than either could see. Both were strong in their own way. "Would you two like me to go, or should I stay and referee?"

Rheena smiled. Yes, this one was going to be good for Shanna. She waved toward the door. "You may go."

Shanna kissed Reid's cheek. "I'm a big girl now, Reid."

Even big girls got hurt. He gave her hand an encouraging squeeze. "I'll be down the hall if you need me," he told her as he closed the door behind him. There were a few things he wanted to see concerning her campaign before he left tonight anyway.

"So, where is she?" Rheena asked impatiently.

"Jessica?" Shanna turned to face her mother. "Jane took her to the park. You actually came all the way to see her? I'm touched." It wasn't like her mother to go out of her way like this.

Rheena didn't answer for a moment, emotions scrambling within her. She wasn't an open person by nature. But nature had whimsically changed some of her rules. "No, I actually did come to see you."

That was even more unlike her mother. "Why?"

Rheena turned, defensive. She wasn't used to being questioned, especially not by Shanna. "Why not? A mother has a right to see her own daughter."

An ocean of hurt feelings came flooding back to Shanna. Where was her mother when she had needed her? When she had been afraid of the dark and just the touch of her mother's hand would have helped? Where was she when her approval had meant the world to her? "You didn't exercise that right very often, as I recall."

Explanations rose and faded. A lifetime of not apologizing for her actions kept Rheena from giving voice to any of them. "You're giving your father a second chance, why not me?"

Was her mother serious? Something *was* wrong. Shanna could feel it. "Is that what you want? A second chance?"

Rheena's eyes held hers. It took a moment for the word to come. It wasn't easy, asking. "Yes."

"Why?"

There was a stubbornness to her daughter that she had failed to recognize. Had it always been there and she just hadn't noticed it? Whatever the case, it made this even more difficult.

"Because I'm your mother," Rheena said, irritated that she had to explain anything at all. Because she couldn't completely explain all this to herself.

Because she had suddenly come face-to-face with her own mortality and it frightened her.

Shanna watched as her mother roamed the room, restlessly, as if searching for a place to hold her. "Because I wanted to tell you that I was proud of you, because I suddenly realized that I don't know this person everyone was talking about—and she was my own flesh and blood." Rheena crossed back to Shanna. "All I really knew was what she looked like and that she had better hands than I did."

Her mother was rambling. Shanna suddenly grew concerned. Why wouldn't she tell her what was wrong instead of meandering like this? "What?"

"Hands, Shanna, hands." Rheena moved close and held hers up. "I have hands like a fishwife." She looked at hers as if she hadn't seen them before, turning them first palm up, then down. "You can do a lot of surgery on various parts of your body, but hands stay large and ugly looking." Her gaze shifted to Shanna's hands. "I've always envied you your hands."

"You envied me?" How was that possible? Shanna could only stare at her mother. "How could you have envied me, of all people? You were always so beautiful." She remembered how much she had ached to look like her mother as a child, hoping that if she suddenly woke up pretty, her mother would have time for her. "Like some sort of a distant fairy princess with an ugly duckling for a child."

"You were never ugly." The words were stated emphatically. Rheena cupped Shanna's chin in her hand and looked at her. She had turned out to be quite pretty at that. "You just insisted on making yourself plain." A quirky smile played on Rheena's generous mouth. "I sometimes thought it was your way of exacting revenge. Looking back, I suppose I can't blame you."

For a moment an awkwardness hung between them. It made Shanna think of the only other time they had actually talked. The afternoon in her mother's room, after Eloïse's funeral. Shanna picked up her speech from the desk and elaborately straightened the pages. "I have two speeches to deliver this afternoon. One of them is at a press conference at a homeless shelter." Shanna looked at her mother hopefully, suddenly wanting her to be there. "Why not come with me?"

She had already displayed too much emotion. It embarrassed Rheena to be that weak. "Well, I—"

Shanna wasn't about to accept her refusal. Not this time. "You're coming. And Mother?"

"Yes?"

Shanna looked at the garment Rheena had thrown on the sofa. "Ditch the coat." She came up behind her mother and placed her hands on the older woman's regal shoulders. "You're one of the most dedicated charity fund-raisers I know, but where I'm going, you're going to look like Marie Antoinette slumming." She hesitated, realizing that this wasn't going to be any good if her mother really didn't want to accompany her. "That is, if you want to come."

"Yes. Yes, I do."

Shanna dropped her hands to her sides. There was an edge in her mother's voice she didn't recognize and it worried her. "Mother, you want to tell me what's wrong?"

Haughty denial was on the tip of her tongue, but she had come this far. What was the point of lying now? "I found a lump in my breast last week."

"Oh, Mother—" Compassion and horror mixed in Shanna's eyes.

Rheena held her hands up, thwarting Shanna's attempt to take her into her arms. "Don't get maudlin on me. It's benign." She saw the relief in her daughter's eyes and it touched her more than she had realized was possible. She had thought herself above ties that mattered. She'd been wrong. "All right, get maudlin." Relenting, Rheena moved toward her daughter and hugged her. "I suppose that's why I came."

"Why did you come?"

"Because, for one week, I saw the end of the road all too clearly. And I don't want to go there alone."

Shanna linked her fingers with her mother's. "You'd never be alone, Mother. Not while I'm around."

She had hoped Shanna would say that. She couldn't have asked it outright, but Rheena was glad Shanna had said what she needed to hear.

"Let's get you ready. You have an image to keep up," Rheena said, nudging her daughter toward the bedroom.

26

If *she had been* in the habit of biting her nails, Shanna was positive she would have had none left. They would have been bitten off over an hour ago.

As it was, she had to stop herself on several occasions from chewing her lower lip as she watched the newscast on the large-screen television monitor in front of her. On the coffee table next to her was a tall glass of diet soda, its ice cubes long since melted, leaving a ring of condensation on the table.

"Stop worrying. You're a shoo-in," Reid assured her.

He said the words next to her ear in order to be heard above the deafening noise in the hotel suite. The room was filled to overflowing with "Brady for Congress" volunteers. They had all gathered together to wait out the results of the months of hard work they had put in, eager to find out if everything they had worked for had been for nothing, or if their goal was still within sight. Victory now meant more grueling months of canvassing, endless campaigning, and late-night strategy meetings, all with an eye out for a greater victory in November.

Optimism and hope rode high in the suite. Everyone felt they had backed a winner.

Everyone but Shanna.

Her eyes glued to the screen before her, Shanna answered, "In the immortal words of Yogi Berra, 'It ain't over till it's over.' " She took Reid's hand as he sat down next to her on the love seat and squeezed hard, unconsciously searching for reassurance. "Remember the newspaper headline that read 'Dewey Wins'?"

Reid leaned in closer. Part of him wished that they were waiting for the results alone, just the two of them, in her room. But she didn't just belong to him. A piece of her belonged to every person in this room and he knew he had to share her.

He took a small whiff. She was wearing a new scent, something light and airy and extremely seductive. "Dewey didn't smell like springtime."

She laughed, the tension leaving her just for a moment. "Lucky thing, or Mrs. Dewey would have been severely suspicious."

Senator Brady pushed his way through the throng to join them. He shook Reid's hand, but his eyes were on Shanna. She looked a little drawn. He remembered his first primary. He felt as if he had gone to hell and back twice while waiting for the final results. "So how are you holding up?"

Shanna rose quickly, abandoning the list of statistics on the screen about the local election in the first district. "Dad, you came!"

He hugged her to him, wishing there was something he could do to ease things for her. "Did you think I wouldn't? What, and miss my daughter's first primary? Not likely." He released her, stepping back. He had been listening to the radio on the way over, monitoring the election. "Your mother's even on her way. Don't worry, you had a good lead in the polls yesterday."

Leads weren't always accurate, or final. "*Some* of the polls," she reminded him. "Pete Fellowes is the one to beat," she pointed out as they flashed the man's photograph on the screen.

In the senator's opinion, the man looked like an aging Boy Scout. He dismissed him readily. "Fellowes is too bland to inspire voters."

"He's bright, he's tough, and he has a couple of unions behind him." Shanna had done her homework before she had started to see whom she was up against. There were three other candidates, all lawyers. One was currently teaching in a law school. Two had run before and lost.

She looked back at the television screen, worrying the corner of her lip.

"You'll win," Brady told her confidently, squeezing her hand. "If you'll excuse me, I'll be right back. I have to see someone." He merged into the crowd again, leaving them alone in a crowded room.

Shanna returned to watching the television monitor. She continued chewing her lip. Reid slid his finger there to stop her.

"Keep that up and your lip'll be too swollen to give your victory speech to the press." He grinned, mischief in his eyes. "If it's going to be swollen, at least let me have a go at it."

Part of her longed to take him at his word and just run away from all this. But she knew that was impossible. She wouldn't do it even if she could. There was too much at stake, too many people involved. And she did want to win. Far more than she had first realized.

She sank down on the love seat, her body so tense it

was almost rigid as another district's statistics flashed by on the monitor. "Later."

There were far too many people present for him to take her into his arms the way he wanted to. "Is that a promise?"

Shanna looked up at Reid, lost in thought. She hadn't said anything remotely close to a promise. Or had she? "What?"

She was too preoccupied to follow their conversation, he thought. She needed a break, however small. He sat down again, his tone low, persuasive. "When you win the primary, why don't you take a couple of days off? I have some time coming to me and—"

How could he even suggest that? "Reid, I can't. Things will be even more hectic than ever."

"Exactly my point." Wanting her, he satisfied himself temporarily by imagining her the way she would be tonight, in bed with him, warm, supple, giving. It was enough to make his body ache. "Get away and store up a little energy for the good fight ahead."

She knew exactly what was on his mind and laughed. "Store up energy?" she echoed. "With you?"

"The thought did cross my mind."

He was tempting her, even though she knew it wasn't the logical thing to do at this time. But they hadn't had any time alone together for what seemed like months. She didn't want to take a chance of losing what she had with him. "If I go off with you, I won't *have* any energy to campaign when I get back."

He wanted nothing more than to go away with her for a little while. Whenever he could get away to be at her side, the pace she kept up was so incredibly hectic that it left no time for them to explore one another as lovers.

"You'd be surprised." He played his ace card. "Actually I was thinking more in terms of the three of us going."

She narrowed her eyes. "Excuse me?"

He grinned. "You, me, and Jessica."

It had a pleasant ring to it, and although she knew it couldn't ever be permanent, she did savor the sound of it. "Like a family."

That was his ultimate goal. To form a family unit. "Exactly like a family."

She was torn between her heart and her head. "I don't know."

It wasn't the answer he had hoped for. He felt frustration building, but this wasn't the time to vent it. "I do. The matter's settled."

She didn't know whether to be annoyed or amused with the way he simply took over. It was a first. Usually he treated her like a complete equal. There had never been a moment during this whole campaign when he had demonstrated any frustrations of ego because the spotlight was exclusively on her.

Amusement won. "I don't get a say in it?"

"Only if you say what I want to hear." He moved closer to her as the din continued to rise behind them. "There's a three-day weekend coming up next week. You can take a break. Do it, Shanna," he coaxed, his voice at the same time seductive and excited. "Win or lose, you need the time off. If you lose tonight, I'll help you nurse your wounds." His eyes slid over her body with familiarity. "And whatever else might need nursing. If you win, I promise I'll help you come up with one hell of a campaign speech." He gave her a hooded, sexy look. "But only if you inspire me."

She could already see herself with him at some isolated cabin. It sounded delicious. Suddenly she wanted nothing else. The hell with caution. "You drive a hard bargain, Reid Kincannon."

He shrugged easily. "I don't like to lose."

Shanna glanced at the screen as new figures were displayed. "Neither do I. Okay, you're on."

Doreen pushed aside several people to reach Shanna. "Shanna," she called out, excited. "Channel Two just projected you the winner, based on two percent of the final tally being in."

A euphoria took hold of Shanna and she fought hard to hold it in check. "Let's hope the other ninety-eight percent feels the same way."

"Chamberlain, here we come." Doreen rubbed her bony hands together as she invoked the name of the front-running candidate on the other ticket. She smiled broadly at Shanna. "You'll beat the pants off him."

"Don't count your pants before they fall, Doreen," Shanna warned. Her heart fluttered slightly as she saw her own photograph flashed on the screen. The totals so far appeared to be good. "We've got to win this one first, remember?"

There wasn't an iota of doubt in Doreen's voice. "We will, sugar, we will."

"So, Madam Candidate, how does it feel to win your very first primary?"

Reid placed a wildflower in her hair. True to her word, they did go away together. For three idyllic days they hid in a cabin that Reid borrowed from a friend and pretended the rest of the world didn't exist.

They were in a meadow. Before them, as far as the eye could see, the grass waved long green fingers in the spring breeze. If the sky had been any bluer, Shanna was certain it would have required paint. Reid was propped up against a tree, his legs forming a warm set of parentheses around her body. She leaned her head against his shoulder, feeling lazy. A few feet away Jessica was gathering a bouquet of dandelions, their white fluffy heads breaking apart in the wind as soon as she pulled them with her chubby hands.

Shanna couldn't remember when she had been this relaxed, this at peace.

"It feels wonderful," she answered with a sigh. "You feel wonderful." She snuggled happily against him, absorbing his warmth, absorbing his very presence. She tried to store it up within her.

The respite would only last another day. The time they had spent together was precious and she would treasure it forever. But it was going to end soon. There was a campaign waiting for her to mount starting Tuesday and people depending on her.

Reid toyed with her hair, remembering the way she had looked last night as the glow from the fireplace in the bedroom warmed her skin. Just the thought made him want her again. He knew he would never grow tired of making love with her. "This can go on, you know."

She rose on her elbow, turning to look at him in surprise. "Are you asking me to give up the election campaign?"

Was what he was implying so difficult for her to imagine? "No, I'm asking you to marry me."

She had been dreading this moment. She had played with the idea more than once, but each time a fear had seized her heart, squeezing it. Fear that pushed aside everything else. "Reid, I—"

He hated the hesitation he saw. "You've had a better offer?" he asked dryly.

"No, don't be ridiculous." Sitting up now, she hugged her knees to her, watching Jessica. The little girl was chasing butterflies in a circle. Shanna ran her tongue along her lips. "It's just that—"

He held up his hand to stop her. "Let me guess. You're afraid."

Her head jerked up, the flower falling from her hair. "I'm not afraid."

He rose to his knees, his hands on her shoulders, his tone urgent. "Then take a chance. With me." He searched her eyes for a sign that she would. "There are no guarantees in life, Shanna, only commitments we want to see through." Didn't she understand? Hadn't she been paying attention these last few months? "I'm ready to commit to you."

Shanna broke away, scrambling to her feet. Why was he making this so difficult? "But I'm not ready."

He rose, slowly, deliberately brushing the grass from his jeans. His gaze was stony when he looked at her and he was fighting to hold on to his temper. "Because of him."

"Who?" His voice was so full of hate when he said "him" that her own voice quavered.

"Give me a little credit," Reid said in disgust. "Jordan." He spat out the name.

She looked at him in horror. She didn't want Reid to believe that. "No."

His eyes were dark as he worked at restraining his anger, his hurt at her rejection. She was rejecting him for all the wrong reasons. Trapping her against the tree with his body, he placed his palms on either side of her head. "He's there, in your head, every time I make love with you." Suddenly aware that he was pressing too hard, Reid released her. "You're comparing us." He saw surprise fill her eyes. "What? Did you think I don't know?"

"I'm not comparing you," she cried in anguish. "Jordan was a horrible lover."

"I'm not talking about that part of it." He struggled to lower his voice. He didn't want to frighten the baby. Did Shanna think that was all he wanted of her? To have her in his bed? Did she think so little of him? Of herself? After all this time, had they made no progress at all?

"I'm talking about the rest of it, damn it. You're waiting for me to walk out on you emotionally. You're waiting to find out about my secret life, that I'm using you for some purpose, the way he was. That I'm only saying things I don't mean, the way he did. Well, you're going to be spending your whole life waiting in vain. And wasting two lives in the process."

He realized he was shouting again, and it was doing no good. Abruptly he turned away. "I'll go see about getting us something to eat."

Shanna watched his back as he walked away. She felt so confused, she didn't know which way to turn. Suddenly she was running after him. "Reid, wait."

He stopped and turned in her direction. "I have been waiting," he said evenly.

Shanna took a deep, shaky breath. "Please, just give me a little more time to sort it out. To think." She touched his cheek, as if somehow to instill patience in him. Her eyes pleaded with him to understand. "I know you're not like he was. In my head, there's this tally and you have all the pluses, he has all the minuses.

"But in here"—she tapped her chest—"I'm still so afraid. I loved him with all my heart, and even when I thought there was something wrong, I refused to believe it. My heart was the last to go, the last to accept his deception. Now"—she smiled sadly—"it's the last to be convinced that it won't happen again."

He wanted to stay angry at her for the frustration he felt. But he couldn't. He loved her too much.

"You know," he said quietly, "when you fall off a horse, they say the best way to stop being afraid of riding is to get back on."

Rising on her toes, she placed her hands on his

shoulders in supplication. "I need a little more time to get back on that horse."

Reid smiled as he touched her mouth with his own. He was hopelessly stuck on her and he knew it. No matter what he threatened, he wasn't going anywhere. He just planned to continue asking until he wore her down. "Just try to hurry, okay? Horses do die of old age, you know."

"I'll try," she promised with a laugh.

"Now go get your daughter." He waved his hand at the golden-haired child in the field. "And I'll see what I can do about tantalizing both your taste buds."

"Pizza would do it," Shanna tossed over her shoulder as she went to get Jessica.

"Exactly what I had in mind," he called after her. A nice, simple meal, he thought. If only the rest of it was nearly as simple.

27

"I'll be about an hour or so."

Reid's voice was intermixed with the crackling sound of static. The sky was filled with lightning. Television and radio broadcasts were all being affected. Two major thunderstorms had hit the D.C. area, one after another. It had been raining heavily for almost three days now, and according to the weather bureau, a third storm was queueing up, waiting to wreak havoc on the city.

The electricity had been winking in and out at Shanna's apartment all evening and now it seemed as if even the telephone lines were threatened. She could hardly make out his words.

"I just have a few finishing touches to make on your father's speech for tomorrow evening."

Shanna toyed with the wire. There had been a restless feeling within her all day and the evening intensified it. "Why can't you do it here?"

"Because, my sweet, in case you haven't noticed, you distract me. And the way I feel tonight, I wouldn't get one word down on paper."

It had been a long, hard day and she ached to feel Reid's arms around her. The storm made her feel like a child again and she needed him to make her feel safe. "Sounds promising. Hurry," she urged breathlessly.

The static cut into his answer. The urgency in her voice worried him a little. Normally she didn't display this sort of vulnerability outright. Did she finally realize that she needed him, or was something wrong? "Are you all right, Shanna?"

She was behaving like a child. "Just edgy. I miss you."

Maybe they were having a breakthrough after all. "I'm halfway there already. A half an hour at most."

She looked out the window. The world was dark and dreary three floors down. The rain was still coming in sheets. She heard a car screech and the sound of a crunch as it apparently hit another vehicle. She shuddered and turned away. "Be careful. The weather's really nasty."

"I'll hire a gondola if I have to. And if you—"

The line went dead.

"Reid? Reid?" She sighed as she hung up the telephone. "Terrific."

She didn't like being without a phone. "Next, the lights'll go out again," she murmured. Her fingers curled around the flashlight she had slipped into the oversized pockets of her flare skirt. If the lights did go out, she didn't want Jessica to be frightened if she woke up. Like her mother had been, the little girl was afraid of the dark.

Shanna looked at Reid's photograph on the piano. She ran her finger along the bottom of the frame. Impulsively she kissed the tip of her finger and pressed it against the glass where his lips were. She loved him, she knew that, but she still hadn't been able to convince herself to accept his proposal. Fear of ruining what there was between them kept her from saying yes. With marriages all around them floundering and her own experience, Shanna didn't want to make the same mistake again. She wanted things to go on just the way they had been. Forever.

It was called having your cake and eating it, too, she supposed.

Checking the phone again, she found there was still no dial tone. With a frustrated sigh, she dropped the receiver back into the cradle and walked into Jessica's room. The little girl was asleep, clutching tightly the stuffed rabbit Reid had gotten her. She called it "Mister Weed" in his honor. Shanna smiled to herself. She was going to miss it when her daughter outgrew her Elmer Fudd stage.

The storybook she had read until Jessica fell asleep was on the chair, another gift from Reid. There was no denying the fact that he would make a good father for her daughter.

A hell of a lot better than the one biology had given her, Shanna thought, her lips twisting in a bitter smile. He hadn't even been to see her once. So far, Jessica asked no questions. She probably assumed that Reid was her father. He was around so much. But someday the questions would be there and Shanna had no idea how she was going to handle it. How do you tell a little girl her father didn't care enough to see her?

No use dwelling on mistakes, she thought. At least Jordan had, however unwittingly, given her this precious jewel, and for that she was very grateful.

Leaning over her daughter in her brand-new, grown-up bed that she was so proud of, Shanna kissed her head lightly and tucked the sheet around the child's small body. "Sleep tight, baby."

Shanna left the door ajar. The small "magic" lamp

next to Jessica's bed remained on "to scare away the monsters." It was a solution Reid had come up with when the night-light had failed to alleviate the little girl's fears.

"Hurry home, Reid," she whispered to the emptiness around her.

She was alone. The three of them had returned to D.C. for several days. Shanna needed to meet with a few of the party leaders who were supporting her. Jane had asked for the night off to visit with her brother and his family, despite the inclement weather. She wished now that Jane was here. She wanted someone to talk to, to drive away this strange, overwhelming sense of anxiety that was inexplicably claiming her.

There were a hundred things she could be doing, but somehow she couldn't focus her attention on any of them. Maybe there was something on television she could watch until Reid arrived. Because of the effect it could have on her reputation, he wouldn't spend the night. But at least he would be here for a little while. It would help.

The doorbell chimed, startling her well beyond a reasonable response. She whirled around. Reid. Had he changed his mind about working tonight? He had a key to her apartment, but because he and Doreen were overly sensitive about the possibility of a reporter seeing him use it, he normally rang the bell. "No need to tarnish the future congresswoman's reputation," he had teased.

Hopeful, excited, she hurried to the door. "Changed your mind, did you?" she asked as she swung open the door. And then, speechless, she took a step back, feeling as if she had received a physical blow.

"Yes, as a matter of fact, I did."

Jordan, looking like a cover of *Gentlemen's Quarterly*

in a smoky full-length raincoat, walked in before she had a chance to shut the door. A few raindrops still clung to his hair, despite the umbrella he had used getting out of his car. The drops reflected the hall light and gleamed like little stars.

A halo. Now there was deceptive camouflage, she thought. They hadn't exchanged a word since that day in the hospital. The divorce had been handled exclusively through lawyers. "What are you doing here, Jordan?"

Dropping the umbrella in the corner next to the door, Jordan casually shrugged out of his raincoat. A small puddle formed on the tile. "I was just in the neighborhood and heard you were back in town, so I—"

It was amazing how clearly she could see through him now, how clouded her vision had been then. "Jordan, you are never 'just' anything. You're probably the most calculating man in Congress." She wished that Reid was with her, or Jane. She felt vulnerable with Jordan here. She had no idea what he was up to. "Now why are you here?"

He'd been watching her progress and been angrily impressed by it. He knew now that he should have fought harder to keep her. She would have turned out to be one hell of an asset to him after all. Some of his ties were turning shaky. One of the people who had heavily funded his campaign by using several holding companies had recently come under suspicion. If the Justice Department decided to investigate, Jordan was afraid that his connections to the man might place his career in jeopardy. There were kickbacks that would be difficult to explain and the man had ties to organized crime. Jordan knew he needed more weight in his corner. Someone who could pull real strings. He needed the aura of a wife and family. Most of all he needed the influence that Roger Brady could exert on his behalf.

Jordan smiled broadly at Shanna as he took her hand. "To see my daughter, my wife."

Shanna yanked her hand away and looked at him coldly. "Your ex-wife. I've been your ex-wife for three years now." She tried to move away from him, but he followed. She felt like prey being stalked. She shoved her hands into her pockets and fisted them to stop them from trembling. "As for your daughter, you never acknowledged her before. Why now? What kind of a game are you playing?"

He looked around the apartment. If nothing else, she had always had good taste. He looked at her coyly over his shoulder. "No games, Shanna." He indicated the sofa. "Mind if I sit?"

"Yes, I mind."

The frost in her voice had no effect on him. He made himself at home, as if he'd always belonged there. "Sorry, can't hear the rest of it. My ears clogged up after the 'yes.' Must be the weather." He patted the seat next to him and waited for her to sit down.

Shanna stood where she was. "It's not charming anymore, Jordan."

He looked at her, his eyes stripping away her bravado the way he had always managed to subtly undermine her self-confidence. "I'm not trying to be charming, I'm trying to be honest."

She didn't think he could be honest even if he wanted to be. And she knew he didn't want to be. "Changed religions?"

She'd gotten a lot harder to deal with, he thought, annoyed. He jumped to his feet and caught her hand as she turned away. "No, but I have changed." He put on the sincerest expression he could manage.

Remember what he did to you. Remember what you found out about him.

She dug down for the wounds that had only recently healed. "Help me out here, what on the evolutionary scale comes after snake?"

He grinned, amused. It was the same boyish grin that had her heart fluttering five years ago.

No palpitations, no flutters. Nothing. There was a deadness in her now. Finally immune, she thought, after all this time. It was a relief, in a way, to have this confrontation and know she didn't care anymore.

"I deserve that," he conceded, slowly rubbing his thumb along her wrist as he held her hand firmly in his. "That and more. I was a fool back then, a stupid fool who was desperately trying to get somewhere."

There had never been anything stupid about him. Jordan had known exactly what he was doing every step of the way. She was trying to forget, but she would never forgive. "And now?"

She was weakening. He knew it would only be a matter of minutes. He looked soulfully in her eyes. "Now I'm a man who sees what he's lost."

Bravo. Nicely done. "Please, Jordan, before I 'lose' my dinner." She tried to pull her hand free, giving him a contemptuous look. To her he was the lowest form of life and she regretted with all her heart that he was Jessica's father.

Jordan wouldn't let her free. He tightened his grip on her hand, even though his expression remained contrite. "I should have never let you go."

It's not working, Jordan, I'm over you. I've had my shots.

"As I recall, 'let' had nothing to do with it. I ran."

She pushed against his chest. The movement surprised him and he let her go. All right, he'd go slower. Her resistance was a revelation to him. He would have thought that after all this time, she'd jump at the chance to get back together. Unless she was getting action from somewhere else.

The thought annoyed him.

Though he hadn't wanted her at the time, the fact that she did walk out had stung his pride. "You wouldn't have if I hadn't wanted you to."

A walking, rutting egotist, she thought, loathing the very sight of him. How could she have been so damn blind and sold herself out for the likes of him? "Still twisting things, aren't you?"

His patience was getting thin. This was supposed to have been easy. The wounds had healed. He was supposed to apologize and she'd fall into his arms, eager for a second go at the marriage. "Shanna. I want you back."

C'mon, Reid, where are you? "Why?"

He spread his hands wide. The matter should be evident to someone with her mentality. Though he had kept close tabs on her progress these last few months, he was confident that once a mouse, always a mouse. "I want to be a family, a real family again."

"What 'again'?" How could he say things like that and not choke on his own words? "Need something for the annual Christmas card this year? Naked women aren't cutting it anymore?"

He had to remember that he needed her father, he told himself, curbing the desire to strike her. "You've become a hard woman."

She raised her chin. "Maybe someone made me that way. Maybe I did learn something from being married to you after all."

She moved away from him again, trying hard not to appear as unsettled as she felt. Maybe it was good to clear the air, once and for all, and tell Jordan what she thought of him. But she would have felt a great deal more confident if someone else had been in the room with them.

He wouldn't let her get away. Each step she took, he matched. Frustrated, he reached for her. If he could just get her in bed, the matter would be settled. This time he'd use patience, whatever it took to get her to be submissive to him. It was his only chance to beat the rap he felt was coming. "I liked you better the other way."

When she thought of herself the way she was in those days, she was almost physically ill. "Of course you did. A rug you could wipe your feet on."

He shook his head, gliding his fingers along her cheek. "A woman I could depend on." He was backing her into a corner.

She slapped his hand away and momentarily saw anger flash in his eyes before he controlled it. "Depend. Funny word coming from you. There was a time I thought I could depend on you."

"You can," he assured her, his voice low, seductive. "Now."

A tiny piece of her wished it could have all been different. But she knew better now. Wishing never made anything so. And leopards never changed their spots. The trite saying was grounded in reality.

"Yes, I can depend on you. Depend on you to lie, to cheat and to try anything you can to get ahead. Your goal was the presidency, wasn't it? What better image than a reconciliation in your past? A realliance to the Brady family. And the Brady money."

No, his goal was survival and she might be the only key. Damn the bitch's cynicism. "You have every right to be suspicious," he began, running his hands along her arms.

Reid, she wanted Reid. Where was he? Outside, the rain beat hard against the window and lightning suddenly creased the sky. What if he didn't come? How was she going to get rid of Jordan on her own?

"I'm not suspicious. I know."

The little bitch had gotten stubborn. He hadn't counted on that at all. "Shanna, what do I have to do to convince you I'm serious? I'll do anything." Holding her against him, he began to lower his mouth to hers. "Just say the word and I'll do it."

She turned her head just as he was about to kiss her, his mouth landing in her hair. "Drink a cup of hemlock."

He wanted to choke her. But for the moment he let her go. "What?"

She took the opportunity to move to the other side of the piano. "Or try throwing yourself on your sword. The Japanese had a custom. Hara-kiri. Death with honor. It'd be a new experience for you."

She was talking crazy. "I've no intention of experiencing death."

She narrowed her eyes scornfully. "I was talking about honor."

Enough of this pussyfooting around. She was his if he wanted her, damn it. Why didn't she just admit it? "Shanna, I love you."

Though panic was mounting within her, she looked him squarely in the eye. "Jordan, the only one you ever loved was the image that you saw in your mirror every morning. Now I really don't know why you're here, but I know it has something to do with furthering the future of that image and I am not interested. I don't want you dead, I just want you out of my life, permanently. That means out of my apartment. Now." She gritted her teeth as his grip on her arms tightened.

"I want you, Shanna," he breathed against her. She could feel his loins begin to pulse as he pressed her against the wall. His eyes took on a dangerous light. "No woman ever walked out on me. *Ever.* I do the walking and I've walked into your life again. Get used to the idea." The grin that came over his face now was sardon-ically evil. How could she have ever thought he was handsome? And how could she have ever loved him?

He rubbed his pelvis against her insistently. "Maybe after you've sampled a little of what you've been miss-ing, you'll change your mind—"

He disgusted her. She felt dirty just being touched by him. "I was missing it even as you jerked spasmodically over me."

Rage took over, breaking his resolve. The pressure he was living with had gotten to be too much. "Why you sanctimonious little bitch!"

Jordan raised his hand to hit her. Suddenly they were pitched into darkness as the lights in the apartment went out. Shanna jerked her knee up. Jordan let out a surprised, anguished yell.

He fell with a thud to the floor. "Bitch!" he bit off, moaning. "You're going to pay for that."

28

"Mama, where are you?"

Jessica's frightened cry echoed in the shadows of the apartment. Adrenaline spurted through Shanna's veins. Her baby. She had to go to her baby. "I'm coming, Jessica. Mommy's coming."

Jordan, huddled in pain on the floor, managed to grab Shanna's ankle as she quickly turned toward the cry. Thrown off balance, she lurched forward. Shanna fell hard and hit her forehead against the arm of the sofa. Although it was well padded, it was firm. The impact jarred her head, slamming her mouth shut and making her catch the tip of her tongue between her teeth. She tasted blood.

"The hell you are." Jordan's voice was menacing. "You're staying right here." He grappled with her as she fought frantically to get away. In the background, Jessica's cries for her continued. Jordan ignored them. "What is it? You've been getting it regularly from somebody else, is that it?"

Though she scratched and clawed, she couldn't get away. He wrestled her until she was under him. "Miss Goody Two-Shoes has been screwing for someone else, is that why you don't want me?"

Jordan's breath was hot on her face and she struggled to escape his hold. "I don't want you because you disgust me, Jordan! Now let me go!" Gaining a little space, she yanked with all her might. He fell on her again, pressing her down with his weight.

Desperate, she braced her hands against his chest and tried to wriggle free. The flashlight in her pocket dug into her thigh. For a moment she stopped struggling, letting him believe that she had given up. She snaked her hand into her pocket.

Jordan pivoted himself on his hands, looming over her. "Good, you've finally come to your senses." His voice had an evil, triumphant smirk. "I knew you couldn't resist."

Swinging with all her might, she hit him on the side of the head, slicing him. Screaming, stunned with the blow, Jordan fell back.

Shanna scrambled to her feet just as the front door swung open, crashing against the opposite wall. The light from the flashlight the man in the doorway held almost blinded her for a moment, but Shanna ran toward it, knowing she had to be safer there than with Jordan.

A sob broke free as she focused on the man's face. "Reid!"

With one arm around her protectively, Reid shone the light on the figure sprawled on the floor. "What the hell's going on here?"

Jordan touched his temple. His fingers felt sticky. Blood. Rage boiled within him, but he managed to get himself under control. His eyes on the two in the doorway, he knew he had to act calmly. He took out his handkerchief from his pocket and dabbed it at his wound. There was nothing but contempt in his eyes when he looked at Reid.

"Nothing much. Just a little misunderstanding," he told him. "Is this the reason?" he asked Shanna. "Is he why you're turning your back on me?"

Her insides were quaking. Any moment now, she felt that her entire body would be shaking spasmodically. Needing comfort, she moved even closer against Reid.

"What happened between us is three years old, Jordan. Reid has nothing to do with it." She made herself look at the man she had once loved. "You have everything to do with it."

Jordan was unconvinced. No woman would turn him down if he asked her. There had to be something more. He rose to his feet. "A two-bit, would-be speech writer?" He turned toward Reid. "How are you doing, Kincannon? Is this why you left me?" He smirked, waving his hand at Shanna. "To have a go at her? Easy pickings, wasn't she?"

Without a moment's thought, Reid dropped the flashlight and swung hard at Jordan's face. The flashlight cast a wild, dizzying arc against the wall and ceiling as it hit the floor. Jordan crumpled down at almost the same moment.

Reid rubbed his left hand over his knuckles before picking up the flashlight. His knuckles were stinging. He didn't even give the unconscious man a second glance. "They always make that look so easy in the movies."

Gratitude and relief mingled with confusion as Shanna let out a shaky breath. The baby was still crying for her. "I have to go to Jessica." She picked up the bloodied flashlight she had used as a weapon and shone it down the hallway. Just then the lights came on again. She switched off the flashlight.

"It's okay, baby," Shanna called, hurrying down the hall.

With the lights back on, Jessica was beginning to calm down. She looked at her mother, bewildered. "Voices, Mama. Jessie hear voices."

She couldn't show Jessica how upset she was. Fear, disruption, chaos were all things that Shanna fought hard to keep out of her daughter's daily life. She smoothed the covers down around her slowly. "Nightmares, honey. Nothing more, just nightmares."

Jessica looked around her room, her eyes already starting to close again. "The lights." She yawned, pointing at her lamp.

"Blinked," Shanna said quickly, then smiled. "They were winking at you. It's okay now." Her voice was calm, reassuring. Jessica was already more than half-asleep. "The magic lamp'll protect you and Mr. Reid'll keep you company." She tucked the rabbit in next to the little girl. "I'll be in the other room, honey, talking to someone." She touched her lips to Jessica's forehead. "Pleasant dreams, sweetheart."

Shanna eased out of her daughter's bedroom. Her heart was still pounding hard against her rib cage. She looked down at her clothing. Her skirt was torn where Jordan had tried to rip it from her. She covered her face with her hands and bit back the sob that rose up in her throat.

Don't let go. Don't let go.

Regaining her composure to some extent, Shanna returned to the living room. Jordan was still lying on the floor, unconscious. She looked at Reid. "What are we going to do with him?"

He knew what he'd like to do, but there were consequences for that. He put his arm around her. She looked white as a sheet. He saw the torn skirt for the first time and rage flared all over again.

"Murder comes to mind, but it won't look good on

your record to have your father's speech writer kill your ex-husband." He took stock. "Pour him into a cab, I guess." Reid kept his voice calm for her sake. "What did he want from you?"

Shanna closed her eyes, wondering when the memory of this evening would fade away. "To pick up where we left off."

It didn't make sense to Reid. "Why? Why would he come now instead of sooner?" She was trembling, he realized, tightening his arm around her.

"I have no idea." She looked at Reid. They had to clear up something. Now, or she would have no peace. "What did he mean, Reid?"

Reid didn't know what she was referring to. "What did he mean by what?"

Shanna moved aside, a chill taking hold of her. "Saying that you quit your job with him to come to work for my father in order to get a 'shot' at me." Uncertainty gnawed at her belly as she rubbed her arms, trying to drive away the cold. "Did you hit him because you were angry or because you wanted to keep him quiet?"

Reid's eyes darkened dangerously, but he took no step toward her. "You have to ask?"

She was shaking and no longer knew what to believe. She needed to be reassured. Jordan had come back into her life, and suddenly there were snakes everywhere. "Yes, I think I do."

"I told you, I have no political ambitions." Reid's voice was even as he controlled his anger.

"But I am well off," she reminded him. She had lived with that curse all her life, never knowing if someone was with her because of herself, or because of her family, her money.

For a brief moment his patience snapped. Reid grabbed her arms, wanting to shake her, wanting to shake sense into her head. But he did nothing but hold her arms. "Have I *ever* asked you for anything? *Ever?*" he repeated, his tone harsh.

She pressed her lips together to keep them from trembling. *Tell me I'm wrong, Reid. Please tell me I'm wrong. I want to be wrong.* "Maybe you're the patient kind."

He looked at her, angry, hurt. "Shanna, if you believe that, then all the time we've spent together has been meaningless." He let her go and turned away.

Pain ate at her. Jordan's insinuations had hit a raw, exposed nerve that had never healed properly. If Reid had nothing to hide, why hadn't he told her about Jordan before? He knew she had been married to him. "Why didn't you tell me you worked for him?"

"It was only for a few months and it wasn't anything I wanted to use as a reference." He swung around. "I left because I didn't like what I saw." Reid jerked a hand at the crumpled figure on the floor. "He's a parasite, an opportunist. I couldn't write speeches for a man like that, knowing they were just empty words to deceive people into voting for him. That's not what I'm about." He looked into her eyes, searching for the woman he loved. "I thought you knew that."

Tears stung her eyes. Yes, she knew that. She dragged her hand through her hair, sucking in a ragged breath. "I'm sorry, he just has me so shaken."

It was all he needed to hear. One apology and all the hurt was instantly washed away. Reid took her into his arms and just held her, letting her draw comfort from his presence.

"Shh, it's okay." He stroked her hair. "It's okay. I won't let him hurt you."

"How very touching."

They both jumped when Jordan spoke.

He was sitting up on the floor, nursing his jaw. Damn,

he was going to have one hell of a bruise there by morning. "Well, now that we've both shared her, we both know she's not much of a lay, is she?" He began to rise to his feet. "When you get tired of her, let me know."

Jordan suddenly felt himself being hauled up the rest of the way and slammed against the wall. Air whooshed out of him as his spine hit the flat surface. Reid was glaring at him, his face thrust an inch from his. Jordan had never seen such hatred in his life and shrank within himself. There was nowhere to go.

Reid wanted nothing more than to choke the life out of him. Slowly. "You are never getting your slimy hands on her again. Never. Do I make myself clear?"

Jordan was a survivor. Against all odds, he had survived before, and somehow, someway, he would do it again. He'd been threatened before. "Want to keep the goose that lays the golden eggs all to yourself, huh? You're smarter than you look."

Reid tightened his grip around Jordan's throat until panic set into the latter's eyes. "If you so much as look at her, there'll be so many little pieces of you around, nobody'll ever figure out how to put you together again."

Jordan's face turned a horrible shade of red as he frantically tried to pry Reid's fingers from his throat. He couldn't get in any air.

A little longer, Reid thought. It would only take a little longer.

"Reid, Reid, you're choking him," Shanna cried, pulling at his arm. She couldn't budge it. New fear sprang up. She couldn't let him kill Jordan. Reid's whole life would be ruined. And all because of her. "Reid, please, he's not worth it. He's not worth it!"

Sense returned. "No, you're right. He's not." Reid shoved Jordan toward the door. "Get out before I change my mind."

Jordan stood, one hand on the door to hold himself up. He rubbed his throat with the other as he gulped in air. "I could have you arrested, Kincannon," he finally managed to say.

Reid knew it was just Jordan's word against theirs. And Shanna counted. But the scandal could hurt her. "I don't think you want the full story of your attempted rape to get on the six o'clock news now, do you?" Reid asked malevolently.

Jordan retreated, but as always, he tried to save face. He squared his shoulders. "Those must be some speeches you write these days. You've got a hell of an imagination."

His shoulders ached where he had hit the floor and his jaw and temple were throbbing fiercely, but he managed to straighten his tie. And with effort, he picked up his raincoat and placed it over his arm. "Maybe I should have tried a little harder to hang on to you, too. More money, eh?"

There wouldn't have been enough money in the world to make Reid stay with someone of Jordan's ilk, once he had realized what the man was about.

"We all make mistakes, Calhoun," Reid said, referring to his having come to work for Jordan at all. "Yours was in coming here. Don't let it happen again. Ever."

Jordan gave Reid a final, contemptuous look, taking care to do it with the front door open, then turned to look at Shanna. "So you finally got your knight in shining armor, Shanna. Too bad you had to lower your expectations to do it."

"They couldn't have been lower than when I was with you." So saying, Shanna slammed the door in Jordan's face. She turned and threw herself into Reid's arms.

29

Reid stood silently holding Shanna in his arms for a few minutes, allowing her time to pull herself together. When he felt that she could answer him, he asked gently, "Did he hurt you?"

She was acting like a fool, she thought, but she couldn't help it. Being with Jordan had brought everything back, the insecurities, the shame at the end. And, for a few terrifying moments before Reid appeared, she had thought Jordan was going to rape her. It was going to take her time to work all this through.

Shanna looked up at Reid and shook her head. "No. Just scared me, I guess."

He still didn't understand how all of this had happened when it could have been avoided so easily. "Why did you let him in?"

She shrugged helplessly. She had been too eager to stop to look through the peephole. Her mistake. And she had paid for it royally. "I thought he was you."

Reid shook his head. There was no use in telling her

that she should always look before opening the door. She knew that better than he.

There was a bemused smile on his lips as he said, "I could take that as an insult, you know."

She let out a long, jagged breath, trying to calm down. The tremor within her wouldn't be stilled. Shanna doubted she would be able to put all this behind her anywhere in the near future. The almost maniacally angry look in Jordan's eyes was going to take a long time to erase.

"When he rang the bell, I was hoping you'd changed your mind and decided to stop working. I opened the door without thinking."

Reid stood facing her. With his hands resting against her shoulders, he slowly stroked the sides of her neck with his thumbs. "You need a keeper."

"No, no keeper." She didn't want to be taken care of. Not anymore. She didn't want to give up the independence she had struggled to forge for herself, against all odds. Against her own inclinations. "I keep myself." She smiled up into Reid's face. She knew every ridge and line now by heart, and just the sight of him could excite her. "But I do need a hero riding in once in a while to help out. The way you did tonight."

"Rent-a-knight?" he suggested with a grin.

She loved the way he made her feel. The way he made her smile. "What's your fee?"

Instead of answering her, Reid nibbled on her ear. Her pleasured moan aroused him. God, he was so glad that she was all right. "The fee's negotiable."

It was happening again. He was drugging her senses even as he was stirring them, working them up to a fever pitch. She wanted nothing more than to be with him tonight, lost in his arms, in his scent. "When do we start negotiating?"

He took her hand and led her to her bedroom. "Now."

It was to have begun slowly, as it always did. But after what she had been through, something within Shanna didn't want it to be slow, didn't want to wait. She was eager for Reid's touch, eager for his love. She wanted to lose herself blindly in it. She wanted to make love with him so that it washed away everything that had just happened. She needed to get so totally steeped in him that she couldn't think, or feel, or know anything but Reid.

She had never needed anyone the way she needed him tonight.

As soon as they were within the bedroom, Shanna began to tug off his shirt, her hands shaking as she tried to work the buttons free. Reid caught her trembling fingers, surprised. She had never taken the initiative before. "Hey, hey, where's the fire?"

"Here." She pointed at her chest, where her heart was. "Inside me. Take me, Reid. Take me fast, take me now." *Make me forget everything else.*

"Don't do this, Shanna," Reid warned her. It had taken coaxing on his part, but she had told him what Jordan had been like as a lover. Insensitive, demanding, and much too quick to take his pleasure. Reid didn't want to somehow fall into a trap where she could compare the two of them and find him lacking.

He grazed her temple with his lips. "You know the best part of it for you is to draw this out."

He didn't understand, she thought. He couldn't begin to fathom her need for him. "No, it's not." Her eyes spoke silently to him, telling him of her need. "The best part of it is you."

It was as close as she had ever come to telling him she loved him and he savored it. Reid laughed softly as he framed her face gently with his hands. "I don't think you need anyone to help you with your speeches after all." He kissed her lips lightly, trying to coax her toward the inner peace she sought from the demon that had been raised tonight. "You do fine just on your own."

No, not without you. "Guess again." On her toes, she drew his mouth to hers. Her kiss was hungry, searching, wanting.

She had never been like this before with him. He could do nothing but try to hold on and give her what she needed. All of himself. There was no holding back for either of them.

Shanna set the pace. Clothes were quickly shed and forgotten. Naked, they fell into bed as the hunger flared between them like a dried piece of wood touched with a match. It all but exploded, incinerating them both.

Her hands were everywhere along his body, touching, stroking, reveling in her own boldness. It was as if she needed to reassure herself physically that he was here, with her. And that he wanted her.

She couldn't get enough of him.

Her mouth savaging his, she straddled Reid and heard him moan her name against her mouth as she moved eagerly against him.

He wove his fingers into Shanna's tangled hair, drawing her away, holding her face an inch from his. "Something new?"

She could hardly breathe. The frenzy taking over her soul was stealing her breath away. She didn't even recognize herself. It was as if she had died and been reborn tonight. "Am I doing it wrong?"

She was so precious to him, so very, very precious. "Shanna, you couldn't do anything wrong. Except leave me." He brought her mouth down to his.

Shanna shifted slightly to receive him. He gripped her buttocks hard as she began the ride up the steep incline. The pace increased, the stars and heat radiated as she ascended. Faster and faster until the final sensation burst upon her. Shanna's head fell back as the explosion racked her, then set her free. She slumped down against Reid's chest, her breathing shallow.

He could feel her heart pounding against his. It comforted him just to have her like that, with him. But he knew that she needed more. She needed to be loved and shown that she was.

Reid stroked her hair, wondering if she would ever be completely his, without the ghosts, without the fears that still haunted the recesses of her mind. He didn't want her money, her family, or her name. He just wanted her. For always.

"Now that we've done it your way," he murmured against her ear, "I'd like a crack at it."

It took effort to raise her head. Shanna tried to focus on Reid's face, still dazed from her ascent. "You're kidding."

He grinned and his eyes shone. "I never kid when I'm naked."

Easily, he reversed their position. As she lay back into the cover they had just twisted up, Reid made love to her slowly, by inches, with his hands, with his lips. With his tongue. He raised his head for a moment and watched in fascination as she began to move with anticipation that overpowered her exhaustion.

It was happening again. The excitement was bubbling, pulsing, seeking release. How could that possibly be after she had just used up every shred of energy she had? "Reid?"

"Shh, no interrupting." The words were murmured against the quivering muscles of her belly. His tongue languidly forged a moist path as he created an arc along the tops of her thighs. Each pass brought him closer and closer toward the center.

Shanna groaned. Lava was pouring through her veins. She grabbed fistfuls of the blanket as her body went hurtling toward first one peak and then the next. He pushed her thighs apart. Very slowly, gently, he stroked her with his lips, each time a little closer, a little deeper, a little longer. When he plunged his tongue to her very core, she had to bite her lip to keep from crying out.

Frantically she strove to hold on to the sensation Reid created, and just as frantically she reached for the end, the final peak, the final explosion. They just kept flowering into another one. There was no end.

Her body sleek with sweat, she was draining beyond belief, still twisting against the bed. Against his mouth. "No more. I can't," she gasped.

Reid drew himself up until he was next to her, his eyes on hers. He ran his fingers through her hair. "The human body is amazingly resilient. You'd be surprised what it can withstand."

Kissing only her lips, he slowly worked her up into a fever pitch again.

She had thought she was too tired even to move. She was wrong. He was right. The human body was amazingly resilient. Her heart pounding crazily, she began to move urgently against him until he entered her again. Together, they reached another plateau in paradise.

And Shanna felt safe. For now.

There wasn't a single cloud in the sky. It looked just the way it had the day of her grandmother's funeral. It should have been raining then. It should be raining now.

Shanna brushed away fresh tears as she looked at the gathering for Annabel Whitney's funeral. Half of

Congress had turned out to pay their respects. The senator's wife had died of cancer of the pancreas, succumbing almost as soon as she was diagnosed. Death had been swift and devastating to all those who had been left behind.

It was a beautiful funeral. Annabel had touched many lives, had made many friends. Shanna doubted that the senator, cocooned in his sorrow, had really noticed any of it. Shanna's parents were with him and he was supported on either side by his two sons. A legion of grandchildren and assorted nieces, nephews, and their families all attended. All were grieving the passing of a gentle lady.

But Whitney was alone in his pain. It was a place no one else could enter.

There were so many tears, maybe there were none left for the rain, Shanna thought, wiping her own away again.

When they lowered Annabel's coffin into the ground, Shanna squeezed Reid's hand tightly. She looked toward Senator Whitney. The wide shoulders were slumped and he seemed like a little old man to her instead of the larger-than-life figure who had always populated her world. She watched as he cried, unmindful of his tears.

Eventually the funeral was over. The beautiful words of tribute had all been said and the condolences had all been given. But the pain, Shanna knew, having suffered through Eloïse's passing, would last a very long time.

The crowd began to disperse as everyone went on to pick up the thread of their lives.

"Wait for me," she said to Reid. He nodded as she began to make her way over to Whitney. His sons stood off to the side, allowing their father privacy with the people who came to offer a few more words. They were all wrapped in their own shroud of grief.

What could she say that she hadn't already said? Yet she had to come by one last time. Senator Whitney turned just as she approached and they hugged one another.

"Senator, I'm so very, very sorry." It wasn't enough. It was the truth and all she had, but it wasn't nearly enough to help fill the dark abyss she knew had been created by Annabel's death.

Whitney nodded his shaggy white head. He took out his handkerchief and dabbed at his eyes. It was a useless effort. They misted again as soon as he stopped.

"Thank you." The senator took a deep breath, as if to stabilize himself. He tried to smile, but couldn't. "She was younger than me, you know. By ten years." His voice was hoarse and cracked occasionally as he spoke. "She was supposed to take care of me in my old age. I married her thinking I'd never be alone." He pressed his lips together. He was talking more to himself than to Shanna. "Guess you can't make plans like that. God's gotta have His say and He doesn't have to tell us first." He sighed heavily. "I'm going to miss that lady every day for the rest of my life."

Shanna wanted to tell him it was going to be all right. She wanted somehow to help mitigate the pain, if only by a little. But she knew there wasn't any way now. Only time would do that. And never completely.

"Is there anything I can do?" she asked him.

He was silent for a long moment as he watched the black cars pull away from the cemetery without really being aware that he was looking at all. Then he turned to Shanna and took her hands in both of his. His were large and wide and so cold, as if the very life's blood had been stolen from them.

"Yes," he said to her quietly. "There is something you can do." Whitney's eyes held hers, as if suddenly seeing her there for the first time. "Don't miss out. Enjoy everything now. We never know if there's going to be tomorrow." He dropped her hands as he looked toward his wife's grave. "I had a lot of plans for tomorrow that aren't going to happen now."

And then he walked away, a broken man.

Shanna felt Reid's hands on her shoulders. She knew it was he without having to turn around, and was grateful for the bond that existed between them.

"Let's go home," he said.

Shanna nodded as he slipped his arm around her. His touch had never felt dearer.

30

Bedlam.

The best word to describe what was taking place around her this evening was bedlam, Shanna thought. Pure bedlam. Six floors below, in the Excelsior Hotel's main ballroom, her campaign workers and well-wishers were partying as if the votes were already all tabulated and she had already won the congressional seat for which she had worked so hard.

Here, in the suite she had reserved for the occasion, there was enough noise and confusion to rival the Mardi Gras celebration in New Orleans. But no matter how large the cluster of people was in any corner of the room, all life was centered on one thing. Everyone kept an eye on one or more of the three television monitors scattered throughout the room, each tuned to one of the three major networks.

Everyone who mattered to Shanna was here, stuffed into this ornately decorated suite. Her family was here, her friends, key staff members of her campaign.

And Reid.

There was no category for him. He had turned out to be all those things to her and so much more.

Ever since Annabel Whitney's funeral, Shanna had had trouble getting the elderly senator's parting words out of her mind, even during the last few hectic weeks of her campaign. Was she being a fool, refusing Reid's proposal? She knew she had turned him down because she was afraid of change. Afraid to change what there was between them by altering their situation. She was afraid that change would take the man she loved and make him into someone she didn't know. Jordan turned out to be someone he hadn't initially appeared to be. It didn't seem possible that the same would happen with Reid. But things were going very well between them. They might change if they were married. And one traumatic experience was enough.

Yet Whitney's words kept echoing in her mind. And there was the fact that changes kept happening, no matter what. Life went on. There was no doubt in her mind that she wanted to spend hers with Reid.

Figures toggled on the screen she was watching, bringing her attention back to the immediate present. Nerves jangled close to the surface as she watched the early lead that had been projected for her during the first hour slip a little as they entered the second.

But that was only on one channel. The other two stations, her father told her as he stopped to see how she was holding up, still had her leading by a reasonably healthy margin over the challenger, Edward Chamberlain.

"Want to bring out the champagne early?" Reid asked, coming up behind her. Shanna only shook her head as she continued watching Channel Four's projections. "Hey, you're stiff as a board." He leaned closer and whispered in her ear. "That's my role."

She laughed, the tension that had her in its grip loos-
ening for a moment. "Not here."

Instead of the aforementioned champagne, Reid
handed her a glass of diet soda. She took it gratefully
and sipped. She might as well have been sipping water.
She didn't taste anything.

· She was a beautiful nervous wreck, Reid thought.
"We'll win," he assured her. ·

And after that, he had no idea what was going to happen. Shanna had been almost continuously busy before.
How frantic would her pace become after she took
office? And where would his place be within the structure of her life? He had his own clearly defined career
with the senator. He was there to give Shanna moral support and help edit her speeches on occasion. But beyond
that, he hadn't a clue. She had turned down his proposal
once, asking for more time. Time had gone by and she
had said nothing. Was there an unspoken message in
that?

Though he wanted to settle things between them, he
wasn't going to spoil the evening for her. It was hers to
savor and enjoy.

"Remember Dewey," she reminded him, the way she
had on the night of the primary. Then she had won, but
she was afraid of counting on lightning striking twice in
the same place.

He gave her an encouraging smile and whispered.
"I'd rather remember you and the way you were last
night."

Shanna didn't say anything. She just took his hand
and held it, her fingers wrapped tightly around his. Having him here with her would see her through this
evening, win or lose.

She looked over toward the sofa on the far left of the
suite and saw Jane standing over Jessica. The little girl

was apparently giving an animated rendition of a story to Senator Whitney. Instead of being sleepy, Jessica appeared to be completely awake, her eyes open wide as if she had somehow stumbled into some sort of strange wonderland. Shanna had felt the same way at her father's election-night headquarters the first time she had been there.

In a way, Shanna thought, she felt a little like that now.

She smiled as she saw Whitney take the child and place her on his knee, bouncing her gently up and down. Jessica clapped her hands together in glee. Shanna could remember another evening just like this one, years in the past. But then she had been the little girl on Whitney's knee and his hair had been a deep, chestnut brown. She smiled as the memory warmed her.

"Well, the son of a bitch finally got exactly what he royally deserved."

Rheena's voice, etched with triumph, surprised Shanna. She turned just as her mother dropped a copy of a Virginia newspaper on the marble table in front of her. Shanna looked at her mother quizzically. "What are you talking about?"

"Front page, dear. Always read the headlines, if nothing else." Rheena looked at her daughter. There was no criticism in the statement, only a small note of affection. "That way they'll always think that you're well read."

Shanna looked at the big block letters across the top of the newspaper. CONGRESSMAN INDICTED. JORDAN CALHOUN CAUGHT TAKING BRIBES.

Rheena only smiled as Shanna raised her eyes to her mother's face in utter surprise. This time there was a touch of vindictive pleasure in the older woman's eyes. "It was about time that he got what was coming to him."

There was something about the way her mother

looked as she said the simple statement that immediately had Shanna suspicious. The scarlet smile was just a tad too self-satisfied. And why would her mother have even bothered to look at a copy of a Virginia newspaper anyway? Why would Rheena think to keep such close tabs on Jordan now?

"Mother, you didn't have anything to do with this somehow, did you?"

Rheena looked at her only child and delicately placed her manicured hand to her breast, the picture of injured innocence.

"I? The Justice Department was investigating him. Do I look like a member of the Justice Department?" And then the generous, scarlet mouth curved ever so slightly. "Of course, I do *know* people in the Justice Department. But then," she said with a vague, weary sigh as she began to move toward someone she had just noticed in the room, "I know people everywhere."

Somehow, someway, her mother had set the wheels in motion. A whispered word there, a hint here. Shanna still had no idea just how many strings her mother had at her disposal when she needed them. Just as in Hollywood, where more deals were struck at cocktail parties than in studio offices, more business was taken care of at Washington parties than could ever be managed on the floor of the House or Senate.

Reid picked up the newspaper and reread the headline. He shook his head as he let the paper drop again on the table. A hint of admiration was in his eyes as he looked in Rheena's direction. "I certainly wouldn't want her holding a grudge against me. Do you really think she had something to do with all this?"

Shanna nodded. "I don't 'think.' I know. I know what Mother is capable of." She looked at the grainy photograph of Jordan surrounded by several of his lawyers. There wasn't a single note of sorrow within her. No sadness for what he was going through, no memories of the past to soften her. He was, as her mother had pointed out, getting what he richly deserved. Shanna wouldn't have done anything to him on her own. It wasn't her way. But a part of her was secretly glad it was her mother's. "Can't say I'm sorry."

The evening dragged on, each minute slowly dripping into the next, despite the pulsating excitement all around her. It took another agonizing hour and a half before the torture came to an end. The soda and tension mixed badly, sending Shanna off to the ladies' room far more frequently than she would have liked. And her stomach was threatening to make short work of the one hastily consumed sandwich she had eaten all day.

As she walked out of the bathroom for the third time, Reid grabbed her hand and pulled her toward him before anyone else had a chance to claim her attention.

"Missed me that much?" she asked, caught off guard.

"Always." His grin told her that he had news.

"What? What?" She was in absolutely no mood to play any games. Tension had completely shredded her nerves into confetti.

He placed his hands on her shoulders and turned her in the direction of the closest monitor. "Channel Two just declared you the winner."

She wasn't sure if she gasped. It was growing too noisy for her even to hear herself. Shanna's hand went to her lurching stomach. She turned toward Reid. "It's only what, nine-thirty?"

He checked his wristwatch. "Nine twenty-nine." Didn't she understand the magnitude of what he was saying? "Time has nothing to do with it." He pointed toward the monitor as the figures flashed on again. "You've got a clearly impressive lead."

She tried to keep it all in perspective. "What about the other channels?"

As she asked the question her father approached her from her left, his smile broad. Frantic movement to her right drew her attention toward Doreen, who was eagerly waving at her from across the room. The campaign manager was pointing to the television monitor directly in front of her and giving Shanna the high sign.

"Channel Seven says the job's yours," Senator Brady informed his daughter. "Shanna." He placed his hands on her arms in lieu of an embrace. Outright displays of affection in public were hard for him. "I've never been more proud of you than I am at this moment."

"I haven't done anything yet," Shanna replied nervously. "Be proud of me when I manage to get something accomplished."

Reid let out a sigh. "Don't you know by now that you will?"

There was something in Reid's tone that bothered her. It had a touch of exasperation in it. She was going to ask him what was wrong when Doreen shoved the portable telephone receiver into her hand.

Doreen covered the mouthpiece with one hand. "It's Chamberlain. I think he wants to concede."

Numbed, Shanna placed the receiver against her ear and listened to the stern, gruff voice congratulate her on "a campaign well run."

The words were perfunctory. Shanna knew that Chamberlain thought her an upstart, a usurper. Still, the game had to be played. "Thank you, Edward. It was a good race. You were a very difficult man to beat." A curt thank-you and the line went dead.

Shanna handed the telephone back to Doreen. "We

won." She said the words, but she didn't quite believe them.

A feeling of euphoria began to take hold of Shanna. It started at her toes, working up from her toes, swirling up her ankles, through her legs, up her body, like a shadow that was lifting from her by measured inches.

"We won." She turned to Reid, excitement now throbbing through her. "We really won!"

Cheers went up throughout the room as people were hugging, crying, vicariously sharing in Shanna's triumph. Her father kissed her cheek and several people embraced her, saying things she couldn't quite hear.

Reid waited until the initial furor had died down somewhat. When it came to Shanna, he didn't want to be part of the mob. "Is a member of Senator Brady's staff allowed to kiss a congresswoman-elect in public?" Reid laughed as she threw her arms around him and squealed.

Shanna looked up into his eyes, his soft, wonderful green eyes. "He'd better!"

"Later, you two." Doreen came between them, splitting them apart. "There's a ballroom full of people downstairs who need to hear you tell them the news." Excited, triumphant, Doreen was laughing and tugging Shanna toward the hallway.

Shanna looked over her shoulder at Reid, and suddenly everything became clear to her. All of this was wonderful. It was everything she had dreamed of, but it was nothing without him. She made up her mind, hoping that it wasn't too late.

"No, wait," Shanna pleaded. "Not later." She pulled her hand from Doreen's. "Give me a minute, please." The woman gave Reid a measured glance, then stepped out into the hall.

Shanna waited until the suite had all but been cleared as people went down to the ballroom below.

Only her parents and Jane and her daughter remained and they stood off to the side.

Suddenly afraid that she had waited too long, Shanna said in almost a whisper, "Is your offer still open?"

He wasn't sure he understood. He didn't want to jump to a conclusion that had no foundation. "What offer?"

It was too late. She swallowed back the bitter bile of disappointment. "The one you made to me in the meadow," she said without enthusiasm. Why had she waited so long to come to her senses? "In Virginia."

She didn't have to explain any further. Why did she look so stricken? "Always."

Shanna's mouth dropped open. It *wasn't* too late. It wasn't. It was all right. She grinned, not even noticing the tears that were sliding down her cheeks. But as she moved toward Reid Doreen was whisking her away down the elevator.

"C'mon, already," Doreen urged.

"Bring the baby, please," Shanna called to Reid, hoping he heard her.

Red, white, and blue balloons were everywhere, with identical streamers strung in between. Laughter flowed as easily as the champagne. There was a stage set up on one side of the ballroom with a podium in the middle. Shanna took the two steps up to it shakily, her cheeks flushed, her spirits exploding within her. As she came up to the microphone the applause was deafening.

"Wait," she cried, hands outstretched, quieting them. "Like I said to my father when he congratulated me, I haven't done anything yet. Save your applause for then." She tried to still the urge to shed happy tears. "Right now the applause belongs to you."

Shanna looked at the sea of upturned faces, so many people she didn't even recognize, so many who had self-lessly helped her because they believed in her. "Because if it wasn't for you, your hard work, your faith, and your time, I wouldn't be here."

As she waited for the next burst of applause to die down, she saw Reid enter the ballroom through the rear door, holding a sleeping Jessica in his arms. Love flooded through her and she felt so grateful to be given this second chance at life.

Their eyes locked and held as Reid made his way slowly toward Shanna.

"I promise to try to live up to all my promises. And to not make promises unless I can live up to them. I promise to justify your faith in me." She smiled and stretched out her hand toward Reid. Behind her were her key campaign workers. In front of her was her whole world.

"I feel very humble now, very proud, and very happy. Outside of the evening my daughter was born, this is the happiest night of my life." She drew in a long breath as Reid joined her with Jessica. "Not just because you've elected me your representative, although that's pretty heady stuff for a woman whose only credentials for the job up to three years ago was eavesdropping on political discussions in her father's den."

Blinking back tears, Shanna looked at her father in the front row. He was standing next to her mother. The senator's arm was around Rheena's shoulders and they were smiling. It was the most natural show of unity Shanna had ever seen between her parents. Shanna could have sworn there were actually tears in her mother's eyes, but that might have been due to the lighting.

Shanna waited again for the laughter and noise to dissipate.

"As I said, this is the happiest night of my life not only because you've elected me, but because a wonderful man, who's very aware of every one of my faults, my flaws, my shortcomings, still wants me to marry him."

She turned to look at him, the man she loved holding the child he had helped to deliver. "The answer is yes, Reid." Her voice softened but still carried throughout the ballroom because she whispered the word over the microphone. "Yes."

Anything else she might have said was drowned out by the cheers and the clapping of the crowd. The balloons were released and fell down upon the ballroom occupants like colored raindrops.

Stepping away from the podium, Shanna murmured, "I'd like that kiss you promised me, please."

Reid handed the sleeping child to Jane. Because of the din, Reid read Shanna's lips rather than heard her voice. And then he wasn't reading them anymore. He was too busy kissing Shanna as the cheers and balloons engulfed them.

AVAILABLE NOW

LORD OF THE NIGHT by Susan Wiggs

Much loved historical romance author Susan Wiggs turns to the rich, sensual atmosphere of sixteenth-century Venice for another enthralling, unforgettable romance. "Susan Wiggs is truly magical."—Laura Kinsale, bestselling author of *Flowers from the Storm.*

CHOICES by Marie Ferrarella

The compelling story of a woman from a powerful political family who courageously gives up a loveless marriage and pursues her own dreams finding romance, heartbreak, and difficult choices along the way.

THE SECRET by Penelope Thomas

A long-buried secret overshadowed the love of an innocent governess and her master. Left with no family, Jessamy Lane agreed to move into Lord Wolfeburne's house and care for his young daughter. But when Jessamy suspected something sinister in his past, whom could she trust?

WILDCAT by Sharon Ihle

A fiery romance that brings the Old West back to life. When prim and proper Ann Marie Cannary went in search of her sister, Martha Jane, what she found instead was a hellion known as "Calamity Jane." Annie was powerless to change her sister's rough ways, but the small Dakota town of Deadwood changed Annie as she adapted to life in the Wild West and fell in love with a man who was full of surprises.

MURPHY'S RAINBOW by Carolyn Lampman

While traveling on the Oregon Trail, newly widowed Kate Murphy found herself stranded in a tiny town in Wyoming Territory. Handsome, enigmatic Jonathan Cantrell needed a housekeeper and nanny for his two sons. But living together in a small cabin on an isolated ranch soon became too close for comfort . . . and falling in love grew difficult to resist. Book I of the Cheyenne Trilogy.

TAME THE WIND by Katherine Kilgore

A sizzling story of forbidden love between a young Cherokee man and a Southern belle in antebellum Georgia. "Katherine Kilgore's passionate lovers and the struggles of the Cherokee nation are spellbinding. Pure enjoyment!"—Katherine Deauxville, bestselling author of *Daggers of Gold.*

COMING NEXT MONTH

ORCHIDS IN MOONLIGHT by Patricia Hagan
Bestselling author Patricia Hagan weaves a mesmerizing tale set in the untamed West. Determined to leave Kansas and join her father in San Francisco, vivacious Jamie Chandler stowed away on the wagon train led by handsome Cord Austin—a man who didn't want any company. Cord was furious when he discovered her, but by then it was too late to turn back. It was also too late to turn back the passion between them.

TEARS OF JADE by Leigh Riker
Twenty years after Jay Barron was classified as MIA in Vietnam, Quinn Tyler is still haunted by the feeling that he is still alive. When a twist of fate brings her face-to-face with businessman Welles Blackburn, a man who looks like Jay, Quinn is consumed by her need for answers that could put her life back together again, or tear it apart forever.

FIREBRAND by Kathy Lynn Emerson
Her power to see into the past could have cost Ellen Allyn her life if she had not fled London and its superstitious inhabitants in 1632. Only handsome Jamie Mainwaring accepted Ellen's strange ability and appreciated her for herself. But was his love true, or did he simply intend to use her powers to help him find fortune in the New World?

CHARADE by Christina Hamlett
Obsessed with her father's mysterious death, Maggie Price investigates her father's last employer, Derek Channing. From the first day she arrives at Derek's private island fortress in the Puget Sound, Maggie can't deny her powerful attraction to the handsome millionaire. But she is troubled by questions he won't answer, and fears that he has buried something more sinister than she can imagine.

THE TRYSTING MOON by Deborah Satinwood
She was an Irish patriot whose heart beat for justice during the reign of George III. Never did Lark Ballinter dream that it would beat even faster for an enemy to her cause—the golden-haired aristocratic Lord Christopher Cavanaugh. A powerfully moving tale of love and loyalty.

CONQUERED BY HIS KISS by Donna Valentino
Norman Lady Maria de Courson had to strike a bargain with Saxon warrior Rothgar of Langwald in order to save her brother's newly granted manor from the rebellious villagers. But when their agreement was sweetened by their firelit passion in the frozen forest, they faced a love that held danger for them both.

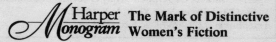 **Harper Monogram** **The Mark of Distinctive Women's Fiction**